THE ONES THAT GOT AWAY

THE ONES THAT GOT AWAY

LISA HILL

www.blkdogpublishing.com

CHAPTER ONE

'I can't hear the telly,' Gran moaned.

Tilly Henshaw opened one eye and discovered the world was sideways. Gran – stooped in her chair as usual, one shoulder of her beige, chunky knit cardi sloping down her arm – looked like she was hanging from a suspended rollercoaster ride. She was right though; the telly was quiet. In fact, Tilly could hardly hear it over the thudding sound reverberating in her head.

A pair of twenty denier clad legs appeared, also at a ninety-degree angle.

'You'd better get a chivvy on, young lady.' The air of mounting irritation in Elaine Henshaw's voice was palpable.

'Ugh, Mum.' Tilly groaned, shutting her eyes and turning over on the sofa. *Ouch*; ooh, even moving hurt. 'Don't go on at me,' she mumbled, pulling the sleeping bag further over her tangle of ringlets.

The sleeping bag was thrust back leaving Tilly, still in last night's little black dress and heels, feeling insecure and freezing. 'What are you doing that for?!' She tried grabbing it back, but a wave of sickness decided to join the thumping party in her head, rendering her defenceless from the tirade which was inevitably about to rain down upon her.

'Tilly, you are due in work in half an hour and look at you!'

Slowly propping herself up on her elbows, Tilly rubbed her forehead, avoiding her mother's gaze. She knew she was a massive disappointment to Elaine; she didn't need it reconfirming.

'I can't believe you carry on behaving like this, when—'

'Oh, I've spilt me tea.'

Both women turned around to see Gran pouring tea into her lap.

'Oh, for Christ's sakes mum!' Elaine erupted. Tilly couldn't help but feel that the lid, which had just popped, on Elaine's temper was much more to do with Tilly's perceived misbehaviour than Gran spilling her drink; something she would do at least another five times today.

Dropping the sleeping bag Elaine rushed to take the mug from Gran's hand and disappeared out of the living room. Tilly flopped back on the cushions, instantly regretting it as her hangover notched up another gear.

'You could help you know,' Elaine said, reappearing through the door having donned a pair of rubber gloves and carrying a washing up bowl.

'Okay,' Tilly whispered, tentatively inching her legs off the sofa. Gingerly she stood up, holding onto the arm of the sofa in case her legs wouldn't support her. She might only be five foot, four inches tall but she had drunk pretty much her body weight in vodka and coke last night. 'Woah.' Tilly took a deep breath as the floor rushed towards her. She sat back down.

'You are pathetic, do you know that?' Elaine said, sponging at Gran's skirt.

'I'm wet,' said Gran.

'I know, Mum, don't worry, we'll pop you in some dry clothes in a minute. Can you stand, so I can take you to your room?'

Tilly took a deep breath, getting up again, trying to ignore her pounding head.

'I'll get Gran changed.' She teetered across to Gran, trying to supress the queasiness in her stomach.

'Thank you,' said Elaine. 'Then you'd better head off home and patch things up with Simon.'

Tilly hooked her arm through Gran's. 'No way.'

Elaine whipped Gran's sanitary sheet away from the chair.

'Oh, Tilly, stop being so childish! Can you actually remember what happened last night? You were so drunk, *again*! So, Simon put you in a taxi to here! You'll have to go home and apologise; you're going to lose him, Tilly.'

'I am not apologising,' Tilly said, through gritted teeth, concentrating on leading Gran to the bathroom.

'I need the toilet,' said Gran.

'Come on then.' Tilly quickened her pace.

'Tilly, are you taking your medication at the moment?' Elaine had stopped scrubbing the armchair and was following Tilly and Gran into the hall.

Tilly ignored Elaine's regular jibe about her meds and instead focused on getting Gran to the bathroom. In some respects, with Gran's dementia, it was a blessing that Gran and Mum lived in a bungalow. On the other hand, if Gran couldn't manage stairs, she may have been forced into a home, leaving Mum to lead a life of her own.

Then, perhaps, she wouldn't feel the need to constantly interfere in Tilly's.

'Turn around then, Gran,' Tilly said, reaching the toilet.

'You're not taking them, are you?' Mum persisted.

Tilly rolled her eyes. 'Why does everything have to come down to whether I'm taking my medication? Am I not allowed to have feelings and emotions? Am I supposed to take my pills and live a partially sedated life, making semi-conscious decisions on the things that really matter?'

Now it was Elaine's turn to roll her eyes. 'Not this again! Bored, are we? Five years in a steady job, living with your boyfriend for three years and suddenly life's become a little dull, has it? Need a change of scenery? Or is it the thought of getting married next year which scares you?'

'No.' Tilly helped Gran onto the toilet, avoiding Elaine's gaze, acutely aware that she wasn't just lying to Mum, but to herself.

'Well, don't expect me to pick up the pieces this time when you get into debt or go cruising around the world and expect somewhere to crash when you finally decide to grace us with your presence again.' Tilly watched as Elaine's yellow marigolds waved theatrically all over the place. 'You're not living back here again!'

Tilly wanted to say that she had no intention of living with a dementia patient – who co-incidentally had been diagnosed with schizophrenia forty odd years ago – or a neurotic fifty-something who thought she had manic depression but, in fact, – in Tilly's humble opinion anyway – just needed to get a life.

But she didn't. 'Aren't I allowed to be *un*happy?'

'I've finished!' Gran said, like a toddler wanting its bottom wiped.

Tilly tore off strip of toilet roll. There was no dignity in old age, she reflected, handing over the paper to Gran. Here they were, having a discussion about her future, all standing in the bathroom with Gran sitting on the toilet.

Elaine leaned against the bathroom doorframe and folded her arms across her skinny frame.

'Tilly, it's Thursday morning and you're standing there in last night's clothes, having got so drunk that your fiancé wouldn't have you in the house. I understand you're unhappy, but ask yourself, why?'

Silence. Even in Gran's Alzheimer-infected mind an argument could cut through, leaving her sensing not to say anything. An anxious feeling, an all too familiar feeling, settled in Tilly's stomach. Her eyes frantically scanned Elaine, as if her mother might have held the answer to this monumental question. She bit her lip, afraid to admit to herself, let alone aloud. 'I don't love him.' She closed her eyes and waited for the fall out. The tirade of what an ungrateful brat she was, but deep-down Tilly knew she hadn't been in love with Simon for some time. The problem was that everyone – her mum, Archie next door, her friends at work -were all so happy for her, there was no-way she felt she could break-up with Simon.

Until now, perhaps.

'But why?' Elaine's voice was softer than Tilly expected. 'Because the two of you aren't getting on, or because you're not taking your medication?'

Tilly's settling anxiety was being pushed out by the queasiness of her hangover again.

'Who said I'm not taking my medication?'

Liar, liar, pants on fire.

'Because you're behaving like you always do when you don't take your medication; you go off the rails.'

Something ignited in Tilly. Something she hadn't felt for many years, or at least something she tried very hard to avoid from feeling around Elaine. Anger.

'Why do you feel it's acceptable to say things like that?' She asked, calmly, belying how she was seething underneath.

'What?' Elaine shrugged. 'Come on, Mum,' she said to Gran, edging past Tilly, 'let's go get you changed.'

Although Tilly was beginning to feel like death warmed up, there was a spark of fight left. 'No,' she said, blocking Elaine's path between her and Gran. What gives you the right to say that to me? When a train derails, there's an initial panic to ensure everyone is okay, then they clear up any spilt cargo, before its winched back on the rails so it can happily chug off again. No-one refers to the train ever again as *the train that went off the rails*. It's just a train which continues to work like it did before. In fact, the fact it derailed in the first place was probably due to some external factor like an obstacle in its track—'

'Tilly.' Elaine started before breaking into a nervous titter. 'You haven't had much sleep; you probably need to go home and vent your frustrations at Simon. I was—'

'You were only what?!' Tilly roared. Scaring herself, not to mention practically blinding her vision with this agonising headache. 'Belittling me, like usual? You were suggesting that I've come off the rails, that I'm causing *you* trouble again. Well,' Tilly said, folding her arms, trying to protect herself from what was inevitably going to be a falling out with her mum, 'let me finish my analogy.' She swallowed hard. 'When humans derail, they are most likely to be labelled that way for the rest of their lives. And whatever obstacle derailed them is never to blame. It will be the human's fault for being *mental*.'

'I am not calling you mental!' Elaine blustered.

'Then what are you saying?' Tilly snapped. 'That I'm just being me and going to cause you grief and anxiety *again*?'

'Tilly.' Elaine closed her eyes and took a deep breath.

Tilly knew Elaine was trying hard not to lose it.

'You are getting this out of proportion.'

'Am I?' Tilly replied. 'Why must you always assume that the answer to all our problems lies in a packet of pills?'

Elaine's neck took on that tense look of a tortoise straining to reach its head out of its shell. Every muscle in her was constricted and turning puce, to match the colour of her face. 'I do not!'

'But you do!' Tilly knew she sounded exasperated and the thudding in her head was beyond bearable now, yet she needed to get her point across. She needed to be heard. '*You* had me put on pills for ADHD when I was fourteen! You live on Lorazepam for *your nerves* which might just be anxiety, something you could try to sort out by addressing what's causing it, and yet you think we've both inherited Gran's mental health issues and, so, automatically *pills* are the answer!'

Elaine, whilst supporting Gran's weight, was opening and shutting her mouth like an apoplectic puffer fish.

'How dare you say such things, Tilly! My anxiety *is* an illness.'

Tilly leant on the bathroom sink for support and clutched her stomach.

'If you say so. But having fun is not a sign of requiring attention. Wanting to escape a loveless relationship with a control freak is not having a manic episode. It's life, mum; what happens to people every day. They are unhappy in a situation and want to change it. No-one accuses them of having ADHD or bi-polar disorder, or schizophrenia, like Gran. They don't need admitting to The Priory either; they just confront their issues and get on and do what needs to be done.'

Her mother looked scared. Frightfully underweight – almost skeletal – her short, feathery blonde hair looked limp and lifeless. Her blue eyes shone, blinking back tears. Tilly's heart reached out to her mum; she had always put Gran and Tilly in front of her own needs. She had put her life on hold for too many years, or so Tilly thought. Tilly couldn't make Elaine change her ways.

But Tilly could change hers.

Elaine pursed her lips, her face now a bright shade of fuchsia. 'Fine, you go break up with Simon then, but you won't find better than him. He's given you stability Tilly; he's given you a chance of a happy, *normal* life. Go and throw that all away if you want but don't expect me to pick up the pieces when you go back to your party girl ways.'

Tilly wanted to argue that she didn't see why breaking up with Simon meant the rest of her life was going to go to the dogs; she still had a job. Although after that hissy fit she rather suspected Mum wasn't going to have her back here to live. Bile began rising in her throat brought on by an equally rising feeling of panic. 'Bleuugh,' her voice made that involuntary sound when retching as she threw up into the toilet.

'Pathetic, Mum. Never had any sense of responsibility, that one.' Elaine muttered, leading Gran into the hall.

'Well, at least I have the strength to actually admit I might be fucked up,' Tilly muttered, turning on the tap.

CHAPTER TWO

1966

Ruby looked down at her stomach and noted that the new fuchsia pink, Capri pants she was wearing – which had cost four-shillings-and-six-pence and she had painstakingly saved up for each week out of her wages for the past two months – weren't likely to fit her in another two months' time. She was sitting on the sofa, trying hard to focus on anything apart from the ensuing row between her parents over the monumental news she had just delivered them. In fact, she was beginning to wonder if she could carefully slink out of the door and pop around to Mary's and listen to the new record player which she'd bought with her first wage packet. Mary was lucky; her parents didn't make her pay rent.

'You know abortion is illegal?' Her father rounded on her. The whites of his eyes were almost illuminous, especially against the puce of his face.

Ruby recoiled as far back into the settee as it would go. Over her father's heavy breathing and her mother's sobbing, The Beatles *Do you want to know a secret?*

floated out of over Radio Caroline. She didn't want this to be a secret; that's why she'd told them. It was a mistake, a big one, but she wasn't prepared to pretend it wasn't happening. Stella Groves, who had been in her year at school, didn't tell anyone she was going to have a baby until it popped out. When the father didn't support her, they carted her off to the unmarried mothers' home. Ruby wasn't going to let that happen to her or the little person inside her.

'I wasn't planning on an abortion.'

'Why you!' Bob Mackenzie's voice echoed around the living room before the *thud* came of him punching the living room door. 'Arrgh!'

'Oh, Bob!' cried Jean Mackenzie. 'What have you done that for? There's a hole clear through now!'

Ruby put her index finger to her lips and started biting her nail. That punch was meant for her and no mistake.

'You've brought shame on this family, young lady! What were you thinking?!'

Ruby reflected that there was precious little thinking involved at the time of this conception but telling her father that would be to really pour oil on troubled waters. She did know it involved love but there was precious little point admitting that for her father to scoff over, especially when it didn't matter how much she loved the father of her baby; he wasn't choosing her.

Perhaps if she had told him about the baby, he would change his mind.

Ruby stared at her pink suede court shoes which matched her trousers.

'I don't know,' she said, quietly.

'Bit late now, isn't it?' Bob shouted. 'Would have helped if you'd thought with your head not your knickers at the time!'

'Bob!' Jean cried.

'What's going on?' Lil appeared in the doorway.

Bob looked at Jean who looked at Ruby. Lil looked from one pink face to another. Ruby stared at Lil and in one flash of inspiration the idea fell into place. A wash of relief spread over her. 'I'm pregnant,' she said, jumping to her feet.

'What?' Ruby saw the colour drain from Lil's face as she gripped the back of the settee for support.

The carriage clock on the mantelpiece chimed quarter-past the hour before ticking on. Ruby could almost feel her dad's heavy breathing down the back of her neck. She kept looking directly at Lil.

Lil looked on the brink of tears and she lowered herself down into the green velour sofa. She was twenty-nine but looked like a six-year-old, vulnerable and forlorn. She was twelve years older than Ruby – Ruby knew she was a mistake but there was no point throwing that in her parents face at this precise moment in time – and had just celebrated her eighth wedding anniversary to Stan. All Lil's friends had two or three children hanging off their apron strings by now. Ruby knew how much it pained Lil not to have a child of her own.

'You can have it.' Ruby blurted out. There, it was said; no going back now.

'You what?' Bob shouted.

Ruby turned on her father, suddenly empowered by this practical solution.

'I can't have an abortion,' she counted on one finger, 'I don't have a time machine like that Doctor Who bloke on the telly, so I can't go back in time and put this right,' she counted on her second finger, 'and Lil and Stan can't have children,' she counted on the third. 'What would you suggest? Doesn't this fix everyone's problems and keep your wholesome reputation intact?'

Her mother collapsed into the arm chair in a fit of tears. Bob stared at Ruby with his fists clenched. Ruby turned to look at Lil. She was leaning on the arm of the sofa, rubbing her forehead.

'Are you sure about this?' Lil asked, with the faint glimmer of a smile on the corner of her lips.

'Absolutely,' she nodded, feeling rather less confident than she was portraying.

Bob took a step towards Ruby and looked down at her. His usually smooth, brill creamed black hair was flopping into his eyes.

'Fine. You go through with this.' His eyes narrowed. 'But don't expect to ever live under my roof again.'

Ruby watched as he stalked out of living room and into the hallway. Her legs felt like jelly. Lil was getting up from the sofa and embracing Ruby in a hug.

'I can't thank you enough!' she squealed. 'I promise you; I'll look after it like it was my own.'

'It will be yours,' Ruby whispered. There was no going back now.

Good thing Archie knew nothing about their baby.

CHAPTER THREE

Archie folded up his paper and placed it down next to his empty breakfast plate.

'Has it ever occurred to you that your mother just cares about you?' he asked.

Tilly swilled her last piece of fried bread in the remnants of eggy, baked bean sauce, popped it in her mouth and chewed down to refrain herself from snapping at Archie. She had come around to off load. She didn't need to fall out with him as well as everyone else. Tilly licked her sticky fingers, one by one, as she carefully considered her reply.

'I hear what you're saying—'

'But you think I sound like Phyllis?' Archie interjected.

Archie and Phyllis had lived next door to Gran and Mum for as long as Tilly could remember. Her earliest memories were of tip-toeing over the garden wall, calling out, 'Mister Fairclough!', and asking him if she could help him with his gardening. They were like proper grandparents, which was silly in a way because Gran and Grandad had been her real grandparents who she'd lived with, along with Mum, until Grandad died when she was sixteen. Gran had still been relatively normal then. Normal for her, anyway. Her Alzheimer's didn't really kick-in until Tilly was twenty-one and had left home. But Archie and Phyllis were like grandparents should be, proper grandparents, who were always pleased to see you and took you on walks to the park, and day trips to Weston-Super-Mare, and were as excited as you were when you did well at school.

'Sorry, but you do a bit.'

There was an awkward silence where Archie fiddled with the corner of the newspaper and Tilly dipped her finger in her sauce and licked it.

'I miss her too,' Tilly said, quietly

'It's been two years now,' Archie said, clearing his throat. 'You think I'd have got used to it, by now.' He picked up his coffee and took a swig.

'There is a difference between accepting someone's not coming back and still missing them.'

Archie raised one of his white eye brows and looked directly at Tilly.

'Wise words from someone so young.' He smiled and his face creased with wrinkles. Tilly thought Archie still looked handsome for an older man. He'd celebrated his seventieth birthday last year but still had a suave demeanour about him and good posture. He was a real silver fox. She was mildly surprised he hadn't met someone by now; a widower, or a divorcee, but it made her realise that just because someone wasn't here anymore didn't mean you loved them any less. It was an observation she'd made over the past few months which had drawn her to the conclusion she didn't love Simon anymore. It was awful to admit, even to herself, but if – *heaven forbid* – anything did happen to him, she didn't see that she would miss him.

She knew it was a nasty, horrible, bad thought to have, but it really would be a relief.

'Not that young Archie; I'm thirty-four now. Mum thinks Simon is my one and only chance of *getting it right;*

you know? Marriage, a family, all that.' Tilly pushed her plate away.

Archie detached himself from the table and crossed one immaculately creased, trouser leg over the other. 'Your mother had you very young. She wants you to have all the things which she never had the opportunity to have.'

This was true. Elaine had never revealed the identity of Tilly's father. She'd got pregnant at eighteen after, she maintained, a one-night stand. However, Tilly had never really bought that story. After having Tilly, Elaine had never left the family home, opting to raise Tilly under the same roof as Gran and Grandad. Fifty-three years old and never left home. At least Tilly could say that she'd escaped home and lived a little. But Tilly suspected Elaine's reasons for never leaving home ran deeper than the stigmatism of a being a single mum in the nineteen-eighties. Tilly was pretty sure it was where all Elaine's anxieties stemmed from. Shutting yourself away from the world because you'd been rejected by it was a far more likely appraisal of what had happened. Tilly's suspicions were that Elaine had told her father about her pregnancy and he hadn't wanted to know. He'd walked away. Not that she'd ever voiced this opinion to anyone, least of all Elaine.

'She just wants me to be settled so it's one less thing for her to worry about,' Tilly muttered.

'Hmmm.' Archie rubbed his hand over his chin. 'And what do you want little Tilly Henshaw? What would make you happy?'

'I don't know.' Tilly pursed her lips and thought. 'Do I sound like a brat?' She winced, waiting for Archie's reply.

Archie laughed. Hector, his little wire-haired, Jack Russell, who had been snoozing on the sofa, suddenly burst to life and started yapping.

'Oi, shush you,' Archie said. He looked at Tilly and grinned. 'Well, Hector thinks you are.'

Hector jumped off the sofa and sprang onto Tilly's lap. She pulled at his collar to stop him licking her empty plate.

'Gee, thanks Hector, so what do you suggest?'

Hector looked at her with big soulful eyes.

'I think Hector would tell you about the code of dog.'

Tilly frowned. 'Which is?'

'Dog does what's best for dog. He will suffer the consequences later.'

Archie and Phyllis had always had Jack Russells. There had been Patch when she was very little and when he passed away, they had had Tatty and Scruff, together. They treated them like children. Probably the children they had never had, Tilly reflected.

'So, what are you saying? Jump, then worry about how to swim?'

'Well, if we could stop talking in clichés for a moment, then, yes. It doesn't matter how much you train a dog, if he doesn't want to do something or he wants to do something different to your command then he will, no matter how high the reward is for following your instruction.'

'So, what you're saying is, that if I carry on with a relationship with Simon it will just be to please Mum?'

'That's how you feel, isn't it?'

Tilly idly stroked Hector's silky ears. 'Yes, I guess it is.'

'You went out last night, had a blast, got drunk and didn't give a jot what Simon thought. You didn't want to stay in with him.'

'Whoah, that's a bit harsh.' It was true but hearing it put into plain English made for uneasy listening.

'Is it? Wasn't that behaving by the code of dog? Doing what you wanted?'

Tilly sighed. 'Yes,' she said, quietly.

'So, what are you going to do about it?'

'I don't know!' Tilly wailed. This was scary stuff. She knew she wanted to extricate herself from her relationship with Simon and she hated her job, but she didn't have a plan either. 'I've got nowhere to go Archie! I earn enough to get a little flat in Southville or Bedminster, somewhere close to work, but I loathe being a secretary, it's so boring!'

'It's a far cry from cruise ships and ski chalets.' Archie nodded in agreement.

'I don't want to go back to that either.' Tilly buried her head in Hector's wiry fur. She'd loved her life as a cruise ship entertainer in summer and chalet girl in winter, but she was past that. She wanted to do something meaningful and fulfilling that wasn't sending email's, checking invoices and counting down the seconds until her lunch break.

Archie leaned across the table and peered into Tilly's gaze.

'So, what do *you* want?'

Tilly held his gaze. What she would really like was to move in with Archie, he was the nearest thing she'd ever had to a father figure. But he didn't need her drama and what was he to her anyway? A kind, next door neighbour who had always treated her like the granddaughter he'd never had. But they weren't related. He had no obligation to help her.

'To escape,' Tilly whispered.

'Then you're in luck,' Archie said, standing up.

'Luck?' Tilly followed his movements across to the old mahogany bureau.

'Yes, luck.'

His native, guttural, Yorkshire accent came out in the word 'luck'. Tilly knew Archie had moved from Leeds in his late teens when he had taken an engineering apprenticeship with British Aerospace. Tilly presumed that in order to avoid developing a West Country accent over the five decades he had lived in Bristol he had developed a posh person's accent instead, but when he was agitated or nervous the Yorkshire lad rang through. Instinctively, Tilly knew that whatever Archie had gone to retrieve from that bureau was important.

Archie pulled down the hatch and rooted through a line of old envelopes, fingering them one by one, as he went. Eventually he pulled one out, shut the bureau back up and dropped the envelope on the table before sitting back down.

Tilly peered at the envelope suspiciously. In blue, inky, swirly writing it said *Miss T Henshaw*.

'Who's it from?' She looked up at Archie.

Archie leaned forward, resting his elbows on his knees. 'What this letter will tell you, will change your world. I suggest you open it when you are ready.'

Tilly frowned. 'Change my world? Why, am I not who I really think I am? Was I adopted, or—'

Archie put a finger to his lips and Tilly stopped talking.

'The correspondent once tried to befriend your mother, but Elaine refused to have anything to do with her.' He averted his gaze from Tilly. It's not really my place to tell you. But the writer has written to you every year since you turned eighteen. I've always told her that I would only pass the letter on if, or when, I felt the time was right.'

Tilly's mouth dropped open. 'Sixteen years? You've taken your time, Archie. You know this *her* then?'

'I do.'

'Are you related to them?' Frustratingly, this was turning into a game of *Guess Who?* Tilly felt she should be asking if they had ginger hair and glasses.

'No, but she is, and always will be, a good friend. She's watched you grow through mine and Phyllis' eyes.'

This was getting a bit creepy. 'But she has *my* interests at heart?'

'Yes.' Archie's expression was very serious. So only open if you are prepared to live with the consequences. Your mum will be furious with me, but I think this is probably the moment I've been waiting for. If you want your escape, Tilly, then this is your opportunity.'

Tilly stared at the envelope with its exuberant and enticing writing.

'Stuff it.' She picked up the letter, grinning as she ripped it open. 'Hope Home,' she began to read aloud…

Hope Home,
Gull Island,
Hope Cove,
Cornwall
PL29 1TH
1ˢᵗ January 2019

Dear Matilda,

If you are reading this then Archie has finally told you about me. I say finally because I have been writing the same letter every year for the past sixteen years, since you became an adult and were old enough to make your own mind up.

I am pleased to finally introduce myself to you. I am Ruby, your Great Aunt, Lil's sister. I know you are likely to wonder why you have never heard of me before but it's what you young ones call 'complicated' and I hope that one day we can be great friends.

The purpose of this letter, originally, was to let you know that there is someone out there who cares about you. It may sound daft seeing you have never met me, but just because I don't have anything to do with our Lil or your mum anymore, doesn't mean I don't care. As the years have gone by and your gran's health has deteriorated, I can imagine life must be difficult and I wanted you to know there is somewhere you can come if you ever need to escape. Not forever, necessarily, just a few days perhaps. My door is always open to you. My cottage in Hope Cove is always standing empty and ready for action. The address is:

Hope Cottage
Island View
Hope Cove,
Cornwall
PL29 1EH

I've enclosed a key, but Archie will phone ahead; let's hope this year is the year!

Love and hugs

Auntie Ruby X

Tilly's eyes bulged wide with excitement before narrowing in confusion. 'Make my own mind up? What's she got; three heads or something? She can't have done anything as bad as I've done with my life; why has she been a social outcast all these years?'

Archie shook his head, his lips purse. 'I've done my bit, lass. If you want to know more, you need to speak to Ruby. But, tell your mum first.'

Tilly watched Archie swallow hard as she did the same. What was it with her family and secrets? The Henshaws were full of them. 'Oh, Archie, why do I feel like Pandora and you just handed me the key?'

Archie set his sparkly blue eyes directly at Tilly's gaze. 'Why do you think it's taken me over a decade to do it?' he said, a provocative smile twitching at the corner of his lips.

CHAPTER FOUR

2nd *April 1965*

Dear Archie,

I put off writing this letter until after the first of April as I didn't want you to think it was a practical joke.

I feel it is my duty to tell you that on Wednesday 24th March, I gave birth to a baby girl, our daughter. She has my blonde wispy hair and your bright, blue eyes. She is perfect.

She doesn't have a name yet, as I'm not keeping her. If it was up to me, I'd call her Marilyn as she looks like a little version of Marilyn Monroe. My parents were angry when I told them that I'd fallen, so I came up with a plan for my sister to take her. Lil and my brother-in-law, Stan, have been married over ten years without catching so it's seems a sensible solution.

I am going to London to see if I can get a job as a secretary there, where no-one will know me. I will miss our little Marilyn, but Dad will never look at me the same and now you and Phyllis are living in Bristol, I don't want to bump into you and face painful memories.

I know I can confide this secret in you, Archie, because I have done the same for you. Phyllis knows nothing about me, and I understand why you chose to go ahead and marry her. That is why I will never tell her what happened between us. In return, our little Marilyn, or whatever Lil and Stan decide to call her, mustn't know about you. Lil and Stan are officially adopting her, and I will be known as Auntie Ruby.

I know I can trust you not to do anything rash, Archie, after all, Phyllis knows nothing about us. Lil and Stan live at 22 Southfield Close, Westbury-on-Trym, Bristol. In case you might like to see our little Marilyn from afar.

I am going to stop writing now, Archie, as it is too painful. You were my first love. Who knows, under different circumstances perhaps you, me and Marilyn could have been a happy little family. You have hurt me Archie, but I wish you luck and happiness. Know that there will always be a part of my heart that loves you.

Ruby xxx

Archie finished reading and tears sprang to his eyes; the same way they had the first time he had read this letter over fifty years ago. The paper was discoloured now and there were splits in the folds, but then it had spent five decades being carried around in his wallet. Carefully he folded the paper and popped it back in its place of belonging, in the back compartment, next to his emergency twenty-pound note. He sighed as he pushed the wallet firmly down in his back trouser pocket. He had wronged two women. He had not been fair to either of them. And the consequences of his decision had not only affected both Ruby and Phyllis but Elaine too, and now Tilly. If only Ruby had told him she was pregnant. Archie looked down at Hector who was looking expectantly up at him.

'I know,' Archie said. 'No point going over old ground, is there? It is what it is; there's no changing history.' Nor did he want to. He had enjoyed a very happy forty-eight years of marriage to Phyllis.

Although it didn't mean he didn't wish things had turned out differently. Elaine knowing who he really was, for one.

'Better not put this off any longer,' he said, picking up his keys from their hook by the front door and stepping out of number twenty-four. He glanced at the half-packed suitcase lying open on his bed. He had a feeling Tilly would be back this afternoon and itching to go. He'd better get this over with and make sure he left the bungalow in order. He had no idea how long Tilly would want to stay in Hope Cove, but he wasn't leaving her to her own devices; he owed Elaine that much.

It was a bright April morning and the daffodils in Archie's front garden uniformly swayed as he walked down his driveway and around to number twenty-two. Since Stan had died the front garden had become dowdy and bedraggled. Archie tried to help to start with but then Elaine had got defensive that she wanted to do it. That was before Lil's health took a turn for the worse. Poor Elaine really had become Lil's carer; no life for a woman just turned fifty. Number twenty-two and twenty-four mirrored each other. Archie strolled up the long concrete driveway with its shingle centre strip, laced with weeds. Where Archie and Phyllis had updated their 1960s bungalow over the years, Stan and Lil had kept there's neat and tidy but little of its appearance had changed. It reminded Archie of the first time he had walked up this driveway. Nervous as hell, coming to introduce himself as the new next-door neighbour. Then he had rung the front door and a little girl had opened it, his little girl, only a tot. He had knelt down and asked if her mummy was in, fighting back tears, knowing that her real mummy had run away and had not been seen since.

'Only me,' Archie called out, opening the back door into the kitchen of Lil's bungalow.

'Is that you Archie?' Lil called out.

Hector followed Archie through the door, tail wagging excitedly as he knew Lil would feed him tit-bits.

'It is,' Archie called out, noting the dirty clothes lying in a pile on the kitchen floor. 'Where's Elaine?'

'Here!' she called, scurrying into the kitchen with a pile of crumpled up sheets in her arms. 'Wet bed again.' She raised the sheets in explanation.

There she was, still his little girl. Ruby was right; she did have Ruby's petite features, but her eyes were so like his. There had been times in the past when he was worried, she would notice the similarity and guess. But then, as far as Elaine was concerned, Stan was her dad and Lil was her mum.

'Oh dear.' Archie watched Elaine squash the sheets into the washing machine. 'And a set of dirty clothes too?'

'Yes, that was Tilly's fault,' Elaine said, standing up and rolling her eyes.

'Really?' Archie knew how Elaine could be down on Tilly. But then she had learnt to be a mother from the highly critical, Lil.

'Well, maybe not entirely Tilly's fault but she ended up staying here last night and I was arguing with Tilly, not watching mum and then...' she trailed off, catching a glance of Archie's face. 'You know all this, don't you? She's been round to off-load, hasn't she?'

'She might have.' Archie leant on the kitchen worktop and folded his arms.

Elaine huffed and ran her fingers through her short hair. 'I don't know what to do, Archie. I think she's getting out of control again. She doesn't know how lucky she is finding someone like Simon. I can't cope with it all; Mum takes up all my time, I'm exhausted! I haven't got time to worry about Tilly too.'

Archie glanced at all the medication boxes on the counter. He knew most were Lil's but a fair few were Elaine's too. He knew what he had to tell her was going to break her heart but, for Elaine and Tilly's sake, he knew that he had done the right thing showing Tilly the letter.

Archie rang his finger along the counter. 'Perhaps, you need a break.'

'Laney!' Lil's voice rang out from the living room. 'You there, Laney?'

Archie often wondered whether Lil's memory wasn't as far gone as she made it out to be. She had a canny knack of claiming Elaine's attention right at the most inconvenient moment.

'Won't be a minute, Mum,' Elaine called out. 'You must be joking, Archie, who would look after Mum?'

Archie felt Ruby's home for geriatrics on Gull Island would be perfect.

Persuading Elaine to go was another matter entirely.

'Laney!' Lil sang.

Deciding it was easier to cut to the chase, Archie walked across the kitchen tiles and shut the door. 'I gave Tilly a letter this morning.' He knew what he had to say was going to hurt Elaine whether he sugar coated it or not. 'It was from Ruby.'

Elaine gasped. Archie watched her grip the work surface. He hoped she wasn't going to have a panic attack.

'Why? Why would you do that Archie? She's a liar! What on earth are you doing keeping in contact with her?'

Archie took a step forward towards Elaine and looked down into her deep blue eyes. There was a time when they had shone. These days they looked like the murky English Channel, always full of woe.

'Whatever you believe or don't believe about what she's told you in the past, she is still a member of *your* family.'

'Yes, a family member who stirs up trouble!' Elaine snapped. 'In fact, her and Tilly are very alike; both attention-seekers.'

'Nevertheless, Tilly is *unhappy*—'

'She is not unhappy!' Elaine's voice was rising. 'She's attention-seeking *again*, like she always does. Everyone goes through bad patches; it doesn't mean they have the right to go around destroying everyone else's happiness. She should try being a single mum at her age, bringing up a thirteen-year old girl, putting your own life on hold for so long that you end up with no life and, oh…' Elaine broke into a sob and began to cry.

Archie moved-in and put his arm around her Elaine. Surprisingly she didn't push him away; she leant into him and continued to cry.

'Ssssh,' Archie said into soothing tones. In the silence of their embrace Archie pretended Elaine knew he was really her father and was grateful for his support.

'So, how does Saint Ruby plan come to the rescue, this time? More to the point, how do you have a letter from her to Tilly? Have you been keeping Ruby abreast of our lives?'

'She sends me a card every Christmas. In it she puts a letter to Tilly, hoping one day I'll give it to her.'

'Saying what? How long has this been going on for?'

'Since Tilly was eighteen.'

Elaine's eyebrows almost shot off her forehead. 'What? Oh, Archie, I thought I knew you better than this!'

'Sometimes,' Archie paused, choosing his words carefully, 'I am not sure we ever really know anyone at all.'

'What does that mean?' Elaine's tearstained face searched Archie's for an answer.

'Helloooo!' The back door swung open and Tilly appeared, grinning from ear-to-ear.

'Come to tell me about your escape to Cornwall?' Elaine asked sarcastically. 'What about Simon; does he know you're going?'

Tilly averted her gaze from Elaine's and blushed. 'I've left him a note.'

'Pah!' Elaine laughed, sounding slightly unhinged. 'I said to her earlier, Archie, she's pathetic and to prove the point she's dumped her fiancé by letter.'

Archie swallowed hard and concentrated on his breathing. He had possibly made the wrong choice giving Tilly that letter. But then, Tilly needed help as much as Elaine did; wasn't Tilly allowed a fresh start if it helped turn her around from the rut she'd got stuck in?

'You're going to stay with *her*, aren't you?' Elaine spat, sounding wounded.

'If by 'her' you are referring to Ruby, then, yes, *we* are.'

Elaine's head swung around at Archie. 'You're going too?'

The reddish anger had faded from Elaine's face, leaving a pale and frightened pallor. Everyone was leaving her, or that's how it must seem. Archie swallowed hard. 'I thought,' he could hear his voice wobbling, 'that if Tilly is going to go anyway, it would be best if she had a chaperone.'

'Oh, great, so you two get to swan-off on a little holiday and I'm left looking after Mum, like usual. Thanks a lot.'

Archie watched Elaine's eyes brim with tears. He went to put his hand on her shoulder, but she brushed him away, making him feel like the traitor he knew he was.

Elaine folded her arms and fixed Tilly with a stare. 'You know she tore this family apart? She's a *liar*.'

Tilly frowned. 'How? I guess that explains why I've never heard of her.' She flicked her long ringlets over her shoulder. 'She's still family.'

'She claims she's my biological mother.' Elaine spat.

Archie felt the muscles in his stomach clench.

'Pardon?' asked Tilly.

Elaine's lower jaw jutted out. 'You heard.'

'How long have you known this?'

'She turned up when I was pregnant with you.'

'What?!' Tilly's voice had notched up an octave. 'Were you ever going to tell me?'

'No!' Elaine shouted. 'Because it's not true! She's a fantasist. She turned up wanting to stir up trouble for your Gran and Grandad, but I sent her packing. I've told you before, Tilly, there's clinical mental health issues in our family. Ruby's mad and look at Gran, she's—'

'For goodness sakes, Mum, we're not the Saxe-Coburg's!'

'Who?'

'George the Third? You've must have heard of the madness of King George?'

'Actually,' Archie interjected, 'they now think King George the Third was suffering from porphyria which is something to do with your blood and liver I think and—'

'Makes you present like a mad person?' Tilly raised her eyebrows.

'Well, um, yes,' Archie reluctantly conceded. 'But lots of physical symptoms too,' Archie rushed on, keen to keep talking technicalities and avoid talking about the elephant in the room; he had just caused a massive ruction between his daughter and granddaughter.

Neither of which had a clue who he really was.

Probably best to keep it that way.

Elaine rubbed her forehead. 'Tilly, I still don't get what you're talking about?'

'You make out like we're a dynasty of mad people when, really, we aren't. All you are is stressed out from dealing with Gran! If Ruby really was your mum, then it means that you haven't inherited any mental health issues from Gran and neither have I!'

'I have had enough of this!' Elaine shouted. 'Get out! Both of you! You go on your little adventure and leave me to care for my sick mother. *My* mother Tilly. I warn you now, no good will come of you seeing Ruby. And,' Elaine's voice wobbled, clearly distressed, 'if you go now, there's no coming back here for you.' Archie watched Elaine swallow back her tears. 'Never.'

Tilly looked down at her hand resting on the door handle. 'Fine,' she said, eventually, turning the handle. The door opened and Hector flew out in front of her.

Archie slowly walked to the door, listening to Elaine's heavy breathing. He turned to see the hurt and anguish at his betrayal in her eyes.

'I don't know what made you keep in contact with Ruby, Archie,' she said, the whites of her knuckles showing as she gripped the kitchen side, 'but I will never forgive you for this.

If Tilly ends up in a worse mess, I'll blame you entirely.'

Archie kept her gaze and nodded. 'Best make sure I take good care of her then,' he said, stepping over the threshold. He hesitated and looked back, suddenly compelled with an urge to say what he felt. 'Tilly is right about one thing though. Whatever Ruby is to you, she is still *family*.' He paused, uncertain to whether to pour more oil on trouble water. 'And, I for one, thinks families should stick together.' He pressed his lips into something resembling a smile and closed the door behind him with a very, heavy heart.

CHAPTER FIVE

1981

Ruby stepped out of her cottage and looked across to the island. It was late November and the angry waves battered the Cornish cliff edges. Seagulls could barely fly in a straight line against the early winter winds. She pushed her hair out of her face and squinted. There were men on the island with a Land Rover, erecting a large sign. It looked like the same colour as Hardwickes; the estate agents down in the village. Locking the cottage door behind her, she wrapped her mac around her waist and tightened the belt. She was going down to the village for milk and bread, she would call into Hardwickes and ask.

'Morning, Ruby Mac!' called Eric, out of the window of his battered, old Defender, as he towed his latest catch of fish up the hill, towards Newquay.

'Morning Eric!' she waved back, laughing to herself. All the locals called her 'Ruby Mac', shortening her name from MacKenzie, but also a nod to the fact that come rain or shine, she had her mac on her. The weather in Cornwall was unpredictable; it was best not to get caught short. The locals saw her as a soft Londoner and teased her affectionately for it, not knowing that she grew up much closer to their home.

She'd moved to Hope Cove in January; her fresh start. After her divorce from Max had come through, she'd wanted to run away. Get away from London, from the bustling busyness of it all, from all the gossipers and the lying, cheating husbands. She was thirty-three and what had she ever achieved with her life? A daughter she had given up out of shame, running away from the one and only man she'd ever loved, and now a divorcee. She'd gone to London in search of a career, to make something of herself. So that, one day, she could return to Bristol and tell everyone what a success she was. That was the dream. The reality was that she'd got a job as PA to the Editor of *The Reporter*, the most successful newspaper on Fleet Street in the late sixties, and within six months he'd left his wife and Ruby had found herself living in the lap of luxury. She'd wanted for nothing; clothes and shoes from Carnarby Street, a sexy E-type Jaguar to zoom around in and supper out every night in the fanciest of restaurants.

But it didn't make her happy.

If she'd have ploughed herself into work, perhaps she wouldn't have been so bored. Upon reflection, if her and Max had had a child together, perhaps it would have worked. Of course, she would have had to have stopped taking the pill for that to happen. He'd wanted children but Ruby couldn't risk anymore heartbreak where babies were concerned. It had been safer to go along with the pretence of trying for a baby. Plus, Max was always working or drinking in clubs to get the next juicy story; a child in that marriage would have been a disaster. She would have been trapped.

Not like here, Ruby smiled, passing the church and lighthouse on her way down into the village. The sun was trying hard to find break through the fiercely dull, cloudy November skies, with just a tiny glint of hope shining on the church spire. She was free here. It was a jolly good thing that, after six years of marriage, Max had embarked on an affair with his new PA. She should have seen it coming; once a cheat always a cheat.

It made her realise she was a fool for keeping a torch alive for Archie.

The children were on their break time at the school, all running around the playground like lunatics, not noticing the biting cold wind. Not a care in the world. Oh, to be a child and do it all again. But it was time to face facts; she wasn't a child, nor was she getting any younger. She needed a challenge.

She'd started coming to Hope Cove when things were beginning to go wrong with Max. She'd seen a little offer in in *The Lady* and, upon arrival, had found the long walks over the cliff tops cleared her mind and the cosy evenings in The Lobster Pot, where she stayed, were filled with fun and laughter. There was always a fisherman or his wife to chat to. Soon she was coming nearly every weekend and as soon as her divorce settlement came through, she made an offer the first cottage which became available. Luckily, Hope Cottage had one of the best views in the village. Unfortunately, it was up the hill and around the corner, on the outside of the cove, but the views went all the way to Newquay and beyond. On lighter days, she fantasised of Captain Poldark riding along the sand dunes, towards the cottage, come to rescue her like he did in that TV programme a few years back. But she had come to the conclusion that it wasn't a man who was ever going to rescue her; she needed to rescue herself.

The harbour was busy with fishermen bringing their catches ashore. She briskly walked past the lifeguard station and The Lobster Pot, making her way up the hill to the north of the cove, where all the little shops lined up in a row. Hardwicke's was the third on the right, next to the Post Office. Ruby stopped. There it was in the window; an auction of the old Majestic Hotel on Gull Island was to take place next week. A frisson of excitement stirred within her. An excitement she hadn't felt for many years, probably not since those special few months when she had first met Archie. She pushed the shop door open and was faced with a room of crammed desks, for spacious shop premises in Hope Cove did not exist.

'Morning,' she said, breezily, to the girl behind the nearest desk.

'Good morning, how can I help you?' She was wearing a high neck, pleated blouse and jacket and she reminded Ruby of a newsreader. Her thick, red hair was cut into a Princess Diana style, page boy cut, framing her face.

'I'm interested in the details in the window, for the hotel on Gull Island.' Ruby beckoned to the window.

The girl looked her up and down before catching glimpse of her Chanel handbag. She visibly relaxed. Ruby rolled her eyes at how judgemental people were.

'Of course,' she smiled, getting up from her desk walking to a filing cabinet at the back of the room. 'Here you go,' the girl said, walking back and handing Ruby a glossy brochure, which meant it was an expensive property because most other property details Ruby had ever seen were black and white print on a scrappy piece of A4, even in London.

Ruby smiled and took the particulars. The front page gave her all the same information as the card in the window, so she whipped the cover open where she found more internal pictures and a guide price.

'Two Hundred and Fifty Thousand?'

'Yes, I know, it's quite steep,' said the girl, sitting back down at her desk. 'Do you think you'll be interested? It's just that we were only sent twenty copies from the printers and so we need to reserve them for genuinely interested bidders.'

Ruby looked up from the brochure she'd been fingering. She pulled out the chair opposite the girl's desk, sitting down with a forceful *thud*.

'What makes you think I wouldn't be interested?' Ruby raised a threatening eyebrow. She was fed up with people making assumptions about her. Just because she made the most of herself, dressed well, did her hair and make-up regularly, it didn't make her a gold digger. It was why she had fled London; she didn't need negative people thinking she'd only married Max for his money. She was a true romantic and if she managed to secure a bid on the old Majestic it would be with love in mind too.

'Well, no offence—'

'Why do people say that? It only caveats the fact you're about to insult me.'

The girl blushed furiously. 'I'm sorry Mrs Mac, I...' the girl trailed off. She looked as if she was about to burst into tears.

Ruby up held a hand. 'Don't apologise, it's my fault. I'm just a bit sensitive when people make assumptions based on appearances. My affairs are private, suffice to say that I could certainly afford to pay more than the starting bid at the auction. So, could you add me to the list of attendees, please?'

'Yes, of course,' the girl, her Cornish accent thicker than before, pulled a notepad out of her drawer.

'It's Ruby Mackenzie, as you know.' Ruby leant over the desk.

'Right.' The girl forced a smile. 'What will you do with the property if you secure it?'

'Turn it into a retirement home.'

The two other staff members in the office, mute until now, turned to stare at Ruby.

'Oh wow! My Nan can barely cope with the stairs in her cottage, we have to take it in turns in our family to help out. It would be amazing if she could go into an assisted home.'

'And do you enjoy helping?'

'Oh, yes, I love my Nan. She is so grateful when we go to visit; it makes her day. She can't get out of the house no more. An old people's home would be brilliant for her; all those other old people to talk too.'

Ruby viewed the girl through different eyes. 'What's your name?'

'Julie, Mrs Mac.'

'Call me Ruby,' she smiled, standing up. 'Thank you for your help, I'll be in touch if I'm the lucky bidder.' She waggled the particulars and with that disappeared through the door, knowing the office would erupt the moment the shop bell tinkled behind her.

Ruby smiled to herself as she set off down the street. If she could secure the old hotel for less than five hundred thousand, her million-pound divorce settlement would more than cover refurbishment and get the business off the ground. The words in Archie's recent letter rattled around in her head as she crossed the road to take in the view of the cove. *Your mum is getting quite forgetful now and Lil has little patience. Poor Stan, I don't know how he copes. Lil is just as absent minded. Last week she thought Elaine was trying to poison her tea. How Elaine can concentrate on her O Levels with all that drama is beyond me. Although she does escape around to ours to revise.* Well, Ruby couldn't do much to practically help in Bristol but she could take the added stress of her mum out of the situation. She looked across to Gull Island. She just needed to make sure she could secure that property.

CHAPTER SIX

Tilly dropped her battered, old VW Golf into second gear as the lane suddenly lurched downhill. The ferny banks parted to reveal little cottages nestled in a valley and the choppy sea beyond, glinting in the weak, April sunshine.

'Oh, it's so pretty!' Tilly said, gently easing on and off the brake as they continued their descent into Hope Cove.

'It is,' Archie said, still holding on tightly to Hector in the front passenger seat.

'That's the first thing you've said since we left Taunton Deane services.' Tilly said, rounding a corner lined with pretty, whitewash cottages.

A hint of summer warmth might have been in the air today but the atmosphere inside Tilly's car on the journey from Bristol had become decidedly cooler the further they had travelled. It had started off with a heated debate leaving Bristol and continued on the M5 with Archie fretting over how much he had upset Elaine.

'We're coming into the centre of the village.' Archie's voice was very matter-of-fact. 'If you turn left at the T-junction, opposite the harbour, and head up Church Lane.'

Tilly sighed. 'Okay,' she said, rolling her eyes. Did all men sulk? She carefully made her way down the narrow lane with houses dotted either side, glad that she didn't have a bigger car as the cottages were very close in places. No wonder there had been that width restriction at the top of the lane, when they'd come off the main road.

The harbour came into view and she flicked her indicator on. People bustled about in the road, going about their business. The harbour had a little, shingle beach beyond its sloping concrete, with four-by-fours pulling fishing boats in from the sea. To the right of the harbour was a tall building with fishermen huddling around outside, holding pints and laughing. The sign swinging on the wall indicated it was a pub; The Lobster Pot.

Beep! Went the car behind her.

'Left, Tilly,' Archie commanded, impatiently.

'Sorry, just taking it all in.' Tilly put the car into first gear and pulled out into the road, carefully navigating people going about their business. Evidently little Cornish fishing villages didn't do pavements.

'Where next?' she asked, pushing the car into second gear, trying to keep her eyes on the road and not on the beautiful view of the craggy cliffs with waves breaking gently against them.

'Go up past the school, then follow the road around to the left, past the church and lighthouse. We're the first cottage on the left after the school playing field; opposite the surf shack.'

'Surf shack?' Tilly's head swung around to Archie. 'Is there another beach around this hill then?' They were going steeply uphill again. Tilly noticed a disused building to her right with washed out windows. A sinking feeling swirled in her stomach. The building looked like a closed down restaurant; a long, single storey building with a canopy. Not encouraging when you were moving somewhere and would need to find a job. 'Ohhh!' The brow of the hill had peaked, and the island came into view. 'Is that Gull Island?'

'It is.'

Tilly could see a long, golden, sandy beach sneak into view below the road with great big, white, foamy waves crashing onto it. They were travelling parallel to the school playing field and she could see a double fronted grey stone cottage coming up on her left. She indicated and pulled in, finding it hard to tear her eyes away from the mesmerising coastal scene in front of her.

'You can see why Ruby settled here,' Archie said, quietly, focusing on the view in front of them.

Tilly unfastened her seatbelt and turned to Archie. 'So, you can say something unrelated to directions, then?'

Archie nodded his head and smiled. 'I can,' he said, still fixing his eyes on the view across to the island. 'When the tide is out you can walk over there.'

'That's where Ruby lives?' Tilly asked, squinting to make out the large looking manor house with smaller buildings dotted around it.

'Yes, Hope Home. Bringing hope for those who feel they're past it.'

Tilly laughed. 'Is that her mission statement?'

'Something like that. I imagine she runs it to try and work off what she sees as her penance for giving your mother up.'

Now they were getting somewhere. Archie had refused to discuss Elaine's paternity on the way out of Bristol. He seemed preoccupied with his guilt over leaving Elaine and Gran behind.

'So, you do believe Ruby is Mum's mother, i.e. my grandmother?'

'I do.'

Tilly looked up at the cottage; her new home for the foreseeable future. 'How long have you been coming here?'

Archie hesitated, looking at the cottage too. 'A couple of years. Come on, Hector,' he hurried on quickly, opening the car door, 'we'd better show Tilly around her new home.'

It had occurred to Tilly that Archie and Ruby had been friends for several years, as Ruby had said she'd been writing the same letter ever since Tilly was eighteen. But exactly how long? And the most important question of all…

'So, how did you and Ruby meet?' Tilly jumped out of the car and followed Archie to the front door.

His hands were all of a jitter as he ignored her question and focused on finding the right key.

'Here, let me.' She took the keys from Archie's hands and tried the first one that came to hand. The blue front door swung open and a delicious smell of vanilla wafted over her.

'Oh, wow!' Tilly's jaw dropped as she stepped into the airy hall with highly polished, oak floorboards. She moved from room to room, taking in the well-furnished, spacious cottage; its little nautical trinkets here and there, bright white walls, a wood burner in the living room, an archway through to a massive kitchen-cum-diner-cum-snug and wide, bi-folding doors onto an idyllic garden full of borders with flowers yet to bloom.

'It's awesome!' she called out to Archie. 'Why does she have such a fabulous second home?'

Hector's claws tripped over the floorboards as he padded along after Tilly.

Archie shrugged. 'Somewhere to escape, perhaps?'

'Well, it will do for me. It certainly makes me glad I escaped.' Tilly grinned. For the first time in a long time, all her worries about Simon, Mum and Gran simply were simply melting away.

CHAPTER SEVEN

Elaine pulled the soaked sheets off the bed and held her hand to her mouth at the overpowering smell of urine. Mum was in the lounge watching Jeremy Kyle. She stripped the mattress protector too, dumping everything angrily into the washing basket, knowing she was taking out her frustrations of Mum, Tilly and Archie on the innocent laundry. A black and white framed photo, nestled in amongst many on Mum's bedside table, caught her eye. It was of Mum and Ruby. Mum was in her mid-twenties and Ruby couldn't have been more than fifteen. Funny that there was such an age gap between them. No-one had explained why, but then no-one ever explained things in the Henshaw family. Apart from turning up out of the blue when Elaine was pregnant with Tilly, Ruby hadn't featured in Elaine's life at all. She was the black sheep, the proverbial bad penny; she was never mentioned when Elaine was growing up. She picked up the picture and studied Ruby more closely. They had the same nose and possibly the same eyes. Only Ruby's sparkled. But then, perhaps hers had sparkled when she was fifteen? Not now. They were dull now, worn down by life. They certainly shared the same petite frame, something Tilly had inherited too. Ruby was fair haired, like Elaine, although in this picture it was long and wavy whereas hers was short and limp.

Elaine put the picture back carefully and bit her lip. Was Ruby her real mother? She had always considered it unthinkable, but Tilly had accepted it the moment she was told. Tilly could see it was plausible. Elaine certainly looked more like Ruby than Lil, but then they were sisters. Ruby certainly looked like Jean, Elaine's grandmother, from what Elaine could remember of her anyway.

'Laney!' called mum from the living room.

'What?' Elaine snapped back, still appraising photograph.

'Is it elevenses yet?'

'Ugh.' Elaine sighed. 'Once I've finished your bed,' she called, putting the photo frame back and pulling a fresh cream fitted sheet from the pile of linen she'd taken from the airing cupboard.

'Can I have a teacake?'

'Bloody, infernal woman,' Elaine muttered, pulling down the elastic of the sheet over the corner of the mattress. 'Can't remember which day of the week it is but can remember what a teacake is and how much she likes them.'

The collection of photos on the bedside table caught Elaine's eye again. Next to the one of Lil and Ruby was another of her grandparents, also in black and white, on their wedding day. It was probably not long before the second world war. They looked so happy, smiling at each other, completely in love. Elaine had experienced that once, briefly. And there was Tilly throwing away her opportunity, leaving Simon and running off to Cornwall. She reached for the duvet cover and started the awkward process of trying to get her little arm span into the corners of the king size cover. She wished she could run away. She looked back at the photo of her grandparents and a distant memory stirred in the back of her mind. Her grandfather, Bob, had died when she was quite young, in the late seventies, she must have been about thirteen. But she couldn't recall Nana Jean passing away. Why couldn't she remember that? Why wasn't it significant like Grandad? Nana Jean had lived with them for a little while, in this house, but one day Lil had said she was going away. She could recall Lil telling her when Nana Jean had passed away, but Elaine hadn't long given birth to Tilly and her memories of that time were very haphazard. She'd always assumed that's why she hadn't gone to the funeral, but now she tried to recall it she couldn't remember anyone actually inviting her. Nana Jean had just moved away and a few years later, passed away. Lil had never been close to her mum so perhaps Elaine had just presumed that she lived far away, and it was too much to get to the funeral and back in a day.

Had Nana Jean run away too?

Elaine dropped the duvet and dashed into the living room. Lil, as always, was stooped over in her chair, intensely watching the television.

'Mum,' Elaine approached calmly, knowing that if she went about this the wrong way, she wouldn't get any useful information at all.

'Is it elevenses now?'

'Yes, in a minute.' Elaine knelt down and took Lil's hand.

'Mum, could you try and remember something for me?'

'I'm not very good at that,' said Lil, still focussing on the television, drool escaping from the corner of her perpetually open mouth.

'What happened to your mum? What happened to Jean? Nana Jean?'

Lil turned her head to Elaine and looked out from under her bifocals. 'Our mum? Mine and Ruby's?'

'Yes, yours and Ruby's?'

'She went to live with our Ruby.'

'When?' Elaine snapped, forgetting she was trying to take the calm approach.

'When she kept forgetting things.' Lil continued to stare at the box.

'Like you?'

Lil laughed. 'I don't forget things! Now, where's my teacake? Plenty of butter for me, please.'

Elaine rolled her eyes, stood up again and wearily made her way back through the hall to Mum's bedroom.

So, Nana Jean had started to forget things too. Instinctively, Elaine stood in front of the pictures again and concentrated. The third picture was a colour one taken in the early seventies of her mum and dad, with her sitting between them on the bench in Archie and Phyllis' garden. She was about seven or eight. It was around the time Lil began behaving peculiarly. She would get up in the night to bake or dust the house. Then she began imagining that the television was telling her to do things.

Elaine peered between the three photo frames. Something wasn't right. Ruby didn't feature at all in her life until after Grandad Stan died. Then she went from having nothing to do with her family to having Jean come and live with her. Why? Ruby ran an old people's home on an island in the middle of the sea. She knew that because it had been featured a few years ago in the psychology magazine Elaine subscribed to. The home specialised in dementia patients and had won lots of awards. Elaine dragged her eyes away from the pictures and went across the hall to her bedroom. She picked up her iPad and flipped over the cover. She was still getting used to navigating her away around it. Tilly had bought it her for Christmas because apparently, she needed to *join the 21st Century*. Elaine had been reluctant at first; all these things like Facebook and Twitter seemed another way of giving yourself low self-esteem if you asked her, however, she had to admit she used the Kindle app every night and it was useful to iMessage with Tilly instead of spending her mobile phone credit on text messages. Simon had installed the wi-fi at Christmas too. He was such a handy chap; what Elaine would give for a handsome man who could help her around the house!

Stupid girl.

Navigating the home screen, Elaine found the Safari app she needed to open to look on the internet. She typed in 'residential home Cornwall' and the first search to pop up was a link to 'Ruby Mackenzie's Hope Home'. She clicked the link and an illustration, reminiscent of a Daphne Du Maurier novel cover, sprang up. A list of awards littered the right-hand side with an oval framed photo of Ruby below welcoming the reader to the Hope Home website. Elaine clicked on the 'about' section and was taken to the history of the home. It had opened in 1983, the year before Tilly was born, by Ruby and had focused on dementia patients from the outset, now boasting to be one of the top ten dementia and mental health respite homes in the country.

Elaine clicked back to the home page and tried to remember what Tilly had taught her to do in order to zoom in on a picture. Put your fingers together and slide them out, that was it. Ruby suddenly became enlarged and Elaine focussed on Ruby's dazzling smile, expensive tailored suit and large pearl necklace around her bony neckline. What Elaine would give to look as glamourous as that. Although, as Lil had always reminded her when she still had all her faculties; wall flowers don't look glamourous, they just blend in. She was fed-up with blending in. She was fed up with always doing the right thing. Tilly defied doing the right thing and had decided to end it with Simon in the pursuit of happiness. Why couldn't Elaine do the same thing? Sitting down on her bed, she still focused on the smiley, happy photo of Ruby. She had given Tilly an escape route to Cornwall, how come she hadn't done the same for Elaine? A warm tear escaped from the corner of Elaine's eye and dropped onto the screen, distorting Ruby's face. Maybe it was because Ruby had tried to rescue her when she was pregnant with Tilly, but she'd refused to believe Ruby's claims? Whether she was her real mum or her aunt, it didn't matter. Elaine had been blind; Ruby had cared after all. She must have taken Jean off of Lil's hands and looked after her in her home. She had kept in contact with Archie in order to keep check on them all and whatever had caused the big rift in the past, she obviously still wanted to be part of their family.

'Laney! Laney! I need the toilet!'

'Coming,' called Elaine, reaching for a tissue and popping her iPad back on her bedside table. She took one last look at Ruby. 'Well, if you want to help that much, have I got a big problem for you,' she said, switching the device off.

CHAPTER EIGHT

Tilly skipped across the causeway the following morning, towards Gull Island. The tide was out, and she couldn't resist collecting shiny shells, vacant of their sea life occupiers, stuck to the damp sand. A moment of guilt lapped over her as she thought about him coming home to their empty house to find her note. But she didn't want to think about that now. He had suffocated her with his incessant budgeting for their home, for the wedding; there was never any spontaneity, not even to go out to dinner once in a while. They were always saving for something but never living for now; just existing.

She couldn't carry on living like that.

The morning was grey and drizzly, a far cry from the almost blinding sunshine when they had arrived yesterday afternoon. Mist clung to the craggy island rocks and seagulls flew in out of view, clearly unfazed by a bit of visual disturbance. Tilly bent down to pick up another scallop shell and cleaned it in a shallow pool of water before stuffing it in her pocket. Of course, the shell collecting was really all aiding in her prevarication to actually arrive at the island. She had been so eager to meet

Ruby, but after she had unpacked last night and made some supper for her and Archie – Ruby had even gone to the trouble of stocking the fridge and cupboards with food – the enormity of what she had done really struck her. Guilt had started to seep in. She'd simply emailed her boss her resignation, citing a break down in the relationship between her and Simon, packed all her essential things up and got in the car to go and collect Archie and Hector. She hadn't given Simon's feelings a single thought, and she hadn't much cared to worry about what her boss and colleagues would do when she didn't arrive for work this morning, either. She certainly wouldn't get a reference now, which might make getting a new job slightly tricky and, deep down, although she hated to admit it, even to herself, it was all very irresponsible.

It was her all over.

And now, as she made her way up the beach to the steep, winding drive leading up to Hope Home, she was worried of what Ruby would think of her. Grandmother, Great-Aunt, it didn't really make any difference; Ruby was still family. Tilly was really hoping too that she was normal. As in not like Mum or Gran; just a normal, happy-go-lucky person, that didn't give off an air of the unhinged, nor moan constantly about her problems and how they had affected the rest of her life. Tilly felt weighed down by the constant feeling she'd ruined her mother's life just by being born.

Her pace slowed as the driveway got steeper, but it quickly tapered off to reveal a car park and a sprawling, old house. It had a porch with columns and the entire house was pretty much covered in ivy, bar the windows and roof. It looked old, possibly Georgian, with newer one-storey buildings extending off in all directions. With the choppy sea waves as its backdrop, it looked very much like something out of an Agatha Christie novel, adding to the feeling of foreboding she was already experiencing.

Suddenly the double glass doors swung open and there stood a very excited looking lady, dressed head-to-toe in red, waving energetically as she ran towards Tilly.

Surely this couldn't be Ruby? Surely pensioners didn't run.

'Tilly, darling.' This glamourous, Helen-Mirren-lookalike-type-creature enveloped Tilly in a breath-taking hug. Tilly stood still, like a statue, not used to such over enthusiastic displays of affection and wallowed in Ruby's Chanel-infused embrace.

'Hello, you must be Ruby,' Tilly squeaked.

'Of course, I am darling.' Ruby released Tilly from her clutches, took a step back, placed her bejewelled hands on Tilly's shoulders and studied her face.

Tilly looked into Ruby's sparkly, blue eyes which looked like they were alight with mischief. Her hair was a neat, wavy white-blonde bob and her, remarkably, minimally wrinkled face was made-up and beaming with a smile. Tilly was suddenly overcome with a sense of belonging. She recognised those eyes, full of excitement and anticipation of what life might have to offer. It was like looking at an older version of herself.

'Er, hello,' Tilly said, awkwardly, beginning to feel a little overwhelmed by Ruby's surveillance.

'Hello,' Ruby said, hooking her arm through Tilly's and guiding Tilly towards the entrance of the home. 'Come with me and I'll show you around.'

'It's a lovely place you have here,' Tilly said, looking up at the home.

'Thank you. I like it to feel like a home-from-home for my residents.'

Tilly looked up at the first-floor windows and saw an elderly lady waving down at her. Tilly waved back.

'Who's that?'

'Hmmm?' Ruby looked up. 'Oh, that's Shirley. Terrible Alzheimer's; spends most of her time living in 1942. I expect she thinks you're a land girl.'

Tilly looked up at again at Shirley, still waving, looking clean, tidy, presentable with her glasses on and her white hair set in a perm. In spite of feeling awkward, Tilly found herself waving back. 'This is just the sort of place that would benefit Gran.' Tilly said, without even thinking.

She stopped walking and looked at Ruby, furiously blushing. 'I'm sorry, that just came out.'

Ruby laughed. 'Don't be silly my dear; Lil is my sister after all.'

'But,' Tilly hesitated. She knew she liked Ruby already, she didn't want to upset her.

'Yes?'

'Are you my aunt or my gran?'

'I'd prefer be a nana, like my mother was. But we've got a lot of ground to cover before that. Why don't you just call me what you feel comfortable calling me for now. Ruby is fine.'

Ruby smiled and Tilly instantly felt relaxed.

CHAPTER NINE

1971

'You two look like you're having fun,' Phyllis said, as Archie stepped over the back-door threshold. He had come in to pour himself and Elaine some lemonade. They were potting-on seedlings in the weak, late March sunshine.

'She used the money we gave her for her birthday last week to buy some children's gardening gloves and a little gardening set. It's a bit early to be potting-on really but we're only doing the hardy things like geraniums and petunias. Right little chatterbox she is; needs to know what I'm doing every step of the way. Very bright for just turned six, I'd say.'

'She's inquisitive, like you.' Phyllis continued with drying up the dishes, not looking at Archie. He took the bottle of pop from the larder, thinking of what to say next. It was the way Phyllis said it. *Like you.*

Archie laughed nervously. 'Nothing wrong with wanting to know things, it's how we learn.'

'Very true.' Phyllis set another breakfast bowl down on the side.

They both stood in silence watching Elaine out the window. Escaping wisps of hair, from her mousey ponytail, were blowing in the spring breeze. Archie turned and walked across the kitchen to the cupboard where Phyllis kept the glasses. 'Would you like some pop?' he asked, reaching for a glass.

'She's got your nose, hasn't she?'

'What?' Everything happened in slow motion. He turned to see Phyllis still staring out the window, her head cocked to one side in contemplation. The glass fell from his hands, smashing into hundreds of tiny pieces on the floor. His heart raced liked the first time he'd seen his precious Concorde, the one plane he had helped design, soar into the sky. But not in the same way. Fear kept him stuck in the same place, unable to move.

Phyllis turned and smiled. 'She is yours, isn't she?'

'I...' he couldn't move. He could hardly make his face and mouth move to speak. Was he having a stroke? 'How? How did you work it out?' he stammered.

Phyllis smiled. 'I put two and two together.'

'How?' Archie looked over Phyllis' shoulder to see Elaine was still engrossed in planting the seedlings. This wasn't how he had imagined his secret coming out. He wasn't prepared. He gripped the swirly cream Formica worktop for support.

'Lil has a sister called Ruby.'

Archie grimaced at the mention of Ruby's name. That was all dead and buried. He had told Phyllis before they wed that he had had a fling and she'd forgiven him. Perhaps she was mad to, but she had confessed herself that she wasn't sure whether to marry Archie or her childhood sweetheart.

Phyllis smiled at Archie from under her thick fringe. She was wearing a shirt-waister dress with a half-pinny, wrapped around. She always looked immaculate. She was so beautiful with her chestnut hair piled up in a ponytail. He loved her so much.

She put down her tea towel and tripped across the kitchen in her little kittle heel stilettos. 'Don't look so panic-stricken; I'm not about to divorce you,' she said, reaching up and planting a kiss on Archie's lips while her arms enveloped around his neck.

'When did you find out?' Archie asked, still stuck to the floor tiles, unable to move from the shock that his secret, a secret he thought he hoped he would take to the grave, was out.

Phyllis released herself from their hug and walked back across to the kitchen sink. 'When we first moved here, how long is that now?' She asked, bending down into the cupboard and pulling out the dustpan and brush.

Archie gasped. 'You've known all that time and not told me?'

'No, silly,' Phyllis laughed, crouching down to sweep up the broken glass. 'Whenever we moved here—'

'Three years ago, last Christmas.'

'Yes, well, Lillian invited me in for coffee and biscuits one morning, just before Christmas actually. Elaine was still a toddler then and we were sitting on the carpet playing with some stacking cups and Elaine went over to the mantelpiece and took down a photo of Lil and another girl, somewhat younger than Lil. Anyway, Elaine just kept saying, Ruby. I froze on the spot.

'But how did you know it was my Ruby?'

Phyllis momentarily stopped brushing and Archie cursed himself for saying *my*. She wasn't his Ruby; he hadn't wanted her and had discarded her like an old crisp packet once he'd had his fulfilment.

He really was a bastard.

'I didn't, but I just knew. It was too much of a coincidence, us moving here.'

Insensitive bastard.

'So, I had my suspicions that Lil's sister might be *your Ruby*—'

Archie inwardly cringed.

'—but I had no way to prove them.' Phyllis continued drying a glass and avoiding his gaze. 'Then last week, I was round next door having a catch-up with Lil and we were talking about Elaine's birthday, which brought us on to whether we were going to have children, which led to me explaining we were trying without much luck and Lil told me that her and Stan had had lots of trouble conceiving. So, I asked her long it had taken her to conceive Elaine.'

Archie felt his face beginning to blush furiously. They had been trying for six years now, ever since they had got married, but nothing had happened, as yet.

Total, utter bastard.

He put his hand on her shoulder and she grabbed his hand and squeezed it.

'Anyway, Lillian got all funny and I could see she was getting upset, so I tried to change the subject, but then she blurted out that she wasn't really Elaine's mum, that her and Stan had adopted her sister Ruby's baby. She said she felt terrible because she thought Ruby would have some input into Elaine's upbringing, but Ruby was so heartbroken that their dad wouldn't speak to her, and you had chosen me, that she ran off to London and now they barely hear from her.'

'Lillian knows I'm Elaine's father?'

'No!' said Phyllis, standing up. 'And keep your voice down, the back door's open.'

'But you just said—'

'Because I worked out that Ruby was heartbroken over you, not that Lillian knows who Elaine's father is.'

'Oh,' Archie said, pulling out a kitchen chair and seating himself at the table. He suddenly felt very dizzy.

Phyllis emptied the dustpan into the kitchen bin, placed the pan and brush neatly back in the cupboard and came to sit with Archie. She took her hands in his. 'Don't you see what this means, Archie?'

Archie searched Phyllis' face for answers. The only conclusion he could come to is that she would want a divorce. Only she was smiling.

'We know now that the baby making problems must be with me, not you! So, we can go to the doctors and tell them that, and they can investigate me.'

'No way.' Archie shook his head vehemently. 'I'm not letting the doctor know I've got an illegitimate child!'

'And if I can't have children—'

'Please don't say that, Phyll, love, it makes me ever so upset.' He took her hand and squeezed it.

'But if I can't,' Phyllis persevered, 'then at least we have Elaine.'

Archie stared at his wife, stunned to the core. In later life he would reflect that if they had lived in a different era, where divorce was less shameful, she surely would have wanted one.

'She's Lillian and Stan's, not mine,' he said, quietly.

'Then why did you move us here? Our little flat in Clifton was more than adequate. Much more suitable for a lifestyle without children.'

'Because this is our family home and one day, we will fill it with children, *our* children.'

'And because you know your daughter lives next door.'

Archie traced his finger along the crack in the middle of the table. He sighed. 'Yes. When this house came up for sale, it seemed like fate. But she can never know.' He looked directly into Phyllis' eyes. Her beautiful, chocolatey brown, innocent eyes. 'Lillian and Stan might stop us seeing her.

Phyllis nodded, her eyes welling with tears.

Archie rushed to hug her. 'Oh, Phyll, I'm sorry, this is all my fault.'

'Don't be,' Phyllis sobbed, her whole body shaking like a trembling bird. 'This might be a blessing in disguise. Elaine is such a lovely girl.'

Right on cue, footsteps clattered through the back door.

'Uncle Archie, can I, oh!' Elaine's little face was full of worry seeing Archie and Phyllis embracing. 'Shall I go home now?' she asked, quietly.

'No dear,' Phyllis said, reaching in her pocket for a hanky and quickly dabbing her eyes. 'Aunty Phyll is a bit upset.'

'What about?'

'Uncle Archie broke one of my glasses. Silly of me to get so upset.'

'Silly Uncle Archie for breaking it.'

'That's what I said,' Phyllis said, crouching down to Elaine's level. 'Now, why don't we get you cleaned up and you and I can make some rock cakes and leave Uncle Archie to tidy up the garden. How does that sound?'

'Can I lick the bowl?'

'Yes, just don't tell your mum.'

'Okay,' said Elaine, taking Phyllis hand. 'It can be our secret.'

'Yes,' said Phyllis, looking at Archie. 'Our little secret.'

CHAPTER TEN

Tilly trailed her fingers down the highly polished, oak staircase and dreamily imagined living in such ostentatious surroundings.

'Can you take me to the toilet?' an elderly lady asked, as Tilly almost crashed into her at the bottom of the stairs.

Perhaps without all the geriatrics then.

'No, Eileen,' Ruby interrupted, Tilly is my granddaughter. 'Julie,' Ruby called, 'can you take Eileen to the ladies please?'

Julie, a plump lady, probably in her mid-fifties with cropped auburn hair, wearing the same checked dress as all the other staff, smiled as she appeared from the communal living room and guided Eileen away.

'I could have done that,' Tilly said, feeling a bit like a spare part.

'If you had a CRB check you could.'

'What's that?' Tilly asked, following Ruby behind the reception desk and into a little office with lots of keys hanging on the wall.

'Criminal Records Bureau check,' Ruby said, sitting down in a worn, brown leather swivel chair. 'You need one to work with vulnerable people; children, the elderly etc.'

'Oh, I see.' Tilly looked around at all the greetings cards littering the walls. 'Who are all these from?' Tilly asked, peering underneath one of a costal scene.

'They're from all the relatives that write and thank me when their relative has moved on or passed away.'

'You must be very popular,' Tilly said, trying to count how many there were.

'We help a lot of people, especially those with dementia and mental health problems, who sometimes need more than straight forward care. Not psychiatric care, we don't go that far. Just individuals in need of some TLC.'

'Like Gran,' Tilly said, reading some of the kind comments.

'Like your great-grandmother too. Here she is, look.' Ruby turned around and picked up a frame of an old lady, sitting in a pale green armchair, smiling back at her.

'Is that your mum?' Tilly asked.

'Yes, she was my first inmate.' Ruby laughed. 'Probably ought not to call them that but we do occasionally get the odd escapee.'

'Really? I suppose it's no different to me wanting to escape Simon, is it? Although, I hope your residents actually like it here, it's so grand.'

'It's more they forget where they are   and   go out thinking they're on their way to work or to do some shopping. We have alarms to alert us when someone is coming in or out but there isn't one member of staff per person and we don't have eyes in the backs of our heads.'

'Ha, it sounds like when Gran goes walkabouts.'

'You keep mentioning Lil.'

Tilly frowned and put the picture of her great grandmother back on Ruby's desk. 'I suppose it's because I feel bad leaving Mum to deal with her. Gran's got worse this past year and Mum's the one suffering. She gave up her job at the local supermarket five years ago when Gran was diagnosed with Alzheimers and that really was her lifeline to the outside world. She doesn't have any friends she sees regularly; she just stays in and cares for Gran.'

'It sounds utterly miserable,' Ruby said, raking her hands through her wavy bob.

Tilly sighed. 'It is, but I can't seem to make Mum understand she's entitled to a life. I guess you must have felt the same if you looked after your mum?'

'Ah, well that was a different. I caught wind of the fact my father had died, and that Lil wasn't coping very well. You know Lil has schizophrenia?'

'Yes,' Tilly laughed. 'Before she got dementia she wasn't allowed to watch TV because she thought the television was telling her to do things, like flush all the cereal down the toilet, but since she's been diagnosed with the dementia, it's like it's altered her brain again; the TV's her best friend now, she sits and stares at it nearly all day.'

'That can happen. Her brain will be constantly changing, deteriorating.'

'It is.'

'Oh dear.' Ruby pursed her lips together sympathetically.

'So, how did you know that Lil wasn't coping with your mum? I guess it must be Archie? Did Archie live next door to Gran before you left Bristol?'

Tilly watched Ruby's face momentary flicker with what looked like a glimmer of panic. 'What? Oh, yes, he's been ever so kind over the years, keeping me abreast of the goings-on in the family.'

Tilly picked up another photo frame. This one was a picture of Ruby and Lil when they were younger, possibly just before Ruby had got pregnant with her mum.

'Is that why you turned up when Mum was pregnant with me?'

'Yes, it was. I felt it was an opportunity to get her away from Lil, but I handled it all wrong.'

'By telling her you were her mother?'

Ruby gazed at the photo in Tilly's hand. 'Amongst other things.'

'Is that why you kept writing those letters to Archie? To give me the same opportunity?'

'I did,' Ruby smiled at Tilly. 'But it was for my own selfish reasons as well, I'm afraid,' Ruby rushed on. 'I don't want to die a lonely old spinster. I want to be part of my family again; whatever relation you believe I am to you.'

Tilly nodded, her mind racing with a million questions. 'What about the father; did he ever know Mum existed?'

Ruby's elbow jolted, hitting her mouse, springing the screen of her computer to life. 'Ah!' Ruby said, over enthusiastically. 'That's what I was going to talk to you about; these are my staff timetables. We've got a few shifts where we're a bit short staffed and I wondered if you would like some work? I take it you'll be looking for work?'

Tilly wrinkled her nose. She was going to sound really like a brat now.

'That's ever so kind of you,' she stumbled over her words, 'but, er, I know from Mum looking after Gran how much patience you have to have and, well, I'm not sure I'm that person.' She winced at Ruby's blank expression.

Ruby burst out laughing. 'My girl, I'm not going to be offended! I was just trying to help you out.'

'I know, and *thank you*.' Tilly popped the picture frame back on the desk. 'Is there anywhere in the village who might be looking for work?'

'There's my rival residential home, you could always try there.'

Tilly eyed Ruby up and down. Had she offended her and now she was hurt?

Ruby laughed again, stood up and enveloped Tilly in another Chanel hug. 'I was only joking,' Ruby said, detaching herself from Tilly and reaching for a set of keys hanging alongside all the other hooks. 'Come on, I need to go over to the village for supplies; if we hurry we can make it over before the tide turns.'

'Okay,' Tilly said, watching Ruby gather up her handbag – also Chanel – and her Burberry mac from the back of her chair.

'Can I ask you something?'

'Of course,' Ruby said, smiling as she made her way through the office door.

Tilly followed like an obedient child. 'How did you afford this place? Please don't feel you have to answer that,' Tilly rushed on, 'only it must have cost a small fortune, even over thirty years ago.'

'Ha!' Ruby strode down the corridor to a rear entrance, Tilly still following. 'A very rich ex-husband and an excellent solicitor.'

'Oh.' Tilly didn't know what else to say. She felt a bit foolish for asking but if she was going to be successful herself, she needed to know how others went about it. She didn't fancy acquiring a husband just to divorce him though, she could have stayed in Bristol for that.

'Come on, I'll tell you about it on our way over to the mainland.'

Tilly had forgotten she was on an island, having walked. The sea breeze swept her long hair over her face. She pulled it back as she stepped into Ruby's Land Rover and took in the landscape of the mainland. 'Wow, it's breath taking.'

'Now you can see why I wanted to live here,' Ruby said, starting the ignition.

Tilly nodded, still taking in the view. She could just make out the little cottage her and Archie were staying in.

'I think you should go and see Winstone at The Lobster Pot.'

'Is that the pub on the harbour?'

'Yes.' Ruby made the descent down the long, steep drive to the beach. 'It's about the most happening place around here. He's always looking for bar staff; it'll tie you over until you decide what you're going to do.'

Tilly wasn't sure what that meant. Did that mean the cottage wasn't on offer forever? She hadn't been in

Hope Cove twenty-four hours, but she already knew she loved it here. She would have to work hard and decide what it was exactly that she wanted to do. In the meantime, she would go and see this Winstone. Although, she found it hard to imagine that with an old-fashioned name like Winstone, the pub was going to be either hip nor happening.

CHAPTER ELEVEN

'Ugh, there is never anywhere to park in this village,' Ruby grumbled as she tried to turn her cumbersome four-by-four around in the teeniest of car parks. She peered out of Tilly's window. 'Never mind the tide's still out; we'll go and park down on the harbour.'

'Won't the fishermen mind?' Tilly peered as far as she could out of the Land Rover window to see the harbour littered with little fishing boats which were stranded on the sand along with empty trailers and the odd tatty Defender.

'Probably.' Ruby swung the car out onto the tiny street. 'But they forget that the reason they go out to fish is because we, the great Cornish public, come to buy it. This car park is meant for patients, but I bet it's full of tourist's cars. That's the doctor's surgery there,' Ruby nodded to a building on their right which looked as if it must be built on the cliff, it was so precariously close to the sea.

A pang of guilt stabbed at Tilly's stomach. At least she knew where the surgery was now. When Mum had phoned last night, sounded calmer, she'd promised making a doctor's appointment would be first on her list of things to do today.

'There are quite a few shops for a village,' Tilly commented, as they drove slowly down the hill towards the harbour. Out of her window she has spotted a clothing boutique, a gifty looking shop, grocery, pharmacy, estate agents, post office, little supermarket, another gift shop and a fish and chip shop. Her eye was caught by the most delicious looking bakery on the corner as they turned onto the slope of the harbour.

'Wow, those Danis pastries look awesome.' Tilly craned her neck around to keep looking as Ruby kept on driving.

Ruby pulled up on the sand, wrenching up the handbrake. 'Ah, that's our very own Master Baker, James, and his wife Emma; they've won awards for their baking. They supply bread and cakes at the home. I'm going in there now to place next week's order. Why don't you pop in the Lobster Pot and introduce yourself to Winstone,' Ruby said, opening the driver's door.

Tilly looked up and squinted at the crooked, white wash, three storey building. Beyond it, the bleak spring sunlight was trying to peep through the clouds. Perhaps that was a good sign? Perhaps this Winstone might have a job going? Tilly jumped out of the car to properly appraise the pub. It certainly had charm. It wouldn't have looked out of place in Diagon Alley.

'Go on in,' Ruby called. 'I'll go and see Emma, then I'll join you for lunch.'

Tilly's stomach rumbled. 'Okay,' she said, glumly, 'but what shall I say?'

Ruby shrugged, before throwing her head back and laughing. She must have been in her sixties, possibly nearer seventy, but she was full of such life and vivacity. With her tousled hair blowing in the wind she wouldn't have looked out of place modelling in a perfume advert. 'How should I know?!' she exclaimed. 'I'm not you! Now go on, he won't bite!'

Tilly smiled and waved, as she made her way towards the pub entrance. What she would have given for Elaine to be like that, instructing her to be independent, instead of constantly fussing over her. Perhaps she wouldn't have spent her entire adult life trying to run away from Bristol then. Pushing the long, gold handle the door flung open and Tilly went hurtling in the pub. Okay, so it wasn't as heavy as she thought. All pairs of eyes – not that many locals at just before midday, but enough – fixed on who had just entered with a crash.

'Sorry,' Tilly mumbled, aware she was blushing furiously. Which was curious because normally she didn't care about making a clown of herself. Perhaps it did matter to her what the people of Hope Cove thought of her? Especially if she was going to be sticking around. Her eyes scanned the olde-worlde bar, full of small rounds tables with battered spindle chairs, dented stools and bare, dusty floorboards. It was like walking back into a pub from her childhood where her grandad used to take her on Sunday lunchtimes, before they won't home to Gran's roast. All that was missing was that ingrained tobacco smell which all English pubs had lost since the smoking ban a decade ago. Her eyes landed on a tall, dark figure at the bar polishing glasses with a crisp, white tea towel. His chocolate eyes locked on her and he smiled. Cascades of butterflies erupted in her stomach. He looked like a cross between Idris Elba and Richard Blackwood. His biceps rippled as he made a final twist of the glass with the towel. Tilly swallowed hard.

'Can I help you?'

He sounded like Idris Elba too; a thick east London accent.

'Hi,' Tilly said, taking a step forward, aware that her voice had suddenly become high pitched. 'I, er,' oh, heck, why was it so hard to get any words out? 'I, um,' she took a deep breath. 'Hi, I'm Tilly,' she said, extending her hand. He shook her trembling hand as she tried hard to collect her thoughts.

'Hi, Tilly.' A faint glimmer of a smirk whispered at the corner of his lips.

Tilly frowned, trying hard to focus. Why was this so hard? 'I was looking for your Grandad, Winstone?'

The smirk won. 'Right.' He placed the glass back above his head. Around them customers continued to chat amiably while music tinkled softly over the sound system. 'And why would that be?'

'Well, I was hoping to introduce myself.' Her breathing was going back to normal now. 'I've recently moved to Hope Cove and my, er, Ruby, suggested that I came and enquired whether you had any shifts available here?'

'Ah, there you are darling!' The door swung open and Ruby suddenly appeared at the bar a la Willow the Wisp. 'I see you've become acquainted with Winstone?'

Tilly looked blankly between Mr Muscle and Ruby. Mr Muscle was trying his hardest to supress his laughter.

The penny dropped.

Tilly wanted the ground to swallow her up.

Winstone began sniggering.

Ruby looked between the two perplexed. 'What's wrong?'

Tilly looked down at her boots.

'Tilly thought Winstone was my grandfather,' Winstone managed, between guffaws.

'Sorry,' Tilly muttered, feeling utterly stupid.

'Oh, darling, don't be sorry.' Ruby put her arm around Tilly and rubbed Tilly's shoulder.

'Are you staying for a drink?' Winstone asked.

'Lunch, actually. We'll grab a couple of menus and set up in the corner over there.'

'Great. I'll be over to take your order shortly and we can have a chat about bar work.'

Tilly looked up Winstone, hopefully. 'So, you do have vacancy then?'

'I'm always in the market for people with experience.'

'I used to work on the cruise ships,' Tilly blurted out. She felt eager to overcome her faux pas.

'Cool, well in that case, why don't you hop behind the bar and show me what you're made of while I have a drink with Ruby?'

Tilly's smile dropped as Winstone flung an apron at her.

'We're kind of desperate,' he continued. 'I think this is what you'd call perfect timing. If this shift goes well there'll be plenty more to come.'

'Okay,' Tilly sang, grabbing the apron, trying to process what had just happened. She really needed to make her next priority the doctor's surgery; her ADHD must be making a resurgence. How else could she explain running away from her fiancé yesterday and the way her body was reacting to the fit, pub landlord a mere twenty-four hours later?

CHAPTER TWELVE

I t had been tricky to even navigate his Maserati down the windy lanes into the village. Now, parked on the slope of the harbour, Winstone watched the lapping, gentle waves of the Cornish sea innocently ebbing and flowing, and his mind was instantly transported back to Ibiza. He closed his eyes, as if that would block out the pain. Instead her face, her beautiful, sun kissed face stared back at him with those accusatory, vacant eyes.

He gasped, opened his eyes and scrambled to get out of the car, as if he could leave the memories parked in there until he was ready to deal with them.

'Are you okay?' A concerned voice called.

'What?' Winstone turned to see a glamorous woman, probably in her late fifties, carrying a basket full of fresh bread, peering up at him. She used her free hand to push her golden, wavy locks away from her face. 'You look like you've just seen a ghost.'

He had.

'I, er—'

'I was just coming over to tell you not to park there; take it from me the fishermen around here don't take kindly to sports cars cluttering up their harbour. You can park up in the doctor's surgery, if you're not going to be long.'

'Oh, thanks.' Were these all signs? The sea reminding him of Ibiza, the friendly yet officious lady telling him where he could or couldn't park. He thought coming down here, doing what he knew, running a pub, would be his escape; his fresh start.

'Sorry, I'm not telling you off.' The lady hitched the basket up her hip.

'No, it's fine, I think I might have made a mistake coming here anyway—'

'You're not from around here, are you?' The lady put her hand to her forehead to block out the sharp, June sunshine as she appraised Winstone, her eyes dancing like she knew something he didn't.

'No,' he said, looking down at the particulars he had in his hand.

The lady followed his gaze. 'Ah, you've come around the Lobster Pot, haven't you?'

'I had,' Winstone said, distractedly. Perhaps this was all too soon. Perhaps he needed keep on staying with his mother in Dagenham, until he was stronger.

'Nonsense! Don't let first impressions put you off; I didn't.' The woman smiled.

'You're not from around here either?' He found himself asking.

'Bristol originally, but I lived in London before emigrating down here.'

'Pah. You make it sound like another country.'

'Oh, it is! There's only one thing Cornish folk dislike more than tourists and that's strangers that settle here.'

Winstone's eyebrows shot up.

'But, as I say, don't let that put you off. Look, you move your car up to the surgery car park; you can't miss it, it's just around the corner, back up the high street from the pub, and I'll dump these,' she gestured to the basked of loaves, 'in my car and go and grab the keys from Hardwickes, the agents.'

'They'll let you do that?'

'Oh, yes, old Edward Hardwicke is still living off the commission of the property I bought through him.'

'Oh?'

'Yes, over there,' the lady pointed out to sea.

Winstone followed her gaze to the island out in the sea, with a not unsubstantial looking manor house prominently glinting in the sun. He let out a low whistle. 'Woah, that *is* a house and some. Do you own the island too?'

'Ha,' the lady chuckled. 'No, just the land. Although, I guess that sort of means I do! Either way, you're going to like it here, er—'

'Winstone.' Winstone held out his hand. 'Winstone Chambers. And how do you know I'm going to stay? I haven't even looked around the pub yet.'

'Ruby,' the lady said, taking his hand and shaking it. 'Because I know a lost soul who needs saving when I see one.'

Winstone pursed his lips and fought back the tears. How could this woman, he'd only just met, be so perceptive?

'I thought you said they weren't very friendly around here?' Winstone chuckled, nervously.

'That's the good thing.' Ruby smiled. 'When others won't befriend you, you only have one choice; to learn to like yourself again.'

Winstone swallowed hard and nodded. He hadn't seen the pub yet, but he knew he was going to take it. What Ruby had just said was exactly what he was looking for.

CHAPTER THIRTEEN

Archie took another sip of his pint and looked across the harbour. The sun had come out and so had the tourists with it. It was only mid-April but that didn't stop the flocks of tourists all wanting to experience a quaint, quiet little fishing village. Although it was anything but quaint and quiet with all these tourists.

'Better get used to it,' he muttered, 'only going to get worse when summer arrives.' He looked down at Hector who was snoozing on the patio of the little veranda at The Lobster Pot, oblivious to Archie's dejected mood.

'By getting used to it, I take it you're stopping for a while.' A thin, pale hand jangling with sparkly bracelets placed a fresh pint glass down on the table and the head sloshed over and down the glass.

Archie looked up to see Ruby smiling down at him. With the sunlight behind her, creating a halo effect around her crown of white blonde curls, she really didn't look much different to the day he'd met her. All life had thrown at her and she never failed to smile.

'Thank you,' he said.

'Winstone told me you'd been nursing your one so long it had probably gone flat.' She squeezed herself around the table, sitting down on the little concrete wall before leaning back on the balcony railings.'

'Yes, I doubt I'm his most lucrative customer; I'll get Tilly the sack.'

'Oh, don't worry about Winstone, he was only joking. That's his 'thing', having a laugh. I suspect it's hiding what's really going on the inside.'

'Taken up amateur psychology, have we?' Archie bit his tongue for being so cantankerous. He was in a miserable mood, but it wasn't Ruby's fault.

'And you're turning into a right old git.' Ruby took a sip of her glass of wine.

'Touché.' Archie twisted his pint glass around idly watching the bubbles fizz to the top.

'So, are you going to tell me why you've been avoiding me for the past week?'

There it was; the reason she had tracked him down. He took a sip of his new pint and swallowed hard, biding himself some time. He had been avoiding Ruby but then, he'd been avoiding Tilly wherever possible; only getting up when she'd gone to work, cooking her supper then disappearing off to watch television in his room. He was feeling guilty. Although seeing he had suffered with a feeling of guilt nearly all his adult life, it should really come as no surprise nor hardship to him anymore.

'I've been avoiding everyone.' He stared out to sea, wondering if he should just hire a boat and go and discover the rest of Cornwall by coast for a few days.

'By sitting in the pub?' Ruby raised a sceptical eyebrow and rested her head in her hand. 'Don't do this to me Archie.'

'Do what?'

Hector, seeming to instinctively know a row was brewing, hopped up into Archie's lap and covered his eyes with his paws.

'Shut me out. You do it all the time.'

Archie almost choked on his lager. 'I beg your pardon! How do I *always* shut you out?'

'You come down here when you want to escape the situation at home then, when you've had enough and begin missing Elaine and Tilly, you up sticks back to Bristol without as much as a by your leave.'

'I think that's a little unfair,' Archie said, feeling stung, most probably because Ruby did have a point. It was exactly what he did, although it pained him to admit it.

'Well, it's true. It's been the same since Phyllis passed. You dropped me for her all those years ago and now you think you can pick me up and drop me again, whenever it suits you.'

'Now steady on and keep your voice down,' Archie hissed.

'Well, it's true.' Ruby's bottom lip jutted out just like Tilly's did when she was being defensive.

Archie took Ruby's free hand. It was freezing cold. He squeezed it. 'You know, just because Phyllis isn't here anymore doesn't mean I love her any less. Or miss her for that matter.'

'I know.' Ruby massaged her forehead. 'But I loved you once too and I had to get over that Archie, I had to move on.'

'And now I'm back and messing with your feelings.'

'Did I say that?' Ruby snapped. 'I'm on about the girls.'

'Yes, and that's what's bothering me the most. Poor Elaine stuck at home, looking after Lilian. She has no life of her own, you know. Day-in, day-out; feeding her, washing her, washing those urine-soaked sheets all the time. Perhaps I shouldn't have given Tilly that letter. Poor Elaine is stuck on her own now with no support.'

Ruby drew her hand away. 'Then why did you?'

'Because Tilly was being suffocated by Simon and Elaine. She was going to settle down to a life of mundanity and Tilly is too creative for that. Only, now I'm overcome with guilt that I've left Elaine in the lurch with no support.'

Ruby shrugged. 'I can't help you there. I've tried. I've offered to help Elaine before, but she refuses to see me as anything more than an interfering aunt who wants to stir up trouble.'

Archie chuckled. 'And yet Tilly was willing to embrace you the moment she found out. Funny how they're so different.'

'No different to Lil and I, really.'

'You're right there.' Archie took a hefty swig of his pint, feeling better for unburdening his vexations.

'You know, we could always tell them the truth.'

Archie put his pint glass down with a resounding *thud*. 'And what good would that do? After all these years. I'd risk neither of them speaking to me ever again!'

Ruby leaned across the table. 'But if we told them,' she hissed, 'we could all move on. All of us!' Her eyes were bright like always but pleading.

Archie swallowed hard. He had a feeling he knew what Ruby really meant by 'move on' but he wasn't ready for that. 'I can't risk losing them,' he said, not feeling able to meet Ruby's gaze.

'At the moment, they're not really yours to lose.'

'What's that supposed to mean?'

'They think you're their kindly next-door neighbour.'

'How can you be so cold about this, Ruby?'

Ruby's gaze turned from pleading to dull, disappointed perhaps. 'Not cold, Archie, just weathered. I've had years to come to terms with being shut out of my family's lives.' And with that, she took a final swig of her wine, picked her handbag and walked back through the French doors to the pub.

Archie went back to gazing out at the harbour. The tide was on the turn, going out. All the little fishing boats were abandoned for the day. Was that what he had done? Abandon everyone one? He'd certainly abandoned Ruby for Phyllis and, in turn, inadvertently abandoned

Elaine to an adoptive mother whose mental health had meant she had not really been fit enough to look after Elaine. But he had done the next best thing, he had moved next door and together he and Phyllis had given as much support as Lil and Stan would allow. But Ruby was right; since Phyllis had passed, he did come to Hope Cove to escape Bristol and abandoned Ruby every time he felt the pull to return home. Now he'd brought Tilly here and abandoned Elaine all over again.

It was time to change, Archie decided, putting down his pint and placing Hector on the floor. No more letting people down like he'd been doing all his life.

CHAPTER FOURTEEN

Tilly took off her apron and hung it up. Grabbing her bag from under the counter, she took a quick hop, skip and jump across the creaky floorboards of the lobby, where the stairs led up to the restaurant room above, and she was out the door which led onto the high street and straight into the hustle and bustle of the village. She was half way through her sixth shift at The Lobster Pot since her ad hoc interview last Friday and here she was, yet again, with every intention of going and registering at the doctor's surgery but finding a shop window on the way there much more interesting to disappear into. For the first time in a week her stomach was rumbling too and the fresh smells coming from the bakery opposite the pub were making it difficult not to be enticed across the cobbles. There were rows of fresh buns, pastries, and delicacies. Her eyes fell upon the Cornish pasties; in neat rows, all plump and alluring with a shiny egg wash over their tops. Her stomach groaned again. She'd decided last week that if she didn't want to end up looking like a pasty she was going to have to limit her intake of local delicacies such as pasties, fish and chips and scones with clotted jam and cream. Or take up running. But so far, she'd been really good and lived off salad from the local supermarket and fresh fish from the fishermen's market, by the harbour, and her jeans were actually feeling a little loose; she was going in. The door tinkled and she nearly walked into the person standing right in front of her. The shop floor was heaving.

'Er, is this the end of the queue?' Tilly asked the elderly man wearing cardigan and slacks and leaning on a stick.

'I think it's that lady with the buggy, my dear,' the man said, pointing over to the other side of the bakery.

'Thank you.' Tilly smiled and squeezed herself between the lady with her sleeping baby and the counter. She counted up the customers in front of her; seven, eek. There might just be time to run up the hill to make a doctor's appointment and chuff on the pasty on the way back down. Although, who was she kidding; this was the perfect excuse and bury her head in the sand for another day. She studied the counter inside the bakery. Some of the mini tartlets were so intricate, delicate and moreishly inviting. No wonder there was such a queue; who would have thought a little fishing village like Hope Cove would have such a high-class patisserie? She could never attempt anything like that; she wouldn't know where to start. The queue moved forward, and Tilly's eye was caught by a sign on the notice board she was standing right next to.

Beginners Baking

Join Emma at Harbour House Bakery for our beginner's bakery course starting Tuesday 16th April at 6pm. For complete novices through to those wanting to learn a few more baking skills. Wow your loved ones with fluffy rock cakes, chewy meringues and pack a punch with our signature pasty recipe. £60 for six weeks of classes — enquire at the counter.

Tilly's heart rate soared. She could do that! She could actually do that; it was her night off. She looked in front of her and the queue had gone down to four. She could barely keep still, she felt that excited. She would keep it a secret, tell Archie that she'd got an extra shift at the pub and then she would surprise him with what she'd baked. Life had been hard for Archie since Phyllis had passed away, Phyllis had pretty much all the cooking all their married life. He had mastered basic meals, but he missed Phyllis' baking. He'd been really down in the doldrums this past week too; it would be nice to do something to cheer him up. Plus, who knew where else it might lead?

'Can I help you?'

So caught up in her plan to become the next Mary Berry Tilly hadn't realised she'd standing at the front of the queue.

'Yes, please, I'd like one of your medium traditional pasties and I'd like to enquire about your baking classes.' Tilly pointed to the notice board behind her.

'Oh, I'm sorry,' the lady, presumably Emma, said taking a paper bag and sliding a hot pasty into it. 'I should have taken that sign down; the course is full now.'

'Oh.' Tilly fumbled in her bag for her purse to hide her disappointment.

'We'll be doing another class in June, though, shall I put your name down for that?'

'Yes, please,' Tilly said, handing over her change.

'Thanks. You're, Tilly, Ruby's niece, aren't you?'

Tilly frowned. 'Yes, how did you know?'

'You're living in a village now; we villagers know everything!' The lady laughed.

Tilly smiled. 'Okay, well if you could put me down for your next course that would be great. Shall I give you my number?'

'Write it on here. I'm Emma by the way.' Emma held out a pad and paper for Tilly.

'Thanks, well you know I'm Tilly.' he picked up the pencil and began to scribble her name on the pad. 'Could you recommend a recipe book I could start off with? I'm rubbish as cookery. I could start practising before the next course starts.'

'You don't need any experience at all to learn on our courses, but there's my book in the window, if you wanted to have a play at something easy?'

Tilly swung around to see the display of books in the other little window which faced out onto the lane they had driven down the day she and Archie had arrived in the village.

'You have your own recipe book?' Tilly asked, in awe.

'Yes, I only launched it a few weeks ago; that's what the lessons are about, to tie-in with the book.'

Tilly went and picked one up from the window. There was a lovely picture on the front cover of a delicious looking carrot cake on a cake stand, with Emma cutting a slice while a man holding a baby looked on, rather adoringly.

'Is this your husband?' Tilly asked.

'Yes, that's James and our son Finn.'

'Aww, he's cute!' Tilly smiled. 'How much?' She held up the book.

'Tell you what, have it on me.' Emma smiled. She had a friendly face with golden blonde hair tied back in a short ponytail. She looked suspiciously slim to be a good baker though, just like Mary Berry.

'That's so kind of you! Are you sure?'

'Yes, I could see how crestfallen you were.'

'Thank you!' Tilly beamed. 'That's ever so kind of you; I will go home and practise. I want to bake for Archie, my, er…' Tilly faltered. Archie was technically just her mum's next-door neighbour, but that just sounded weird. 'He's a bit like a grandad to me. We're staying in Ruby's cottage on the mainland.'

'Yes, I've met Archie a few times over the past couple of years. They make quite a striking couple, don't they?'

Tilly paused for a moment. Then nodded, unusually for her at a loss for what to say.

'I expect we'll see quite a lot of each other; we live in the cottage next door to yours. You back onto the school playing field and we back onto the allotments.'

'Oh! I thought that was part of your garden.'

'Gosh, no, don't think I could manage all that gardening!'

'Are there any available plots at the moment?'

'I'm not sure, you'd have to ask Mrs Coleman, next door to us.'

The door tinkled and another customer strolled in.

'Okay, and thanks very much for this!' Tilly held up the book.

Emma waved as Tilly jingled the doorbell again and stepped back out onto the street, her pasty still warm in the bag. She looked up at the doctor's surgery. Stuff it; she had ten minutes before she had to be back in the pub and the sun was shining. She would sit on the harbour wall, eat her pasty and read through Emma's recipes. She would go to the doctors, of course she would, but she'd read in the paper at the weekend that one of the best ways to aid mental health issues was through mindfulness; getting creative, going for walks, connecting with nature, drawing, colouring-in. Tilly had scoffed once when mum had bought a colouring-in book. But baking would fall into this category surely? Another reason to keep her away from the medication for a bit longer.

CHAPTER FIFTEEN

It always surprised Winstone that the pub was so empty on Fridays. Saturdays, and Sundays even, were lively. Okay, not Ibiza lively but certainly there was hustle and bustle all day and evening with a never-ending queue at the bar. You'd think people would stay in mid-week, keeping their alcohol allowance down after a boozy weekend or keeping their money in their pockets until the next one, but no, Fridays – with the exception of the school holidays – were pretty dull and boring.

So boring.

He checked his watch and folded up the local evening newspaper he'd been reading. He had no interest in local current affairs, but his punters did, so it was always good to be abreast of what was going on in the village and local towns. He'd found himself checking his watch more frequently since Tilly had started working for him. He had come a long way in the six years he had lived in Hope Cove. He could smile now at that first encounter with Ruby telling him he'd need to learn to like himself again. He had achieved that, if nothing else. But he kept his heart protected and his feelings locked up to anyone apart from his mum and Laura, his counsellor. Then, out of the blue, Ruby's niece had arrived and, suddenly, he was experiencing a feeling he thought was pretty much lost to him. A stirring of excitement at the thought of a shift with Tilly. Funny, enthusiastic, a hit with the customer; there was nothing not to like. She was intriguing too; she kept her cards close to her chest. In the week she'd been working here he'd found out little about her personal life. She was certainly having an enigmatic effect on him.

He glanced at his watch again; one-minute past seven-thirty and like clockwork she whirled in through the pub door bringing a cool blast of sea air with her. He looked at her, pursing his lips, shaking his head and tapping his watch. Her smile dropped. He winked. She rolled her eyes.

'Whatever,' she said, pushing her bag up on her shoulder and grinning from ear to ear. 'I was having a few domestic issues.'

'Go and put your things away and you can fill me in,' he said, walking behind the bar to crank the stereo up. Perhaps some lively music might entice a few stragglers outside.

He served a customer wanting a refill of cider and went to collect some empties all the time impatient for Tilly's return. She was the most interesting thing to happen in Hope Cover for years.

'So, I pretty much managed to make the oven catch fire,' Tilly said, breaking through Winstone's thoughts.

He laughed. 'Why doesn't that surprise me Little Miss Accident Prone?'

She picked up a tea towel and threw it at him. 'Oi!'

'What?' He spread his arms wide. 'I've lost three pint glasses and two wine glasses in the past week.'

Tilly looked bashful and fiddled with the bar taps. 'Sorry,' she muttered.

'Don't be,' he said, feeling a twinge of guilt that he might have gone too far with his teasing. He didn't know enough about her yet to know where her limits were. 'So,' he continued, trying to rein in the flirting, 'what happened.'

'Well, I tried to enrol on a cookery course at the bakery today with Emma but this next course is full, so she gave me a copy of her new recipe book to start on in the meantime and—'

'Tilly, slow down; there's no customers waiting, you can take your time.' Winstone interrupted, noticing Tilly's speech was speeding up. It was something he'd learnt in counselling, something he'd been guilty of himself in the past; talking too much and too fast.

Tilly blushed and looked down at the bar taps. 'Sorry, my head's still rushing from being late.'

'Well, you're here now.' Winstone smiled.

Tilly managed to look up and smile back awkwardly. 'Thanks, well, I had a go at homemade soup and cheese scones. I thought that would be easy enough. I invited Ruby too; talk about embarrassing! The kitchen was full of plumes of smoke.' She covered her eyes with her hands. 'Poor Archie and Ruby are on their way down here for supper, after they've cleaned up my mess.'

Winstone waited for her to uncover her face from her hands. He raised his eyebrows questioningly. 'Not the next Raymond Blanc then?'

'No.' Tilly's shoulders slumped. 'But the good news is that Emma knocked on the door, as I was on my way out, to say she'd had a cancellation so I can start next week anyway.' Eventually, Tilly managed to meet his gaze with a smile.

He was itching to ask. It was none of his business, but he just couldn't help himself. 'So,' he rubbed his hand along the bar, 'you didn't have anyone to cook for you back in Bristol then?'

'Ha!' She laughed. 'Chance would have been a fine thing. No, my mum's a bit of a control freak, we all had to stay away from *her* kitchen and Simon was the same; he liked to do all the cooking.'

He really mustn't. He shouldn't. But it was like a spot that needed to be squeezed. 'Simon?'

Tilly made an awkward face. 'My ex. We were going to get married.'

'Oh?'

'Yeah, but we weren't really suited. When Archie gave me the letter from Ruby, I knew I'd found my escape route.'

Winstone pursed his lips together as somewhere in his stomach, somewhere deep down, he hadn't felt for a long while, he felt a twinge. He knew that feeling of wanting to escape all too well. He frowned, trying to focus. 'Hang on, you're telling me you've only recent found out about Ruby?'

Tilly smiled and nodded, her ringlets bouncing around on her shoulders.

'You are very intriguing, Tilly Henshaw.'

'No more than you, Winstone Chambers. Like how does a man in his – what late thirties?'

'Yes, steaming towards forty.'

'End up living in a dead-end place like this?'

'The same reason as you, I guess.'

Tilly looked into his eyes, her vibrant green ones full of questions. They suddenly dulled. Whatever she was about to open up to him, she changed her mind. 'Talking of dead; that's exactly what it is in here tonight.'

Damn. Avoiding giving away too much. It reminded him of what he used to be like. 'It always is on Fridays and I can never figure out why.'

'People need a reason to come out, perhaps?.'

'Other than my dashing looks, incredible wit and our excellent menu?'

'Or your inflated ego.' She winked.

'Well, Little Miss Après ski, what do you suggest?'

'Stop calling me a Little Miss for a start. Yes, please,' she said to one of the locals, Fred, who had approached the bar.

Winstone watched Tilly pulling the pint and laughing and joking with Fred. She was like a ray of sunshine with everyone but from what she'd just told him, there was something going on under that façade. People didn't run away for nothing. He, for one, was well aware of that.

'There you go, Winstone.'

'Hmmm?'

'A pub quiz! That will bring the locals out; I can't believe you don't hold one all ready?!'

His heart sank. Why did he open his big mouth and complain about it being quiet? Anything but a pub quiz. He sighed and shook his head. 'Because they're so cliché.'

'Oh, come on now,' Fred said, in his thick, Cornish accent, 'we're in here all the time watching the sport, wouldn't harm us to talk to one another a bit.' He beckoned to his companions in the corner; the regulars who came in every night to escape their wives and hardly ever said two words to each other during the course of an evening.

'Oh, go on Winstone, it would be a laugh! We could run an accumulator, so the prize money builds up over a few weeks. I'll get Ruby and Archie to make up a team; it'll be fun!'

Winstone inwardly groaned. 'Sounds like it's already been decided.'

'You won't sound so negative when your profits are up,' she said, handing Fred his pint and taking his money.

Winstone watched her move graciously, laughing with Fred over what he and his mates might call his team. He shouldn't be so negative; Tilly was trying to help. It wasn't as if he hadn't thought of a pub quiz before. He just preferred the gentle hum of chatting punters to being the centre of attention. He'd been the centre of attention before and look where that had got him. It was what have driven him here, to quietly live out his existence is sleepy, non-eventful Hope Cove.

That's what he wanted out of life; no drama.

85

CHAPTER SIXTEEN

1973

'Thank you for this,' Stan said, standing at the back door in hushed tones.

'It's never any bother,' Phyllis said, putting her hand on Stan's shoulder and squeezing it.

Archie pursed his lips together and tried to supress his feelings of anger and frustration. It was gone midnight and Stan had just come back from the hospital where Lil had been sedated.

'I don't know what possessed her.' Stan was staring at the ground, shaking his head.

Archie wanted to snap that they had spent the best part of the last hour going through different scenarios as to why Lil had decided to lock Elaine in the bathroom for at least an hour – allegedly because she wouldn't eat her liver and onions – leaving Elaine frightened, scared, lonely and looking for an escape route which had consequently led to Elaine climbing up onto the bathroom sink to reach the window, slipping and fracturing her collar bone when she fell in the, thankfully, empty bath. The only conclusion

Archie kept returning to was because Lil was a bloody mad woman.

'Would you like me to come over to yours with you and make you some hot milk?' Phyllis asked. 'Might help you drop off to sleep?'

Stan rubbed his eyes. He was in his late thirties, if Archie recalled, but he was looking like a man on the brink of drawing his pension this evening with all the weight of worry on his shoulders. Archie sincerely hoped he didn't have flecks of white hair around his temples and ears in a few years' time.

'That's kind, but I'll be fine. I'm sorry to do this Phyllis, but would you mind looking after Elaine tomorrow and taking her for her check-up at the hospital? I don't know whether I'm coming or going. I'll have to take the day off work and go to the psychiatric ward to be with Lil. They're going to assess her in the morning.' There was a long pause where Archie was pretty sure he was thinking what Stan was too scared to say. 'I think they might section her,' Stan said, quietly still looking at his feet.

Phyllis put her hand on Stan's upper arm and squeezed it. 'It's not your fault, Stan.'

Stan continued to look down. 'Feels like it though.'

Archie's irritation made way for sympathy. What had this poor man ever done to face this hellish scenario. Having a mad wife was the sort of thing that could make a man lose his job.

'Look, don't worry, Stan,' Archie said, firmly. 'We won't say anything. The school need only know Elaine fell over in the bathroom.'

Stan looked up. 'But what if social services get involved?'

'Then send them around to us, we'll vouch for you, won't we, Phyll?'

Phyllis nodded in agreement.

'We'll tell them we're your back-up. Phyll doesn't work, she'd be happy to do school pick up and things like that, if Lil's too ill, won't you love?' Archie could hear the pleading in his voice. It wasn't a desperation to help Stan, not really. It was the dawn of realisation that he could lose Elaine all over again.

'Of course.' Phyllis smiled, reassuringly.

'Thank you,' said Stan, 'I don't know what we did to deserve you two, but I am truly grateful for all your help.'

Archie couldn't bring himself to look at Phyllis. It wasn't fate which had brought them to live next door to Stan, just plain, selfish, infidelity.

Stan pursed his lips and opened the back door. He hesitated as he stepped out onto the drive. 'What happens if they don't allow Lil to come home? I'm not sure I'll be any good at looking after our Laney on my own.'

Archie bit his tongue.

'I just said, Stan, we're here,' Phyllis said, in a soothing, reassuring tone. 'They'll do something for Lil, I'm sure. She might need her medication changed or perhaps they'll say she needs some of that therapy they keep talking about on Woman's Hour, what do they call it?' She snapped her fingers. 'Counselling.'

'I think we're way beyond talking. That's the problem really; she's quite often silent, like she's in her own little world.'

Phyllis exchanged a worried glance with Archie.

Stan shuffled, as if he wanted to go but something was urging him to stay. 'She's not ours, you know,' he muttered. 'Well, in our hearts she is but we adopted her.'

Phyllis nodded. 'Lil told a while ago.'

Stan bowed his head. 'I just wonder if the guilt has made her go mad.'

'Oh Stan!' Phyllis exclaimed.

'Sssh,' said Archie, 'you'll wake Elaine.'

'Stan,' Phyllis whispered, 'you mustn't think like that! What have either of you got to feel guilty about?'

Archie swallowed hard.

Stan rubbed his eyes again. 'We adopted Laney from Lil's sister, Ruby. She's a fair bit younger than us, more your age, and old Bob, my father-in-law, was pushing her into having a backstreet abortion.'

An icy feeling of guilt trickled down Archie's spine as he thought of a pregnant Ruby, all alone with no-one to turn to for support. Why hadn't she told him? Because he had told her to go away. He had told her that he had decided to wed Phyllis and that their relationship was a mistake. What a tangled web of secrets and lies it had turned into.

'Well, you go home and get some sleep and we'll catch up with you when you get back from the hospital.'

Phyllis closed the door and drew her dressing gown tighter around her waist.

'Goodness me, what a mess! That Ruby has a lot to answer for.'

Archie could tell the moment the words were out Phyllis regretted them. The colour drained from her face and her pupils became as wide as tea saucers.

Her hand shot to her mouth. 'I'm sorry, I just meant, you know, that if Ruby had kept the baby then perhaps Lil wouldn't be so ill.'

Archie wanted to say that he couldn't see Ruby had any other option. She would have been forced into having a bodged abortion and would have probably ended up barren. Who knows, by now she might be married with three children. Either way, he certainly wouldn't have had any opportunity to be in Elaine's life. At least Ruby had given him that.

'I'm going to check on Elaine,' he said, kissing Phyllis on her forehead and heading out of the kitchen and down the hallway.

The little lamp in the guest bedroom was still on and Elaine was reading a book.

'Ah, Enid Blyton,' he said, sitting down beside her. She winced as her body moved with the mattress. 'Sorry, Uncle Archie needs to learn to be more careful now you're broken.'

'Did mum break something too?'

Archie smoothed the quilt down and tucked it in around the mattress. 'I guess you could say that.' He paused, trying to choose his words carefully. 'I guess you could say that her brain is a bit broken.'

Elaine used her good hand to smooth her blonde hair away from her face. 'Is your brain in your head?'

'That's right.'

'So, did she fall and break it, like me?'

Archie smiled. 'No, our brain is a bit different to the rest of our body, it sends messages to to do things like move our arms and legs and go to the toilet, but it also helps us to have feelings too. I think perhaps the messages your mum's brain is sending out is making her feel unwell and do silly things.'

'Is that why she locked me in the bathroom; because her brain told her to?'

Archie nodded and looked down at his beautiful daughter. She was a bright little button. She could achieve great things if she was directed on the right path.

'I think so,' he said softly, taking her book out of her hands and placing it on the bedside cabinet. 'The Naughtiest Girl in the School,' he said, reading the cover. 'I hope that's not you at school.'

'No,' said Elaine, stifling a yawn. 'So, I wasn't locked in the bathroom for being naughty?'

'No, darling, you most certainly weren't naughty. It was just those messages in your mum's brain thinking you should be shut in the bathroom. I promise it won't happen again.'

'Really?'

'So long as your Uncle Archie lives next door, I promise you will be safe.'

'Thank you. Sometimes I wish I was like Elizabeth and could go away to school with other girls and not stay at home.'

It was like someone had torn Archie's heart in two.

'Oh, and why's that?' Archie asked as nonchalantly as he could.

'Then perhaps when Mum saw me in the holidays, she wouldn't be so cross with me.'

Archie took Elaine's little hand and squeezed it tight.

'Just remember that me and Auntie Phyll are always here if you need us. If you are ever scared, you only need to come next door to us.' He looked down at this frightened little creature with her sleepy eyes trying to keep awake to hear what he was saying. Although what he really wanted to say was that he was her daddy and he loved her so much that nothing would hurt her ever again.

But he couldn't.

'Thank you.' Elaine yawned again.

'Right, missy, you've had an eventful day, time you got some sleep. Shall I sing you a bedtime song?'

'Yes, please,' Elaine said, closing her eyes.

He didn't know where it came from, but he started:

You are my sunshine, my only sunshine
You make me happy when skies are grey
You'll never know dear, how much I love you
Please don't take my sunshine away

When she was breathing heavily, Archie crept out of the room, leaving the light on in case Elaine woke in the night, disorientated.

He pulled the bedroom door behind him. In the chink of light, he could see Phyllis, her face wet from crying.

'You only sing Johnny Cash when you're sad,' she said, bursting into sobs.

'Come here you daft thing,' he said, pulling him to her and kissing the top of her hair. 'It just seemed appropriate, but it's exactly the same way as I feel about you. I don't want to lose either of you ever, Phyllis. Never.'

CHAPTER SEVENTEEN

Archie knocked the back door and waited. In the past he would never have waited, just bowled straight in after that first knock but it didn't seem appropriate today. The amount of times he had stood on this threshold and enquired to Lil and Stan about Elaine over the years and now he was here to enquire to her himself. What if she didn't want to speak to him? It was a question he'd pondered the entire train journey back to Bristol. But, for some inexplicable reason, the time she had fallen and broken her collarbone was weighing heavy on his mind at the moment. It had woken him at night these past few nights and he couldn't let it prick his conscious any longer. He had once promised that he would always be there for Elaine, but he had failed her; he had abandoned her in favour of Tilly. One could argue that he was putting his granddaughter first, but that didn't stop the promise being broken. Not that either of them knew who the hell he really was anyway, but it didn't stop him feeling responsible. For both of them.

He continued to wait but no-one answered. It was odd but he couldn't hear the usual hum of the washing machine resonating through the door or Lil's television blasting out. Tentatively, not wanting to scare Elaine, he tried the backdoor handle. Locked. Very strange. Strolling around to the front of the bungalow, he quelled the urge to go to his bungalow and check the post. He'd had to ignore the over growing front lawn and weeds in the shrubbery border when he'd stepped out of the taxi too, for fear his need to orderliness would kick in and he'd put off coming to see Elaine a little longer while he tidied up his own home. He walked across the front lawn and peered through the windows. The curtains were closed with only a crack to peek through. It was dark and very empty looking.

'She's not 'ere,' came a voice over the low fence. Iris, whose bungalow neighboured Elaine's was standing on her driveway in her usual knitted cardigan and tweed pleated skirt, peering over her spectacle rims. 'She left this morning.'

'Where? What about Lil?' Archie could hear the panic rising in his voice.

'Taken her with her. She's renting the place out for six months.' Iris gestured to the big pink and blue 'Let' sign, tied to the lamppost at the front of Elaine's garden. How had he missed that?

'What?' Fear was greeting panic and rising in his chest. 'Why? Where have they gone?'

'She said Tilly's relocated to the coast, so she's gone to stay with her for a while.'

The hot air in Archie's chest was turning into icy condensation running down his spine.

'What?'

'Yes, she said something about her aunt running a retirement home and she hadn't thought about it before, but it made sense to leave Lil there for a few months so she could have a break. I'll tell you what,' Iris said, folding her arms and puffing her enormous chest out like a robin, 'she deserves it, that girl. Nothing but bad luck! It's funny though because Stan only had brothers and I can't remember Lil mentioning a sister once and I've lived here longer than you and Phyllis.'

'Perhaps,' said Archie, absently, for his mind was racing at one hundred miles per hour, 'they didn't get on.'

'Then why take Lil to her old folk's home? I'll tell you now, Elaine's in danger of going the same way as Lil if she's not careful.'

'What do you mean?' A surge of protectiveness surged through him.

'You know,' Iris made a loop movement to the side of her head. 'Gah, gah.'

'Lil has schizophrenia; it doesn't make her a lunatic,' Archie found himself snapping. 'And Elaine is just run down from looking after Lil, that's all.'

Iris bristled, pushing her spectacles back up her nose. 'Been on your holidays?'

'No, visiting family. Actually, I'm going to have to go back again as one of my relatives is unwell and has no dependants.' Archie had no idea where he was spinning these new lies from but what did it matter with the lifetime's web of secrets and lies he had already woven?

'Could I write down my mobile number and drop it through your door? I'm not sure how long I'm going to be away this time and if anything, untoward should happen, I would rather know.'

'Course,' said Iris, smiling, appearing unfazed by Archie's earlier abruptness. 'Pop it through the letterbox and I'll keep an eye. Who knows what kind of reprobates are moving in next door?' She cocked her head in the direction of Elaine and Lil's.

'Thank you, Iris.' He turned to walk towards his own driveway and stopped. 'Oh, and sorry I was rude. I am a little sensitive at the moment, what with my family problems.' That wasn't a lie; Elaine, Tilly, Lil, Ruby, they were all his family, of sorts.

'I'm sorry too, Archie,' Iris said, beginning to walk back down her own driveway. 'Times are a changing; you can't go around calling people nutty no more, can you?'

Archie wanted to reply that it would have been helpful if people didn't refer to those with mental health issues as 'nutty' in the first place, but he didn't want another argument. Instead he just waved and scurried to his front door. He had a more pressing engagement with his house line to phone Ruby and warn her that Elaine would be arriving any second with Lil.

CHAPTER EIGHTEEN

The little ferry boat rocked back and forth but Elaine kept her eyes fixed directly on Gull Island. It was a murky day, but the Hope Home looked striking against its gloomy, grey background.

'I didn't know our Ruby lived in France,' Lil said, clinging onto Elaine's arm like a child would their mother's.

'No, mum, *I explained*.' God she might as well *be* the mother, she was forever treating Mum like a child. It had been that way for as long as she really could remember. Ever since she'd fell off the bathroom window ledge and fractured her collar bone on the bath. She'd been the one looking after Lil, not the other way around. Phyllis had been more like a mother to Elaine than Lil ever had.

'You didn't say we'd need to come on a boat. *You* just said the train and we've been on the train.'

'Yes, mum, I know.' It was like living with a toddler *all the time*. Not for much longer though, Elaine smiled to herself as the craggy cliffs became clearer. She could see gulls nesting in coves and cliff flowers swaying in the sea breeze. It felt like she was seeing life again for the first time, through a fresh pair of eyes. Instead of being cooped up in that dreary bungalow which had felt like a prison.

'You know Ruby Mac then?' asked the ferryman.

Elaine smiled. 'Yes, she's family.' She wasn't going into the finer details with the ferryman. If their little corner of Bristol was full of gossips – and she should know having worked in the Co-op most of her life – then a tiny place like Hope Cove was bound to be awash with it.

'Oh, aye.' He nodded and concentrated on guiding the boat to shore.

Relieved that she seemed to have got away without disclosing any further information, Elaine focused on the beach and braced herself for the landing which was surprisingly smooth.

'Are we here then?' Lil asked, looking around confused. 'I can't see our Ruby. Does she live in a cave?'

'Here, come to this end of the boat and I'll help you both out,' said the ferryman. 'You won't get your feet wet that way.'

'Thank you,' Elaine said, pulling Lil up and guiding her.

'It's a bit wobbly, Laney,' she said, clinging onto the side of the boat.

The ferryman helped Elaine get Lil's legs over and out onto the sand. Elaine followed.

'Dementia is it?' the ferryman asked.

'Amongst other things,' Elaine said, going careful not to get her new patent court shoes sandy. It seemed silly but she'd bought an entire new outfit to deliver mum to Ruby. Elaine knew what a glamourous woman Ruby was, and she didn't want to feel inferior.

'Oh right. So, this is Ruby's sister is it?'

Elaine wanted to snap at this impostor, what business was it of his, but then she remembered she was going to be living here for a while and it wouldn't do to go offending a fellow villager on the first day.

She decided just to smile and nod. 'When will there be a ferry back again?'

'I tend to run them ad hoc most of the time as it's only the home staff; the residents don't go out much. Ruby drives across when the tide's out.'

Elaine was alarmed. 'Is that safe?'

'Oh yeah, nothing wrong with the sand. ''tis ever such shallow water really but enough to warrant the boat at high tide.'

Elaine nodded, not really understanding. She'd worked out where Hope Cottage was and shoved her suitcases over the garden wall, praying it didn't rain before she returned from the island.

'So, how do I get back?'

'Oh, I see! You're not staying tonight then?'

Elaine glanced at Lil who was engrossed in picking up shells.

Elaine lowered her voice. My mother is, but I'm not.'

The ferryman looked at his watch. 'Well, it's three now. I usually come over at six for the shift change; would that suit you or would you like me to come earlier?'

'Six will be fine.' And if Ruby showed her a cold shoulder, she would simply leave Mum and swim back to land. 'How much do I owe you?'

'No bother, it's your first time; we'll call it your welcome gift to Hope Cove. Where're you staying then?'

'Thank you.' Elaine smiled at the man. He was an elderly gentleman who probably ran the ferry to supplement his pension. He had little bear like eyes shining out from his craggy, tanned face. He looked like he had always worked the waves, possibly a retired fisherman. There was something in his nosey, yet friendly way that reminded her of Archie. 'I'm staying at Hope Cottage.'

'Oh, with Tilly!'

'Yes,' Elaine replied, unsurprised Tilly had made a hit of herself in the village already. 'She's my daughter.'

'Well, aren't you the lucky one. Smashing girl that one; works in the Lobster Pot. You brought her up lovely;

she's both funny and polite. Not something you see that often in young 'uns these days.'

'I guess not,' Elaine said, tying her mac around her waist a little tighter.

'Tell, you what, in that mac you do look just like Ruby; you can tell you're all family. Tilly has that same, what's the word?' He looked at Elaine for inspiration.

She looked on blankly.

He clicked his fingers. 'Vivacity, that's it. She's got the same vivacity as Ruby.' He winked and waved. 'I'll see you later then, love,' he said, passing over Lil's suitcase. 'Hope your mum enjoys the home, she'll be in safe hands with Ruby.'

'I hope so,' Elaine called, over the waves as the boat launched into the sea. She turned and tottered up the shore towards Lil feeling almost shell-shocked. So, she looked like Ruby and Tilly had Ruby's personality. It was a shame it wasn't the other way around; she could do with some of Ruby's abundance of confidence. Still, it was a compliment to know that she hadn't done a bad job of bringing up Tilly. Hopefully that meant Tilly had made that doctor's appointment and got on top of her medication.

'Come on, mum,' she said to Lil, hooking her arm through Lil's. 'Looks like we've got a bit of a climb up to Ruby's.'

'Am I staying with our Ruby then?'

'*Yes*, mum, like I told you before. You're going to live with Ruby for a bit. It will be like when you were children.'

'I hope not, Laney.'

Elaine felt a sinking feeling in the pit of her stomach. 'Why?' she asked, feeling tired and frustrated.

'She never shared her teacakes.'

'Oh,' Elaine laughed, feeling relieved. Perhaps there was hope for both of them in Hope Cove after all.

CHAPTER NINETEEN

Tilly watched Doctor Dare tap his Parker fountain pen up and down repeatedly – impatiently almost – on his prescription pad. She wondered whether she had been transported back to her childhood. She couldn't remember the last time she'd seen a doctor *write out* a prescription. In fact, he didn't even have a computer, just a heavily polished mahogany desk with green, leather inbound and a pile of patients notes is those brown open envelopes which she certainly could remember from her childhood, when her mum used to take her to see Dr Pearson at the Falcondale surgery in Bristol. She'd stayed with that surgery all her life. Even when she'd been abroad in French Alps, or on the cruise liners, she'd kept herself registered there with Dr Pearson. Like some sort of security blanket for when she knew things were starting to go wrong again and she inevitably needed to go home. Deep down, she knew that's why she had prevaricated over coming here today. Even when she'd moved-in with Simon in Southville, she'd still stayed with Falcondale.

Doctor Dare took a sharp intake of breath and exhaled loudly. Tilly held his gaze, keen to appraise this man and consider whether she could trust him with her health. He was a slim man, probably in his fifties, with greying dark hair, which was neatly cut at the sides, longer on top so it swept to the back. His charcoal grey suit was crisp and expensive looking, and his crimson tie was neatly attached to his collar, hanging straight down his chest. He was cleanly shaven but wore no wedding ring, although Tilly could clearly identify a white mark one once had been worn. He looked thoroughly modern and yet was living in antiquity. The sun streamed onto the cliffs and the sea shimmered out of the window beyond, yet they were sitting in this gloomy room, with NHS cobalt blue walls, and he was using a stain-glass Art Deco looking desk lamp to read the notes in front of him. This man clearly had problems and yet they were here to discuss hers.

The doctor sighed again and scratched his head. He looked up at her.

'You're a very interesting case.'

'Thank you,' Tilly replied, deciding to take that as a compliment.

'Your records show bouts of ADHD as a teenager, but I have no idea why you're still on medication for Strattera in your early thirties. At least it's the only non-amphetamine-based drug. Do you have a tendency to be impulsive? Do things on a whim?'

Tilly had made the effort to try and discreetly explain in a waiting room full of patients that it would be worth having her medical records transferred from Dr Pearson to Hope Cove when she had made the appointment last week. At the least the receptionist had a computer so Falcondale must have emailed them through.

Tilly wrinkled her nose and tried to resist being honest. But she was never going to break her patterns of behaviour if she kept lying to everyone, not to mention to herself. She took a deep breath. 'I find out I had a long-lost aunt living in Hope Cove two weeks ago, so I wrote my fiancé a letter, packed my stuff up and moved here, to start a new life. I think we can probably agree that is impulsive.'

The doctor nodded sympathetically.

'Can I be brutally honest?' Tilly asked.

'I think you should,' he said, leaning back in his padded leather chair. It made a deflating sound as he crossed one leg over the other.

'I haven't taken any medication for eighteen months.'

He nodded again. Over her years of dealing with medical professionals and psychiatric units, she had become accustomed to the *what the fuck do we do with her now* nod.

'And how does that make you feel?'

'Absolutely fine.' Which was true. She was pretty sure it was true. 'I'd be lying if I said that I haven't been behaving like a brat recently; late nights out, that sort of thing. But I was unhappy with Simon and I didn't know how to fix it. My mum thinks I've got,' Tilly raised her hands to make speech marks with her fingers, *"issues'*. She says that I've run away to Cornwall and it's a downward spiral until I get completely out of control.'

'And what does out of control mean to you?'

Tilly flopped back in chair and sighed. She focused on the seagulls casually floating in and out of the cove as she considered the question. 'Funnily enough, out of control means going home to me; needing to be looked after. Every time I've messed up before, got into debt, got my heart broken, I've gone home. I hate relying on my mum.' She shrugged and looked at the doctor. 'But this time, I haven't run home, I've run away. That's how I know it's different this time. I'm not on the medication, perhaps, if I can bear to concede it, I was on the brink of starting to get *out of control* again but moving here is an opportunity.' She grinned. 'To finally make something of my life.'

'May I ask why you've run away and not tried to work things out with your fiancé?'

'Because he's boring,' Tilly said, without thinking.

The doctor tried to suppress a smile.

'It's okay, you can laugh, it's true! He had a spreadsheet for everything; Christ, I'm surprised he didn't try to schedule in our love making.' Tilly blushed. 'Sorry, TMI!'

'Not at all,' the doctor smiled. 'Can I ask why you were diagnosed with ADHD in the first place?'

Tilly hesitated. It all stemmed from when she was a teen. She had spoken to her mum a few times on the phone since she'd been living in Hope Cove this past month. Guilt made her call to check Elaine was okay. Worry made her call to check that Elaine wasn't having a mental breakdown herself, having to care for Gran every day.

Tilly shrugged. 'My behaviour started to change when I was a teen; I became a delinquent. You know, a stop-out, drinking, boys. I never did drugs though,' she rushed her words, not wanting the doctor to get the wrong impression. 'I've always been told it's probably because my periods started and because my gran has schizophrenia. Alhtough, I've just found out she isn't actually my gran but my great-aunt.'

If the doctor was taken aback by this revelation, he hid it very well. He tapped his pen on his pad again. 'Have you ever considered CBT?'

'What's that?'

'Cognitive Behavioural Therapy. It's where you go and see someone, usually a counsellor or a psychotherapist, and have some sessions, talking really.'

'Therapy?!'

'You needn't sound so horrified; it's really no different to what we're doing now.'

Tilly eyed him sceptically. 'So, *if* I did decide to go through with it, I wouldn't need to take any medication?'

'I'm not convinced you need medication. You've been living without it for eighteen months quite successfully by the sounds of things.'

Tilly supressed a smile thinking that she wasn't as mad as Elaine made out; she was surviving.

'What you've explained about your family life and your upbringing,' the doctor continued, 'brings me to the conclusion that talking about some of this may help you explore why you've behaved this way in the past and prevent you continuing those patterns of behaviour.'

'Like dumping your fiancé by letter.' Tilly laughed nervously.

The doctor raised his eyebrows.

'Yes, then,' Tilly said, quietly. She did the nodding for a change. 'Okay, what have I got to lose?'

'I think it's more about what you've got to gain.' Doctor Dare smiled at her and Tilly found herself smiling back, aware this was the quickest she'd come to like a medical professional for as long as she could remember.

'We'll have a review appointment after you've had six sessions and see whether we need to review any medication. Book in with me around the time of the last session, is that okay?'

'Yes, thank you. How do I book the sessions?'

'The local health trust will write to you.'

'Okay, many thanks!' Tilly picked up her bag and made her way to the door.

'Good luck,' he said, not looking up from writing his notes.

Tilly shut the consulting door as a familiar, uneasy feeling settled in the pit of her stomach. She knew she needed to do this; she knew she needed to talk to a counsellor. It wasn't the first time it had been suggested. But talking to someone meant telling them everything, if she was going to get to the bottom of the problem. And there were some things that Tilly couldn't help but feel were better off buried.

CHAPTER TWENTY

2011

'Thanks again,' Anthony Dare called as the lorry trundled back up the hill towards the Delabole road. He closed the door and allowed the silence of the surgery to wash over him. He could hear the settling, floorboards creaking, after the disturbance of the removal men. Outside gulls cawed and the waves swished as the tide came in for the evening. It was all very peaceful and yet very unsettling. He made his way into the kitchen and flicked the kettle on, the first thing to be unpacked. All around the kitchen table were boxes, everywhere. It surprised him how much stuff he'd actually accumulated over the years; he felt like he'd left all his life in Bracknell. He'd certainly left the most important things there.

Filled with impulse, he decided he would grab the framed photo of X and X he had on the front seat of the car, while the kettle boiled. He pulled the kitchen door, which led out ot the garden and onto the surgery carpark and came face-to-face with a large spray of floral bouquet.

'Impeccable timing!' The bouquet called out. It lowered to reveal a glamorous looking lady, probably in her late fifties, with a wavy white bob and lots of bangles jangling on her arm as she reached to push her hair out of her face. 'Ruby MacKenzie,' she said, extending her hand.

Anthony went to shake it feeling a lurching feeling in his stomach that he wasn't ready to talk to people yet. He wasn't ready to be ingratiated into the ways of the village. He wanted to get used to being on his own first.

He cleared his voice. 'Hello, I'm—'

'Anthony,' Ruby finished for him. 'I know because I was on the panel who appointed you.'

'Were you?' He frowned. He was pretty sure he'd remember someone as stand-outish as Ruby.

'Yes, after the interviews, there was a panel of us who had to sign off. I liked the fact you'd done a course on the menopause.'

Anthony laughed, suddenly feeling at ease. 'Where are my manners; did you want to come in? I haven't unpacked anything.'

'Oh, I won't keep you,' Ruby said, stepping over the threshold. 'I just came to give you these—' she dumped the cellophane wrapped flowers in Anthony's arms, '—and welcome you to Hope Cove. Welcome!' she said, undoing the belt of her beige mac and hanging it over the back of one of the breakfast chairs. She rolled up the sleeves on her expensive looking, cream, cable knit jumper. 'Now, where would you like me to start?'

'Start?' Anthony said, aware of the wobbly rise of panic in his voice.

'You can't unpack this all on your own! I'll help.'

Anthony wondered if all the villagers would be this forthright. 'How do you know I'm on my own,' he asked, knowing how defensive he sounded.

'Because I read through your application thoroughly. Still wearing your wedding ring, I see.' Ruby pulled the nearest box towards her and ran a long, red finger nail down the tape.

Please don't make me talk about Francesca.

'I moved to Hope Cove after my divorce. It was nearly thirty years ago.'

'Oh? There was something worth staying for?' Anthony said, making his way towards the safety of the kettle. He could busy himself making tea – how very British – and not get absorbed into Ruby's Spanish Inquisition.

'Oh, I love it here! Home from home, almost. The closest thing I'll ever get to it, anyway.'

'Where are you from originally?' Anthony asked, mentally cussing himself for getting drawn into conversation. He was wary. Conversation could potentially mean talking about feelings and he wasn't ready for that. He preferred to stick to sterile conversations about atrial fibrillations and the like.

'Bristol,' Ruby said, beginning to unravel cutlery from packing paper and put it neatly away in a drawer.

He was about to argue that she shouldn't put it there when he realised that was exactly the drawer he would have chosen too. Perhaps he was going to get on with this overbearing mother hen more than he had initially thought.

'Ah, I was at uni at Bristol! Well, medical college actually, I was attached to X.'

'Oh! I loved growing up there. I worked for British Aerospace when I first went out to work; most young people did.'

'What made you leave?'

'Long, boring story—'

Anthony knew by the way Ruby was rolling her eyes that there was definitely nothing boring about it, but if he enquired more, it might give Ruby the green light to ask about his recent divorce and he certainly didn't want that.

'—followed my dreams of becoming a top dollar PA to London and met a chap who worked on Fleet Street.'

'Oh, right,' Anthony said, popping some teabags into some mugs. He noticed Ruby hadn't mentioned *fell in love*.

She paused from transferring the cutlery to rub her forehead. 'Yes, doomed from the start really; he was my boss and married to someone else to start with. Ironic, really, that it ended when he went off with his latest PA; my just desserts shall we say.'

Anthony paused his lips together and nodded. He knew all too well the pain of someone cheating on you. 'Must have been hard,' he said, adding boiling water to the mugs, acknowledging how more relaxed he felt since Ruby had arrived.

'Probably no more than I deserved. Anyway, luckily, I married a rich man who paid me handsomely for a divorce. I'd been coming down here for weekends, to escape, towards the end of my marriage and, so, I decided to escape for good. The old hotel on the island came up for sale not long after I moved here and then I knew what I wanted to do; run a retirement home for dementia patients.'

'Ah!' Anthony clicked his fingers together, choosing to focus on who Ruby was instead of the echoes running through him of the need to escape. 'That's who you are; you run Hope Home. I've read so much about your efforts over the years; you welcome mental health patients now, as well, don't you?'

'Yes.' She pushed her hair out of her face as she pulled another unpacked box towards her. 'Not clinical mental health issues, more for those that require rest and recuperation and receive talking therapies. I found that creative projects like crafting work well with the dementia patients and it appears to be working out well with those who need to escape from life for a while too. Luckily the NHS are getting better at funding cognitive therapies for those suffering anxieties, stress, that sort of thing and my bursary which I set up and fundraise for every year makes up the rest.'

Anthony nodded, in awe of what Ruby had to say. He had worked in the NHS ever since graduating, twenty-five years ago and had been an advocate of helping those in crisis ever since. It was why he became a GP; an opportunity to be on the front line, listen to his patients and the problems that they presented. That, and the fact that when he still lived in Bristol he hoped, beyond hope, that he might bump into her at his surgery one day. But then he met X and life had taken him to Bracknell and he had lost hope of ever finding her again.

'You better take those tea bags out, dear, you've obviously made too much removal men's, industrial strength tea today!' Ruby tittered, perhaps unsettled by Anthony's enduring silence.

'Sorry,' he said, quickly fishing out the bags, 'I was miles away.'

'Want to talk about it?' Ruby said, unpacking saucepans and stacking them away neatly in the deep drawer beside the sink.

'I'm not sure there's a lot to talk about,' he said, without thinking. 'Er, just wanted a change, a fresh start. By the sounds of things half your residents' runaway to Hope Cove.'

Ruby pursed her lips together and appraised him through narrowed eyes. He suddenly felt very transparent.

'We can talk about it when you're ready,' she said, returning to the unpacking.

'Oh?' Anthony heard his voice wavering, acknowledging that he felt relieved to have found someone so welcoming in his new village of residence but also fearful at the thought about having to talk about any of it. 'You're thinking we might bump into each other again then.'

'Oh, yes.' Ruby's waves jiggled up and down and she nodded her head vigorously. 'You're the village GP and I run a home for geriatrics. Old Doctor Finney used to make a daily trip to the island, except for Sundays when he visited his daughter in Port Gaverne.'

No-one had mentioned *that* during the interview process.

'So, you see,' Ruby continued, 'we are going to be colleagues, so I thought it was best to hit it off on the right note.' She gestured to the flowers.

Anthony got the impression that perhaps Ruby hadn't always seen eye to eye with old, Doctor Finney.

'Okie doke,' Anthony said, not sure what else to say. 'I shall look forward to working with you,' he rushed to add.

'Brilliant, stuff.' Ruby shut the pan drawer with a flourish. 'So, let's get a bit more unpacking done, then I'll take you for supper in The Lobster Pot and you can be initiated with a few of the locals.'

'Oh, I don't know—'

'Nonsense. Yes, they'll be your patients, but this is where you live now; some of them will be your neighbours too.'

'It doesn't sound like I'm getting a lot of choice in the matter.'

'Not really.' Ruby grinned. 'And over supper you can tell me a bit more about that ex-wife of yours.'

'Perhaps,' Anthony said, handing Ruby her tea and smiling to himself. But on high on his agenda would be to find out what gave Ruby the need to mother all these waifs and strays which, apparently, included him.

CHAPTER TWENTY-

ONE

'Ruby, there are two ladies in reception for you,' Julie said, craning her neck around Ruby's office door.

Ruby detached herself from the accounts she'd been updating and checked her diary. 'That's funny, I've not put an appointment in my diary for a home viewing?' It always bothered her when things like this cropped up. Living and breathing dementia patients only heightened your senses to your own behaviour.

'No, I checked, and the younger lady said she didn't have an appointment—'

Ruby breathed a sigh of relief.

'—she just said she had come to visit you. Like she was family!' Julie laughed. She might be in her fifties now, but she still had the same infectious laugh she'd had all those years ago when Ruby had first met her working in the estate agents. 'She's got an elderly lady with her,' Julie continued, lowering her voice, 'who definitely has onset dementia, I reckon. She just asked me whether this is where you keep your baby!'

Ruby froze. 'Right,' she said, taking a deep breath and pushing her glasses up onto her head. She plastered on the biggest smile she could muster. 'I'll be right there.' She'd been waiting for this day all her adult life; now was the time to embrace it, not go to pieces. Only a part of her was a tiny bit afraid of Elaine. And as she walked out of the office and came face-to-face with her daughter in the lobby, she realised that even after thirty-odd years, she was right to still carry out that fear.

'You always said you wanted to help.' Elaine glowered through narrowed eyes.

Ruby could feel waves of hatred emanating towards her.

'So, now's your chance,' Elaine continued. 'I need you to look after Mum.'

'Okay,' Ruby nodded, eagerly, trying to keep the smile on her face and not give in to the look of total disgust on Elaine's. 'What about you, would you like to stay here too?'

'No, thank you.' Elaine folded her arms.

'Oh, there you are Ruby!' Lil had been wandering along the corridor, peering at the costal watercolours on the wall and had come to halt by Ruby.

'Hello, Lil.' Ruby put her arms around Lil and squeezed her tight. She was a tall woman, much taller than Ruby but she felt so frail. Poor Lil, it wasn't fair that she'd developed so many health problems.

'Where've you put your baby, Ruby?' Lil asked.

'My baby?' Ruby asked, softly. She had so many years' experience with dementia patients, now, that she knew better than to question their thinking. Whatever memory Lil was living, it was real for her.

'Your baby, the one you were going to give me. Have we come to collect it?'

Beneath Lil's glasses, beyond the saggy, wrinkly bags under her eyes, past the bottom lip hanging out with dribble, drooling off the end, Ruby could see the sister she had once known. She had given Elaine to Lil and Stan out of pity, but mostly love, and not just because it was a quick fix to an inconvenient problem. Had it been the most terrible mistake she had ever made? Rationale assured her that Lil would have developed schizophrenia whether she had adopted Elaine or not. But had that responsibility agitated Lil's condition? Had being a mother brought about the bouts of depression? Had it addled her brain and brought her to the way she looked and behaved now; unable to decipher past from present?

'So, it's true then?' Elaine said, quietly. 'I've never wanted to believe it, but I guess Mum's just confirmed it; she isn't *my* mum, is she?'

At that moment Julie bustled through with the tea tray, faltering in her steps at Elaine's cliff hanger. She smiled awkwardly at Elaine and carried on through to the resident's living room.

'Why don't we take you up to your room, Lil,' Ruby said, hooking her arm through Lil's and guiding her towards the staircase. It was a wide, wooden staircase with a low gradient but there was stair lift too. 'Can you the manage stairs?'

'I'll be fine,' Lil said, striding up them. There was certainly nothing wrong with her physical health.

Ruby looked back to see Elaine standing in the lobby still, her coat hanging off her shoulder bag. 'Will you come up too?'

'What's the point? She'll be fine with you. I'll be on the mainland with Tilly if you need me.'

Two thoughts passed across Ruby's mind, but she said neither, instead focusing on helping Lil around the ninety-degree-turn on the stairs. Elaine didn't want to stay in the home but was happy to go and stay in the cottage which *she owned* and, secondly, did Tilly know about this? Surely, she would have mentioned something about such a monumental decision on Elaine's behalf. Now wasn't the time to go throwing accusations about though.

Ruby smiled over the staircase. 'Perhaps it would be nice to help Lil settle into her room though? Assure her you're not going to be too far away.'

Ruby watched Elaine's glistening eyes.

'Okay,' Elaine said, before sighing and following Ruby and Lil up the stairs.

'Along here,' Ruby said, guiding Lil down the upstairs corridor and through a fire door which led to a newer part of the building and Ruby's private quarters. She stopped at her front door and grabbed her keys from her dress pocket.

Elaine followed them into the room and gasped. 'This is your apartment?'

It was a pretty spectacular view if Ruby said so herself. She had had the large aluminium frames installed so that she just had two large sheets of glass in the corner of the open plan living-cum-dining-cum-kitchen. All the sofas faced out at the view which stretched down the Cornish coastline.

'Sure you don't want to stay?' Ruby asked.

'I'll be fine with Tilly and Archie, thank you.' Elaine snapped.

'Do they know you're coming?'

Elaine walked across to the living room to look out at the view.

'Where's this baby then?' Lil asked.

'She's standing in the window, Lil!' Ruby said, exasperatedly, beginning to lose her cool. 'Can't you remember when I handed her over to you in the hospital?'

'Aye, at Queen Mary's.'

'Yes, well, that's her now, Elaine, standing in the window. Do you remember taking her home with Stan?'

Lil stood still and peered at Elaine. Elaine continued to look out the window.

'Our Dad was really cross with you.'

'Yes,' Ruby said, blinking back tears. Christ, this isn't how she had imagined her family reunion. A voice in the back of her head kept telling her *they're here; don't blow it.* The fact Elaine had come this far was a start. That was all she wanted. Apart from Archie telling Elaine he was her dad, but that would come in time now, she was sure of it. *Then* everyone could move forward and stop running away from their problems.

Ruby opened the door to the guest bedroom. 'This will be your room, Lil.' She walked Lil into the room and Elaine followed.

Elaine frowned. 'These are all pictures of Nana Jean.'

'Yes, this used to be her room,' Ruby said, guiding Lil to a velour, winged-back arm chair beside the double bed.

'I read on the internet you specialise in dementia.'

Ruby focused on getting Lil to sit down, inwardly smiling that Elaine had taken an interest.

'Yes, your dad, er, Stan, contacted me in the early eighties to say that Mum was declining; forgetting things, I expect you know. One day she could brush her teeth, the next day she'd forgotten how to do it.'

Elaine nodded silently, looking at the photos on the wall.

'Anyway, what with your mum, er, Lil, being as she was, I wanted to help. It coincided that I'd just moved down here with a big divorce settlement. This used to be a hotel before I bought it.'

Elaine looked at Ruby and sneered.

'Looks like life treated you pretty well.'

Ruby wanted to shout that life hadn't been a bed of roses and that giving Elaine up to Lil had been the single most painful experience of her entire life, let alone the biggest regret.

Instead she simply smiled.

'Would you like some tea?'

'No thank you, I'd better say my goodbyes and wait for the ferry.'

Ruby glanced at the clock opposite the bed. 'It's only four; the ferryman won't be back for another hour at least.'

'I don't mind.'

Ruby shrugged. 'Suit yourself. I'll arrange for one of my chaps to bring Lil's things up from the lobby. Is there anything particular she likes to wear to bed?'

'She doesn't know she's wearing clothes half the time.'

Ruby looked at Elaine. She showed signs of ageing beyond her fifty years. Life had treated her harshly. A wave of guilt swept over Ruby.

'Tell you what, once you're settled, perhaps we could have a girly shopping day out? I've promised Tilly I'll drive her over to Truro for lunch and to buy some new summer clothes. Why don't the three of us go?'

Elaine looked down at the floor. 'I've come here for a rest. I'm tired. I've come to spend time with my daughter. I haven't come to make friends with you or rekindle some long lost mother-daughter relationship so you can forget any of that.' She looked up at Ruby with a piercing stare. 'She's my mother.' Elaine pointed at Lil. 'Maybe not biologically, but she raised me, she stuck around, not like you.'

It was like being kicked in the stomach by a hippopotamus. Ruby blinked back tears determined not to show how she felt. She wasn't going to give Elaine the satisfaction of seeing her upset. She may regret the past, but she hadn't had a choice. Her choices were taken away from her. Otherwise she would have married Archie and kept Elaine.

'And on the subject of parentage,' Elaine continued, now into her stride. 'Are you ever going to divulge who my father is?'

Ruby shook her head, standing close to Lil as possible, like her life depended on it. 'Have you ever told Tilly who her father is?' She regretted the words as soon as they were out.

'I asked first.'

Ruby shrugged. 'Maybe we have more in common than you think.' Ruby felt like she was sinking ever deeper into her grave of secrets and lies. The problem was Elaine's paternity wasn't Ruby's secret to tell. Not after all these years, anyway.

'At least I kept Tilly.'

'Ohhhh!' Ruby let out a frustrated sigh and walked to the window hoping the view of the sea might calm her. She turned back and looked Elaine straight in the eyes. 'There was no way I could have been a single mum in 1965; I'd have been packed off to the unmarried mothers' home. Not that that would have happened; it was either adopt you or abort you and I could never have done that.' Ruby put her hand to her mouth to stop herself letting out a sob.

'You could have tried!'

'You didn't know your grandfather; there's no way he would have had the shame of a bastard child in the family. I did what I thought was best.'

'Letting me know the truth would have been for the best!'

'It wasn't my decision to make, was it? It was Lil and Stan's! I tried to help when you were pregnant with Tilly, but you wouldn't let me!'

'Because I didn't believe you!'

Elaine had turned puce. Ruby took deep breaths, not wanting to stress out Lil who was staring between the two of them, almost mesmerised.

'Twenty years might not seem like a long time but in those days, but opinions began to change.' Ruby said calmly. 'Christ, if Tilly had a baby now, no-one would bat an eyelid at her bringing up a baby on her own!'

Elaine, looked away, blinking furiously. Her attention was caught by a photo on the wall. 'This is me,' she said, frowning. 'And this one, and this one!'

The wall was dotted with little 6x4" picture frames all higgledy-piggledy over the William Morris print wallpaper. Some of Lil and Ruby, before Ruby left home, one of Lil and Stan on their wedding day, but mainly ones of Elaine as a child and a few of Tilly too.

'How did you get all of these?'

'Archie,' Ruby said, done with lying.

'Why though? Why keep in contact with Archie and not Lil?'

Ruby shrugged. She didn't really have answer for that – not even a made-up one – apart from telling Elaine the truth.

'Phyllis knew I was adopted by you.' Elaine said, still studying the pictures.

'I know,' Elaine said softly, folding her arms as if to protect herself from another tirade from Elaine.

'Is that why you were friends? Did Phyllis contact you?'

'Something like that,' Ruby said, feeling that all-consuming guilt well up in her again. All her life she had felt guilt towards Phyllis. The poor woman couldn't have children of her own. Fancy having to live next door to your husband's child. Thankfully, Phyllis had never seen it that way, but Ruby still felt guilty at the mention of her name. 'Would you like to help me get Lil unpacked?'

Elaine looked at Ruby, studying her face for what seemed like an eternity. She pressed her lips together. 'Okay,' she said, dropping her bag on the bed. 'If I can remember the way, I'll pop down and get her case.' She walked to the bedroom door. 'I'm sorry, for shouting.'

Ruby, still hugging herself, said, 'that's okay. I think you have a lot to shout about.'

For the first-time Elaine smiled, a proper, genuinely content smile. It took years off her.

'Come on, Lil,' Ruby said, when Elaine had left the room. 'Best get you to the toilet. I expect you're parched too. Shall we make a brew?'

'Okay,' Lil said, standing up. 'Then can I have a cuddle with your baby?'

'If you like,' Ruby said, playing along. It was Ruby's turn to return Lil's favour now. She had looked after Ruby's baby when Ruby had needed her to. Now Lil needed Ruby to look after her. Even if she couldn't make things up with Elaine, she could gain pleasure from paying her debt to Lil.

CHAPTER TWENTY-TWO

'I think for a first attempt at pastry, they look exceptional,' Emma said, shrugging on her raincoat.

Tilly beamed with pride as she looked down at her homemade Cornish pasties, still hot, nestled in their tin, on a bed of baking parchment, all glossy and brown from the egg wash brushed on before popping them in the oven. They smelled delicious.

'I can't believe I've made something edible,' Tilly said, bursting with pride for feeling like she had actually accomplished something for a change.

'Nonsense! You're a natural. Are you walking home?' Emma flicked the lights off.

'Unless I can interest you in a quick drink at the pub first?'

'I'd love to,' Emma said, digging in her satchel bag for her keys, 'but I promised James I'd be back for supper so we could have a bit of evening together before he has to get down here to start tomorrow's baking.'

'How do you two ever have sex?' Tilly asked picking up her pasties and following Emma to the door.

Emma dropped her keys.

'Oops, sorry, I'm being tactless, aren't I?'

Emma laughed, bending down picking up her keys, 'You are just like Ruby, aren't you?'

'Thank you, I think,' said Tilly, walking through the kitchen door and out into the cobbled alley which led onto the High Street.

'To answer your question,' Emma said, locking the door, 'we have to grab the opportunity when it arises; usually when Finn naps.'

'I bet.' They walked in companionable silence down the alley way and out opposite the harbour. 'It's a shame no-one else wanted to go for an after-class drink but I guess everyone is taking what they've made home for supper.'

Emma had purposely said she was making the classes from five to seven o'clock so that people could go home and eat what they'd made straight away but Tilly was hopeful some of her fellow baking students might have welcomed an opportunity to socialise. Tilly still felt like a newcomer and had been looking forward to a chance to get to know some more locals.

'They've all got young families, like me. Most of them are from my mother and baby groups; I expect they wanted to get home before children's bedtimes.'

Tilly had noted that most of the women tonight looked younger than her and, yet, still had at least one child each. She'd felt a creeping panic expand in her chest that she was being left behind. It still didn't make her regret leaving Simon; having a baby with him would have been a big mistake.

As they passed the pub, Tilly could see Winstone talking to a customer as he collected glasses on the balcony.

'What about you, when was the last time you had sex?' Emma said, following Tilly's gaze.

'What?' Tilly almost dropped her pasties. 'That's a very personal question!'

Emma laughed. 'Touché. Don't tell James but he is *really* fit, isn't he?' Emma nodded in Winstone's direction.

Tilly shrugged. 'I guess,' she said, concentrating on her placing one foot in front of the other up the steady incline of the hill towards the lighthouse. Winstone was *hot*. But she'd just come out of a *steady relationship*, as Elaine would put it. Old Tilly wouldn't have cared and would carry on regardless, flirting with Winstone until she got her way; not stopping to consider whether that was what she really wanted, just focusing on her feelings of lust. New Tilly was going to be more conservative, considered and sensible, by focusing on what she really wanted.

It sounded positively boring.

'I've never known him to have a girlfriend. His parents come to stay every so often and his mum told me once that his girlfriend died eight years ago. That's why he moved down here; to get away from it all.'

Tilly watched Gull Island come into view over the brow of the hill and reflected that several of Hope Cove's residents were all running away from something. Ruby certainly had, possibly Winstone and, now, here was Tilly doing the same.

'That's awful. Did she say how she died?'

'She said it was a sudden death and Winstone took it hard. James and I are both good friends with Winstone, he often comes for supper, but he's never mentions much about his personal life.'

'I'd noticed that.' Tilly had tried a few times to bring the conversation around to family but Winstone always managed to keep things jovial and change the subject. Although Tilly was no-one to talk; she had kept Simon, Mum and Gran all close to her chest.

'Ah, so you're interested in him then?'

'I didn't say that!' Tilly defiantly clutched her pasties to her chest.

'I can't get over how much you're like Ruby; she'd be just the same! Nosing into other people's lives but you can never get close to her. She is an enigma with the villagers and I can tell you, your sudden appearance in the village has got plenty of tongues wagging.'

They rounded the corner by the school onto Island View. Tilly bit her lip and looked over to Hope Home which was blazing with lights against the dusky sunset.

'She's not my really my aunt,' Tilly blurted out, wondering where the words were escaping from.

Emma stopped walking and frowned.

'Promise not to tell anyone?'

'Of course,' said Emma, nodded solemnly.

Tilly bit her lip. This seemed something like old Tilly would do; gossip. But then, Emma appeared to be becoming a friend, of sorts, and Tilly had precious few of those. Surely it was okay to tell friends secrets? Friends should be caring, empathetic, perhaps even offer solutions to problems. Tilly made up her mind. 'She's my grandmother,' she said quickly, before she changed her mind again. 'She had my mum but gave her up to my gran. I only found out a couple of weeks ago.'

'What?!' Emma stage whispered, her face theatrically lit up by the street lamp above.

Tilly nodded. 'I know; we're all screwed up in my family. Anyway, my mum's never believed Ruby; she prefers to live in blissful ignorance in Bristol, caring for Gran, complaining how boring her life is but never doing anything about it.'

'Blimey,' Emma said, carrying on walking. 'Ruby's a dark horse. I'd never imagined her to keep secrets.'

'I'm not sure it was hers to keep. I mean, I guess it was up to my Gran to tell Mum, but she has dementia now.'

'And how does Archie fit into all of this?'

'Archie?' Tilly frowned. 'He's our next-door neighbour, in Bristol. He's lived next-door so long he's like part of the furniture.'

Emma shifted her heavy holdall, full of handouts and what she'd baked up onto her
shoulder. 'But there's something between Archie and Ruby, right? I mean, he's been staying down here on and off for the past couple of years, surely they're more than good friends?'

Tilly looked over at Hope Home again and narrowed her eyes. It had crossed her mind a couple of times these past few weeks. Why were Archie and Ruby so close? Tilly knew how devoted Archie was to Phyllis' memory but now she knew where he had been disappearing to the past couple of years *on holiday*, Tilly's mind was beginning to draw the same conclusions as Emma.

They came to halt by Tilly's front door. 'You could be right; I've had the same thoughts myself, but Archie loved his wife, Phyllis, so much; I'm not sure that even if he felt strongly about Ruby now, he'd do something about it.'

'Maybe, it's up to you to play Cupid then?' Emma raised a playful eyebrow and kissed Tilly on the cheek. 'You did great tonight; go and show off to Archie and no doubt we'll catch up before next week.'

'Thanks, Emma, bye,' Tilly said, trying the front door as she didn't fancy holding the pasties and scrabbling to find her keys. To her luck it was open. Usually when she opened the front door Hector came skittering from somewhere to find her, but the house was silent this evening. The nights were drawing out, but it was still dusky, and all the lamps were lit around the cottage.

'Hello?' Tilly called out, wondering if Archie might have popped out and left the lights on. Perhaps he didn't hold out much hope for Tilly's pasties and had gone to the chip shop for his supper.

'In here,' Archie called. His voice sounded strained.

Tilly hurriedly wiped her feet on the mat before dashing up the hallway and into the kitchen. 'I didn't think you were here, it's so quiet,' she called out. 'You'll be pleased with my efforts tonight, I hope you're hungry because, ta-da!' She lifted the box-lid and looked up. Archie was sitting with Hector on his lap looking terribly glum and opposite him – with her back to Tilly – was Mum.

'Hello, Tilly,' Elaine said, slowly turning around.

Tilly almost dropped the pasties.

'What are you doing here?' She sounded accusatory, even to herself.

Elaine's smiled. 'You don't sound too pleased to see me?'

Tilly swallowed hard and risked a glance at Archie. He looked worried. 'Where's Gran?'

'Don't you mean Auntie Lil?' Elaine spat sarcastically.

Great. Always accused by her mum of having 'one of her episodes', Elaine appeared to be on the brink of one herself.

'She's over at Hope Home,' Archie said, standing up and releasing Hector to the floor. The little dog scurried to his bed by the Aga.

'Did you bring Mum and Gran back?' Tilly asked feeling thoroughly confused. She knew Archie had gone to Bristol today to check on Elaine. Perhaps he had persuaded her that she needed a break?

'Archie was just telling me he got the surprise of his life when Iris next door told him I've let the bungalow out for six months.'

'You've done what?' Tilly slammed the box of pasties down on the kitchen table and slipped her satchel off, a feeling of panic rising in her chest.

'You're not the only one allowed an adventure Tilly; I'm fifty now, it's time I started living a little.'

'Did Ruby know you were bringing Gran to live with her?'

'Does it matter?' Elaine snapped. 'They're sisters; why shouldn't Ruby shoulder the burden of looking after Lil for a change?

Tilly winced Mum's use of Gran's real name. As if she'd detached herself from caring for Gran physically or emotionally.

'And, where are you going to live?'

'Here, with you. Why should you have the monopoly, Tilly? Ruby is allegedly *my mother*, so doesn't it stand to reason for me to stay in her house?'

They fixed each other with a stare. Elaine's was defiant, Tilly's was one of incredulity that Elaine could just turn up like this. She looked at the pasties, going cold, and the conversation she had just had with Emma rang through her mind. *She prefers to live in blissful ignorance in Bristol, caring for Gran, complaining how boring her life is but never doing anything about it.* Now, Elaine was beginning to believe Ruby could be her mother and was attempting to make a life of her own. Something Tilly had always wanted for Elaine.

Perhaps it was the old Tilly not taking this news very well. Perhaps the new version of Tilly needed to gracefully accept it. *Perhaps*, if Mum had to spend less time looking after Gran they would have more time to spend together? Although that seemed to leave Tilly with an ever more unsettling feeling in her stomach.

'Well, I wonder if it's time I packed up and went home,' Archie said, standing up with a spine-tingling scrape of his chair across the quarried kitchen tiles.

'What?' Tilly's stare-out with Elaine was broken as she switched to see Archie's woeful expression.

'You don't need me here now, do you? Not now Elaine's arrived.'

'I haven't come here to spend time with Tilly; I've come to have a rest,' Elaine said, shattering Tilly's illusion that perhaps this was an opportunity for her and Mum to build bridges.

'Nevertheless,' Archie continued, 'this place will be a bit crowded with the three of us. I'll get myself back home and keep an eye on those new tenants for you.'

'You can't, Archie!' Tilly wailed, wondering why it was so important for Archie to stay, feeling that it was more about not being left alone with Mum than having Archie stay. 'For a start I've made tonight's supper,' she pointed at the box of pasties, 'and there's the first pub quiz next week; you have to stay and be part of my team, you promised!' Tilly had been busy putting up posters around the village – much to Winstone's disgruntlement – advertising that the pub would be holding a regular pub quiz starting on Friday nights. She was also trying to persuade Winstone to hold a disco afterwards for the younger villagers starting at ten o'clock and going-on until midnight. He had mentioned, in passing, that he used to be a DJ and Tilly couldn't fathom why he was so reluctant to pick up the mantle again.

'I know, but you don't need me and Hector getting under your feet.'

Tilly thought about what Emma had said about Archie and Ruby. Ruby had also agreed to be on Tilly's team.

'You have to; you'll be letting me and Ruby down otherwise. I insist; Mum can make up the fourth team member.'

'What?! I don't know the first thing about pub quizzes. I don't think I've been in a pub since 2005!'

'Here's your opportunity,' Tilly said, watching a faint smile twitch at the corners of her Mum's mouth. 'Now, let's have supper; I'll put these in the Aga to keep warm while I prepare some veg to go with them.'

'They do look delicious,' Archie said, peering into the box. 'Shall I go and get some chips from the chippy to go with them?'

'Why not.' Tilly almost laughed at the relief on Archie's face at being able to escape the two rowing women.

'My God, what's happened to you, Tilly? Less than a month and domesticated already!' Elaine scoffed, as Tilly donned her apron to peel the veg.

Tilly rolled her eyes. 'Whatever,' she said, looking in the fridge for carrots and broccoli. There was no point being bitter; Mum had as much right to be here as she did, and she certainly deserved a break from caring from Gran. Tilly would just have to grin and bear it. She would have to keep Mum occupied and encourage her to integrate with village life. She didn't want Mum sitting around, with nothing to do, slowly slipping into one of her bouts of depression. Tilly had come here to escape and, now, so had Elaine. And Tilly was buggered if either of them let the issues they had left behind dominate them here, in Hope Cove.

CHAPTER TWENTY-THREE

'Here you go, doctor,' Tilly said, placing the plate of crab sandwiches on the table.

'Thank you,' Anthony said, returning Tilly's infectious smile. He didn't usually venture into the local restaurants or pubs for fear of being lynched by a local who didn't understand the notion of 'off duty' and used the chance meeting as an opportunity for out-of-hours medical advice.

'Here, doctor,' Tilly said, whipping a flyer out of her apron pocket. 'Do you fancy coming to the pub quiz this Friday? I can hook you up with some other single players looking to make up a team. Or, er, your wife?'

Anthony smiled at the girl's awkwardness. 'I don't have a wife,' he said, taking some cutlery wrapped in a red serviette from the pot, in the centre of the table, and unravelling them. He looked up at Tilly who was looking at him quizzically. 'Or a significant other,' he added.

'Okay,' Tilly grinned. 'Well, let me know if you'd like to join a team. Enjoy your lunch.' And with that, she disappeared back into the pub.

May had finally brought some welcome spring sunshine. He wasn't sure if it was the sun which had drawn him out of his surgery and down to the pub for lunch or Tilly Henshaw. He had purposely sat out on the balcony overlooking the cove so he could watch her from a distance. He had thought about her a lot since her visit to the surgery last week. She reminded him, incredibly so, of his daughter, Libby. It was silly, really, to want to be near someone because they reminded you of someone else. He couldn't explain it, even to himself; it wasn't rational at all. But Tilly Henshaw's mannerisms, her Pollyanna outlook on life, had left a lasting impression after her visit to the surgery. From a medical point of view, he was particularly curious too. Okay, so a fifteen-minute discussion wasn't enough to analyse her entire mental health history but all he could see was a normal, healthy young woman. Why on earth had her previous doctor diagnosed her with Attention Deficit/ Hyperactivity Disorder? It made no sense. Of course, twenty years ago she may have been a different person, a child at that. He was adamant, however, that whatever it was that had caused her issues then, had resolved itself by now, hence why he had channelled her down the cognitive behavioural route. He would be fascinated to read Laura Steele's report when she finally discharged Tilly.

'Alright, Tony?' Winstone asked, appearing through the balcony door, collecting up empties at the neighbouring table.

'Good, thanks.' Anthony tried to reply through a mouthful of crab sandwich. 'And you?'

'You know,' Winstone said, 'I make a living.'

Here was another troubled soul. That was the biggest problem being a confidant in a small village; you knew everyone's problems but could tell no-one. He often felt that given the opportunity he could make an exceptional master puppeteer. Take Winstone for instance; he needed a girlfriend, someone to share his life with down here. He was a complete alpha male. Only he was wounded by the past too. Another one of Laura Steele's clientele, Winstone continued to see her privately. To the outside world he was the life and soul of the party but on the inside, he was still hurting. Unlike Anthony who privately licked his wounds and didn't try to create an outside persona for the sake of everyone else. Winstone was someone to be admired.

'Young Tilly must brighten the place up.'

Winstone rolled his eyes. 'Stirs it up more like; she's organised this pub quiz and wants me to put on a disco for the youngsters afterwards. You can tell she's related to Ruby; they have the bossy gene in that family.'

There was another revealing secret that he could share with no-one. Ruby was in fact Tilly's grandmother. Anthony had a lot of time for Ruby; she had rescued him good and proper when he first moved to Hope Cove. He had seen dementia patients enter her doors like they had faded away from life and within weeks they were playing bingo and crocheting blankets. She worked tirelessly with her team to ensure that all the lives of her residents were enriched.

'I'm over there this afternoon actually; got to check over her latest patient. Her sister apparently.'

'Tilly's gran?' Winstone sounded astounded. 'Tilly never mentioned anything?'

Ugh, the pitfalls of being everyone's confidant. 'Sorry, best keep that one to yourself; perhaps I shouldn't have told you that. Anyway, the disco will be good; give you the chance to dust off those decks of yours.'

'Maybe,' Winstone rubbed his stubble and looked inside where Tilly was taking an order from a couple who had just sat down. 'How about inviting your two down? They might enjoy a disco.'

Anthony's children, Libby, who was eighteen and Tom, who was fifteen hadn't visited Cornwall since

Christmas. When his marriage to Francesca had ended, he had taken the post of GP for Hope Cove to get as far away from her as possible. He hadn't considered that the distance between Berkshire and Cornwall would put his children off making regular visits. He went up to see them every weekend to start with but nowadays they put him off with excuses about parties and revision.

'I could ask them.' Anthony tried to sound enthusiastic, knowing all the while that there would be some excuse from Francesca about it being too short notice. It was ridiculous when Libby was now, technically, an adult.

'Cool. I'll leave you to it.' Winstone broke away from the table he'd been leaning on.

'Actually, I must go,' Anthony said, glancing at his watch and realising he needed to catch the two o'clock ferry over to the island. 'Delicious as always,' he said, picking up his doctor's bag.

'You're welcome,' said Winstone, standing aside the doorway.

'Winstone,' Anthony lowered his voice. 'Be grateful for Tilly working here. Perhaps a bit of entertainment is exactly what you need.'

'Are we talking about Tilly or the pub?' Winstone raised a playful eyebrow.

Winstone watched the doc leave and his gaze fell back to Tilly for the umpteenth time today. He sighed heavily. The doc was right, Tilly was bringing life to the pub. Quizzes, discos; she was making the pub the hub of the village, which it should be. But it wasn't why he moved here. Which was what Anthony was referring to; she wasn't just good for the pub.

'The Doc ate that fast!' Tilly appeared on the balcony.

Winstone nodded. 'Had to get over to the island.'

'Oh, right,' Tilly looked out at the cove where you could see the peak of the island beyond the headland and the lighthouse.

'What's that old building over there?' she asked, shading her eyes from the bright May sunshine with her hand. 'I noticed it the first day we drove through the village; has it always been empty?'

Winstone grinned at Tilly.

'What?' she asked, looking at him. She was so pretty; she wore minimal make-up, a little concealer and mascara, but she really didn't need to with her abundance of golden ringlets and pale freckled skin.

'I'll tell you, if you tell me your news.'

'Pardon?'

'You don't seem quite yourself today.' Winstone realised he couldn't reveal the source of Tilly's secret.

'Don't I?' Tilly frowned picking up the Doc's empty plate.

'Yeah, you just seem a bit, what's the word,' Winstone scratched his head. 'Melancholy.'

'Oh,' Tilly's shoulders slumped. 'I thought no-one would notice,' she said, sitting down on the bench.

Winstone checked there was no-one waiting at the bar before pulling out a chair. 'Penny for them?' he asked.

Tilly pressed her lips together and looked out over the cove. Seagulls screeched above their heads as Winstone waited for her to speak.

'Oh,' she sighed, 'I suppose you're going to find out soon enough.' She flicked her hair out of her face. 'My mum turned up last night. She's come to stay at the cottage with Archie and I and she's moved my gran in with Ruby.'

Interesting.

'Why's that such an issue? Surely it must be good to have your family down here?'

Tilly raised her eyebrows. 'You'd think,' she laughed, nervously. 'It's complicated.'

Winstone watched her lean, freckly arm rub her dainty collar bone. He got the impression she had no idea just how beautiful she was. She had such striking Celtic looks; she didn't look out of place in a Cornish fishing village.

'My gran has dementia,' Tilly continued.

'Then, surely, she's in the best place, at Ruby's?'

'Oh, yes,' Tilly nodded, 'it's just I kind of came down here to escape and I fear Mum might…'

'Cramp your style?' Winstone finished her sentence then immediately regretted it. What if that wasn't what she was going to say?

Tilly smiled. 'Something like that. Now you have to tell me what the empty building on the other side of the cove. I wondered if it was a seasonal business which only opened in the summer months?'

'Anyone serving today, Winstone?' Came a shout from the bar.

Winstone rolled his eyes, standing up. 'Oh, nothing special; just a restaurant that's failed like a thousand times. There's practically a new owner every season.'

'Is that it?! I tell you my personal secrets and you give me *nothing special!*'

Winstone shrugged and grinned. 'It was your choice.'

'Ugh!' Tilly pulled the tea towel from her waist and flicked Winstone with it. 'Next time I'm asking more about *your* family!'

'Nothing to tell,' Winstone called over his shoulder, as he raced to the bar, glad of a diversion before Tilly prodded any further to his personal life.

CHAPTER TWENTY-FOUR

Elaine stopped by the lighthouse to take in the view. It might be the sort of view many holidaymakers took for granted each year on their annual stay in Cornwall, but to her it was simply breath taking. The sun shone over the cove, across the headlands into the distance and the aqua-blue sea shimmered as the little fishing boats dipped up and down in the gentle waves. The early May sunshine was weak in strength but still warmed her to her bones. *This* is what it felt like to be alive.

She had spent a leisurely morning lying in bed reading one of her favourite romance author's latest novel. When she had heard Tilly go to work and Archie leave to walk Hector, she'd made her way downstairs to make a cup of coffee in one of those fancy plunge cafetierès which Tilly liked so much. She had to admit that ground coffee did taste better than the instant Nescafè they had at home.

Her gaze settled on Hope Home, its windows glinting brightly over on Gull Island. The waves were choppier on this side of the headland and the little ferryboat was casting a trail of foam as it made its way over to the island. Elaine felt a pang of guilt as her eyes sought out the upstairs wing of the property housing Ruby's quarters. Was Mum, Auntie Lil, whoever the hell she was, okay? She had thoroughly enjoyed her leisurely morning – the first one she reckoned she'd had since before Tilly was born – but it hadn't stopped her worrying. Had Ruby put Mum to bed on time? Had Mum woken in the night and worried where she was? Had she left Ruby enough incontinence pants? That rising flight of panic, like caged butterflies beating their wings ready to escape, rose in her chest and she could feel herself panicking. She went back to looking at the view, taking deep breaths and allowing the gentle waves, washing against the little shingly beach in the cove to calm her nerves. She wasn't going to find herself a job if she entered every shop like a nervous wreck. Although it did remind her that she probably should go and register with the local doctor. She'd asked Tilly last night and was relieved to find there was a surgery in the village which Tilly had already visited. She was reluctant to believe that counselling was going to help Tilly but even she had to admit that Tilly seemed, well, normal down here. She would never have imagined her taking up baking either! Tilly was changing. It gave Elaine hope; if Tilly could change, then surely, she could too?

Just remembering the person, she used to be would be a start.

Walking down the hill past the school, Elaine surveyed the high street which appeared to run down into the harbour and then back up the hill on the other side. She could see the Lobster Pot, where Tilly worked, for it had a large painted sign outside swinging in the spring breeze. She wouldn't try there. Tilly might decide to move back to Bristol if Elaine cramped her style any further. She felt implored to get a job though. The bungalow was being rented out for nine hundred pounds a month and, after letting fees, it left her with nearly eight hundred. She was going to give that to Ruby every month towards Mum's care at the home; she may have dumped Mum on Ruby and expected her to take over, but she wasn't going to let Ruby have the satisfaction of paying for everything as well. Ruby had a lot of making up to do but money didn't buy love. So, Elaine was going to get a job to pay her way at the cottage. She couldn't contribute a lot of rent, but she wanted to make sure she paid her way with food and bills, as Tilly evidently was. Archie must be using his pension to pay Ruby some keep for Elaine knew he was too proud to accept handouts. Not for the first time recently, it crossed her mind what exactly the deal was between Archie and Ruby. Why did Archie have so much allegiance to Ruby when it was *her* mum and dad, he had lived next door to for years?

She'd wandered into the village now and was walking past the harbour, humming with tourists. She glanced in through the door of The Lobster Pot but couldn't see Tilly in the dark depths of the pub, so she carried on along the path. It occurred to her that if she went in the pub someone might be able to tell her who was hiring staff, but then Tilly might yet to have told anyone about Elaine's sudden appearance and be embarrassed. She didn't want to make things worse than they already were; she just wanted to have a quiet life for six months, have a break from looking after mum and live a little. Soon she would be known as Elaine, Tilly's mum. Or Tilly's mum who works in such-and-such, if she was lucky enough to find a job.

An index card caught her eye in the bakery window.

> *Part-time holiday staff required.*
> *Customer Service experience essential.*
> *Apply within – ask for Emma.*

Elaine looked at all the scrumptious cakes and buns in the window. She would put on a stone just looking at these delights all day, but then Tilly had said she could do with putting on some weight and she'd also mentioned how nice the couple who ran the bakery were. Plus, all those years chained to a chair on the Co-Op checkout would stand her in good stead, surely? What the hell, Elaine thought, pushing open the shop door. A little bell jangled above her head, just like her nerves jangling around her body. What was she doing? She took deep breaths and vowed the next place she would visit would be the doctor's surgery, to request a repeat prescription.

'Can I help?' smiled the lady appearing through a doorway behind the counter.

'Are you Emma?' Elaine barked, telling herself to calm down.

'Yes,' the girl smiled, her blonde ponytail swinging behind her.

'I'm here about the job in the window, for holiday staff?'

'Oh, yes, is it for your daughter?'

'No, it's for me!' Elaine snapped, indignantly. Good grief, this was not the way to go about acquiring a job. Only this girl had to be younger than Tilly and owned her own bakery, which was slightly intimidating.

'Oh, I'm sorry.' Emma blushed. 'Have you any experience working with customers?'

'Yes, I used to work in a supermarket, until five years ago when I gave up work to become a full-time carer, for my mother.'

'Oh, dear.' Emma was looking at Elaine with a peculiar expression. Elaine's heart was hammering like a steam engine and it was taking all her will power not to run for the door. She needed a job though. She must pay her way. There was no way she was living off handouts from Ruby.

'And, er, how is your mother now?'

'Oh, she's fine; she's staying over on the island at Hope Home.'

Emma frowned again.

'Look, I'm sorry, this was a bad idea.' Elaine began backing-up towards the door, her thumping pulse relaxing slightly at the thought she could escape out onto the street any second. She would just avoid the bakery while she was here; she never ate cakes anyway and…

'No!' Emma rushed around to the front of the counter. 'Please, sorry, it's me, I'm not helping. I keep looking at you and thinking how familiar you look, but I've lived in Hope Cove all my life and I can't remember seeing you in the supermarket? Please, come on through to the back; it's quiet, I can interview you now if you like.'

Elaine's anxiety levels shot up again. She could feel a tightening in her chest. She had to stop being like this! How was she going to cope if she actually got the job?

'Are you sure? I don't want to take up anymore of your time.'

'You're not, please.' Emma held out her arm indicating Elaine to go behind the counter. 'We'll go in the kitchen. Can I get you a coffee?'

'Um, yes please.' Elaine walked through to the rear of the shop to a shiny kitchen full of bright aluminium work surfaces, kitchen equipment and one of those posh looking barista machines.

'I must say there is something very familiar about you. Where do you live?'

'I've just moved into Hope Cottage.'

'Ah! Next door to me!'

'Oh?' Elaine didn't realise that. If she got the job, she would be living next door to her employer. One more thing to worry about. 'Sorry, perhaps I should have said, I'm Elaine, Tilly's mum.'

Emma laughed. 'Well, that makes sense then! I can see the similarity between you, Tilly and…' Emma trailed off.

Elaine just knew Emma was about to say *Ruby*. Everyone else could see it. Why did she always refuse to believe it?

'Strong genes,' Emma continued. 'Tilly looks so much like you. Can I get you a coffee? Cappuccino or Latte or just a flat white?'

'I'll have a Latte please.' She'd never tried one of those.

'Okie doke and now I know your Tilly's mum, let's start again. I'm Emma, pleased to meet you.' Emma extended her hand and Elaine shook it, trying hard not to tremble like a leaf.

As Emma babbled on, Elaine's mind dwelled on Emma's faltering words, again. Had Tilly told Emma about who Ruby really was? Did it matter? This was a fresh start in a new place, even if it might only be temporary. She needed to get out of the mindset of shame; it was Ruby's secret to explain, not Elaine's. She would just like to be Elaine Henshaw from now on, not Tilly's mum or Lil's daughter. This was her opportunity to be Elaine. Elaine who works in the bakery, perhaps. She took a deep breath to calm her nerves and began concentrating on what Emma was saying.

She would get this job because it felt, to Elaine, like her new life depended on it.

CHAPTER TWENTY-FIVE

'Archie, don't you think this is a sign?' Ruby hissed. 'Elaine's found the courage to follow us all down here; isn't now the time to tell her?'

They were standing in her kitchen while the doctor examined Lil in the next room. The weather had changed from glorious sunshine to overcast clouds coming in on the horizon from the Atlantic. It seemed a storm was brewing outside and inside this afternoon.

'Look,' Archie said, firmly, for he did not want the doctor to overhear their bickering, 'she was being truculent and resentful; it wasn't the right time to be saying, oh by the way, Elaine, darling, now you're here, I just wanted to let you know I'm your biological father and have been lying to you pretty much for nigh-on half a century.'

Ruby rolled her eyes and leant on the island which separated the kitchen from the living area.

'She needs to know; we can't carry on like this.'

'I know,' Archie rubbed his forehead. 'Otherwise, what is the point of me being here? They'll guess before long too; I think Tilly already thinks there's something going on between us.'

'And is there?' Ruby raised a playful eyebrow.

Archie stared at her and folded his arms. Damn this beautiful creature; she had played with his heart strings for over five decades and here she was doing it again. He would not submit.

'I need a little time. We should let Elaine settle in. Perhaps after this infernal pub quiz Tilly has planned for next week? Elaine has come this far, she's entrusted Lil to you; let's build up that trust a little bit more first?'

Ruby eyed him suspiciously. The doctor's voice became louder as he walked towards the bedroom door.

'No, Archie. It's like taking off a plaster. You can do it slowly and endure the pain for longer or you can do it in one quick swipe and put up with the stinging sensation for moments after. She *needs* to know. There will be another pub quiz the following Friday which Tilly will expect us at; are we to sit around a pub table and play happy families when they are unaware each week that we are in fact a family?! No.' Ruby shook her head and her perfectly sculpted ash blonde, wavy bob fell into her eyes. 'I'm not doing it Archie; Elaine and Tilly need to know, we can deal with the aftermath afterwards. If you're not prepared to do it in the next week then you might as well pack your bags and move back to Bristol.'

'But—'

'Here we are.' Doctor Dare burst into the room, guiding Lil with one arm, doctors' bag in the other. 'Lil wondered where you were so I said she could come with me.'

'Of course.' Ruby made an effortless-looking smile and walk across to relieve the doctor of his duties. 'She's well then, Anthony?'

'Her body is fit as a flea.' The doctor put his bag down and scratched his head. 'Unfortunately, her faculties aren't, but then I guess you already know that.'

'She's been like it for ten years,' said Archie. 'The dementia, that is. She's had the schizophrenia a lot longer, since the seventies.'

'Are you a relative?' The doctor asked Archie.

'Um, no. I'm, er…'

'This is Archie,' Ruby said, evidently wanting to avoid Archie putting his foot in it. 'He's lived next door to my sister in Bristol for a long time, so he knows the family intimately. More than I do really!' Ruby let out a nervous titter. 'We have all patients assessed when they enter the home, don't we Anthony?'

'Oh, yes, keeps me in business,' said Anthony, smiling at them both.

'I think with your routine here you may see some improvement in Lilian.'

Lil turned at the mention of her name. 'That's what me mum and dad called me, Lilian.'

'Yes,' Ruby said, 'shall we get you a cup of tea, Lil?'

'And the telly,' said Lil, looking around for a television set. 'Is the baby napping, Ruby?'

Archie was startled at the mention of a baby. Lil had never mentioned a baby living in Bristol. He swallowed hard knowing what baby Lil was referring to.

'She gets confused,' he smiled at the doctor.

'She's got some cognitive recognition though; she knew that the photo of Ruby's mum was her mum too.'

'Jean and Bob,' Lil said, reaching for the remote control on Ruby's nest of coffee tables. 'Bob wouldn't let Ruby keep the baby.'

If the doctor was surprised, he didn't show it. A crash came from the kitchen where Ruby had dropped the tea pot.

'Ohhhh! Blast it!' exclaimed Ruby.

Archie went to help her clear up. 'I don't need your help,' she snapped.

He backed off. 'Okay, well I'll be going,' he said, picking up his anorak from the back of a dining chair.

'Me too,' said the doctor, picking up his bag. 'I wasn't sensible enough to bring a coat,' he said, shrugging on his jacket.

'What she's just said, about a baby—'

The doctor put his hand on Ruby's forearm and squeezed it. 'Everything's confidential,' he said. 'Don't worry. Bye Lil!' The doctor waved and Archie opened the front door to Ruby's flat.

'Wait up doctor, I'll come with you,' Archie said, keen to escape more interrogation from Ruby.

'We need to sort this, Archie!' Ruby hissed.

Archie nodded. 'All in good time.' He nodded, closing the door on Ruby's angry face behind him, pretty sure that after fifty years of living in ignorant bliss with the Henshaw family, time was the one precious commodity he was swiftly running out of.

CHAPTER TWENTY-

SIX

Tilly sat looking out at the North Cornish coastline, at the calm Atlantic bathed in sunset, through the large arch window, in Laura Steele's 'consulting room'. It was a big, lofty lounge, sparsely furnished and very relaxing. It was as if the lack of furniture was purposefully intended in order for visitors to empty their thoughts.

Or perhaps it was intended to focus one's thoughts?

Tilly didn't care; she could merrily sit back in this squashy arm chair and take-in that view all day. Only, she had to be in work in two hours so that certainly wasn't on the cards. She tore her eyes away from the view to survey her surroundings again. Laura's home was a luxuriously renovated barn conversion, standing alone on a lane off the road from St Endellion to Rock. It had been a bugger to find. All around were farming fields with the odd sheep. It was too isolated for Tilly, but the house was very inviting. All white walls and sculptures made from artefacts, like driftwood, reclaimed from the sea. It reminded Tilly of Hope Cottage but on a grander, sophisticated scale. What was currently troubling Tilly was that Laura didn't look much older than her and look what Laura had achieved with her life. It made Tilly feel like she had a mountain to climb.

'There you go,' Laura said, returning to the room and setting two steaming cups of tea on the coffee table in the centre of the arm chairs arranged either side of the large, arch window. 'Now, have you been told much about how counselling works?'

Tilly, who had been lying back in her chair resting her feet on the coffee table quickly straightened herself up, all traces of feeling relaxed quickly abandoning her. 'We sit here in silence until I finally crack and tell you what I'm thinking. You analyse the hell out of it and blame it all on my mother for not showing me enough love when I was ten.'

Laura nodded, settling herself into her armchair.

Silence filled the room. 'See, I told you so,' Tilly said, averting her gaze, not wanting to be judged by yet another professional who knew nothing about her. Interestingly, she hadn't felt like that with Doc Dare. She'd actually felt listened to, for a change.

'I've been admiring your view,' Tilly continued, feeling uncomfortable with the silence. 'You have a lovely home. It's a beautiful house *and* in a beautiful setting.'

Laura took a sip of her tea and Tilly could see her eyes dancing over the rim of the mug. 'What does it make you feel?' Laura, finally spoke.

'Well, er…' Tilly tilted her head and her top knot slipped out of its grip. Ringlets tumbled down onto her shoulders. She scrabbled to tie them back up again. 'I'd be lying if I said it didn't make me feel a bit uneasy.'

Laura set her mug down. 'Interesting, because you just said you'd been admiring by beautiful house, in a beautiful setting. So, what's making you feel uneasy?'

Tilly bit her bottom lip. Elaine had always brought her up not to show any weaknesses. Did she tell Laura how she was really feeling? Could she even admit to herself that she was feeling… *jealous?*

'Shall I explain how I see this working, Tilly?' Laura cut across Tilly's thoughts?

Tilly nodded keenly. 'Please, do?'

'I'm a psychotherapist and I usually work with clients over long periods of times, years sometimes. The great thing about psychotherapy, *normally*, is the luxury of time. But, as part of my work with the NHS I also see clients, like you, who we call 'time limited' cases. As you know, we have six sessions. Although, I would normally give my clients the time and space to process what we talk about, you and I don't have that indulgence. You have been referred to me for cognitive behavioural therapy, where we can hopefully look at some of your behaviours of the past and how they are *possibly* affecting you now—'

'Well, that's the thing, they aren't—'

'They aren't or you don't know if they are?'

'Well, er…' Laura had her there. She really didn't know.

'Tilly, you seem to me, from the notes I've read and speaking with the person sitting before me, to be an intelligent, young woman, receptive to processing anything which might need changing in order for you to move forward with your life.'

Tilly nodded vigorously. 'Oh, yes, definitely. That's definitely what I want.'

Laura nodded. 'So, as our time together is limited, what I really need from you is for you to be honest; say what you're thinking. This is your space; it's yours to discuss what's on *your* mind so that, together, we can explore what's going on in your life.'

'And change it?'

'Do you want to change?'

Tilly pressed her lips together and thought hard. She did want to change. 'Yes, I do.'

'Okay,' Laura said, picking up her mug of tea again.

Silence filled the room again. Tilly felt like it was her turn to talk again, but she didn't really know what about. She felt like Laura had just offered her an olive branch, said they could explore what was going on together but that was exactly the problem; Tilly didn't know what was going on.

'I'm not sure what to talk about now,' Tilly offered, feeling confused.

'Let's go back to that uneasy feeling you were having. What do you think that was about?'

'Oh, that's easy, I was feeling jealous—' Tilly clamped her hand to her mouth, feeling she'd said too much.

'Jealous?'

Well, she'd offered up that much, she felt she probably ought to explain herself now. 'Yes, it's silly really, but you can't be much older than me and I don't even own my own home and, yet, here you are living in a spacious barn conversion.'

'Okay.'

Laura did that thing that all therapists did of going silent. Tilly secretly wondered if it was just to let you know that they were in control of the situation or whether it was really to make you think. Any therapy Tilly had had in the past she had mainly focused on looking at the seconds hand on the clock, ticking down the time until she could leave and *not* think about things. Which, actually now as she was sitting in silence, seemed a pretty stupid thing to do, because if she actually stopped to think about the thing she was trying *not* to think about, she might actually resolve the issue and needn't worry about it anymore. That did make a lot of sense.

Tilly cocked her head to one side. 'Actually, I'm not sure it is jealously.'

'No?'

'I think it might be envy.'

'Go on.'

'Well, jealousy suggests I begrudge what I have, and I don't even really know you.'

Laura nodded.

'But I am *envious* of what you have. Not your house; what it signifies.'

'And what does it signify for you?'

'Success, a sense of accomplishment.' Ooh, this was scary, Laura was drawing the thoughts out of Tilly's head and making her vocalise them without her even really thinking about it. But she was really thinking about it, because she was swiftly acknowledging what her life was lacking. 'A sense of purpose, too, perhaps,' she added, meekly.

'You don't feel your life has purpose?'

Tilly screwed up her face. 'Maybe?' She shrugged. 'In some ways. I mean, I'm always there to be my mum's emotional punch bag. She tends to take everything out on me when life gets stressful.'

Laura nodded. More silence ensued. Tilly cursed herself for mentioning again the one thing she had vowed not to mention in these sessions; Elaine. But, if Laura had clocked that Tilly had an issue with Elaine, she hadn't acknowledged it, yet.

'That sounds very hard,' Laura finally said.

'What?'

'Being someone's emotional punch bag.'

Tilly sighed and tucked a loose ringlet behind her ear. 'It is hard. Really hard sometimes. I thought I was coming down here to escape it all.'

'Escape?' Laura almost sounded incredulous.

Tilly nodded. She realised she was opening up to Laura, beginning to trust her. But sharing your feelings with others could be dangerous, in Tilly's experience anyway.

'And what were you escaping?'

Tilly went to open her mouth and paused. Why had she escaped? 'At first,' she said cautiously, frowning as she reached into the recesses of her mind, 'I thought it was my fiancé, sensible Simon, and our boring existence. But lately, I think it's because I want to make something of myself, I want to be me.' She looked at Laura still frowning. 'Does that make sense?'

Laura smiled. 'I think it probably goes hand-in-hand with your desire to change, which you just talked about.'

'Yes,' Tilly agreed.

'Why couldn't you make something of yourself in Bristol?'

'Oh, that's easy, Mum… arrggh!' Tilly gasped and her hand automatically clamped over her mouth.

Laura kept smiling. 'Go on,' she said, her face lighting up with anticipation.

Tilly shook her head. 'I can't. It's not right.'

'What's not right? You've come here to get to the bottom of why you were diagnosed with ADHD, or at least that's what your referral notes said. Is that correct?'

'Yes, and the fact I don't feel I have ADHD.' Tilly found herself speaking like a disgruntled teenager.

'Okay, but you are experiencing the need to change. Which suggests you were something and now you don't want to identify like that anymore.'

Tilly looked on at Laura with her lips slightly parted. It was like this woman could see into her soul. At all the bits that even Tilly didn't want to look at and appraise.

'Did you notice,' Laura continued, 'that you sounded like a truculent teen when you told me you don't feel you have ADHD?'

'Yes.' Tilly folded her arms and slumped down in the chair. 'Oh, God, I just did it again!'

Laura nodded. 'I wonder,' she said, pausing as if to keep Tilly hanging off her every word, 'I do wonder if perhaps I was just speaking with fourteen-year-old Tilly then. The Tilly who didn't want to be diagnosed with ADHD in the first place.'

Tilly found her eyes glazing into the middle distance. She was no longer in Laura's therapy room. She had been transported back to Doctor Pearson's consulting room, when she was fourteen, arguing there was nothing wrong with her but Elaine was there, insistent Tilly was out of control and needed medication.

'I was just being a normal teenager,' Tilly whispered, returning to the present, retreating into the protection of the squashy armchair.

Laura nodded. 'Tell me about you Gran, Lilian?'

Tilly had to hand it to Laura, she had read up on Tilly's notes very well if she wasn't even referring to them.

'She was diagnosed with schizophrenia a long time ago. Now she has dementia and there's very little of the person she was left, really.'

Laura pursed her lips in a sympathetic fashion. 'That must be hard, looking after someone who is a shadow of their former self.'

Tilly bit her thumbnail. 'That's fallen to my mum, really. Gran got worse when my Grandad died, sixteen years ago, but I'd just finished my GCSE's and was only interested in partying. I left home as soon as I could after A-levels.'

'And why was that, do you think?'

Ugh, what was this, Mastermind? Tilly took a deep breath as she remembered why she was here; to get to the bottom of why she had always been labelled with 'issues'. Why she had always got out of control and needed reining back in. Laura was entitled to ask questions.

'To get away from them, to escape, I suppose.'

'Like how you've ended up here in Cornwall, living in Hope Cove?'

Tilly crashed her head back onto the cushioned armchair. 'I guess so.'

'So, what is it you keep running away from?'

Tilly locked her eyes with Laura's imposing gaze. It was exactly that, a gaze. There was no judgement in her face, no quizzical expression either. Laura was trying to get Tilly to answer her own question.

Tilly exhaled loudly. 'Running away. You don't think I'm tyring to escape; you think I'm trying to run away.'

'I'm just trying to understand how all of this feels for you, Tilly.'

Tilly sighed. This was hard. Painful, almost. 'I guess,' she said, trying to focus, 'that I'm running away from Mum and Gran, only this time they've come with me.'

'Have they?' Laura frowned and reached for her file.

'Don't worry, I can tell you've read my referral thoroughly,' Tilly interjected. 'This has all happened since I went to see Doctor Dare and filled in your form. Mum arrived last week; she turned up and left Gran with Ruby. She's moved into the cottage with us, got herself a job at the bakery as well. She's like a different person!' Which was true; since Elaine had got a job and wasn't fretting over Gran every five seconds she had visibly relaxed into a normal, non-neurotic human being.

Laura raised an eyebrow. 'Perhaps your Mum needed to escape too?'

'I think so. I kept telling her she needed to get a life. I still can't believe she's done it though, she's rented the house out and everything!'

'And Ruby is your Great Aunt, who runs Hope Home?'

'Yes, sort of, have you heard of it?'

'Yes, I've met Ruby at various functions; she's a lovely lady, very much the life and soul of the party. You remind me of her.'

'Thanks, well, as you've probably already read, it seems that Ruby is in fact my grandmother and had my mum adopted to gran, Lil.' Tilly glanced at the clock. Over half-an-hour had gone by already. 'Anyway, I'm wittering on; I better let you get back on track.'

'No,' Laura shook her head vigorously. 'These sessions are about you Tilly, not me. We're here to get what you want out of them. Of course, we could explore why someone who ostensibly has Attention Deficit Disorder just tried to deflect the attention away from her.' Laura smiled and Tilly instantly knew that she liked and respected this woman. If Tilly had any hope of sorting her life out, Laura was going to be the one to help her with it.

'I just don't want to take medication anymore. I've not taken my pills for over a year and I've been fine. Okay, so I've split up with the man I was going to marry and moved to a different county, but I'm sure other people do that all the time without being accused of having ADHD or being bi-polar.' Tilly could hear the defence in her own voice.

Laura did that annoying nodding-silence thing again. It was beginning to grate on Tilly. All silence at home, when she was younger, was when she was in trouble with Mum and Gran was staring vacuously into space. Tilly tended to avoid silence like the plague these days.

'Have you ever heard of the self-fulling prophecy?' Laura asked.

Tilly frowned. 'I don't think so. Is it from the Bible?'

Laura laughed. 'No, it's a theory, a psychological theory; there are a few variations, but they are pretty much the same.' Laura placed a piece of A4 paper on coffee table.

'Blimey, I didn't realise I'd signed up for A-Level psychology.'

Laura smiled. 'It's quite simple, look.' She pointed to the diagram.

It was a bit like a flowchart, but it went around in a circle back to where it started. At midday it said 'Our Actions', at three o'clock it said, 'Others Beliefs', at six o'clock it said, 'Others Actions' and at nine o'clock, 'Our beliefs'.

Tilly studied the diagram, but it didn't make much sense. 'Are you saying that I act like how other people, my mum for instance, expect me to?'

Laura clicked her fingers. 'Yes. In the past,' she said, pointing to the 'Our Actions', 'you've behaved in a certain way, perhaps staying out too late with your mates and your mum,' Laura's finger moved to the 'Others Beliefs', 'has interpreted this as more than just truculent teen behaviour, due perhaps to your families' mental health history, and she took you to the doctors.'

'Which is 'Others Actions?''

'Yes.'

'Then I started behaving that way even more because my mum thought I had ADHD?' Tilly had a sudden flashback to when she'd died her hair illuminous pink and Elaine had marched her down the doctors to up her medication.

'Hmmm, I'm not saying that this is exactly how it happened, but I do believe, going on what you've told me and what I've read in your medical history, that you have changed your behaviour based upon others' beliefs.'

'So, it's all mum's fault?'

'I didn't say that.'

Tilly rolled her eyes. 'You didn't have to. Anyway, it would be unfair to blame mum; she's been through the same experience really, hasn't she?'

'I don't know your mum, it would be unfair of me to say without assessing her, which would then be something we couldn't discuss for confidentiality reasons, however,' Laura paused, 'I do think a lot of what's going on at the moment; you coming to live down here, your mum following you, perhaps it all stems back to your grandmother and her mental health. Perhaps your mum has talked herself into having mental health problems too?'

'Oh, there's no doubt about that,' Tilly nodded, still studying the diagram. 'So, could I use this to change my behaviour too?'

'Of course, that was my other reason for showing it to you.'

Tilly's shoulders slumped and she looked out at the calm sea, the sun glinting on the waves. She looked back at Laura. 'That's the biggest problem; I don't know what I'm good at yet.'

The Ones That Got Away

CHAPTER TWENTY-

SEVEN

Winstone looked around the bar and grinned. He'd never seen the place so heaving; it reminded him of heady days, DJing in Ibiza. You could almost see the steam rising off the punters. He had to hand it to Tilly, she definitely had a way with people. She was flitting between tables, handing out question sheets and collecting entry fees.

'Here you go,' Tilly said, reappearing behind the bar with a book entitled *The Ultimate Pub Quiz Book*.

He took it from her. The warm pub had enticed the shirt off her back. She'd tied it around her waist, leaving her long ringlets to flow over her dainty shoulders. He swallowed hard as he could see the lace of her lemony bra teasing its way out from under her white vest top. Tearing his gaze away, he concentrated on flicking through the book. He raised a quizzical eyebrow and folded his arm, purposefully flexing his biceps. 'I hope you haven't been looking up the answers.'

She punched him on the arm. 'Ouch, that actually hurt me!'

He'd barely felt her knock him. 'Well, if you will be a cruel taskmaster,' he said, shaking his head. 'Anyway, you haven't answered the question; have you looked at the answers?'

'No,' she said grinning, 'plus I have no idea which quiz you're going to pick! Now if you excuse me, I shall be over with my family ready to answer questions and will return to serve at half-time.'

'Okay,' Winstone said, watching her step down from the bar, 'oh and Tilly—'

'Yes?' She swung around and the light behind her hair gave her an angelic halo. Winstone swallowed hard again, shame washing over him for even feeling this way.

'Thank you, for all of this.' He extended a hand out across the pub. 'I've never seen it so packed.'

'You won't be thanking me when you have to carry all those empties out onto the harbour for collection in the morning.' She winked and with that was gone over to the little table in the corner where Ruby, Archie and Elaine were huddled.

'Are we all okay for drinks?' Tilly asked, sitting down next to Elaine.

'Fine, thanks love,' Elaine said, lifting her gin and tonic up to show it was still half-full. She couldn't remember the last time she'd drunk in a pub. Possibly her student days, before Tilly was born.

'We're good thanks, sweetie,' Ruby said. 'We were just discussing your mum's new job in the bakery.'

'Oh, yes! It's going well, isn't it, Mum?'

'Yes, thank you,' Elaine said, clutching onto her glass like her life depended on it. She'd had to use her inhaler more than usual this past week. The anxiety of starting a new job had almost made her late on the first day, she could hardly get off the toilet. Today was another hurdle; the unfamiliar surroundings of a public house. Drinking alcohol was something she rarely participated in, apart from the odd Baileys at Christmas.

'How are you getting on with Emma?' Ruby asked.

'Very well, thank you.' Emma had been extremely patient with Elaine while she got to grips with her orientations in the bakery. The little placards for each type of bun, cake, pastry and pasty pointed out towards the customer meaning Elaine had had to quickly familiarise herself with the vast array of different delicacies offered.

'I get on really well with her,' Tilly said, filling-in the name section on the quiz sheet. 'She says my baking skills are really coming along.'

Archie – mid pint swigging – almost spat out his lager. 'You can say that again, that focaccia you made last week was delicious and those pasties in your first week, oh, and that Bakewell tart.' He patted his stomach. 'No wonder my trousers feel a bit tight around the waist; I'll have to lengthen Hector's walks.'

Hector didn't stir from his secure position on Ruby's lap. She was stroking him and looking down with an expression of love, the sort of expression reserved for mothers and their babies. Elaine felt a stabbing sensation in her stomach. Would that have been how Ruby would have held Elaine, if she'd been allowed to keep her?

'Thanks, Archie, I'm really enjoying it. Perhaps that's where my talents lie. No point opening a bakery here though; there's no way I could compete with Emma and James.'

'That doesn't mean you couldn't offer a different type of food experience, does it?' said Ruby. 'Those pop-up thingies are all the rage now; with the summer coming you could easily run a little stall on the beach.'

Elaine watched her daughter's eyes widen and bit her lip. She would be the first to admit moving to Hope Cove seemed to have done wonders for Tilly. What she didn't need was to be encouraged into some hare brain scheme. She had a steady job here at the Lobster Pot; why couldn't she be satisfied with that?

'Oooh, wouldn't I need some sort of licence though?'

Ruby shrugged. 'We'll look into it. Come over to in the morning and we'll sit down in my office and make some enquiries.'

Elaine looked at Ruby, so effortlessly confident, and inwardly sighed. If she really was her mother, then why was Elaine nothing like her? Ruby made life sound easy when all Elaine ever found it to be was stressful and complicated. She looked again at Tilly, practically dancing on her stool, and realised that the confidence had clearly skipped a generation.

'Good evening.'

Elaine froze. It was like being transported back in time. Only how could it be?

'Oh, hi doctor,' Tilly said, standing up. 'Care to join us?'

'Oh, yes, do Anthony; it all got a bit stressful when you visited last week. I'll buy you a drink.' Ruby went to get up but Hector softly growled.

'I'll get them in,' Archie said, standing up. 'Nice to see you again, doctor, what's yours to be?'

Elaine picked up her handbag not daring to look at the impostor with his uniquely comforting voice. She couldn't. How could she? Oh, gosh, she really needed her inhaler. 'I'm okay thanks, Archie.'

Out of the corner of her eye, Elaine could see the man raise his pint glass to confirm he was good for a drink. She was aware she was beginning to take her deep breaths, the ones she knew to do when she felt a panic attack coming on. What was he doing here, in Hope Cove? Of course, if she could bear to look up she could confirm it was him. Not that she needed it confirming; she knew.

'Here, take a seat, while I go to the bar.' Archie said, gesturing the man to his chair.

Oh, gosh, please don't.

'Oh, yes, do Anthony,' said Ruby, 'we'll definitely win with you on our team.'

'Are you sure you don't mind?'

I do! Go away!

'Not at all,' Ruby said, patting her hand on the stool Archie had just vacated. 'It's nice to see you out and about; you're not one for frequenting the pub of an evening, are you?'

So why choose this one?!

'Well, Tilly came into reception last week wielding her poster to go up on the noticeboard and then badgered me into coming. That was her second attempt too. She said twenty percent of the winnings went to the Lifeboats, so I thought I'd wander down and see what it's all about.'

Oh, heck, he's even met Tilly. Of course, he's met Tilly; he's the bloody doctor!

A horrible, unwelcoming feeling crept over Elaine sending her into deeper panic mode; how was she going to get her medication now? She couldn't go and she him. How could she possibly go and see him?

'Unlike you to be over here when the tide's in Ruby,' Anthony continued.

'Oh, I'll stay at the cottage tonight; I'll bunk in with Tilly. If she doesn't end up pulling that dishy boss of hers by the end of the night.'

Elaine would have scowled at Ruby for suggesting Tilly would be that easy but that would certainly be the pot calling the kettle black in the current circumstances.

'He is most definitely off-limits, so you will have to put up with me hogging the duvet,' Tilly said, flatly.

Elaine's entire body was pumping with adrenaline now as she scanned anywhere but where Anthony was sitting for her exit route.

'Oh, so you don't deny you like him then?' Ruby said with eagerness.

'Have you met Mum, doctor?' said Tilly, evidently keen to avoid Ruby's interrogation. 'Mum, this is Doctor Dare, the local GP—'

So, he did qualify in medicine then.

'—He's the one who's hooked me up with CBT. Are you okay, mum?'

Elaine could fight it off no-longer. She routed around in her handbag for her inhaler, burying her face from his appraising gaze.

'Mum?' Tilly asked again.

'I'm fine, love,' she lied, taking the lid off and shaking it.

Anthony was straight to his feet and rushing around the table to Elaine's side. He took her wrist and placed two fingers on the inside to measure her pulse.

'Are you okay? You're breathing is laboured. Tilly, can you find your mother a paper bag?'

He still hadn't looked at her.

'Sure,' Tilly said, jumping up.

Elaine waved a hand to dismiss the request. She took a puff on her inhaler. 'I'm fine but I think I'd better go home now.'

'Well, you should come and see me for an emergency appointment at the surgery in the morning. I insist.'

He looked up at her. Bravely, more courageously that she felt she'd ever had to be in her life, she took the inhaler away and met his gaze. In that instant he knew. Age had given him a few more lines around his eyes and some white hair peppered in amongst his jet-black ones, but the boy she had once known was still there. Still looking as assuring as ever. Still reminding her about everything she had given up.

Elaine withdrew her gaze. 'Can't, working,' she muttered, standing up and hooking her bag over her shoulder.

'Are you sure you're okay mum?' Tilly was looking quizzically between Elaine and the doctor.

Anthony was still staring at Elaine. Still holding onto her wrist.

'I'll be fine,' she said, whipping her wrist away, feeling bereft all over again at the loss of his touch. 'Just had a busy day. I probably need to go home and rest, that's all.' She managed something resembling a smile and she seized her opportunity to escape through the gap between Tilly and Anthony.

'I'll walk you up the road,' Ruby said, standing up, still clutching Hector.

Elaine laughed nervously. 'Honestly, I'm fine! I'll be off now.' She swallowed hard, unsure if she could say his name. 'Anthony,' her voice wobbled, 'can take my place on Tilly's team. Night, love.' And with that she turned and fled, gulping in fresh sea air as she stumbled out onto the harbour. 'Why me?!' she shouted to no-one but the stars as she quickened her pace up the hill towards the lighthouse. Why, when she had just found some long, sought after, independence, when she didn't have to care for Lil twenty-four hours a day, did she find herself opening the door straight into the past?

CHAPTER TWENTY-EIGHT

1983

Anthony leant in behind Elaine and wrapped his arms around her waist, pulling her towards him, softly kissing her neck whilst swaying to Spandau Ballet singing 'True'. He had to bend a little – well, quite a lot, actually – to kiss her neck. She arced, in pleasure, and wrapped her hands around his.

Perfection.

All the hard work and favours he had to pull-in to get his hands on a pair of tickets for this concert had paid off. He'd pretty much worked every evening and weekend shift at O'Reilly's – the Irish Bar he pulled pints in, on White Ladies Road, to try and get him through medical college without the need for a student loan – to pay the extra £100, the Student Union Leader, John, was charging him for the tickets which he'd got hold of from God knew where. He didn't care. He'd only been seeing Elaine eight weeks and when she mentioned it was her birthday this weekend *and* he knew how much she loved Spandau Ballet, he knew what he had to do.

It might not have been that long, but he knew this was love. Tony Hadley sang out in a proclamation of love and the crowd sang along too, but Anthony was barely aware. It was like he and Elaine were the only two people in the room and Tony was singing for them. It was funny how it felt. He'd had other girls; he was twenty-one, of course he had, but this was different. Elaine wasn't like the girls he was used to at his old grammar school in Berkshire or at Uni. She was as intelligent as them, but she lacked their arrogance. She worried about him, turned up at his student share to clean the kitchen and pop his dirty clothes in the washing machine before hanging them out to dry. She was studying to be a nurse – that was how they met – but given the right education she could have been achieving more by now, he knew it. Not that it mattered; he'd qualify by the time he was twenty-five and once he'd specialised, he'd been earning enough money for both of them to live off.

Tony stopped singing and the mesmerised crowd broke into applause, breaking him from his reverie. Elaine turned around, wrapped her arms around his neck and reached up to kiss him firmly on his lips, pressing her pelvis firmly into him.

'That was fantastic,' she said, breaking away but keeping her face inches away from his.

'You're welcome,' he said, 'happy birthday.'

Her birthday was tomorrow. He'd carefully wrapped her presents and stashed them under his bed. Their relationship hadn't gone as far as the bedroom yet, but he knew that Elaine was an honest, wholesome girl and he knew he needed to be patient. It didn't matter anyway, he was in love; he'd wait. Although, secretly he hoped tonight was *the night*.

The band said their thanks and disappeared back stage. The crowd started to filter out of the exits at Colston Hall, leaving a trail of empty plastic beer glasses in their wake. Elaine remained with her arms firmly around his neck, looking up at him like a Disney Princess with those beautiful, blue, doe-like eyes.

'Would you like to go around to the stage door and see if we can get their autographs?' he asked.

'I can think of better things we could do,' she said, sultrily, into his ear.

Green light. 'Let's go,' he said, grabbing her hand and marching her towards the nearest exit, impatiently urging the crowd of remaining concert goers to quickly pass through.

The journey was one big blur. A bus ride from the centre of the city to Bedminster. They stayed entwined, arms, hands, tongues fondling and caressing like they were the only two in existence. He fumbled for his keys in the front door and shoved it open. Remarkably, the 1930s bay-semi was quiet and dark. Perfect. No jeers or letching from Stephen or Mark, his fellow housemates. They embarked the stairs, tugging at each other's clothes, fumbling at the buttons. He backed her into his room and led her to the bed, pushing her gently onto his freshly washed, sailboat duvet. She looked up at him longingly before removing her Spandau Ballet T-shirt over her head, revealing her black, lacy, Wonderbra.

He gasped; she was so beautiful. 'Are you sure?' he asked. He had to be sure. He'd waited so long, so patiently because Elaine was special; she was worth the wait. Loving, kind, Elaine. They'd drank alcohol this evening and he didn't want it to affect her decision.

'Totally,' she said, unbuttoning his Levis and tugging at his boxers.

He revealed himself to her and it was her turn to gasp. He grinned and leaned over her. Succumbing, she lay down, allowing him to unbutton her tight denim, drainpipes. She had matching lace panties and he slowly reached inside, rubbing her gently. She groaned and fumbled to release her bra. Kissing fervently, they pushed each other's jeans away and he tugged her panties down. She smiled as he entered her. He had to concentrate not to explode there and then; his desire for her was so strong. They moved in rhythm, like they were made for each other; perfect timing. He rolled onto his back, pulling her with him and she giggled as she turned, with him still in her, sitting up straight on him to reveal all of her beauty. Her pert breasts, her taught stomach. Again, he held back his urge as she writhed on top of him, gripping her thighs firmly to his pelvis until eventually she climaxed. Only then did he put himself into overdrive and make her bounce up and down on top of him as he came over and over again inside of her. She lay on top of him, kissing him passionately. He returned his kisses with as much intensity, whilst the rest of his load filled her inside. Releasing herself, she lay down next to him, resting her head on his chest as the both drifted into post-orgasmic bliss.

He awoke fired up, ready to go again but most excited about giving Elaine her birthday gifts. The bed was empty and cold. He rose in panic, hoping she'd just gone to the bathroom, but her clothes were gone. Naked, he stood looking around the room, feeling down. There on the end of the bed, lay one of his A4 lined jotter pads he used for lectures.

Had to go. We forgot about protection. Gone to emergency out of hours at hospital. Thank you for a fantastic night. Love Elaine X

'Fuck,' he said, sitting back down on the bed.

CHAPTER TWENTY-

NINE

Tilly arrived at Hope Home early on Saturday morning. Ruby hadn't stayed the night at Hope Cottage as planned, in fact the house had been eerily quiet when she'd got in. Part of her had felt the need to stay until Mum got up, to check she was okay after her abrupt departure from the pub last night, but she had to be back across on the mainland to start her shift at The Lobster by midday. Plus, if Tilly was totally honest, she was impatient to know Ruby's ideas to get Tilly's career off the ground.

She pressed the buzzer and waited for someone to release the double doors. It was just before eight, but she knew someone would be up and manning the reception. Life at the home was twenty-four hours non-stop by all accounts.

'Morning!' Julie sang, wearing her apple-green tabard, as Tilly stepped into the lobby. She was such a jolly lady; she was definitely suited to working with the patients in the home.

'Hi,' said Tilly. 'Is Ruby about?'

'Still dealing with your gran. Go on up to her apartment, if you like.'

'Great, thanks,' Tilly said, taking the stairs two at a time. She'd been up to Ruby's apartment a couple of times to visit Gran since her and mum had arrived. She could only hope that one day she'd earn enough to afford such an impressive pad as Ruby's; the view was breath taking.

She knocked the door.

'Come in,' came Ruby's voice.

'Morning!' Tilly said, bursting in.

Ruby and Gran were sitting at her glass dining table, sharing breakfast. Or more, Ruby was eating breakfast and reading the papers while Gran's eyes were fixed to the television with porridge dribble escaping from the corner of her mouth.

'Look, Lil, it's Tilly,' Ruby said, gently reaching across the table and stroking Lil's hand.

Gran turned. 'Oh, 'ello,' she said, returning to BBC Breakfast.

'Sorry to call so early.' Tilly closed the front door and walked towards the table. 'But I've got to be at work for midday.'

'No problem,' said Ruby, 'it's lovely to see you. Coffee?' she asked, standing up.

'Oh, yes please,' Tilly said, eyeing up the pain au chocolates. In a rush to get here she'd forgotten about breakfast.

'Help yourself,' Ruby said. 'I'll pop the kettle on and make a fresh pot.' She waggled the cafetière. She was wearing white fitted jeans and a pale pink, silk blouse. She looked effortlessly chic for before nine o'clock in the morning. Unlike Tilly, in her hoodie and running gear. She'd skipped a shower and decided to run here as the tide was out. It was all part of her desire to become a different person, having listed to Laura at her first session last Thursday. Laura had said exercise was an important factor in a healthy mind.

Ruby's discarded newspaper was lying open on a page with a large phot of Prince Harry. It was the headline which grabbed her attention. *I totally lost the plot.* Tilly drew the paper towards her and started reading.

'Interesting, isn't it?' Ruby said, returning with a steaming fresh pot of coffee and a cup and saucer for Tilly. Tilly smiled. She had suspected Ruby wasn't a mug type person.

'It must have been hard, losing his mum at twelve.' Tilly had scanned over the first few paragraphs which told of Prince Harry's struggle to come to terms with his mother, the late Princess Diana's, death. Instead of dealing with it at the time it wasn't until his late twenties, sixteen years later, that his life began to spiral out of control, and he'd started to seek help in the form of therapy. Tilly swallowed hard; it was all a little familiar and it made her feel bad because her mum was still alive.

'It's such a great thing the younger Royal generation are becoming ambassadors for mental,' Ruby said, pouring their coffee. 'There's so many stigmatisms attached to being mentally ill when, in fact, we all suffer at some point or other. Some of us live in a perpetual cycle of anxiety—' Tilly watched Ruby pause, as if considering if she said what was on the tip of her tongue. '—like your mother.'

Ruby didn't meet Tilly's gaze. Tilly wondered if there was some guilt lingering there surrounding her relationship with Elaine. Although the way Ruby had said *we*, as if including herself, seemed preposterous; she couldn't imagine composed, outgoing, vibrant Ruby to ever be someone to suffer with anxiety or depression.

She stirred sugar into her coffee. 'I'm not sure everyone does. If everyone suffers then it takes the emphasis off of people like Gran, who have a proper mental illness.'

Ruby burst out laughing. Her coffee cup chinked against the saucer as she set it down. 'My darling girl, if you went to A&E with a broken leg or a burst appendix, would anyone discriminate against you? Would they say, *sorry, your appendix has burst but this person can't walk as they have a broken leg so you'll have to wait.* Both would be considered urgent and would be dealt with accordingly.'

'I don't understand?'

'Well, if Lil turned up in hospital during or after a psychotic episode from her schizophrenia, why should she be treated any differently either? Or if you turned up at your GP suffering from chronic anxiety, preventing you from leading your everyday life, shouldn't that be taken seriously? Of course, it isn't, but times are changing. All, I'm saying is that we are all individuals and we are all battling our own problems.' Ruby shrugged. 'It doesn't matter if everyone in the world is suffering with some sort of mental health issue, we must treat everyone individually and equally.'

'Right,' Tilly said, still not entirely sure she still understood. Although, Doctor Dare had taken her seriously and sent her to Laura Steele, so perhaps she would do well to change her attitude.

'Coverage such as a Royal can provide,' Ruby continued, 'is helping change people's opinions. The days of *pull yourself together* are thankfully being left behind. It's why I decided to set this place up; to deal with mental health issues.'

Tilly had noticed that not all the occupants of Hope Home were elderly.

'I thought you made this place specialise in dementia, because of Nana Jean?'

'I did,' Ruby took a gulp of coffee, 'but then your mother sent me into deep depression and I ended up on anti-depressants.' She shrugged. 'I'm an optimistic person so I found myself having to turn the situation around; to make a positive out of it so I could help others. Of course, all the mental health illnesses have fewer offensive names these days, reducing the stigmatism. Manic depressives now have Bi-Polar disorder—'

'Hang on.' Tilly turned to look at Gran then back at Ruby. If even Ruby had mental health issues, it threw Laura Steele's theory about Tilly out of the window. 'How did you end up depressed? What does mum have to do with it?'

'She rejected me.'

Tilly shook herself, wondering if she was the one who had gone mad now.

'How?'

'I wanted to help her. Lil phoned me to say she was pregnant, with you, and Stan supported her decision to keep you, but Lil wanted her to have an abortion. I didn't' want history repeating itself so I wanted to offer your mum an escape route; something I never had. So, I turned up and went in all gung-ho, explained who I was, told your mum to keep you and that I would support her. I offered for her to come and live here and start a new life. I thought she could still pursue her nursing career that way.'

'Mum wanted to be a nurse?'

'Yes, she was training before she had you, but she gave it up when she fell pregnant.'

Tilly shook her head and marvelled at how little she really knew about Elaine.   'What about my father?'

'Didn't want to be involved, I guess. Anyway, that's all in the past; you can't change any of it. Your mother rejecting me helped me to go on to help others.'

Tilly sat quietly, sipping her coffee, taking in this latest revelation. Her mother had once had career aspirations too. Working at the Co-Op checkout had never been her raison d'etre.

This certainly wasn't turning into the morning she had anticipated.

'I'm having counselling.' The words escaped Tilly's mouth before her brain even engaged that she was saying them.

'Oh?' Ruby's light hearted tone belied her concern as she dropped her coffee cup to its saucer. 'Locally? Or Someone in Bristol?'

'It's a new thing. I went to see Doctor Dare and he suggested I go for CBT with Laura Steele.'

Ruby clasped her hands together. 'Oh, lovely Laura. I'm sure she'll get to the bottom of the problem, or whatever it is.'

'Want more tea, Ruby,' Lil said, banging her plastic beaker on the glass.

'You know, Gran was more independent than this a few weeks ago.' Tilly looked cautiously at Gran. 'She can hold a china mug you know.'

'And spill quite a lot of it.' Ruby pursed her lips as she took the lid off the beaker and began pouring tea from the pot.

Tilly looked around the ostentatious surroundings of the flat and conceded she wouldn't want an oversized toddler making her pristine soft furnishings dirty either.

'Fair point.'

'To be honest, I wasn't sure what level of care your mother was giving your—' Ruby faltered, '—Gran and I had to start somewhere, so I kept to our procedures here. I'm still assessing her, truth be told. Some days she's quite independent, other days she wets her incontinence pants five or six times.'

Tilly grimaced. 'I can call you Nana, if you prefer.' She could tell from Ruby tripping over her words that it was hard to refer to Lil as 'Gran'.

Ruby shrugged. 'It's fine. It's silly to try and change after all these years and it's easier to explain to folk in the village that you're my great niece.'

'Well, just so you know, I do believe you and you would have been a great Nana when I was growing up.'

'Thank you.' Ruby beamed. 'And as your Nana, am I allowed to enquire how you came to be referred to Laura for counselling? Is it something to do with Simon?'

'It's complicated.' Tilly was still trying to compute the confession from Ruby of once having been on anti-depressants. Were they a family of freaks with mental health issues being passed from one generation to the next? Did she actually have ADHD?

'When I was a teenager,' Tilly continued, 'I was put on meds for ADHD. Mum thinks I have,' Tilly raised her fingers to mimic speech marks, '"episodes" where I'm erratic. Misbehaved, generally out of control. I left home as soon as I could, worked on cruise ships in summer and as a chalet girl in winter, got myself into debt and went back home. Mum thinks I'm impulsive.'

'We're all impulsive my dear; look at my flat.' Ruby waved her arm around. 'Full of expensive artefacts I have no need for.'

'Precisely. A year ago, I stopped taking my medication. Now I've run away again and, so, out of respect to Mum, really, I went to see the doctor.'

'And what did Anthony have to say about it?'

'He thinks I was either misdiagnosed, or I've outgrown the diagnosis, so he's sent me to Laura to figures things out.'

'And what does Laura say?'

'I've only had one session. She seemed to follow my lead. She said I seem like a normal thirty-two-year-old; not depressed, just trying to get my life in order. She gave me something called the Self-Fulfilling Prophecy to work on. It's a diagram of behaviour. She thinks that Mum has always thought of me as trouble and therefore I behave like that.' Tilly watched a flicker of horror briefly pass over Ruby's face. 'Well, not trouble, perhaps more exuberant and unpredictable. She'd prefer it if I'd settled for Simon, I think, but I wasn't happy and I couldn't settle for normal and unhappy.'

'Hmmm,' Ruby said, standing up and tidying Lil's discarded porridge away. 'Sounds like this is all my fault.'

'No way,' Tilly said, incredulously. 'How can you draw that conclusion?'

'If I'd kept your mum, perhaps things would be different. Perhaps your mum wouldn't have treated you the way she has. She's bitter and angry with me and it sounds as if she's taken it out on you over the years.' Ruby looked at Lil. 'Your Gran, perhaps, as well.'

'Mum has been nothing but devoted to me and Gran.' Tilly surprised herself at leaping to Elaine's defence. 'And if you hadn't given Mum up to Gran, life might be different; I might not even be here.' Blimey, this morning hadn't turned out the way she had imagined at all. She met Ruby's gaze as Ruby nodded. The silence spoke volumes; an acceptance to draw a line under the matter.

'Very true. So, Tilly Henshaw, what do you think you need to do to be normal *and* happy?'

Tilly slumped down in her chair and raked her hands through her tangled curls. 'I don't really know.' She looked at Ruby and bit her lip, debating whether to tell her how she really felt.

'Go on, out with it,' Ruby said, loading the dishwasher.

'Well, I want to be like you; rich and successful. I want to have a purpose. I don't want a man to rely on; I want to make a difference. Only, I don't really have any skills and so I haven't a clue how to go about doing it.'

'I thought you'd come here to discuss a pop-up restaurant?'

'Yes, but that's nothing compared to what you've achieved.'

Ruby took the tea towel, which was slung over her shoulder, and threw it at Tilly.

'For goodness sakes girl, stop sounding so defeatist! Rome wasn't built in a day and all that. I started this place off on a healthy divorce settlement. Having left Simon before you even got as far as the altar, you don't have that luxury.'

'No.' Tilly pressed her lips together and thought hard. The mortgage they had was in joint names and she had contributed to the hefty twenty-thousand-pound deposit they had put down, plus the mortgage repayments for the past three years. Perhaps she shouldn't have just walked out?

'Luckily for you, though, you do have a newly acquired, wealthy Nana, willing to invest some capital.'

'Really?' Tilly's eyes practically popped out of her head.

'Of course, you're my granddaughter; I want to help. I think you need to enlist Emma's help with what exactly you should be offering in terms of food; you don't want to go treading on anyone's toes.'

'It's fine; I was thinking hot food like paella or something in little cardboard cartons. Nothing like they offer at the bakery. Perhaps something vegan and environmentally friendly; definitely no plastic!'

'And what about that delectable employer of yours? How's he going to feel about you setting-up in competition?'

Tilly blushed. 'I hadn't thought of that.'

'Well, let's go and get Lil settled in the Day Room and go through to my office. We'll have a look on the web at how you get a licence to sell food on the harbour and see if we can source a pop-up stall for you. We'd better set a budget too.'

Tiny butterflies began to swirl in Tilly's stomach. 'Thank you,' she said, coyly.

'You're very welcome,' Ruby said, shutting the dishwasher door. 'But you don't want to be like me; keep your heart open-minded. I've seen the way Winstone looks at you.'

'He's my boss,' Tilly said, fixing Ruby with a firm stare.

'Not for much longer, perhaps.' Ruby winked. 'Come on Lil, you can come downstairs and wee what's on; I think Carol is running knitting club this morning.'

Tilly laughed. 'How will Gran remember how to knit?'

'You'll be amazed how the brain works,' Ruby said, helping lift Gran out of the chair. For such a petite woman she certainly had great strength; Gran was at least twice Ruby's weight.

Tilly glanced at the newspaper, still open on the table. A photo of Prince Harry smiling back at her, caught her eye. Perhaps they all had mental health problems in the Henshaw-Mackenzie family. But if a Prince could suffer too, it showed that anxiety, depression, schizophrenia, none of it discriminated. As she went to hold the door for Ruby and Gran, Tilly contemplated Laura's suggestion that it might be beneficial for Tilly and Elaine to go to counselling together. Perhaps what would be even better would be if Ruby came too. There were too many skeletons in the closet. Ruby and Elaine both kept the paternity of their children close to their chests. Maybe, just maybe, it all needed to come out; ironed out. Then they could all ditch their demons and move forward together.

As a proper family.

CHAPTER THIRTY

1984

The doorbell rang and Elaine jumped, like she did every time it rang these days. She risked a glimpse around the edge of the curtain, but she couldn't see anyone, unsurprising as the bedroom looked out onto the front garden and the front door was to the side of the bungalow.

'Laney! Can you get that?' Mum called.

Panic rose in her chest. 'Sorry, not dressed,' she lied. She couldn't risk opening the front door; what if it was him? What if he'd found her? She clutched her stomach and waited to see if the door rang again. It didn't. Instead, a glamorous lady with blonde curly hair – a faint resemblance to Marilyn Monroe from behind – tottered in her heels and mackintosh back up the driveway towards the path. She glanced at Elaine's window. Elaine took a step back, before watching the woman make her way up Archie and Phyllis' driveway. Probably the new Avon lady, Elaine thought, returning to her bed and her book on pregnancy.

She was fourteen weeks. Last week, after the scan had confirmed that everything was well with the baby, she had told Mum and Dad. Naturally, they had been shocked but there had been no shouting or crying like she'd expected. Dad had been surprisingly calm. He had even asked how she was feeling. Mum had been really strange. She looked at Elaine blankly and said, 'it's just like history repeating itself.' Which was odd, Elaine had reflected.

'Of course, you won't keep it, will you?' She'd continued. 'There's no shame in abortion these days.'

Thankfully Dad had looked horrified. 'She can do whatever she wants,' he'd said. 'We'll support you.' That had almost made Elaine cry.

She had tried to get rid of her baby. She'd been too embarrassed to go to the doctor and ask for the pill in the weeks she'd been seeing Anthony. Mum and Dad were so old fashioned and prudish, she hadn't mentioned to them she had a boyfriend. She hadn't even mentioned it to Archie and Phyllis. Instead, she'd made out she was just out with friends from college when she was seeing him. Which wasn't a lie, that was how she'd met him; in the student union bar which served the polytechnic where the nursing college was based and adjoined the medical college where Anthony was training. He was three school years above her but not like some of the other idiots training to be doctors. He was thoughtful, and kind and never arrogant. He was a gentleman; she'd never met another man like him. Apart from Dad and Archie, perhaps, but that was different. Sub-consciously, she knew she was going to sleep with Anthony that night because she had plucked up the courage to go to the sexual health clinic on campus and get some free condoms, but she was still undecided until they were dancing to *True* that she was going to go through with it. As Tony Hadley sang out *head over heels when toe-to-toe*, she knew. It was exactly how she felt. She'd never slept with anyone before and had assumed Anthony would disappear like the other few brief boyfriends she'd had. Lose interest when she wouldn't give-in and fall into bed quickly enough, but he hadn't.

He'd upped his game. He'd surprised her with the concert tickets for her birthday. It had all felt so right. So right, her body had taken charge of her brain and the condoms had lain forgotten in her handbag. To be fair to Anthony, he'd probably assumed she was using the contraceptive pill. That's why as soon as she'd realised in the middle of the night her mistake, she'd got dressed and fled.

Now, three months later, she hadn't spoken to him since.

The doorbell rang again, more persistently this time.

'Laney!' Came mum's commanding tone again. She would just be watching the TV and dragging on a fag. She wasn't meant to watch television, what with her schizophrenia, but when Dad was at work in the day, Mum had got into the habit of flicking it on for the morning programmes as soon as Dad left for work.

The doorbell went again.

'LANEY!'

Elaine sighed and put her book down on the bed. She risked a glance through her bedroom window but could see no-one. Creeping out into the hallway it occurred to her to ignore the caller and tell Mum it was just the local Jehovah Witnesses doing the rounds again.

DING DONG!

Elaine's stomach muscles clenched but through the frosted window Elaine could see the outline of the lady who she'd seen on the driveway before. She relaxed a little. At least it wasn't Anthony. Although, behind the blonde lady's outline, Elaine could make out another female figure.

Gingerly, she opened the door.

'Yes?' She squeaked.

The lady smiled. A big broad smile. There was something vaguely familiar about her.

'Hello, you must be Elaine,' she said, her big red lips parting to reveal sparkly, pearl teeth.

'Might be,' Elaine blurted out, wondering how this stranger knew her name.

'I'm your aunt, Ruby.' She smiled again. 'Is your mum at home?'

Elaine opened the door wider. She'd heard of Aunt Ruby but couldn't remember her.

Ruby, still smiling, stepped over the threshold and past Elaine, revealing a distressed Phyllis, wringing her hands, tears glistening like snail trails down her face.

'Oh, Elaine,' she cried, rushing towards Elaine and enveloping her in a hug. 'Why didn't you tell us?'

'Tell you what?' Elaine asked, a wave of anxiety rushing over her again.

'About the baby,' Phyllis whispered into her ear.

Elaine drew away, shocked. Phyllis knew. She had wanted to tell Archie and Phyllis, they were like an aunt and uncle to her, but she was embarrassed.

'Who told you?'

'Ruby.' Phyllis was dabbing her eyes with her hanky.

'How does she know?' Elaine looked into the living room where Ruby had disappeared. Raised voices began trailing from the room. Elaine and Phyllis followed them.

'She has a right to know now, Lil,' Ruby said sternly. 'I can help her!'

'What do I have a right to know?' Elaine asked, quietly.

Mum looked panic-stricken as she looked from Elaine to Ruby and back at Elaine.

'Nothing, love. This is your Auntie Ruby; remember her?'

'No. Why did you tell Ruby about the baby?' It didn't make sense. Why tell a distant relative her news but not Archie and Phyllis who they all considered to be like family?

Mum's face paled.

Ruby smiled again. 'Sit down, Elaine,' she said, lowering herself onto the arm of mum's chair.

'Ruby, don't do this,' said mum.

'No, Ruby,' said Phyllis, shaking her head. 'Don't do this now.'

Ruby looked between the two women. Her pearl necklace sparkled in the lamp light Mum had left on, on such a dull January day. She still had her mackintosh on but where it opened, it revealed a well-cut, two-piece skirt and jacket. Her watch was Chanel and her opaque, sheer, stocking-clad legs were well toned and finished off with some extremely expensive looking stilettos. Whatever Ruby had done with her life since leaving Bristol, it evidently paid well. She was the polar opposite of Mum, still sitting in her beige cardigan, knee-length woollen skirt and maroon, moccasin slippers. Mum looked at Elaine, her face full of what Elaine was assumed was fear, because she looked almost on the brink of tears.

'My dear, Elaine—' Ruby began.

'I'm not having this, I'm phoning Stan,' Lil said, standing up and pushing past Elaine, into the hallway.

'Ruby, please don't do this.' Phyllis pleaded.

Elaine frowned. What did Phyllis know that she didn't?

'Firstly, I want to say that I know about your...' Ruby paused, as if searching for the right word, '...*situation* and I have come to offer my help.'

Elaine folded her arms. 'I don't want an abortion, thank you, and you won't make me. Mum wants me to—'

Phyllis gasped.

'—but Dad says he'll support my decision and I'm keeping *my* baby. I know it'll be hard being a single mum but—'

'No, no,' Ruby interrupted, waving her hands and shaking her head. 'You misunderstand me. I'm here to offer my *support*.'

Elaine frowned again. 'Why?'

Ruby glanced at Phyllis before ploughing on. 'Your mum says you've become a bit of a recluse; dropped out of college, not going out with your friends anymore.' She raised a quizzical eyebrow. 'I take it the father isn't going to be involved?'

'*Ruby*,' Phyllis said, sternly. 'This is none of your business. You're upsetting Elaine and Lil and I think it's best if you left.'

Ruby ignored Phyllis and looked directly at Elaine, raising both eyebrows. It was as if she was silently asking if Elaine wanted her leave and, because she was upsetting mum, Elaine did want her to leave, but curiosity was taking over.

'I don't want the father involved,' Elaine said, looking down at her white cotton socks. She could still fit into her stonewashed jeans but there were beginning to feel tight.

'Because he doesn't want to be involved?'

'No.' Elaine's bottom lip jutted out. 'It just wouldn't work.' Why was she telling Aunt Ruby – practically a stranger – all of this? 'He's very intelligent and career focused. He doesn't need a girlfriend and a baby holding him back.'

This was true. She knew Anthony would immediately offer to marry her; he was that type. Honest, reliable. But it wasn't fair on him; he was going to be a doctor, make something of his life. He didn't need her and a baby dragging him down.

'Married?' Ruby asked.

'No!' Elaine shouted. 'What is all of this? Why turn up now out of the blue?'

'I've come to offer you a way out.'

'I've told you; I'm keeping the baby.'

'That's fine,' said Ruby, crossing her legs. 'Come and have it with me.'

'What?'

'I live in Cornwall. I run a retirement home. Come and live with me, start a new life; I'll help you. Once you're ready, you can continue your nursing qualifications. You can even work at the home, if you want to?'

Elaine frowned. That's all she seemed capable of doing, frowning. Why was Ruby doing this? It was a tempting offer, though. No-one would know her, no-one to look and stare and say *oh, there's that Elaine Henshaw from school, in the club with no fella.*

Very tempting, indeed.

'Buy, why?' Elaine asked. 'Why help me now?'

'Ruby, don't,' said Mum, walking back into the room. 'Please don't.'

Ruby ignored her. 'I know what it feels like to be in your position, Elaine, that's why I've come to offer my help.'

Elaine looked between the three women in the room. Ruby looking defiant, Phyllis with her hand over her mouth and Mum looking petrified.

'What? How? I don't have any cousins, do I?'

She looked again between the women. Silence.

'Will someone please explain?' she asked, her heart beat rising. What was so awful that they didn't want her to know?

Mum finally spoke, looking down at her slippers. 'Ruby is your real mum.'

It was as if the room had turned sideways. Phyllis still had her hand to her mouth. Mum continued to look at her moccasins and Ruby looked on at Elaine, smiling. Elaine studied her face. The petite features, the bright blonde hair, the sparkly blue eyes. She looked to mum with her greying perm, tall, masculine frame and in an instant, she knew Mum was telling the truth.

'Liar,' she said, standing up. 'You're lying.'

'She's not,' said Ruby, 'it's true.' Ruby continued to beam.

Elaine scowled. 'My mother is standing there.' Elaine pointed to Mum. 'She's the one who has cared for me, nurtured me, financed me for my entire upbringing. Who the hell do you think you are, coming in here, with your designer clothes and vicious lies? GET OUT!'

Mum burst into tears and Phyllis comforted her. The smile slipped from Ruby's face into one of sheer horror.

'Elaine,' Ruby whispered.

'I mean it,' Elaine said, far more calmly than she felt. She moved to the living room door. 'Sling your hook and don't come back.'

Ruby slowly moved toward the door, blinking back tears. 'You are my daughter and that,' Ruby pointed at Elaine's stomach, 'is my grandchild. I'm not walking away from you both this time.'

'There's the door, keep walking,' Elaine said, trying her hardest to fight the urge to dissolve into tears.

'Fine,' said Ruby, shoving a card into her Elaine's hand, 'but when you're ready, come and find me.' She looked back at Phyllis and Mum. 'Before I go; one last piece of advice.' She locked her eyes on Elaine's. 'Tell the father. Make sure he's involved. He has a responsibility and you will regret it if you don't.' With that she turned on her heel and walked away, just as she had been instructed to.

Elaine's breathing was rapid. Over Mum's sobs she could hear Ruby's heels clack across the hallway tiles before the front door slammed shut. She looked down at the card.

Ruby Mackenzie, Proprietor, Hope Home

She crumpled the card in her hand and flung it in the waste paper basket.

'Selfish cow,' she muttered before rushing to her room, slamming the door and flinging herself, sobbing, onto her bed. Great big sobs thinking of what Ruby had just said and what lay ahead, being a single mum.

Chapter Thirty-

One

Elaine found her breathing relax as she walked back up Church Lane, towards the light house which cornered Island View. The bakery closed at three o'clock on Saturdays and as she enjoyed the warm spring sunshine on her arms, she decided she would go back to the cottage and change into shorts and a vest, find a warm rock on the bay, overlooking the island, and read her book.

She'd almost not made it to work this morning. She'd barely slept after coming face-to-face with Anthony last night in the pub. Of all the places why did he have to be here! She'd come here to escape some of her problems, not create more. Her mind kept wandering to 'what if's'. What if she had told him about Tilly? Would they have made a go of it? Would he have told her to get rid of the baby? If he had, then she wouldn't have carried a torch for him these past thirty-odd years. She would have known his true colours and maybe let her life move on like a normal person. Which mad her question, was she actually pleased to see him? Was he married? Did he have a family? What cruel fate would have him married with a family when their paths were now crossing again.

And the most burning question of all kept cutting through her thoughts; what was she going to tell Tilly? She could barely get off the toilet this morning. Good thing she'd left her scales in Bristol as she was probably underweight by now. She'd just got rid of one worry by handing Mum over to Ruby for a few months and now, here was her past, zooming towards her at one hundred miles per hour.

'Hello.'

Elaine froze. She'd been so wrapped up in her own thoughts, as she'd climbed the path, she hadn't realised she'd already reached the lighthouse.

She looked at Anthony. He hadn't changed. Older, yes, but still had that boyish grin, the one she had fallen in love with. 'Hello,' she stammered, lowering her head, her stomach wringing in knots.

'I didn't like to bother you at work.'

Elaine kept her eyes averted from Anthony's and looked over to the island. 'I'd rather you didn't bother me at all.' She cringed at her own abruptness.

'What did I ever do to you?' His voice sounded strained.

She still couldn't look at him. She wrapped her arms around her, suddenly feeling chilly and fixed her stare on Hope Home. Bloody Ruby. She could easily blame her for all of this. If she hadn't given Elaine up, perhaps she'd have had a normal upbringing.

'I looked everywhere for you after that night. For weeks. I asked after you, went to the nursing college. None of your friends would tell me where you were.'

Elaine slowly turned around to look at Anthony. Tilly had his nose and his wry smile.

'Ugh.' Elaine exhaled. If she blamed Ruby for everything then Ruby got to take credit for Tilly and that was one thing in Elaine's life, she was proud of. If life had turned out differently, she may never have met Anthony and certainly wouldn't have Tilly.

'I'm sorry, I can't do this.' She tried to walk past him, around the edge of the lighthouse. The cottage wasn't far. She could run and be within its safety in seconds.

'*Elaine*,' Anthony pleaded. 'Please, don't do this. You do remember me, don't you?'

Elaine stopped in her tracks, tears brimming in her eyes. Remember him? She had never forgotten him on one day since October 1983.

'I'm sorry, Anthony,' Elaine said, edging past him. 'I've come here to have a break, look after myself. I can't deal with any more stress.'

Anthony looked perplexed. 'Stress?'

'I want to go home. I'd prefer it if you left me alone now.' She kept edging past, her heart beat hammering like she'd just run a marathon. What was she so afraid of?

Tilly. That's what she was fearful of. Losing Tilly.

'Wait!' He said, fumbling in his pocket. He pulled out his wallet. 'I don't know what happened that night but I'm pretty sure I know that Tilly was the consequence.'

'Ohhh! Anthony, just leave me alone.' She quickened her pace, but he caught up with her and pulled at her shoulder.

'Look!' he said, waving a piece of paper in front of her face. 'Look at this.'

She stopped in her tracks and blinked. Through her blurry eyes she could see an unfolded piece of discoloured lined paper. It was in her writing.

'I have kept this in my wallet for over three decades. If you think I ever forgot about you, you're wrong.'

Elaine blinked back her tears and shook her head. 'I can't do this, I'm sorry, I'm not strong enough.'

Anthony put his hand on her forearm and it felt like electricity running up her arm.

'What's wrong Elaine?'

She could easily give in, dissolve into tears in his arms, let him tell her everything would be okay now they'd found each other again, but the thought of Tilly finding out and being angry stuck in the forefront of her mind.

'I must go home,' she said, focusing on Hope Cottage, wondering if she meant the cottage or escaping back to Bristol. She didn't dare look into his wounded eyes. She could feel him appraising her, feel his warm breath on her neck. She wanted him to release her so she could run to the safety of the cottage, but she couldn't bring herself to break away from him either.

Eventually he sighed and released his gentle grip from her arm. 'Okay, if that's what you want. But we need to talk.'

She was about to say there was nothing to talk about but deep down she knew she had to face this. He was the local doctor. He was probably the doctor who had sent Tilly for her CBT.

'I am Tilly's father, aren't I?'

She looked up at him and blinked back tears. 'I can't do this now,' she said, rushing off as quickly as her court shoes would carry her towards the cottage door. She knew he was watching her as she fumbled for her key and scrambled inside the safety of the cottage, but she couldn't look back. Looking back would be facing up to the reality, the past she knew one day would always catch up with her but never wanted to confront. The nagging worry which Elaine always forced to the back of her mind, playfully skipped to the forefront. What if Tilly didn't really have ADHD? What if Tilly was normal and Elaine had brought her up with 'issues', a complex perhaps. Now Anthony knew the truth about Tilly, would he blame Elaine? She couldn't cope with much more of this. She slammed the front door and slumped down against the wall, dissolving into tears and reaching for her inhaler to help her panicky breathing.

Worst of all, she was running out of Lorazepam and bloody Anthony was the village GP.

Archie and Hector were enjoying the sunshine, sitting on the warm rocks, under the cliffs of Hope Bay, looking out towards Gull Island where they were companionably sharing a ninety-niner. Hector occasionally got up to chase away the seagulls which were brave enough to come begging for food, while Archie contemplated whether he, himself, had a enough courage to confront the past and tell Elaine the truth, or be a coward and go back to Bristol with his tail between his legs. Elaine seemed so happy since she'd arrived here. The burden of not looking after Lil was evidently helping her become more like the Elaine he remembered, young, happy-go-lucky Elaine. He didn't feel he had the bravado to burst her bubble.

Although, not telling Elaine was going to provoke a monumental bust up with Ruby, which was a fate worse than death as far as Archie was concerned.

'Ah, just the person!' Ruby's voice sang.

Archie turned to see her trotting down the cliff steps in a pair of thick rubber sole, pink suede shoes, like girls used to wear in the fifties. She bounced like the girl she would have been in the fifties too. Age was just a number to Ruby; she certainly wasn't much different to the young woman he'd met half-a-century ago.

'I want a word with you.'

If a little feistier and assertive.

'Sounds ominous,' he said, feeding Hector the last of his ice cream cone.

Ruby patted Hector on the head and sat down next to Archie on the broad, warm rock he was occupying. Hector scrabbled up into Ruby's lap and snuggled down for a fuss. Archie was beginning to become a little jealous of just how much Hector favoured Ruby every time he saw her.

'Calm down, I haven't come to tear you off another strip.'

Ruby rubbed Archie's thigh and a feeling stirred inside which he hadn't felt for a long time. Certainly not since Phyllis had passed away.

'I'm sorry about last night; I shouldn't have driven off in a strop.'

'It's okay.' Archie said, lying to save enough argument. Elaine had been in bed when they had arrived at Hope Cottage after the pub quiz last night. They'd stopped for fish and chips on the way home but when Ruby had found Elaine was asleep she began taking her frustrations at their secrecy out on Archie and, taking advantage of the tide still being out, had called a taxi back over to the island.

'No, it's not.' Ruby said firmly, still squeezing his thigh. 'I can't take all of this out on you; I have to take some responsibility myself.'

Archie laughed despite himself.

'Oi!' Ruby bashed him playfully on the arm.

'Sorry, but what's brought about this sudden change of heart?'

'Tilly, actually.'

Archie gazed at her. She was as beautiful now as the day he'd met her. Guilt washed over him again for his unfaithfulness to the two women he had loved.

'Oh?'

'Yes. I sometimes think we forget the person we were before life threw a load of crap at us to deal with.'

'If this is about me and Elaine again, then I'm sorry but—'

'It is and it isn't. Tilly is so full of life and vivacity. She looks forward to what she can achieve. She hasn't let life hold her back; she was in a rut with Simon and she's decided to overcome that. You never mentioned to me that she was diagnosed with ADHD?'

Archie frowned. 'I'm not sure I knew that much about it myself?'

'About the illness or about Tilly having it?'

'Elaine always said she was hyperactive and that she needed medication for it. Phyllis and I couldn't see where she was coming from; she was always so polite and well behaved whenever we looked after her. We assumed it was some sort of thyroid problem and perhaps she didn't sleep much at night. Is it a mental health condition then?'

'Yes, it affects behaviour and focus, but I'm not sure she's actually got it. Anthony's sent her off to see a local therapist so hopefully she can resolve any issues the stigmatism has left her with—'

'Stigmatism?'

Ruby rolled her eyes. 'From being labelled as 'mental'!'

'Tilly's not mental, she's the sanest person I know. Luckily, she's not as nervy as Elaine; doesn't seem to have inherited Elaine's anxieties.'

'I know. Could we get back to the point?'

'Point?' Archie was beginning to feel he'd lost the plot.

'What I've come to talk to you about!'

'Oh, right. Something about being young again, wasn't it?'

'*YES!*' Ruby sounded exasperated. 'Tilly has made me realise that it's not too late to chase your goals. So, I've decided. There's no pressure for you to tell Elaine your real identity, it's your secret to tell, not mine. I won't be pressurising you into leaving Hope Cove and going back to Bristol; take your time and decide what you want to do. I've got my own life to lead, Archie Fairclough. We're in the autumn years of our lives and I'm jolly well going to make sure that however much time I've got left on this earth, that's what I do.'

'Right. Good.' Why did he have such an overwhelming feeling of foreboding? 'May I ask what goal it is you're going to chase then?'

'You.'

With that, she kissed him on the cheek, released Hector onto the sand, stood up, waggled her fingers and purposefully strolled off back up the steps from where she had come.

Archie let out a low whistle. Just when he thought life couldn't get any worse than telling Elaine his real identity, it suddenly had. All his feelings for Ruby, the ones he had supressed all these years, came rushing to the forefront. Quickly stamped upon by that feeling of guilt again; a feeling of loyalty for his love of Phyllis.

192

CHAPTER THIRTY-
TWO

'What about Simply Seafood?' Emma asked, taking a swig of her gin and tonic.

Tilly chewed the end of her biro. 'I guess that might work. I kind of hoped I'd have my name in the title though.

'Tilly's Kitchen?'

'A shack with a couple of hot plates is hardly a kitchen, is it?' Tilly grimaced.

'Ugh!' Emma grabbed her pony tail, pulled it out and started smoothing her hair back into another pony tail. 'You're not making this easy.'

'Sorry, I just want to get it right.'

It was Sunday night and they had agreed to meet in the Lobster for a drink before Tilly's shift to discuss her plans to open a pop-up restaurant. Ruby had been most helpful yesterday in providing a budget to buy the trailer stall and equipment, together with some signage and marketing materials. First of all, Tilly needed to get a licence from the council but after that it would be full steam ahead ordering everything she needed. She was planning on requesting a seasonal licence to begin with, one permitted in the summer months. She would sell her wares on Fridays, Saturdays and Sundays when the village had more footfall from tourists. Emma had suggested sticking to two or three dishes and some sort of dessert, like ice creams. So as not to compete with other local trade, Emma had suggested going Mediterranean; Fritto Misto – lightly battered and deep-fried fish and vegetables – served with a gutsy garlic mayo dipping sauce, fish tacos – with whatever had been caught fresh from the sea that day – and vegetable paella, as a vegan option. She'd also told Tilly to source the best Cornish ice cream Tilly could find and offer it in a few flavours, which would certainly appeal to the tourist crowds at any time of the day.

'I know you do, but the tourist season is here, and you need to get your skates on.'

'Yes, you do, Tilly,' Winstone said, appearing from nowhere, carrying empties. 'Your shift starts in five minutes.'

Tilly glanced at her new watch she had travelled to Wadebridge to purchase today. It was one of those fitness watches which told you how many steps you'd walked or run and calories you burned. Thankfully it stopped short of berating you for that donut you didn't really need to eat as an afternoon snack.

'Right you are.'

'Getting fit, are we?' Winstone asked, placing the empties on the table, already crowded with paper from Emma and Tilly's brainstorming.

'Something like that,' Tilly said, not wanting to go into her reasons for getting fit. She still hadn't finished discussing her ideas with Emma.

Winstone peered at the pieces of paper. 'Harbourlicious? What's all this?'

'Tilly's going to open a pop-up restaurant on the harbour.' Emma said, sitting back and detaching herself from the intense brainstorming session.

'Might be!' Tilly interjected as watched Winstone's eyeballs practically pop out of their head.

'What?'

'Erm, well, I was going to tell you.'

'When? When all my customers were queuing up at your stall and not ordering food in my pub?'

'Keep your hair on!' Emma said. 'We're in competition and you're still friends with me and James, aren't you?'

Winstone pursed his lips and kept his stare on Tilly. The whites of his eyes piercing into her. 'I suppose so,' he said, standing up, not taking his gaze off Tilly. 'See you in five, then?'

'Yes,' Tilly squeaked gathering up her paperwork.

They waited for Winstone to disappear into the kitchen with the empties before they both burst into fits of giggles.

'Consider yourself well and truly in trouble, young lady!' Emma pointed her finger at Tilly.

'Did you see how cross he looked?' Tilly said, laughing but feeling nervous inside. The last thing she wanted to do was upset Winstone.

'Sexy cross.' Emma giggled.

'Ssssh, Emma, you're a married woman!'

'Ah, but you're not.' Emma winked.

'He's my boss.'

'Not for much longer!'

'No way, men are strictly off limits in my world; I am totally career focused. Talking of which, I've got a shift to do,' Tilly said, standing up. 'If I've still got a job.'

Winstone watched Tilly turn the bar stools up on the tables, one by one, before she grabbed the mop and started cleaning down the floorboards. Her hair was up in a messy bun, stray ringlets tumbling over her shoulders as she slapped the mop back in the bucket and vigorously wrung it out.

'What did that mop ever do to you?'

'Hmmm?' She looked up.

They had barely spoken all evening, which was mainly down to him. After her bombshell about the pop-up restaurant, he'd been in a shitty mood and not up for conversation. He'd tried to rationalise it in his brain; competition was healthy. She was entitled to start up her own business, so who was he to stop her?

Because she'd stop being his barmaid; she'd stop working at the Lobster Pot.

'Look, I'm sorry you found out from Emma about my, er, restaurant idea. I—'

'It's fine,' he butted in. 'I shouldn't have reacted the way I did, I'm sorry.'

'Really? You've barely spoken two words to me all evening?' Tilly continued to mop the floor, not looking up at him.

'I overreacted; Emma's right, you're well within your rights to apply for a licence to sell food on the harbour. Although, if you'd asked me, I could have got you to help Tom in the kitchen.' Tom was Winstone's head chef. He was no Rick Stein, but he was good at decent pub grub and the punters lapped it up.

'That's very kind of you, but this isn't just about wanting to make food and sell it.'

'Then why do it?'

Tilly sighed and leant against her mop. 'Because my life is going nowhere; I need some purpose.'

'Thanks a lot!'

Her face looked full of worry.

'I'm joking. I appreciate that being a barmaid for the rest of your life might not be the most fulfilling vocation.'

'Precisely.' She set to with the mop again. 'Ruby's made something of her life, you have this place. I want an enterprise of my own so that I can be successful; give my life some purpose, have an identity.'

He nodded. Coming to Hope Cove had all been part of his recovery process, to give him life some meaning and purpose again. He knew where Tilly was coming from.

'Well, I shouldn't have overreacted and I'm sorry. You have my full support; I'll help you with food suppliers if you want.'

Tilly grinned. 'That would be amazing, thank you.'

'I just hope your cooking has improved since that cheese rolls disaster, you told me about.'

'Oi! I'll come and tip this dirty water over you in a minute!'

Winstone laughed. He'd not felt this comfortable in the company of the opposite sex for what seemed like forever. 'Seriously though, are you sure this is the right venture for you?'

'I want to be rich and successful, like Ruby.' Tilly kicked the bucket along in front of her. 'I've got to start somewhere. I will, of course, need to reduce my shifts here, if that's okay?'

'Reduce?' *Not leave?*

'Well, if you don't mind, I would like to still work here. I can't imagine running a food stall in the harbour at weekends is going to earn me a fortune, is it? So, can I still work here in the week?'

'So, you want me to support your new business venture, which will be in direct competition with me, *and* still pay your wages?'

Tilly winced. 'Yes,' she squeaked.

'My pleasure,' he said, turning to check the spirit levels and hide the enormous grin spreading across his face.

He wasn't going to lose his little ray of sunshine just yet, after all.

CHAPTER THIRTY-THREE

2011 - Ibiza

'Winstoooone!' Tory called from the bottom of the stairs. It was late, gone ten and he'd just showered, ready for his set at *Caspar*, his nightclub.

He walked across the bedroom floor to the balustrade, in just his jeans.

'Mmmm,' said Tory, looking up at him. She was scantily dressed as always. When he'd first met her, it had turned him on something chronic that all she used to wear were skimpy silk dresses which left little to the imagination, her pert breasts staying perfectly put without any need for a bra. Now, as he looked down at her, all he could see was a dress hanging off a skeleton.

'You're high again,' he said, trying to keep his voice even. Another row, just before his set, was the last thing he needed.

'And?' She held her hands around the post at the bottom of the stairs and swung playfully from side-to-side.

He folded his arms. 'Tory,' he said, softly. 'You promised.'

'And you promised to do less late-night sets and, yet, here you are freshly showered and ready to go!'

'I have to.' He did. It was August; peak season with all the uni students here for their summer holidays. They expected Winstone Chambers' name to appear on the set somewhere between midnight and 3am. He'd been a successful DJ when they'd met; he still was. At first Tory had accepted it, enjoyed the attention that came with being a DJ's girlfriend but overtime she'd got distracted; slipped in with the wrong crowds. Her addiction was the result. He was trying to change, trying as hard as he could, but it was difficult when you were in demand. If he stopped playing when the clubs wanted, soon he would be a has-been, a nobody and the money would dry up. That's why he'd bought *Caspar*; an attempt to be his own boss, whistle to his tune and no-one else's. But it was Saturday night on August Bank Holiday weekend; he had no choice.

'You know this is a one-off.' He said softly, looking down at Tory, taking in the hurt in her eyes.

'Huh. Whatever,' she turned and walked towards the mini-bar in the corner of their living room.

He raced down the stairs. 'Tory, no, you don't need a drink, you're high.'

She pulled down the cabinet and reached for the vodka. 'Does it matter?'

'Babe, you know it does. You *promised* me.'

'And you promised me!' she spat, turning around to look at him, her once thick and glossy hair now dull and lank, swinging angrily over her shoulder.

'It's just this weekend. Next weekend I'm not even working! We can spend the entire weekend checking out wedding venues, can't we?'

She hovered with the vodka bottle over the glass, as if contemplating what he'd just said. The silence was agonising. He needed her *not* to have that drink though. He needed her to come down from her high, see sense, not take more skunk, or whatever it was she'd taken to trip out this time.

Eventually she put the bottle down. She looked up at him. 'Promise?'

'Of course,' he grinned, opening his arms out to her.

She walked from behind the bar and rushed across to him. He picked her up and stepped out onto the balcony. The night was hot, oppressive almost, but there was a gentle breeze outside. Ibiza town was lit up and buzzing. Mopeds humming in the street and the waves beyond gently crashing against the shore.

'We will get through this,' he said, still holding the bag of bones Tory had become in his arms, 'I promise.'

'Good,' she said, smiling up at him. She trailed her finger down his naked chest. 'So, don't go out tonight. Stay home with me.'

He sighed deeply as her dull eyes shone with hope, expectancy, lust almost. 'You know I've got to go,' he said, reluctantly.

She immediately started to wriggle and jump out of his arms. 'Fine,' she said, stalking back into the living room and retrieving her clutch bag from the sofa. 'Then I'm going out too.'

'Come with me.' He rushed through the French doors, determined not to let her go out. The company she kept, the socialites of Ibiza, were killing her. She knew it as well as him.

'Pah! And watch women fall at your feet and practically expose their breasts to you, while you lap it up?'

'What? Tory, you know I'm not like that.'

Her shoulders slumped and she turned to look at him. 'I'm sorry, I shouldn't have said that. It's just...' her bony chest expanded as she took in a deep breath before exhaling.

'What?'

'This place, here,' she flung her arms open. Her skinny, sinewy arms, with tattoos to cover up the needle marks. 'Ibiza. I think I've had enough.'

'Enough?'

'Yes, it's eating me up.'

He walked towards her and took her hands. 'Then we'll go home.'

'Home? This is home to you isn't, it? This is the only place we've ever lived together.'

'London.' He looked deep into her eyes as she searched his.

'Your London and my London are very different.'

This was true. His London was Dagenham, hers was Chelsea. East end boy, west end girl. Ibiza was classless; it was all about the music. On the rare occasions he had gone home with Tory, he'd been met with a frosty reception by her parents and brother who thought she could do better.

'We'll buy a big house in Cricklewood and live on neutral ground.'

She laughed and for a brief moment there was that sparkle in her that he had fell in love with.

'Oh!' she reached up on tiptoes and kissed him. 'This is why I love you Winstone Chambers; you are ever the diplomat.'

'I mean it. I'll sell up here and we can go home. I can make a living DJing in London.'

There was that sadness back in her eyes again.

'What?'

'It's like I am your wife-to-be and the decks are your mistress.' She shrugged. 'Sometimes I feel like I can't compete.'

He pulled her to him and kissed her head. 'It's my livelihood. I don't know how to be good at anything else. No DJing, no income and then you won't want me either.'

'Oh Winstone,' Tory stifled a sob, 'don't say that. I will always want you. It's just this life is no good for me.'

'I know.' He hugged her bony frame. She really was so frail. 'Let me get tonight over with and let's talk. We can sort out moving back home; I'm not happy if you're not happy.' This was true. She needed to get away from Ibiza. She needed to get clean. What was money and success if it didn't bring you happiness?

'Okay,' she rested her head on his chest. 'I won't go out tonight, I'll stay here.'

He looked down at her. She looked so lonely. His heart strings pulled as he debated whether he should phone the club, get one of the other DJs to cover his set. But he was the crowd puller and if he didn't turn up the profits would be down, and his investors would go ape shit.

'Do you want me to stay?' It was wrong to put the onus on Tory. Of course, she wanted him to stay.

'It's fine, I understand. I'll text Anabelle and tell her I'm not feeling so good. Get an early night. It's nearly eleven now, by the time I've had a bath and fallen asleep, you'll be home.' She smiled. A sad smile which didn't meet her eyes.

His eyes narrowed. 'If you're sure?' His business brain was telling him he needed to go but his heart was telling him to stay. Tory wasn't herself and he didn't feel it was the effect of the whatever she'd taken.

'I'm fine,' she said dreamily. If we're going to talk in the morning about leaving here and going home, I'll be fine. I've got something to focus on, now; leaving Ibiza.'

'Good.' He checked his watch. 'I'd better get going.' He cupped her face in his hands and kissed her slowly. 'Come on, let's get you upstairs and run that bath before I go.' He took his hand in hers and she followed him up the stairs to the bedroom like a lost lamb. He ran the bath, adding some lavender, to help her relax, and went back in the bedroom to pick up his t-shirt.

'Perhaps you can get back into modelling when we're back in the UK?' He didn't know what had made him say it but the look of sheer horror on her face said it all.

'And hang around with a similar druggy bunch to the crowd I hang out with here, no thanks.'

'I didn't mean it like that.' It was like treading on egg shells. 'I just meant, you could have something to focus on at home; a career, you know some purpose.'

They had met when Tory was on a photo shoot in Ibiza four years ago. It had been love at first sight when he'd singled her out in the crowd one hot summer's evening. She had glided like a swan, through the energetic, sweaty club goers until she had been below his station. He'd lifted her up by his arms and let her dance behind him at the decks until his set had been over. They'd gone for a drink, before a walk along the beach to see the sunrise. It had been perfect. She was going home that morning, but she'd arrived back in the airport less than a week later and kept coming as frequently as she could between shoots until he'd asked her to give it up and move in with him.

A decision he'd regretted ever since.

'So, my life has no purpose, being your fiancé?'

'I didn't say that.' Here it was; another argument. It was all they did these days. He should have made her keep modelling. He wasn't interested in anyone else. With so much time on her hands in the evenings, when he was working, she had become an Ibiza socialite. It was inevitable that she'd ended up doing drugs like the rest of them.

'All you ever think about is earning money, Winstone.'

He went to argue but couldn't. He did always think about bringing in the money, but it was the way he had been raised. His father had been a factory worker at Ford in Dagenham. He'd made a decent wage, enough that his mother had always been a housewife and raised him and his sisters, but his father was sixty-one now and still not retired. Winstone wanted more out of life than that. He was thirty this year; he wasn't planning on working his bollocks off for the next thirty years.

'So, we can have a future!' He shouted. He mustn't lose it, he mustn't. They mustn't have another plate smashing row; the apartment was minimalist enough as it was.

'You are so busy living in the future, *Winstone*, that you can't see what's happening right under your nose, right now!' Tory scowled at him and with that stormed past him into the bathroom, slamming the door behind her.

He stood there, fists clenched, taking deep breaths. Slowly he walked towards the door and raised his fists to knock gently but something stopped him. Instead he leant his head against the door, hoping she was on the other side doing the same. How had they grown so far apart? He felt like such a failure. He'd concentrated on his career, his success and in the process had alienated Tory and let her down. Badly.

'I'll see you in the morning, then,' he said.

Silence.

'We'll talk. Get this sorted.'

Still nothing.

'Love you.' Tears sprang to his eyes. This was ridiculous, he never cried. He grabbed his wallet, stuffed it in his back jeans pocket and fled down the stairs, feeling useless.

CHAPTER THIRTY-

FOUR

'The thing is what if I am like the rest of my family? What if I do have mental health issues? Would I need to go back on medication?'

It was now two weeks since Tilly's first session with Laura and she was back for her second one. The calming effect Laura's consulting room had had on her last time didn't seem to be working today. Even staring out at the view of sloping fields, framed by the Atlantic Ocean, waves calmly shimmering in the bright May sunlight, weren't working either. Instead, she was sitting crossed-legged, winding ringlets round and around her finger as she tried her hardest to relax.

'Tilly, firstly, ADHD is a mental illness. I think it would be best to view it as that, *in the past,* you had a mental illness but what we are attempting to uncover is whether you are still suffering from this illness or whether you were misdiagnosed in the first place. Essentially, does your behaviour now surmount to you actually suffering from ADHD.

'Oh, see!' Tilly cried as panic rose in her chest.

'Tilly,' Laura said, calmly, 'put your hands down on the arms of the chair for a moment and close your eyes.'

Tilly eyed Laura sceptically but did as she was told.

'Now, breath in deep through your nose and out through your mouth.'

Again, Tilly did as she was told, wondering what on earth she had let herself in for with Laura but after about four deep breaths she started to feel a little heady.

Relaxed even.

Laura kept quiet while Tilly continued. Tilly wondered if it was going to go on forever but after about twelve deep breaths, Laura said, 'now, take your breathing back to normal and open your eyes.'

Tilly smiled nervously, as she opened her eyes, feeling self-conscious.

'Good. Now do what I'm doing. Draw your shoulders up as far as they will go, wiggle your neck from side-to-side then release.'

Tilly tried not to giggle as she did as Laura had done. All the vertebrae in her neck and spine went click, click, click as she repeated the exercise.

'Okay and stop. Better?'

Tilly thumped herself against the back of the arm chair and allowed herself to fully assess whether her body felt better.

'Was that your way of telling me I'm stressy?' she asked.

A faint smile twitched at the corner of Laura's lips. 'Maybe.'

'Sorry, was I annoying you?'

'Annoying?'

'I annoy most people. I annoy my mum and Simon always said I was hard work.'

'And what does annoying look like for you?'

Tilly cocked her head on one side as she considered the question. 'Erm, well, you know, just generally getting on people's nerves by being energetic and enthusiastic. Perhaps that's why I was considered to be hyperactive? I think I've always annoyed mum, been a burden, you know? Simon and I just weren't compatible so I'm happy to chalk that one up as a personality clash and, now, I think I've hurt Winstone by starting up Tilly's Kitchen. I'll be selling food on the harbour, right outside the pub; I suppose it was insensitive of me not to ask his permission first.'

'And why do you feel you need his permission?'

'Um,' Tilly tucked a stray strand of hair behind her ear. 'I's in direct competition with him, isn't it? I mean, it's taking potential customers away from his business. He can't actually stop me; I've got my licence now, but it was a bit rude not to tell him before I made a start on my plans.'

'So, how did he find out?'

'He saw me and Emma making marketing plans in the pub.'

'Emma lives next door to you, right?'

Tilly nodded. 'Yes.'

'And she also runs a food outlet in the village, doesn't she?'

Tilly rolled her yes. 'Yes, that's what she told Winstone.'

'So, instead of inviting Emma around to yours to discuss your business plans, you decided to meet her in Winstone's pub.'

'It was before my shift.' Tilly's bottom lip jutted out. 'Plus, she wanted to get away from the baby, you know, meet socially for a drink.'

'There are places to meet in the village, yes?'

Tilly looked at Laura through narrowed eyes. 'You're good. You're saying my sub-conscious wanted Winstone to find out, aren't you?'

'I think that's what you're saying, isn't it?' Laura smiled. 'So, how has Winstone taken the news that you are embarking on a different pursuit?'

'Actually, he's been fine.' He really had. He'd put her in touch with his suppliers for catering and the printers, he used in Delabole, for her business cards and flyers.

'So, you felt you needed his permission, but actually it's all turned out okay. How did that feel? You clearly didn't annoy him.'

Tilly pursed her lips together. Laura was right; why was she worrying about a situation that had turned out okay in the end? 'Oh, I don't know! I annoy everyone eventually.'

It was Laura's turn to cock her head to one side.

'Mum always finds me annoying,' Tilly continued. 'Only this morning she was telling me off for not stacking the dishwasher properly. I'm thirty-two! I should be able to do whatever I want!'

'I think you are, aren't you?'

Tilly frowned.

Laura crossed her legs and leaned-in. 'Tilly, the last time we met, the first time we met actually, you wanted to disassociate yourself from your families' mental health issues. You wanted to make something of your life. I gave you the diagram of the self-fulfilling prophecy and told you to go away and work on it. Today, you walked in here, sat down and told me that not only have you come up with a business model but you have found an investor, some suppliers, got yourself a licence and are planning to launch that business a week tomorrow, which will be less than a month since we met. Not only that, but you're now running and are averaging five kilometre runs at least three times a week. Do you not think you might want to give yourself a break? That's a lot of achievements; what are you being so hard on yourself?'

'My investor is Ruby,' Tilly said, sitting up straight, 'so that hardly counts, and it brings me back to what I was telling you earlier. Ruby had a breakdown; she got depression. If Ruby can have depression, then anyone can! What hope have I got of beating all of this?'

'Beating?'

'Well, you know, fighting off what's inevitably coming for me.'

Laura rubbed her finger down the arm of her chair. Her expression looked conflicted, as if she was holding back whatever she was really thinking.

'Say it,' Tilly said. 'I've come here to talk but I've come to listen to. I'm open to suggestions on how I fix myself.'

Laura smiled. '*If* you feel you need fixing.'

Tilly nodded, knowing what Laura was getting at; that she was beating herself up again.

'What was I deliberating over telling you was my thinking on depression.'

'Pah! Well, that's one thing I know I haven't got, but if even Ruby could get it...' Tilly trailed off and shrugged. It frightened her more than anything in the world; she didn't want to end up a jangly, bag of nerves, like Mum.

'I often find, with clients, that depression is often anger turned in on itself.'

Tilly frowned. 'Supressed, you mean.'

Laura nodded and appraised Tilly with a knowing stare.

The cogs started whirring in Tilly's mind. She shifted in her chair, hooking one leg under the other. 'So, what you're saying is that Mum and Ruby have both been depressed because they've been angry but not aired it.'

'It's possible,' Laura said, swiftly.

Tilly's mind was reaching into its recesses. 'Well, it makes sense; Ruby was angry that she couldn't help Mum make a better life for herself when she found out she was pregnant for me, but Ruby had nowhere for that anger to go; Mum sent her away. And Mum has been perpetually depressed looking after Gran but, then, Gran's lost her marbles so she can't really have a proper conversation and get angry with Gran, because Gran doesn't understand.'

Laura gently nodded, her gaze not dropping from Tilly's.

'Oh!' Tilly flung herself back in the chair again. 'But it's all inherent; it's going to get me. It already has with the ADHD, not to mention the schizophrenia.'

If Laura was frustrated that they seemed to be going around and around in circles she most certainly wasn't showing it.

'I do wonder if our family is all just secrets and lies,' Tilly continued. 'And I often wonder if those contribute to the 'issues' we all have. Secrets could cause anxiety, don't you think? The same way you were suggesting depression is anger turned inwards.'

Laura simply nodded. Tilly found it mildly irritating when she did that, but even Tilly had to conceded she didn't need someone to tell her if she was right or wrong; she should be able to figure that out for herself.

'I gave up asking mum who my father was years ago.'

Where had that come from?

'Your father?' Laura sounded surprised.

'I've never known who he was. I don't have a photo. When I was a child, I used to imagine what he might look like and then, when we went out shopping in Bristol City Centre, I would look for his amongst a sea of faces.'

'How sad for you, not to know what he even looks like.'

Tilly's eyes welled and she tried hard to beat back the tears. What was the point of getting upset about someone you didn't even know?

'It is.' She could hear her voice wobble. 'But then, Mum doesn't know who her dad is either, so I'm not the only to feel that way, am I?'

'With the greatest respect, Tilly, I'm not here for your mother's welfare, I'm here for yours. What matters to me is what it feels like for you to ever have known your father.'

She couldn't hold it back any longer. The torrent took hold. Tears for the father she had never known. Laura handed Tilly the box of tissues, from the table between their chairs.

'Thanks.' Tilly sniffed. 'How is it possible to be so upset about someone you never knew?'

Laura settled back in her chair and appraised Tilly. 'Perhaps you are grieving the loss of the father you've never had? Perhaps you're allowing yourself to do that for the first time?'

Tilly nodded vigorously. That's exactly what this was. 'Do you think that's why I had ADHD? Is that why it's coming back? Because I'm desperately needy of attention, because my Dad abandoned me before I was even born?'

'Do you feel abandoned?'

Tilly rested her head back on her chair and let the tears silently fall. 'It does feel a bit like that.'

'In my experience, Tilly—'

Laura drew a deep breath and Tilly just knew whatever was coming next was as monumental as their discussion about depression.

'—individuals with ADHD often experience something traumatic in their childhoods. Something they bottle-up, don't talk about, perhaps don't even realise the significance of but it begins to affect their behaviour over time. That is why it's one of the most responsive illnesses to treat. Indeed, you may have already begun the process of reconciling whatever event traumatised you which—'

'Nothing traumatic happened in my childhood.' Tilly's bottom lip jutted out. Why did everything need to be about her childhood, for goodness sakes. 'It was a pretty mundane, boring childhood, living with my grandparents and my single-mother.'

Laura narrowed her eyes. Her expression oozed *I'm not buying this.* 'Did all your other friends have single mothers when growing up.'

Tilly rolled her eyes. 'No,' she almost groaned, 'but that doesn't make me abnormal either.'

'Sure. But perhaps you haven't ever really thought about the gravity of that situation. Having never met your father, not knowing his identity; that's a really, big thing.'

Tilly closed her eyes and let more tears escape. Laura was right, of course she was. But that didn't help her sort this whole sorry mess out, did it?

Laura crossed her legs and leaned. 'Look.' She held Tilly's gaze. 'If you think finding out who you father is will resolve some unanswered questions *for you*, then consider pursuing this. But it must be for you and your own self-development, no-one else.'

Tilly nodded and blinked back tears. She had come to the conclusion in early adulthood that if her father wasn't concerned enough to be involved in her upbringing then he wasn't worth concerning herself over.

A sudden thought flashed across her mind; one she hadn't considered before. What if Elaine had lied? What if her father had known nothing about her in the first place? Blissfully unaware of the child he had spawned thirty-two years ago. He might even have a family of his own by now. He might actually be a good dad to those children and not the pantomime villainesque character she had always painted in her mind.

'I could think about finding him. But that would involve asking Mum questions and she's behaving oddly again at the moment.'

Laura glanced at her watch. 'As I say, concentrate on you, Tilly; that's what these sessions are for. And there's something I'd like you to think about in particular over the coming week—'

'Ugh,' Tilly groaned. 'My head is jumbled up with all the thinking!'

'— I'd like you to focus on what you've been doing so far with the self-fulfilling prophecy. You've got the business launch next week so that should help you feel like you're achieving—'

'Oh, good, well that's easy enough.'

'— and I'd like you to explore your feeling of guilt.'

'What guilt?'

'We touched on Winstone and your mum, and how you feel you annoy them. Why do you feel you irritate them? Is it because you actually are annoying them? Or is it because they have short tempers? *Or* is it because of something you feel about yourself?'

'Blimey.' Tilly sighed. 'How do I go about doing that?'

'I'm not expecting you to *do* anything. Just think about how you feel; get a notebook and write down when you've had conversations with them. Winstone is your boss, your mum raised you; they are both significant relationships to you.'

'Are you sure I couldn't do this with Archie's dog, Hector? We get on great together, he sleeps at the end of my bed every night.'

'By all means. Write down why you don't have a feeling of guilt or responsibility towards him.' Laura's face was expressionless. She clearly wasn't prepared to give-in to Tilly's joviality.

'Okay,' Tilly said, gathering her belongings together with a heavy heart. She was sure these sessions were meant to be helping her think more clearly. So, why was she left with a feeling that she was going to spend the next week over analysing every, single, little thing?

CHAPTER THIRTY-

FIVE

It is not unreasonable to register with a new GP for medication when your prescription has run out.
It's not unreasonable.
It's not.

Elaine pushed open the heavy front door of the Doctor's Surgery with an equally heavy heart. Which was hammering like a piston on a production line, but what could she do? She had overthought that question every day since her run-in with Anthony at the lighthouse. She knew she was running low then but up until that night of the pub quiz, she had just thought it would be a case of going and registering with the local GP, getting her notes transferred and booking the appointment to discuss a repeat prescription. Not in a million years had it occurred to her that the local GP would be her ex-boyfriend; Tilly's father.

She cringed again as she thought about Tilly making an appointment of her own, having discussed her ADHD with Anthony. Would he think she was a bad mother? How much had Tilly told him about Lil and Ruby? Would he assess Elaine and decide she was as messed-up in the head as Lil, and needed more than medication? It had kept her awake at night ever since and she thought she'd come to Hope Cove to escape her worries, not take on new ones.

'Good afternoon.' Tina, the receptionist, a petite, plump lady, probably a similar age to Elaine, greeted her with a welcoming smile, much the same way she had when Elaine had popped into register last week. She had purposely checked Anthony's car wasn't in his allocated space in the surgery car park before plucking up the courage to go in and ask.

'Hello,' Elaine stammered, feeling her face go bright red. Why was she being like this? Nowhere on God's earth was there anything written down revealing her relationship with Anthony or that Tilly was his child. Apart from that note he'd kept all these years. That was pretty incriminating.

'He's been called over to the island and is running a little late. He should be back by four.'

Elaine glanced at the clock above the window. It was three-thirty exactly, her appointment time. 'No bother,' she said, taking a seat in the corner furthest away from Tina's desk. 'I've brought my book.' The wait would give her time to debate whether she ran out the door before Anthony returned and tried her luck with Ruby. It had crossed her mind more than once this week that somewhere at Hope Home, there must be a medicine cupboard, fully stocked.

Only, Elaine's mind kept coming back to that crumpled old note Anthony had pulled from his wallet and the feelings he must have kept folded up inside with it all these years.

'You settling in all right?' Tina asked.

The waiting room, with its non-matching collection of spindle chairs, all neatly lined around the walls, was empty apart from Tina and Elaine; there was no way of avoiding conversation.

'Fine, thank you.' Elaine smiled and reached for her latest Mills & Boon in her handbag. She could at least pretend to be reading whilst suffering the all-consuming anxiety of having to come face-to-face with Anthony again.

'Your Tilly's fitted right in; takes folk round 'ere a while to get used to newcomers but they all love her in the Lobster Pot.'

Elaine nodded, and supressed the pang of jealousy that her daughter could take naturally to any situation. No doubt a skill inherited from Ruby as Elaine hated meeting new people.

'You go in there often, do you?' Why was she engaging Tina in conversation? WHY?

'Oh yeah, we all do. Not much to do around here of an evening except stay home and watch the telly. Much better to have conversation, don't you think? Makes you feel better when you've had a good old chinwag with someone. Well, that's how I feel anyway. Probably good thing I've got different people to talk to in here all day!' Tina laughed and Elaine supressed her inclination to tell the woman to stop wittering.

She needed to think.

'Sorry I'm late,' Anthony's voice called out.

The surgery door slammed behind him and there he was, all suited and booted and looking every bit as handsome as the day she had first met him on the wards at Bristol Infirmary, when she had just started her second year of nursing college.

He smiled, the same warm, kind smile she had always recalled in her mind whenever life was tough. 'Elaine, lovely to see you again, come through.' With his medical bag in one hand and a raincoat draped across the other, he extended his arm, signalling for her to go in front of him.

Standing up, Elaine smiled at Tina. She couldn't bring herself to look at Anthony, but she knew he was watching her every move.

It is not unreasonable to register with a new GP for medication when your prescription has run out.

The door closed behind her.

'Have a seat,' he said, pointing to the chairs in front of his desk. He walked towards the coat stand in the corner of the room and hung his coat up.

Elaine, slowly lowered herself into one of the half-back chairs, trying to calm her breathing and focusing on the coastal view, out of the window, to try and steady her nerves.

'I am so glad you've come to see me,' he said, thudding into his office chair and waggling his computer mouse.

'I, er...' *deep breaths,* 'I've come to see you about my medication. I, um...' she could feel her face was turning the colour of a ripe beetroot. 'It's not unreasonable to register with the local GP when your prescription runs out. It's a long way back to Bristol!' she snapped.

Anthony pulled at his tie, smoothing it down, over his chest.

His smile dropped. 'I thought, perhaps, you wanted to talk?'

Her eyes practically popped out of her head. 'No! I genuinely need some medication. You must realise how hard it is for me to come here, but what other choice do I have? If I wanted to see you socially, I could have come to your house.' She blurted it all out without really thinking. 'If I knew where you lived,' she added quickly.

He laughed and pointed to the ceiling. 'Above the surgery, actually. Well.' He exhaled loudly. 'That is disappointing. I thought perhaps after our conversation the other day, you were feeling differently. Tina gave me your registration papers last week and there was a glimmer of hope, for me, that you were open to talking to me.'

'I wasn't sure you'd allow me to see you.' Elaine looked down at her hands which were still clutching her handbag on her lap.

'Allow? You don't need my permission?'

'I wasn't sure if our previous, er, *connection*, might have a bearing over if you could be my GP.'

Anthony raked his hands through his hair and crossed his legs. 'Oh, I see. I hadn't thought about that. So, you concede you remember me now?'

Elaine eyes filled with tears. Her voice caught in her throat, but she carried on. 'How could I forget you?'

Anthony pursed his lips together, perhaps to prevent him becoming watery-eyed too. 'And Tilly?'

Elaine felt herself shutting down again. 'I didn't want to come here today; I just came to discuss my medication. I'm on Lorazepam and I've nearly run out. Will you be able to prescribe me some more?'

Anthony narrowed his eyes as if he was trying to see inside her; she suddenly felt incredibly naked. She looked away, out of the window again. The tide was in and little fishing boats were bobbing up and down on the shimmering waves. That was the one thing she didn't regret about moving to Hope Cove; the sea, the scenery, it all had a soothing effect on her jangly nerves.

Anthony took his gaze away and began tapping on his keyboard, wiggling his mouse and peering into the screen instead of into her soul. Eventually he spoke. 'You didn't want to come and yet here you are.' He raised his eyebrows up to her.

She swallowed hard. She knew what he meant; like the moth drawn to the flame, part of her must have wanted to come, otherwise she could have just gone to register at the practice in Wadebridge. Something buried deep down inside of her wanted to see him again, even if she was too scared to admit it to herself.

'This is awkward for me,' Anthony said, breaking their silence.

'Well, how do you think I feel?'

He paused and looked at her again, as if he was searching for answers to questions he couldn't find the words to ask out loud.

'Are we talking about us or our doctor-patient relationship?' He asked flatly.

Elaine bit her lip. The two were intertwined. 'I don't know.' She sighed.

He leant over his desk. 'Look, as your,' he paused as if he needed to find the right word, '*ex*-boyfriend, you're right; it isn't really appropriate for me to be your GP.' He must have acknowledged the look of horror on her face because he hurried on. 'However, as we are the only two people, I think, who know about our past, so I am willing to overlook this, *for the moment.*'

Elaine exhaled a big sigh of relief. 'Thank you, I can't tell you how relieved I am to hear that.' Sitting back in the chair she tried to regulate her breathing.

Anthony crossed his forearms over. His gaze was commanding again, like he was trying to peer into her soul, again. 'What happened to you?'

Elaine's blood started thumping around her body again, the rhythm of her heart thudding through her ears. 'What do you mean? Nothing's happened to me; I stayed living in Bristol and—'

'Had *our* baby.'

'It wasn't like that,' Elaine stammered, 'I...' she rose from her chair, eager to get out of the room, escape from the most momentous decision she'd ever made which had affected her life ever since, only just remembering at the last second that she had yet to get what she came for; her prescription.

'Stop!' Anthony reached over the desk and grabbed her hand. It was like he was giving her an electric shock, an actual spark, a zap which made them both jolt away from each other.

'Sorry, I didn't want you to leave without your prescription,' he said, lowering himself back into his chair.

'No,' Elaine said, rubbing her wrist where he'd grabbed her. It was funny but it was like that panicky feeling had been zapped out of her. She suddenly felt calm.

'I didn't mean to sound truculent,' he said, focusing on his computer screen. 'I was actually on about you. What happened to you? The Elaine I remember was full of fun and vitality; she loved life. Not a bag of nerves, addicted to anti-depressants.'

'I am not addicted!' She snapped.

He looked at her over the rim of his glasses.

'Okay,' Elaine conceded, 'maybe I am. But I'm trying hard to get on top of things. Not be so panicky and stressed all the time. That's why I came to Hope Cove; to try and sort myself out.'

'Which brings me back to my question,' he said, reaching behind to the printer. 'What happened?'

Elaine shrugged. 'Life I guess.'

He continued to gaze at her whilst whipping the prescription off the printer.

'My mother has schizophrenia.' The words were escaping out of Elaine's mouth before she had time to engage over what she was saying. 'She was diagnosed with it when I was a child. It was one of the reasons I wanted to become a nurse; I wanted to use my experience of living with someone with a serious mental health illness to help others.' She averted his gaze and fiddled with the buttons on her pleated skirt. 'Only I hadn't bet on getting pregnant. My focus changed; I was a mother. Somehow bringing up Tilly was my priority and before I knew it, she was gone; flown the nest but at the same time Dad died and Mum began to deteriorate. Now she has dementia, on top of the schizophrenia, and I had to give up my job five years ago to look after her full time.' She slapped her hand on the wooden arm of her chair. 'I'm fifty-three for Christ's sake! Aren't I allowed a life too?'

She dared to look up at him. If he was taken aback by her outburst he gave very little away.

'I take it by your mum, you're talking about Lil?'

'Yes, I suppose you've heard that she is not my biological mother, and, in fact, Ruby is?'

He nodded solemnly. 'When did you find out?'

'When I was three months pregnant with Tilly. I didn't want to believe her though, so I sent her away. Ironically, the one piece of advice she did give me was to tell you, not knowing that one day you would be her GP!'

He smiled. A gentle, sweet smile. The wrinkles at the corners of his eyes creased.

He sighed. 'So why didn't you?'

'I didn't want you to know.'

'You didn't think I had a right to know?' He voice was soft, but underneath Elaine could sense an air of irritation. He had every right to be angry. He had every right to be shouting at her for denying him thirty-three years of his daughter's life.

She shook her head. 'It wasn't like that; I didn't want you to ruin your life. You were on your way to becoming a successful medical professional, a surgeon even. You didn't need holding back by a partner and a baby.'

'And you didn't think I had the right to make that decision?'

He was stung. Elaine closed her eyes and tried very hard not to cry.

'I wouldn't have been able to cope if you'd rejected me.' A tear escaped and slid down her cheek.

'I would never have done that; I would have supported you. I loved you!' His voice was still calm, but she could tell hear the anguish in it.

Elaine looked at him through her blurry eyes. 'But I would never have known if you were supporting me through obligation, or through love, and I couldn't live with that. I am not a very strong person. Tilly needed a mum that could look after her; my own mother was incapable of that. In fact, both of them, Lil and Ruby failed me. I couldn't do that to Tilly; I needed to be strong for her sake.'

Anthony sighed heavily, leant back in his chair and studied her face. 'You know, I think you're a lot stronger than you think you are.'

The flood gates opened. 'No, I'm not, ohhh!' Elaine sobbed.

Anthony reached for a tissue and handed it to her.

'Thank you,' she said, trying to wipe up any spilled mascara.

'You have single-handedly brought up Tilly whilst caring for a mother with severe mental health issues and held down a job, by the sounds of things; what on earth makes you think you're not strong?'

'I don't know.' She sniffed. 'I don't feel I've achieved anything with my life, I feel stressed and anxious all the time; I never seem to enjoy anything, I just worry incessantly – that's why I'm still on anti-depressants.'

Anthony looked at his watch.

'Sorry, I'm taking up all your time and I expect you have other patients,' she said, standing up.

'Please, Elaine, I was just checking the time because the baby drop-in service starts at four, that's all. Look, let's make you another appointment to come back and discuss this further. We need to consider all the options.'

'Options?' What was he suggesting? Sectioning her?

'Like Tilly, you could consider some counselling. I think we need a thorough review of your medication anyway; I wasn't convinced by your last practice's diagnosis of Tilly.'

'There's nothing wrong with Doctor Pearson,' Elaine snapped. 'He's been our GP for years.'

Anthony raised his eyebrows. 'And yet you still feel anxious and stressed all the time?'

Elaine's shoulders slumped. 'Fair enough.'

'When you leave, book a double appointment with Tina.' He handed her the prescription.

She took the paper and she felt that same tingle of a spark again as their fingers briefly brushed by each other's. 'Thank you,' she managed in a wobbly voice, feeling relieved he hadn't rejected her; he wanted her to come back again. Perhaps only as her GP but he hadn't shouted at her and condemned her for all eternity.

other's. 'Thank you,' she managed in a wobbly voice, feeling relieved he hadn't rejected her; he wanted her to come back again. Perhaps only as her GP but he hadn't shouted at her and condemned her for all eternity.

223

CHAPTER THIRTY-

SIX

Ibiza 2011

It was a funny night. The crowd were loving him, but he just wasn't into it. The beat of the rhythm just went straight through him, pounding his head and stabbing at his heart. Images of Tory's tearstained face as she'd rushed to the bathroom kept flashing in front of his mind. He checked his phone again. Still no answer. He'd text over ten times. She was angry with him, he knew, but it wasn't like her not to reply; she wasn't one for the silent treatment, she was needy. Needy of him. Guilt washed over him again that he'd left her when she was coming down from a high and looked so vulnerable. It was so hot in the club, so oppressive, he was sweating buckets. He grabbed a bottle of water one of the runners had left him and broke the seal. He lifted it above his head and poured it over him to cool down. As it washed over his face and tee-shirt, a horrible thought crossed his mind.

Water.

The bath.

'I've got to go,' he said, to one of the other DJs, due on straight after him. 'Now.' He didn't stop to explain, he was down the steel stairs, pushing through the swarms of club goers, like a surfer breaking waves to reach his abandoned surf board. He needed to get home. He reached the club doors and took in the late-night air. It was cooler than in the day and he paused to take in big gulps of fresh air before setting off at the speed of light. Luckily, their apartment was only at the edge of the main stretch; on an outcrop of land at the end of the bay. He fumbled for his keys in his jeans pocket and swiped the fob against the communal entrance panel. He had never run so fast upstairs before, taking three at a time. Their apartment was the penthouse, but he was in too much of a hurry to take the lift.

'Tory!' he shouted as he broke through the front door.

Silence.

The flat was in darkness and he ran straight for the stairs to the bedroom, around the spiral staircase.

Please be in bed, please be in bed.

He fumbled for Tory's bedside lamp, turning it on to reveal their untouched bed. Perhaps she'd left? Perhaps that was it, packed her things in a fit of anger to catch a flight. He opened the wardrobe, but all her clothes were there. Slowly he turned to look at the bathroom door, still closed like how it was earlier. The light was on.

'Tory?' he called, softly, praying that she lightly replied that she was reading a good book in the bath.

Silence.

It was a horrible feeling of foreboding. The smell of lavender, meant to relax Tory, was making him feel sick. He rushed for the door and turned the handle, taking a deep breath to confront what was on the other side.

Perhaps she'd slipped and knocked herself unconscious. *Please let it be that.*

She was lying like an angel, her arms out to either side of their stand-alone, copper bath. The view of the harbour, with its twinkling lights reflecting back into the dimly-lit room, making her look almost ethereal.

'Tory?' Winstone rushed to her, perhaps she had just fell asleep? He skidded and looked down. Blood, not water. 'Oh, my God, Tory,' he sobbed, turning to look at her, ready to perform CPR. It was way past that though. However, much he willed her to survive, she was gone. Her pale little body in a pool of bloody bath water, her wrists slit several times. Her eyes were wide open, staring at him. She looked scared. On the floor, lay a pink tinged, wet, folded piece of paper. In her writing it simply said, *Winstone.*

***

'And now she's talked me into this hare-brained idea to hold a disco on Friday night after the pub quiz! How have I let her infiltrate her way into my life, get a job working for me, persuade me to start holding a regular quiz night, persuade me allow her to keep her job while she's sets up a part-time enterprise *in competition with my business* and now convinced me to get behind the decks; something I haven't done for ten years!'

Winstone looked up at Laura expectantly. He was sitting in her visitors arm chair, like it was a bucket, his legs dangling over one arm and his head reclining on the other.

Laura took a deep breath and rallied as much self-control as she possibly possessed not to shout at Winstone. 'Is it, and this is just *a possibility*, but is it possible that you *might* have feelings for Tilly?'

'Woah!' His eyes almost popped out of his head. 'What makes you suggest that?' he asked, sitting bolt upright.

BECAUSE IT'S SO BLOODY OBVIOUS!

Having come to her four years ago as an NHS patient, Winstone had become one of her regular, private clients after the NHS funded sessions had run out. He now saw her five or six times a year to 'keep his head in check' as he put it. In her entire career, as a psychotherapist, she had never come across an issue of patient confidentiality.

Until now.

'When was the last time you got behind the decks?' She asked.

'You know when it was; the night Tory died.'

'Right, and have you had any desire to have a go at playing them since? Even in the privacy of your bedroom?'

Winstone clasped his hands together, concentrating hard at intertwining his fingers. 'You know I haven't. I couldn't.'

'So, shall we explore the sudden change of heart?'

He grinned. 'I've said it before, but you're good. You're wasted out here in the sticks; you should be up in London, raking it in.'

Laura smiled but said nothing. She never gave anything away to her clients, which mainly infuriated them but went with the territory when you were carrying out such intimiate, confidential work. It was difficult down here *in the* sticks, as Winstone put it; so often you bumped into clients as events. Winstone was right; she could earn a lot more in London, but she was happy in Cornwall. It wasn't just patients that needed to practise the art of mindfulness. A happy mind, a happy soul and a happy body came from being in a relaxing place and nowhere was more relaxing to Laura than the Cornish landscape.

'Just so I'm sure, what you're saying is that because Tilly persuaded me to get behind the decks again, I must have feelings for her?'

Laura cocked her head to one side. 'Do you?'

Winstone pursed his lips and began beating the life out of the cushion behind him before settling himself back into the chair. 'I've tried hard not to.'

Laura nodded. 'So, what shall we explore? The feelings you have for Tilly, or why you're supressing them?'

'Ugh,' Winstone groaned. 'This is exactly why I don't like coming here.'

She had known Winstone long enough not to be offended by him. 'And, yet, you still do.'

'Yes, because you make me face up to the thoughts and feelings I like to bury. It's much easier to go down the gym or keep on serving customers all evening than be alone with my thoughts.'

Laura kept her legs crossed and placed her hands in her lap, patiently waiting for Winstone to open up a bit more.

'I think I probably know why I'm supressing my feelings for Tilly.'

'So, we're at least establishing that you *do* have feelings for Tilly?'

'Yes, I do. There I've said.' He grinned.

'And how does that feel, to acknowledge them?'

The smile slipped from Winstone's mouth. 'Like I'm betraying Tory,' he whispered.

Laura nodded. In the entire time she had been Winstone's therapist, Tory was his ongoing battle; it seemed he would never relinquish himself fully of the burden of guilt and responsibility he felt surrounding Tory's death. All she could do was to help him live with it.

'What do you think Tory would say?'

Winstone looked down at his hands again. 'I don't know. I *think* the old Tory would tell me to go for it, but the drug addicted Tory was more insecure. She would be jealous, betrayed perhaps, at the thought of me moving on with someone else.'

'Winstone, identifying feelings for Tilly is a massive step forward for you; you know that, don't you?'

Winstone nodded.

'Ever since I've known you, you've lived in the past. Now, you're talking about DJing again, feelings for another woman; this is progress! Surely part of you must feel proud for coming this far?'

He looked up and held her gaze. 'Then why does the other part of me feel like a total bastard?'

CHAPTER THIRTY-

SEVEN

'Budge out the way Archie,' Ruby said, wiggling her bottom in Archie's direction as she shuffled past him with a wooden bowl full of crusty bread rolls. Archie inwardly groaned. It had been like this for over a fortnight now. Giggling, turning up unexpectedly – which had now become predictable – putting her arm through his at any opportunity to stroll along together. She'd taken to buying him gifts too. The latest was a swanky Canon long lens DSLR camera as he'd mentioned there was so much wildlife on the cliffs outside the cottage, he should consider photographing some of it.

It was all very flattering, but he mustn't give in.

'Archie,' Tilly said, reaching up from underneath her new pop-up-stall-thingy, Ruby had invested in for her, 'would you be able to go and handout some flyers around the village for me?'

'Gladly,' Archie said, a little too enthusiastically as he rose from the harbour wall he had been perching on while Ruby helped Tilly set up for the day.

'I'll come with you,' Ruby said cheerfully, plonking the serviettes she had just retrieved from a drawer onto the work surface.

'No need, really.' He would be glad of some peace and quiet.

Tilly turned around from where she was setting up her pans and dishes and looked between Ruby and Archie. 'What is wrong with you two?'

'I don't know what you mean?' Archie blustered.

'You're behaving like a pair of children; either stuck together like glue or wanting to get away from each other. Don't think I haven't noticed; it's been going on since that first pub quiz where Mum walked out, and we had to play with Doctor Dare.'

Archie blushed. Ruby did what she always did and plastered a big smile to her lips.

'Nothing, darling,' Ruby said breezily. 'You know what old friends are like; take each other for granted, don't we Archie?'

Archie studied Ruby's face. Was she implying that's what he'd done all these years; taken her for granted?

He laughed, nervously. 'I guess so. Right, where are these flyers?'

Tilly eyed them sceptically. 'Here,' she said, grabbing them from a drawer.

'You've got this new stall well organised,' he said, not wanting to leave with an atmosphere.

'I know.' Tilly lovingly stroked the granite worktop. 'I'm so lucky Ruby's bought it for me, well, er, loaned me the money to buy it anyway.'

Ruby laughed. 'It's an investment sweetie. We've set it up as a business, *your business*. No doubt you'll be paying the business back in no time.'

A pang of jealousy struck through Archie at Ruby's bragging. Tilly was *his* grandchild too. 'You should have said Tilly, I could have helped you out with your start-up.'

Tilly blushed. 'You're too kind Archie. Ruby's family; perhaps that's why I accepted her help.' Tilly grinned at Ruby.

It was like someone was twisting a knife into his gut. He wanted to say *but I'm family too!* 'Perhaps when you expand, I can help you out then?'

Tilly reached up on tiptoes and kissed his cheek. 'I would love that; you know you're like a Grampy to me.'

Archie could see Ruby scowling at him from the corner of his eye but all he could do was fight back the tears fast approaching. He held the colourful flyers embolden with TILLY'S KITCHEN and a summary of her menu up. 'Best get off and send some customers your way. Come on Hector,' he said, gruffly, pulling Hector's lead. He didn't look back, he couldn't. He batted the tears from his eyes as he made his way up the sun-baked harbour concrete. He would persuade every person he came across to support *his* granddaughter's debut outing in her new business today. He was proud of Tilly, proud of Elaine and truth be told, proud of Ruby too for embracing the opportunity she had been given since Tilly and Elaine and arrived in Hope Cove.

If only he could find the courage to do the same.

Ruby watched Archie wander up the causeway with a heavy heart. She knew she was putting stress and pressure on him but neither of them knew how much time they had left; what was the point of spending it apart? She'd banished any thoughts that Archie didn't want her to the back of her mind. They had kept in touch all these years, he had visited regularly after Phyllis had died and, although she understood that he was most probably still grieving, she knew he still had feelings for her. Most importantly, she still loved him. Couldn't they spend their autumn years – however long that was – in happiness?

'So, what's going on there, then?' Tilly asked, turning on her heat plates.

Ruby kept her eyes fixed on Archie's tall, slim figure with Hector trotting along obediently beside him.

'I don't know what you mean, darling?' she said, idly rubbing her neck. 'As I said, he's an old friend and us oldies don't have as much patience to be polite to each other as you youngsters.'

'Oh, I'm not buying that,' Tilly said, now busying herself with her kitchen prep. 'Everyone asks me what the deal is between you two; now I'm asking you.'

Ruby couldn't stop her reflexes from turning around to face Tilly. 'Who's everyone?'

Tilly bent her head over her chopping board and focused on slicing onions. 'I don't want you to think the village has been gossiping about you.'

Ruby's long string of pearls swung angrily over her peony patterned tunic top. 'Pah! That's all villagers do; gossip. Come on? Who was it?'

'Well, Emma planted the idea in my mind over a month ago. She said you seemed *more than friends*. Then Doctor Dare asked me in the pub what was the deal between you and Archie.'

'Oooh! Did he, indeed.' Ruby set about taking plastic cups out of their packaging and inserting them into their holder for ease of access when serving customers. 'I really would have expected better from Anthony.'

'Well, Doctor Dare and Emma are both intelligent people so at least you know that it isn't just idle village gossip.'

'Huh. More like gossip that's spread like wildfire if even Anthony and Emma are making enquiries. Why can't people mind their own business?'

Tilly stopped slicing and looked over her shoulder. 'What, like you, you mean?' She winked and went back to her slicing. 'Anyway, you're still avoiding the question. Do you have feelings for Archie?'

Ruby busied herself refolding the already neat pile of folded tea towels Tilly had freshly washed and brought down with her from the cottage. It was silly; she could admit it to herself and to Archie, but she couldn't say it out loud. Perhaps it was because theirs had always been a covert relationship. Perhaps, she was meant to have this conversation with Tilly to realise how silly it sounded to want a relationship with a seventy-one-year-old man when she was sixty-nine herself.

'You do, don't you? You have feelings for Archie.'

Ruby looked out across the empty harbour where the tide was far out. Seagulls squawked, tourists chattered on the harbour road and the odd car hummed as it drove down Church Lane and through the village. Of course, she had feelings for Archie; she'd never stopped having feelings for him.

She couldn't tell Tilly that though, could she?

She looked at her watch. 'My goodness, ten-thirty already and you open at midday! We'd better crack on.'

Ruby could feel Tilly surveying her as she began unpacking paper plates and stacking them under the serving counter.

'Fine but we will return to this conversation because as your granddaughter, I think I have probably inherited your meddling gene.'

Fingers crossed, thought Ruby, she could do with a fairy Godmother to sort things out between her and Archie.

CHAPTER THIRTY-

EIGHT

The lights were dancing all over the cellar walls at the Lobster Pot and the music was thumping so loud the floor boards were reverberating and spouting out dust particles which were bouncing off each other in the colourful disco lights. Tilly watched Winstone rehearsing; his large headphones clamped to one ear, mixing one set into each other, a look of concentration on his face like she had never seen before. It was as if he was one with the decks, his lithe fingers gently rubbing the records one way, then the other.

A little shiver extended down her spine. He was good. She was no expert in the art of DJing but she'd spent enough time cruising around the Mediterranean with the odd stop off in a coastal club, in Ibiza, to know a good set when she heard one. She reached for her phone out of her back pocket and opened up her Instagram account. She snapped a quick pic of the master at work, filtered the image so it looked ultra-trendy and typed it up with *The Great Winstone Chambers @thelobsterpot #HopeCove tonight 9pm – Midnight, come and have fun! Join us for our #pubquiz at 7pm, great #foodanddrink on offer #Cornwall #disco #winstonechambers #DJ #party*. She added the pub as the location and posted the photo. Slipping the phone back in her jeans pocket she marvelled at the fact everything had to have a hashtag. She wasn't a big fan, but she knew that people looked up the hashtags. She was using them left, right and centre to promote *Tilly's Kitchen* but it seemed so impersonal. However, if you wanted people to rock up and make use of your services, they needed to know where to look and if people were looking up food and drink in Cornwall, it was the only way to grab their attention. Which was why she was sneakily promoting the disco online. Winstone may have been reluctant but she felt sure if he saw how popular it was, he'd make it a regular thing. Tilly loved dancing. She couldn't wait to have a bop with Ruby later and she relished the prospect of a regular Friday night feature to look forward to every week, even if she was out on the harbour working hard all day, then working her evening shift in the pub. The music felt good; it made her feel alive.

The music suddenly stopped.

'Ah, there you are,' Winstone grinned. 'Enjoying yourself?'

Coming to her senses, Tilly realised she had unconsciously shimmied into the centre of the dance floor. She blushed. 'Yes, thank you, just enjoying your craft.'

'Thank you. I'm just warming up.'

'If that's warming up, I can't wait to see you on your game.'

'All in good time.' He smiled, putting down his headphones and with one swift move, jumping over the decks and down onto the dance floor.

'So, how was your day? I meant to come and see you, but we were busy behind the bar and we're a woman down on Friday lunchtimes now.' He winked.

Tilly rolled her eyes. 'I guess I deserved that one. It was really good, thank you.' Tilly smiled, recalling the feeling of serving her very first customer with the food she had made. Two months ago, she could barely cook! What Laura had taught her about the self-fulfilling prophecy had really worked; it was all about a change of mindset and not convincing yourself that you were as mad as a box of frogs, like the rest of your family, all the time. 'I'm glad your trade wasn't affected by me being on the causeway drumming up business.'

Winstone raised his arms behind his head and stretched. 'Not at all, actually, I was quite surprised. Ruby did say that a little competition might be healthy. Our drinks were definitely up too, so perhaps the tourists were eating with you then coming to us later for a drink.'

'I hope I haven't affected Emma's trade at the bakery.'

'Well, judging from what I could see, Ruby was selling half of Emma's stock so I'm sure she's had the trade one way or another.'

'Oi!' Tilly playfully punched him in the stomach. His core was rock hard. What kind of six-pack lay beneath that Superdry T-shirt, she wondered? 'I saw you catching a few rays on the balcony,' she continued, fighting back to prevent herself from finishing her sentence. It was no good. 'With Laura Steel.'

Arrggh! Why give away you know her Tilly, WHY?!

'Oh, did you now?' He grinned. 'She was in having lunch with her husband. He works in London in the week and stays down here at weekends.

Interesting. Laura gave nothing away about herself; absolutely nothing. So, how did Winstone know so much?

'I didn't know you knew her?' Winstone continued.

'Yes.' She could feel herself blushing now as she cursed herself for bringing Laura up in the first place. 'I, um...' she trailed off. Should she tell him? Could she tell him?

'It's okay, you don't have to tell me.' Winstone said, scratching his neck, looking as awkward as she felt.

'It's okay, you might as well know—' because if she couldn't face up and tell people herself, then surely, she was ashamed of what she was doing with Laura? And at the back of her mind was Laura's question surrounding guilt. If she didn't tell Winstone, was it because she perceived him as a person in authority, as her boss, and would he judge her. Would he sack her? Did she care? '—I'm seeing her, as a client. Just as for six weeks, I'm on a course of CBT.'

If Winstone was taken aback, he didn't show it. He just placed his hands-on hips and nodded, looking down at her with the deep, brown eyes, like pools of melted chocolate. 'That's how I met her,' he said, eventually.

Tilly wasn't able to hide her surprise, like Winstone so tactfully had. 'Oh! Um, right, I didn't—'

'Think I was someone in need of therapy?'

'Um, well, I wouldn't put it like that,' Tilly said, stalling for time, 'but, um…'

Winstone bent double laughing. He rested his hands on his knees. 'You are a bloody awful liar, Tilly.

Tilly blushed, not knowing what to say. She was torn between not giving too much away about why she was seeing Laura but, also, why Winstone had seen her.

He shook his head, standing up. 'It's fine. Sometimes, we all need a little help and that's what Laura's there for.'

Tilly nodded. She was desperate to ask what help Winstone had needed. 'You seem so…' what was it? 'Together.'

He grinned. 'That's what seven years of therapy does for you. I don't see her as frequently now, just when I need her. She's good. Whatever's going on for you, she'll help you through it. And I hope you sort through it too.'

He appraised her with that knowing stare of his. She wanted to say more, but something was preventing her. Probably the stigmatism of ADHD; she didn't want him thinking she was a fruit loop. 'Crikey, is that the time?' she blustered. 'The pub quiz starts in half-an-hour; I'd better get back up there and help Rosie behind the bar.

Winstone nodded. 'Yep, of course.'

She smiled and self-consciously scurried to the stairs which led back up to the pub, all the while wondering to herself whether therapy had made Winstone's problems go away or whether he had some sort of metaphorical wound, which had healed, and he really didn't want to open back up.

CHAPTER THIRTY-

NINE

The basement was packed. His blood was pumping in time to the beat and the adrenaline was flowing through his veins.

Winstone hated to admit it but he was *loving it*.

'Oh, my goodness, I can't get over how busy it is!' Tilly said, sidling up to him behind the decks with a chilled bottle of cider in her hand.

He grinned at her. Laura was right, he couldn't try and hide it; he *did* have feelings for Tilly. Unfortunately, it didn't stop the overwhelming feeling of guilt he had for feeling this way. And in the midst of all of that was the nagging thought that he'd told Laura how he'd felt about Tilly and she was flipping seeing Laura herself!

'Here, this is for you,' Tilly said, thrusting the bottle into his hand. 'Can you play something disco next, so I can have a quick boogie before I head back up to the bar? I've left Rosie up there on her own.'

'Sure.' He'd been playing a mixture of club hits with the occasional *Wham!* and *Steps* thrown in for good measure, to make sure he had all generations covered. It was a world apart from Ibiza, but it was giving him the same buzz.

And he had to admit, it was all down to Tilly.

'Bit of Sister Sledge do it for you?'

'Cool!' She reached up on tiptoes and kissed him on the cheek before jumping down the steps and swirling her way out into the crowd.

He watched her twirl around the dance floor. There were youngsters, teens being silly, linking hands and trying to limbo, there were baby boomers all grooving like mods, there were a few young lads hitting on the local girls and there in the middle swayed Tilly, like a mermaid shimmying through water, her long frizzy hair moving in time, arms above her head, totally lost to the music.

For a brief moment it was Tory. Under strobe lighting, dancing her way through the crowds towards the decks, seducing him with her body and her eyes. He shook himself and found Tilly, dancing like no-one was looking, without a care in the world. He smiled to himself and loaded up *Thinking of You* by *Sister Sledge*. He watched her, as he mixed it in to the last song, as the beat came through, she jumped up and down, waving her hands in the air then blew him a kiss before starting to dance energetically, not to mention pretty well choreographed, to the song.

He smiled. Perhaps Laura was right; perhaps what he needed in his life was a Tilly. A little ray of sunshine who saw the good in everyone. Perhaps if he told her about Tory, he could move forward? They'd gone as far opening up to each other about seeing Laura; that was a big step for him. Could he tell about Tory and move on with his life? She'd just kissed him; she must like him, right?

Or what if he was reading her signals wrong?

Elaine couldn't sleep. Admittedly, she might have given it longer, but after a lavender bath, finishing her latest Mills & Boon and a hot milk to try and soothe her raging thoughts, she decided to give-in, get dressed and see if the waves gently lapping against the shore might calm all those inner-panicky-thoughts.

She didn't dare walk the long stretch of shore adjacent to Gull Island, in the dark, on her own and instead had opted to walk out around the headland by the light house, and down Church Lane, into the village. There were some benches on the harbour by the cellar door to the Lobster Pot; one of those would do nicely to while she whiled away her insomnia into the wee, small hours.

Her pace slowed as she reached the harbour. Forgetting that it was the launch of Tilly's *Disco Friday*, as she kept referring to it, she hadn't betted on all the benches being overcrowded by village youths and the like. She smiled to herself when she realised that one bench was being occupied by a couple, older than her, necking like a pair of teenagers. She settled herself on the harbour wall and watched the intimate pair, her thoughts turning once again to Anthony. She had thought of barely little else since her appointment with him a couple of weeks ago. He had been respectful and kept his distance, but her next appointment was looming the following week and her anxiety levels were creeping up the closer it got. Even the lorazepam didn't seem to be making any difference these days, but then, even she had to concede that a packet of pills was not going to make the father of her child magically disappear.

Her gaze settled on the disco in the cellar of the pub and she smiled as she identified her daughter twirling around; away with the fairies, not a care in the world, as usual. Elaine had to concede that Tilly had become surer of herself these past couple of months. She didn't know if it was the effect living in Hope Cove was having on her, or the sessions Tilly was having with her therapist. Tilly had opened a little – Elaine was pretty sure Tilly gave her an edited version whereby she omitted how much complaining she probably did about Elaine to Laura – and this business of a self-fulfilling-wotsit, whatever it was called was making her, well... more self-fulfilled. Elaine knew she was envious of Tilly. Of course, she had her job in the bakery, which she loved, but Tilly had her own business now, which Ruby had helped her with. Why didn't Ruby give Elaine the same support. Because she'd blown it, that's why. She'd rejected Ruby all those years ago and, in turn, Ruby was keeping her distance from Elaine now. What she'd give to just be able to go over the island and say *Mum, help! The man who fathered my baby is living in the village and I don't know what to do?!* But she couldn't. She'd refused to believe Ruby was her mum and what if Ruby just turned around and said *told you so. I told you to tell the father all those years ago.* It was all such a bitter pill to swallow.

The music slowed, the crowd dispersed, and Elaine's ears pricked as she listened to the opening chords. The boppers on the dance floor were replaced by loved-up couples, dancing crotch-to-crotch, let alone toe-to-toe as she awaited Tony Hadley's opening line of *True.* The outline of a figure – an unmistakeable figure – came striding out of the wide cellar doors as he purposefully made his way towards her.

Her entire body began to shake. 'You requested that, didn't you?' The glimmer of a smile twitched at the corners of her mouth at the thought he had remembered.

Anthony smiled back. 'I did. Winstone was obliging, as usual. May I?' he said, beckoning to the wall.

She nodded, every fibre of her body one thousand times more wired-up than when she'd departed from the cottage to try and relax herself. She'd never sleep now.

'You didn't forget, then?'

Anthony shook his vehemently, as he sat a reasonable distance away from her. 'I'd never forget.' His voice sounded choked. 'It remains the best night of my life.'

Her heart swelled and her nerves started to calm. He'd never forgotten her! It was just like in one of her romance novels. Although, in fiction they'd skip over all the unpleasantness to the hero and heroine could be together, whereas, in reality, as soon as Tilly found out about Anthony, she would probably never speak to Elaine ever again.

She might as well forget any notion – a fantasy she had thought about quite frequently these past couple of weeks – she had of a future with Anthony right now. It was either Anthony or Tilly and she would always choose Tilly.

They sat in companionable silence watching the disco-goers sway in time to Tony.

'Why didn't you tell me?' Anthony finally asked. 'We could have been so happy, the three of us; a little family.'

Elaine's eyes welled with tears. It was funny but now she was actually having this conversation all her anxieties were beginning to flow away. As if the tide next to her was washing them out to sea. 'I couldn't bear the thought that you might not want to know. I dropped out of college, avoided the city centre for weeks. There were moments when my heart ached to go find you, tell you but, then, the day Ruby turned up and told me who she really was, was the day I finally decided to give up on any stupid notion that we could be a family; if my father didn't want to help Ruby when she was pregnant with me, I felt it increased the probability that you'd feel the same way. We'd only been seeing each other a few weeks; it wasn't as if we were even on the verge of getting engaged.'

Anthony nodded and looked down at his Chelsea boots, he was wearing with a pair of jeans. In thirty-odd years, his style hadn't changed. Elaine's had; it had become dowdy. Worn down by years of raising a child single-handedly before taking over the reins of your deranged mother.

'That does make sense.' He looked at her and smiled, those little crinkles at the corners of her eyes warming his expression.

'Oh!' Elaine said, bursting into a series of sobs.

Anthony edged along the wall towards her, putting his arm around her. She didn't hesitate to bury her face in his cotton shirt, breathe in his familiar scent; it all took her back to being nineteen again. She felt protected.

Eventually her sobbing subsided. 'What about you?' she asked, pulling away to find a tissue in her jacket pocket. 'What did life dish out for you, apart from a thirty-three-year-old daughter you knew nothing about.'

Anthony threw his head back and laughed. 'Well, nothing quite as exciting as that!' He pushed his glasses back up the ridge of his nose. 'I finally gave up on looking for you, qualified, met Francesca and, as she was from Berkshire like me, we moved back towards London. I became a GP, as did she, we had two kids, an idyllic four-bedroom house in suburbia, got a dog and the next thing I knew she was telling me she was having an affair and wanted a divorce.'

Elaine swallowed hard. She wasn't the only one who life had dealt a rough pack of cards, then. 'Sounds painful.'

'It was, but if I'm honest, my heart was never in our relationship; I was always looking amongst the sea of faces, wherever I went, for you. Francesca was competing with someone she didn't even know about.' He shrugged. 'I guess it was doomed from the start.'

Elaine fought back more tears, guilt settling on her conscious that she had managed to break up a marriage she didn't even know about. 'You still had feelings for me, then?' she croaked.

'I've never stopped.' Anthony held her gaze.

The guilt was too much; she looked down at her hands which were busily tearing her tissue to shreds. 'I'm sorry, about your marriage,' she mumbled.

'As I say, don't be; I could have tried harder to look for you. I could have written a letter and asked the nursing college to send it onto you. I just assumed you thought it was all one big mistake, or you were disappointed in my performance that night and—'

'Never!' Elaine shook her head vehemently. 'Not one day has gone by in thirty-three years where I haven't thought of you!'

Anthony nodded and smiled. He looked suspiciously close to tears himself. 'Ironically, it was Ruby who helped me get over the end of my marriage.'

'Pah!' Elaine let out a hollow cackle. *Bloody Ruby.* Nearly all her problems stemmed from Ruby's actions. 'Why doesn't that surprise me? *Saint* Ruby.'

'I understand why you're cross with her, but she is probably the most empathic person I know. I think she had it pretty hard when she was pregnant with you, by all accounts.'

Elaine took a deep breath and nodded. 'I know. Perhaps if my father had been involved things would have been different.' She managed to take Anthony's gaze. 'But, perhaps, then I wouldn't have met you and Tilly wouldn't be here.'

Anthony smiled. 'Well, that's something we can both be grateful for then. Do you think she'll be glad to know she's got a half brother and sister, when she finally founds out?'

It was like her entire body had been blasted by ice. Her anxiety returned from the sea in crashing waves, sweeping over her. 'Finds out?'

Anthony frowned. 'Well, now you've found me, I assumed you were going to tell her. I can't wait to be properly introduced.'

She couldn't run away, not this time. She'd come to Hope Cove to runaway for goodness sakes!

Her expression must have said it all.

Anthony took her hand and squeezed. 'When you're ready, of course.'

CHAPTER FORTY

The loud knocking on the door the following morning woke Tilly in a panic. Sitting bolt upright in bed, sun streaming in through the gaps in her nautical curtains, she grabbed her phone in a panic, sure she must have missed her alarm.

'Five am! Ugh.' She flunked back onto the pillows. She had at least another hour before she needed to get up.

The knocking started again. 'Come on sleepy head!' The familiar voice called up to the window. Tilly threw back the duvet and reached for the window latch.

'You have got to be kidding me! What is so urgent to wake me up before dawn and, oh—' Tilly stopped to take in the full effect of Winstone's bulging biceps in his illuminous yellow running vest and even more prominent thigh muscles peeping out from under his black, lycra shorts. She swallowed hard as her eye couldn't resist following his thigh muscles all the way up to his lunchbox area.

My word.

'Come on,' he said, leaning against the wall, pulling one foot up behind him to stretch his thigh. 'You said you were serious about this running stuff, so I thought I'd put you through your paces.'

'Okay, I just need—'

'To get dressed,' he said, fixing her with one of his best *I'm the boss* stares. 'I'm sure you showered before you went to bed last night so just chuck your running gear on; you'll be needing a shower when you get back from being put through the full Winstone experience.'

'Okay,' Tilly said, trying not to groan as she closed the window and began gathering up her running gear from the back of her dresser chair. Winstone was right, she was taking exercise seriously on Laura's advice, but was running *this early* in the morning really that advisable? She showed her teeth some toothpaste – there was no way she was going out with Winstone for a run with bad breath – and crept down the wooden stairs to the front door, so as not to wake Archie or Mum. She quickly tied up her trainer laces and quietly closed the front door behind her.

Winstone grinned, still standing on the pavement, stretching. He checked his watch. 'That was pretty good timing for you.'

'Haha,' Tilly said, locking the door quietly behind her and slipping the key into the tiny zip pocket of her runners. 'I'm never late for work.'

'By the skin of your teeth.' He winked. 'Got that fancy watch of yours on.'

'Yes.' Tilly waved her wrist at him.

'Great, you'd better do some stretching?'

Tilly swallowed hard watching Winstone's lean, toned body stretch in all directions. She nodded and followed his lead, too mesmerised at how fit his body was to actually speak.

'So,' he said, in hushed tones, still stretching. 'What's the deal between your mum and Anthony?'

'Who's Anthony?' Tilly asked, trying to keep up with Winstone's manoeuvres, realising she was nowhere near as flexible as he was.

'The Doc!'

'What?' Tilly stopped stretching and frowned. 'Nothing, they don't really know each other, I don't think.'

'They looked pretty close, sitting on the harbour wall, talking last night.'

'What?' Tilly, half-stretching on one leg, almost toppled over.

'Ssssh! You'll wake your mum and Archie,' Winstone hissed.

'You are kidding me?'

'Nope. Seemed pretty heavy, whatever they were talking about.'

Tilly narrowed her eyes. 'Hmm, I wonder if it's to do with her medication?'

'Isn't that what his surgery's for?'

Tilly's focus wandered from stretching and running to the nagging, worrying feeling she used to experience as a child when anything was up with Mum. 'I wonder if she's okay. I hope she wasn't going to do anything stupid.' A thought flashed across her mind, a fleeting one of a memory she preferred to keep locked away, in the basement of her mind, on the top shelf, where it was almost unreachable.

'They looked fine; quite intimate, if anything.'

'But if you had a problem and were telling someone about it, you'd look quite intimate too, wouldn't you?'

'Are we talking about me or you?'

Tilly averted her gaze from Winstone and looked across to Hope Home. Did this have something to do with Ruby? Was Mum struggling, being in close proximity to Ruby but not having anything to do with her? Ruby had commented that Mum was visiting Gran less and less.

'Why don't we stop talking about talking and do some running?' Winstone cut across her thoughts. 'Let's get those endorphins flowing. Here.' He handed her a bottle of water and started off at a jog.

'Thanks,' she said, taking the bottle and following his lead. She hoped he wasn't going to go too fast; she'd only been doing this running lark for a few of weeks, she still had a long way to go.

'I won't go too fast just yet,' he said, heading off down the coastal road which ran adjacent to Gull Island.

'Yet?!' Tilly exclaimed, realising that running and talking probably didn't come naturally to her as her lungs started to feel like they were struggling for air.

'Yes, we'll do a gentle 3K today and if you find that okay, we'll book another one in for mid-week. I find it's best not to run two days in a row, doesn't do your hamstrings nor calves any good.'

'How do you know all this?' Tilly asked, determined that her little legs should at least try to keep up with Winstone's extremely long ones.

'Years of training,' he said, looking behind him before crossing over the road and down a lane that went over the hill to the rear of the village.

Tilly followed. 'Where do you train? Or have the time for that matter?'

'I train at a gym in Wadebridge most days. If I get up and do all the chores early, there's time to go between eight and ten in the mornings, before I need to be back to open up at eleven.'

'Do you know,' Tilly said, grimacing as the lane inclined, 'I didn't even know you had a car.'

'Ha!' he laughed, his breathing shallower too as they tackled the hill. 'I rent a garage at the top of the hill; I don't like bringing the car down the narrow lanes into the village, it's too big and low.'

Tilly thought about Ruby's Range Rover which she managed to navigate okay. 'What sort have of car have you got then, a Lamborghini?!'

'A Maserati, actually.'

'Oh,' said Tilly, suddenly feeling foolish. The pub wasn't exactly fine dining; what had Winstone done in the past to afford such luxuries?

'Have you thought about a running goal? Something to work towards?'

Tilly felt heartened that Winstone had chosen to change the subject and not labour the point.

'I don't know.' Tilly hesitated. Should she bring up Laura again? She felt it had given them a connection last night, so much so she'd been brave enough to kiss him on the cheek when he said he'd play a song for her. 'It was Laura's idea, really,' she said, feeling brave.

'Oh?' Winstone took a swig of his water.

'She told me that if I wanted to change, I needed to change the way I viewed myself and how I behave. Which is what *Tilly's Kitchen* is all about; trying to make a change.'

'I see.' He sounded nonchalant but underneath Tilly could sense an undertone of intrigue. 'How have you ended up seeing Laura anyway?'

'Doctor Dare sent me, it's a long story.' They had reached the brow of the hill now and were running along the back of cottages all nestling in the valley with Hope Cove stretching out at the bottom. Tilly could see the Lobster Pot, shining in the early morning sun, its distinctive pot of lobsters sign, swinging in the breeze.

'Oh, right.'

There was that undercurrent of interest again. She carried on running, unsure how much to tell him. If he knew she'd suffered with ADHD in the past, he may have thought twice about employing her, such was the stigma surrounding mental health.

'Was is it to do with your ex?'

'Oh, no, nothing to do with Simon; that was one of my better decisions, to leave him!'

They kept running in amiable silence, Winstone clearly jogging to keep at Tilly's pace. Tilly kept her eyes fixed on the beautiful Cornish coastline. She only ventured out of the village occasionally, mainly on her visits to Laura's but it wasn't the same taking in the scenery from the car. It was invigorating.

Even if her lungs felt like they were about to collapse.

'Phew!' She said as they turned out of the end of the lane and into the main road which led back into the village via the Penrock Hotel.

'Do you want to stop for a moment?' Winstone asked, now running backwards so he could face her.

Flipping heck, the man could look effortlessly cool even running backwards.

'I'm fine. I've got my mind set on the harbour, so my legs won't give up just yet.'

'I do that too! I give myself a goal in my head and work towards it when I'm running and as soon as I get near it, they feel like they're gonna give up on me.'

Tilly nodded and smiled, too short of breath to talk.

Winstone turned and fell into pace with her again. Thankfully the road began to decline, and her breathing became more comfortable.

'That's how I'm viewing everything from now on; working towards goals. I think that's what the running's about; it's easier to visualise and accomplish than my career is.' I still haven't figured out why I have this burden of guilt towards you and mum though, she silently added.

'Why are you so hell bent on this career of yours? Money isn't everything you know; it can't buy you happiness. Look at Ruby.'

'What does that mean?'

'She's got everything; she may have bought Hope Home off a lucrative divorce settlement, but she's worked really hard to achieve the rest. She's so well thought of within her profession. She wears designer clothes, has an expensive car, has the means to dine out whenever she likes, but she's not happy.'

In Tilly's mind's eye she could see Ruby smiling and laughing; she was the life and soul of the party, what made Winstone think she wasn't happy? Was it all a guise? Had she been suffering depression for longer than she'd let on?'

'What makes you say that though?' Tilly asked, as they passed the row of shops in the High Street. 'She's always happy and positive; she's got more energy at nearly seventy than I have at less than half her age.'

'She's lonely.'

Why did Winstone sound like someone speaking from experience?

'In what way? She lives in a nursing home; there's always someone to talk to.'

'No-one to share her life with though,' Winstone said, as they reached the Lobster Pot and turned onto the harbour.

Tilly slowed her pace and came to halt, leaning over and gripping her thighs for dear life. Winstone took her wrist and looked at her watch.

'Three point four kilometres in twenty-four minutes; not bad considering how steep that first third of the run is.'

He dropped her wrist and she felt suddenly bereft.

'So what time are you setting up today?' He asked, using the low wall, adjacent to the pub to stretch out on.

Tilly followed suit. 'Erm, as soon as I've showered, I guess.' Her mind wasn't thinking straight. Perhaps it was a lack of oxygen from running. 'Ruby's helping me again, just to set up, then I'm on my own after lunch which might be interesting.' She wasn't sure how she was going to serve food and make coffees at the same time, but it was day two of her little enterprise and there wasn't enough income yet to cover employing a spare pair of hands, so she would just have to learn to be quick and efficient. She'd served enough punters behind the bar in the Lobster now to know how to keep people occupied by chatting to them, so they didn't realise how long the wait was to get served.

'I'll come over after the lunchtime rush and give you a hand, if you want.'

'That's very kind of you.' Tilly bowed down to stretch and conceal her blush. Why was Winstone suddenly so keen to see her? Getting her up at the crack of dawn for a run, offering to come and help in his downtime *and* on a busy Saturday. There came the guilt creeping in again.

Maybe he likes you Tilly Henshaw? Maybe he wants to spend time with you?

'Is that a yes, then?'

She managed to stand upright again. 'That would be lovely, thank you.' There. That wasn't that hard. 'Can I ask you something?'

'Sure,' he said, stretching one arm up and over his back.

Tilly swallowed hard. 'If you think Ruby is unhappy, underneath, what can I do to make her feel better?'

Winstone released his arm and vigorously shrugged his shoulders. 'I don't think there's anything you can do. I think that's something only Archie can resolve.'

'Archie?!' Tilly exclaimed, loudly. Her voice echoed around the harbour.

'Yeah, don't you think she's holding a torch for him? Sounds like they've known each other for eons.' Winstone shrugged again. 'Perhaps she knew him before he married Phyllis, I guess; perhaps that's why her marriage didn't work out?'

Tilly's mind was racing now. Every time she spoke with Archie about Ruby, he was evasive. Elaine had said that Ruby was Archie and Phyllis' friend but what if Ruby had known Archie first? She lowered herself onto the wall.

'You ok?' Winstone said, sitting down next to Tilly and putting his arm around her.

She looked up at him, searching his eyes for answers but why would Winstone have answers to questions no-one in her family could answer.

'Ruby's really my grandmother.' She didn't know where her words were escaping from, but she had to vocalise what she was trying to piece together. 'That's why I came here, because I eventually found out. Mum told me. She's always refused to believe it, but Ruby says she gave Mum to Gran because Mum's real father didn't want to be involved.'

Winstone rubbed Tilly's back. 'Well, that can't be Archie then, can it? That man dotes on all of you! You'd think he was your real Grandad!'

'Precisely. What if he is?'

CHAPTER FORTY-

ONE

Elaine turned the sign on the bakery door over from 'open' to 'closed' and looked out of the window across the harbour. It was a busy, sunny, May Saturday afternoon and, outside, the village high street was teaming with tourists. Her eyes settled on Ruby, helping Tilly over at her new stall and a pang of guilt washed over her that she hadn't been to visit Mum all week. Instead her mind had been preoccupied with thoughts about Anthony and, this morning, had weighed heavily on the inevitable truth; she was going to have to tell Tilly.

'I think I might take Finn to the beach this afternoon, it's such a lovely day,' Emma said, standing alongside Elaine.

'Oh, definitely,' Elaine said, sounding more enthusiastic that she felt. She'd hated taking Tilly to Weston when she was a child; all that sand to clean off their feet and fresh clothes which she got instantly wet and required washing again as soon as they got home. Yuck.

'Tilly's doing well, isn't she?' Emma said, starting to clear the empty baskets out of the window.

'Yes, I have to concede that I was sceptical; I thought she'd at least ruffle Winstone's feathers, but he seems supportive, even though she must be in direct competition with him.'

'Yes, he was a bit resistant to start with, understandably, but I think he's come to see that those that don't want a sit-down meal at the pub are grabbing a bite to eat with Tilly, then venturing over to the Lobster for a drink, and Winstone makes much more profit out of alcohol than food.'

'I think he's sweet on Tilly; he called for her this morning to go for a run before she started work.'

Emma raised a playful eyebrow. 'Oh, did he now? I felt from the moment I saw them together that they're made for each other.'

Elaine popped the empty baskets behind the counter and headed to collect some more. 'Tilly's always been a bit unlucky in love,' Elaine bit her tongue to stop her putting Tilly down. She wanted to vent how stupid she'd been to ditch Simon. 'I'm glad she's focusing on her career.' Which was true, although what Elaine hoped Emma would interpret this to mean was *don't encourage them*.

Emma shrugged and looked out the window again. 'Well, perhaps cupid's got his arrow aimed at another couple for the moment.'

Elaine froze in the middle of taking the wax sheet out of the bottom of a basket, ready to chuck in the bin. Had Emma seen her with Anthony last night? Or someone else had seen his comforting embrace of her on the harbour?

'Who?' She asked as nonchalantly as she could muster.

'Ruby and Archie; look at them.' Emma signalled to the harbour where Archie had arrived with Hector on his lead and was making a fuss of helping Ruby put her cardigan on.

Elaine wasn't sure whether to be overcome with relief that Emma was not referring to her and Anthony, or more panic-stricken than she'd felt before.

'I think they make such a sweet, elderly couple.' Emma smiled, still watching out the window. 'He's such a gentleman; I love James, but he'd never make a fuss of me like that. He's too wrapped up in his own little, baking world.'

Elaine narrowed her eyes and watched Archie and Ruby, a hundred questions racing through her mind. He *was* being a gentleman and she was reciprocating, flirting with him almost, hooking her arm through his as they wandered off with ice creams in hand, just purchased from Tilly.

Exactly how long had that been going on?

***

'Are you sure you're going to be okay, darling? Your mind seems a little preoccupied today?' Ruby asked, as Tilly scooped honeycomb ice-cream onto the cone.

'I'll be fine. The lunchtime rush is over now.' Tilly smiled, handing Ruby her ice-cream. 'What are you having, Archie?'

'A ninety-niner for me thanks, love,' Archie said, pulling Hectors lead in as he had wandered off to torment the seagulls. 'Are you sure you can spare Ruby, love? I don't mind rolling my sleeves up and helping out, if you think you need another pair of hands?'

'I'll be fine.'

Archie handed over his tenner and eyed her sceptically.

'Thanks,' Tilly said, digging in the till for his change. 'What are you two up to, now?'

'Oh, just taking Hector for a walk.' Ruby took a lick of her ice cream. 'Mmmm, delicious!'

'Don't you need to get back to the home?' It was like a spot that you knew you shouldn't squeeze, because the consequence was a gigantic, sore and obvious mess once you'd popped it, but you couldn't resist having a little go anyway.

Ruby waved a dismissive hand. 'Oh, no, sweetie, Julie's in charge today. Anyway, I love being over here on the harbour with you in all the hustle and bustle!'

Tilly frowned but said nothing. In her peripheral vision she could see the silhouette of Elaine hurtling towards them.

'What's going on here, then?' Elaine said, rushing straight up and standing in between Ruby and Archie.

Archie looked as if he was about to jump out of his skin. 'There's nothing going on. We're just having an ice cream.'

A family of customers wandered over and started perusing her menu. Tilly shifted down to the hot food end of her shack and helped them to pick what to eat, then served it up, all the while trying to listen to the bickering going on between Archie, Ruby and Elaine.

'Could you all keep the noise down or you'll frighten away my customers!'

'I was just saying, Tilly, these two spend a lot of time together, don't you think?'

Tilly was tempted to agree but she had a lot more digging to do if she wanted to uncover her suspicions. Putting Archie and Ruby's guard up was not going to be the way to unearth the truth.

'They're retirees with lots of time of their hands; aren't they allowed to enjoy each other's company?'

'Quite right, Tilly, and if you don't mind, I think Hector would like this walk now so we'll finish our ice creams off over the headland. Thank you, see you later!' Archie waved with his free hand before hooking it through Ruby's arm and dragging her off, looking like she wasn't finished with their conversation.

Elaine drew herself into Tilly's stall and whispered over the counter. 'There's something going on there. Emma thinks so too.'

Tilly silently nodded, avoiding Elaine's gaze by focusing on cleaning the steaming wand on the barista machine.

'I should have thought of it before really,' Elaine continued, 'all this coming down here once Phyllis passed away. I expect Archie's lonely.'

Tilly wondered how long it would take Elaine to make the connections forging in her own mind.

'Would it matter if they were becoming close?'

Elaine kept her gaze fixed on Ruby and Archie as they strolled up over the headland. Eventually she turned to Tilly and surveyed her through narrowed eyes. 'I suppose not, but it all seems a bit secretive to me.'

'Hey, Mrs H! How's it going today Tilly?'

Both engrossed in conversation, neither had spied Winstone strolling over from the pub.

Elaine jumped on the spot. 'Oh, Winstone, you gave me a fright!'

'Sorry, Mrs H, just here to give your daughter a helping hand.' He was donning himself in a navy blue and white striped apron.

'It's been busy, but it's calmed down now; don't feel you need to help me if you've got stuff to sort out at the pub.' There it was; guilt. Feeling like an inconvenience, pushing him away. Here were the two people, stood in front of her, who Laura had tasked Tilly with questioning why she felt such a burden to them, and still she hadn't a clue.

'I wouldn't be here if I didn't want to,' he said, navigating his way along the front of the stall and in through the door at the end by the hot food. 'So, what were you guys deep in conversation about?' He asked whilst peering and poking about Tilly's new equipment.

'Oh, nothing much.' Tilly shot Elaine a warning look. After her conversation with Winstone about Archie and Ruby this morning, she didn't need to add fuel to

Elaine's fire. She wanted to find out the answers for herself.

'Was it you cosying up on the wall with the Doc?' Winstone winked, picking up a pair of tongs and twizzling them in his hand.

Elaine looked as red as the strawberries Tilly had out on the counter to make smoothies with. 'I, er, um…' Elaine sounded almost apoplectic, 'I don't know what you mean?'

'Okay,' Winstone said, still twizzling the tongs and grinning.

Tilly smiled, pleased to avoid any further conversation about Ruby and Archie and taking her straight to what she really wanted to ask her mum. 'Oh, come on mum, you can be honest; you've just accused Ruby and Archie of being secretive.'

'I, um, I'd best be getting back home, I haven't had any lunch yet,' Elaine blustered, pushing her handbag up onto her shoulder.

'Mum!' Tilly reached over the counter and grabbed Elaine's arm before she went rushing off. She looked her mum directly in the eyes. 'Are you okay?'

'*I'm fine!*' Elaine sounded sure of herself when Tilly was pretty sure she wasn't.

Tilly slid her hand down Elaine's forearm and took her hand. 'Look, I don't know why you were chatting to Doctor Dare, so if you're not coping—

'*Tilly*, I'm fine. It's not what you think.'

Which confirmed to Tilly it might be exactly what she'd suspected when Winstone told her. 'Look, Mum, you came here for a new start; perhaps this is it.' She smiled, squeezing Elaine's hand.

Elaine nodded, pulling her hand away from Tilly's grip. 'I'd best get back and have my lunch.' She smiled at Tilly, but her eyes looked sad. Quickly, she turned and scurried off up the harbour.

Tilly watched her go, deep in thought. Did the Doc and her mum have feelings for eacht other? How had she missed that? But, how else to explain an intimate moment, late at night, in the harbour. It wouldn't be best practice for a GP to have physical contact with a patient, would it? Except in a consulting room. Tilly smiled. Could this be it? Could this be what she'd always wanted for her mum; someone to care for her, look after her, love her? There was something comfortably familiar about Anthony Dare too; he had set her at ease from that first appointment *and* he'd believed in her.

'Have I upset your mum?' Winstone cut across her thoughts.

'No.' She laughed. 'You did me a favour by bringing it up, though; she had no way of denying it!'

'Do you think there's something going on between her and the Doc?'

'I really don't know,' she said, watching the outline of her mum, huddled over, scurrying up the hill to the lighthouse. And, for some unknown reason, the not knowing was troubling her the most.

CHAPTER FORTY-

TWO

'Do you think Elaine suspects something between us,' Ruby asked, her arm hooked through Archie's as they strolled up the headland, along the narrow coastal footpath toward Port Trillick.

'I fear she might,' Archie said, his head bent low.

Ruby was becoming increasingly frustrated with Archie. She had made it her raison d'etre to reunite them, but nothing was working. She organised their social life, called in on him unexpectedly, took him out for dinner. He always went along with it, like he wanted to be in her company, but there wasn't even a fizz or a spark of passion like they had once known. He'd even lost his flirtatious edge; something she had always loved about him.

She stopped walking and he halted in his tracks, finally looking up at her.

'Do you want to go back to Bristol?' She wasn't one for giving up, but she had a heart; she didn't like to see Archie suffering like this either. The entire situation was literally eating him up.

He looked out to sea, loosening off Hector's lead so he was free to roam the headland. He looked as if he was searching for answers in the gentle waves.

Finally, he shook his head. 'I can't, can I?'

'That doesn't mean you don't want to.'

He looked at her with pain in his eyes, a culmination of the years of living with the burden she had bestowed upon him.

He took her hand. 'I owe it to Elaine to tell her the truth. She's piecing together what's going on; we've hardly been concealed about our courting over the past few weeks.'

Ruby's heart fluttered; *courting*. Is that what he considered all these meals out and long romantic walks? Courting was positive, it suggested a future. She supressed a smile, seeing the anguish which still burned in his expression, and instead gave his hand a little squeeze.

'It's all my fault; I've left you with this burden all these years. I'll be here, by your side.' She risked a peck on his cheek, and he didn't flinch away. Her stomach flipped; it was such progress.

'It's not your fault. Maybe it wasn't handled right in the beginning; if you'd only told me Ruby, then things might have been different!' He was raising his voice now. His hand dropped away from hers.

Ruby's voice caught in the back of her throat. She wanted to say it wouldn't have changed anything but that wasn't true. Only she would never know if Archie would have chosen her, over Phyllis, just because she was having his baby and she would never have wanted to live like that.

'Don't you think I've been paying the price all these years too? I tried so hard to be a part of Elaine's life when she fell pregnant with Tilly; do you not think I could see the irony that the same circumstances have befallen her too?!' She was aware she was shouting but she was hurt. A moment ago, Archie was eluding to a future together. Now he was spurning her for a situation they were both responsible for.

'I think I'd better continue this walk on my own. Come along Hector.' He turned on his heel and carried on along the path, winding Hector's lead in, dragging the dog away from sniffing a patch of wild flowers.

'That's it, run away; don't deal with what's going on in front of your eyes!' She immediately regretted the words as soon as they escaped her mouth, but she couldn't help it. Archie was preventing them being together; guilt for his behaviour in the past.

He turned and started walking back towards her. 'Me running away? That's rich coming from you!'

They were both shouting now, and Ruby was aware that anyone walking on the higher path, which led to the tourist's car park, would be able to hear them, but she didn't dare take her accusing eyes off of Archie's glowering stare.

'Yes, that's right, I did run away. Because I would have had no job once British Aerospace knew about the baby and I'd brought shame on my family, so I'd have had nowhere to live. Lil was my only option to give Elaine at least a fighting chance in life. And, yes, perhaps in hindsight it was a bad decision but what other choice did I have?'

'You could have told me!' Archie roared.

'Why? You had a relationship with me, then you made it perfectly clear that you were betrothed to Phyllis back in Leeds and that you couldn't carry on seeing me! I lost my virginity to you Archie!' She prayed no-one was overhearing this conversation, but it needed to be said before Elaine found out for sure and they all had to deal with the fallout of that bombshell. 'I thought you loved me and that we were going to have a future together; I had no idea you already belonged to someone else, otherwise I wouldn't have gone anywhere near you!' She could see his eyes welling up with tears and she knew she was hurting him but if this was the time for home truths, then she was going to make damn well sure all of hers were heard. 'You say I ran away but only because I had no other choice. And as soon as I had made something of myself; money, a life, some purpose, I came back to my family to support them. I took Mum off Lil's hands and cared for her; I tried my hardest to support Elaine. Do you know I sent money every week to Lil and Stan? And when Tilly was born, I kept on sending it. Because they were *my* responsibility. In fact, they were *our* responsibility but instead of coming clean you chose to move your infertile wife next door and make her go through the pain of caring for *your family* from afar!'

'You bitch.'

Ruby gasped. She'd gone too far, said too much, but it had to be said. Archie needed to know he wasn't innocent in all of this.

'I've never stopped caring.' His voice was softer now; it had lost its angry edge. 'I made a mistake, a big mistake. I feel like I've wasted Phyllis' and your life all these years. I should've called it off with Phyllis, but her father was a powerful man; I didn't want to face the consequences. Yes, it was cowardly, but I was twenty years old and just making my way in the world. I should never have had my way with you and dumped you like that, but I panicked about what was going to happen; I was engaged to Phyllis. And I loved Phyllis, I always loved her.' The tears were brimming in his eyes now, making Ruby well-up too. 'But the months apart, our flirting in the office…' he trailed off and looked Ruby straight in the eye. 'I fell in love with you too Ruby.'

She nodded but said nothing, feeling she had said enough already. She had accepted the situation all these years because she knew Archie was a good and decent man. He'd just got caught between a rock and a hard place when she'd fallen pregnant with Elaine.

'If you'd told me you were pregnant, I would have called it off with Phyllis; you do know that, don't you?'

Silently, she nodded again, twiddling with the long heart pendant hanging from her neck. What she really wanted was him to envelope her in a big hug, but she didn't dare ask for fear of rejection.

'You'd better go for that walk on your own and clear your head,' she found herself saying, going against her physical desire.

'Won't you come with me?'

She wanted to but the harsh words they had just spoken prevented her from moving towards him.

'I think perhaps we both need to clear our heads and decide what it is we actually want. I've always loved you, Archie, you know that. Phyllis isn't here anymore and if you did fall in love with me once, I truly believe you can do it again. I believe that we would be stronger together and we could tell Elaine the truth and support each other through whatever fall out comes our way, but you need to be ready to give up your guilt where Phyllis is concerned.'

He nodded and looked out to sea again.

'Okay,' he said, looking back at her. 'I'll come over to the island tomorrow, okay?'

She nodded and tried to smile but her face just crumpled into tears. She waved and walked back down the hill towards Hope Cove, hoping beyond hope that their argument might be the beginning of the end; a happy end where her and Archie could end their days together, however long they both had left.

CHAPTER FORTY-

THREE

March 2017

Archie watched the daffodils in the garden dance in the breeze out of the spare bedroom window. Phyllis' hospital bed had been delivered yesterday and she had elected to move from their bedroom into the spare, where it was easier to get in and out of this new bed, which moved up and down, also propping her up or down flat without her having to move. It was as if she was accepting the end was near and preparing him for having to sleep alone for all eternity. Perhaps, if he was lucky, he might die soon of a broken heart.

He felt like it had already broken.

Phyllis' breathing became erratic, breaking his thoughts and forcing him to look at her lying so thin and lost in this alien bed.

She came to. 'Oh, hello,' she said. In all these years she'd never lost that comforting Yorkshire burr to her accent.

He smiled. 'I thought you were in pain for a moment.'

She rolled her eyes. 'No more than usual.' Her face contorted with pain as she tried sitting up.

'Here let me help you.' He tried to lift her without hurting her which was futile. Just touching her made her wince in pain. The breast cancer – which had been in remission for five years – had spread and was now into her lymph nodes and bones. The doctors had given her a year to live, eighteen months ago; they both reluctantly knew the end was near.

'Thanks, love,' she said, breathlessly.

'Shall I get you a cup of tea or some more Oramorph? You must be due some more by now.'

'In a minute,' she said, taking his hand. 'Let's just enjoy the peace and quiet together for five minutes, before another of our visitors arrives.'

He nodded, silently acknowledging what Phyllis meant. There was a steady flow of bodies in and out of the house these days. Carers had been coming three times a day since Phyllis had become bed bound a month ago. The community nurse came most days. Elaine called in at least twice a day and Tilly faithfully came every day, straight after work to ensure she got to see Phyllis while she was still awake and make Archie his supper. Archie didn't know what he'd have done without his daughter and granddaughter these past few months, even if they didn't know who they were to him.

'I'd like you to do me a favour.' She asked, resting her head back on the pillow.

'Oh?' He asked, sitting back down in the upright chair Phyllis used on good days when she could get out of bed.

'Yes, you're not going to like it, but I can't ask anyone else and I'm too frail to do it myself.'

Archie frowned as he looked down at his wife. She was still beautiful to him. Her dark hair had gone grey at the edges but not all over. She kept it in that pixie style, she'd had cut in the seventies; it suited her petite frame. Before the cancer had taken hold, she'd looked much younger than her sixty-seven years but now she looked jaundiced and sallow and aged. Cancer was such a cruel disease and he could not help but feel it should be him laid there in the bed; he deserved to die with such fate, not dear, kind, faithful Phyllis.

'Anything, for you.' He tried to smile but found his face faltering, trying his hardest not to cry.

'I want to dictate a letter to you which you have to promise you will send.' She looked at him with such penetrating eyes, full of meaning.

'To who?'

'Ruby.'

'Oh, Phyllis.' Archie raked his hand through his hair. 'Don't bring this up now, please love,' he pleaded.

'This is my final wish; it has to be this way.'

'But why?'

'Because I love you more than anything in this world.' Her eyes brimmed with tears. 'But I'm not long for this world either,' her voice faltered, 'and I want to know you'll be looked after. I know Elaine and Tilly will look after you, but they don't know the truth; Ruby does.'

'I don't need Ruby to look after me.'

Phyllis propped herself up by her elbows and fixed Archie with a defying stare. 'A very long time ago you wronged two women. You did right by me but, in doing so, you left Ruby with a broken heart and an estranged daughter. I always hoped that in my life time I would see that put right but as Elaine refuses to believe who Ruby is, it's never happened. I know Ruby still loves you Archie; I know she'll care for you.'

Archie dropped to his knees and took Phyllis' hands as he leant against the bed. 'I love you. I don't want you to go.'

'But I am going Archie and you have to carry on.'

'What will be the point?'

At that moment Hector stirred from his position at the foot of Phyllis' bed, where he had been curled up sleeping, stretched and padded his way up the bed to nudge both Archie's and Phyllis' hands.

'Hector needs you, see.' Phyllis smiled but Archie knew she was just putting on a brave face.

'I'm sorry,' Archie said. 'For everything.'

Phyllis looked down at him like a mother chiding its toddler. 'What are you sorry for?'

Archie looked at their hands, intertwined, like they had been for the past fifty years. 'My infidelity,' he whispered.

'Archie, how many times must we go over this? You were working down here, I was living in Leeds. It was our fathers who wanted us wed. We'd only been on a handful of dates before you took your apprenticeship; we barely knew each other! Ruby didn't set out to seduce you; you both just fell in love; I can see that.'

'How can you not be bitter or jealous after all these years?'

'You did the right thing, didn't you?'

Archie looked deep into Phyllis' eyes, truly wanting to believe what she was saying. 'The right thing would have been doing right by Elaine.'

Phyllis rested her head back on her pillows and laughed. 'Archie, my love, you didn't know of Elaine's existence! You'd called it off with Ruby before she even knew she'd caught with Elaine. The guilt you should hold is how you treated Ruby, not me or Elaine. She was the one you had your wicked way with then left in the lurch.'

Archie hung his head in shame. Perhaps Phyllis was right; perhaps he had been carrying this burden of guilt for half a decade for the wrong person.

Phyllis ruffled his hair. He looked up and smiled.

'Why do I still feel I did wrong by you though? I should never have let my feelings for Ruby go as far as they did.'

Phyllis shrugged and her face contorted in pain again. 'Shall I tell you something? I've never been able to tell you before.'

Archie's heart started hammering. Please God, don't say Phyllis had been keeping secrets from him all these years too?

'Go on.'

'You weren't the only one fooling around. I went to the pictures a few times with Harry Braithwaite whilst you were working hard down here in Bristol.'

Archie eyed her sceptically. 'You've made that up to make me feel better.'

Phyllis burst out laughing. 'Aye, I have but it's given me such a giggle, it was worth it!'

'It's not funny you know!' Archie said, dissolving into laughter himself.

'Well, it proves a point; you need to lighten up Archie Fairclough. The past is the past and we can't change that; it's only the future we have any influence over. Now go and make me a cup of tea and fetch a pen and paper so we can write this letter to Ruby before I fall asleep again.'

'All right,' Archie said, getting to his feet. He planted a kiss on Phyllis' forehead. 'I love you Phyllis Fairclough and I am so happy that you've been my wife these past fifty years.'

'I love you too and I wouldn't have changed anything for the world.'

CHAPTER FORTY-FOUR

21st March 2017
Dear Ruby,

The time has finally come to have 'the conversation'. The one we should have had years ago. Archie is writing this to you as I am too weak; the cancer has finally got the better of me, Ruby, and I am not long for this world. It is what it is; I accept that, but I must put my affairs in order and, sadly, you are one of those.

I want you to know, I don't blame you. I have told Archie, it's not your fault, it's his. You didn't know about me and I didn't know about you. What I do know is that we have both been in love with the same man for over five decades and I am lucky enough to have shared those with him while you have carried pain and suffering in your heart.

I know you are a good person, Ruby, as you have kept in touch ever since we moved here when Elaine was a tot. I know you've always financially supported Elaine and Tilly, Lil told me, and I know you have never forgotten the family you are estranged from. My one hope was to see you and Archie both reunited with Elaine and Tilly in my lifetime but that hasn't happened as Archie is an old fool – ARCHIE DISAGREES WITH THIS – and Elaine is stubborn; like her father!

Thank you, Ruby, for keeping yourself at arm's length and for letting me have my time with Archie. Now that time is coming to an end, I am writing to ask you one more favour. I have no right to ask you, but I know your steely determination for everything you do will mean that it will happen. Look after Archie for me, please. He may not want your help, I am certain he will not seek it out, but I know when I am gone, he will need support and I know you are the best person to give it to him.

Whatever happens from hereon in, you have my blessing.

All my love,
Phyllis x

Ruby folded the letter back up and looked out of the window through blurry eyes. She hadn't read it since the day she'd received it, it was too upsetting even if it did give Ruby a glimmer of hope where Archie was concerned.

It also explained why Archie still carried around such a burden of guilt.

'Hello?' Archie's voice called out. 'The door was open, so I let myself in.'

'Hello!' Ruby said, a rush of relief flooding through her that he had come. 'I was worried you weren't coming.'

He looked at his watch. 'The ferry was on time; I'm not late?'

She smiled, blinking back her tears. 'After yesterday, I half expected you to pack your things and head back to Bristol.'

He crossed the room to stand next to her and look out to sea. 'That would have been the cowardly way out. I've spent too many years thinking it's okay for Elaine not to go on knowing and things are coming to a head. I can't turn my back on you all now.'

Ruby looked down at the letter in her hand feeling confused. Was he staying for her or for Elaine?

He followed her gaze. 'Is that the letter Phyllis sent you?'

'Yes. I've never been able to bring myself to read it again after I received it. Do you know, under different circumstances, I think Phyllis and I could have been good friends?'

Archie looked out the window again. 'In a way, I think you were. Both respectful of the other. May I read it again, please?'

'Of course,' she said, handing it to him. 'I'll go and check on Lil.'

She left him deep in contemplation and crossed the living room to Lil's door. She knocked gently before popping her head around.

'What are you doing, our Lil?' She burst out laughing at the sight of Lil, in front of the mirror, in a long floral tea-dress, her bra over the top and her hair in rollers. Where had she unearthed a set of rollers from?

'I'm getting ready,' she said, applying some lipstick. It looked suspiciously like Ruby's favourite raspberry Chanel.

'Getting ready for what?' Tears of sadness turned into tears of joy of seeing Lil so happy and not stuck in a chair in her room or the sofa in the living room, just staring out of the window.

'We're going out to Colston Hall, remember?'

Ruby slammed her hand against her forehead. 'Silly me, I forgot! What are we going to see?' she asked, eager to play along with the memory playing out in Lil's mind.

'Herman's Hermits. Do you remember we saw them before you had your baby?'

Ruby clapped her hands together. 'We did! Even I'd forgotten that.'

'We'll go to Spencer's after and have a chippy tea.'

'Now, wouldn't that be wonderful?' Ruby said, wishing it was 1964 again and life was simpler. When she had only just met Archie. 'Now, let's sort your outfit out,' she said, crossing the bedroom and helping Lil out of her extra bra. She took the rollers out of Lil's hair. 'Where did you find these?'

'In the bottom of the wardrobe.'

Ruby had a flash back to doing their mother's hair. There were a few bits and bobs of Jean's which she'd never had the heart to throw away.

'There.' Standing next to Lil in the mirror she could see Lil was beaming with a bit of dribble escaping from the corner of her mouth.

'What's all the giggling going on in here?' Archie asked, appearing in the doorway.

'We're going to see Herman's Hermits, Archie,' Lil said, talking to him through the reflection in the mirror. 'Then we're going for a chippy supper, do you want to come?'

Archie frowned at Ruby in the mirror. She turned to look at him and smiled encouragingly.

'Oh, yes, that would be lovely,' he said, still looking confused.

Perhaps it was years of experience of dealing with dementia patients, or perhaps it was the fact Ruby liked living in a world of make believe, but she had always been able to go with the flow with people with dementia, where others, like Archie, struggled.

'Come on then, Lil.' Ruby put her arm through Lil's and guided her out of the bedroom and across to the sofa looking out over the gardens and the ocean beyond. 'Have a seat here a moment while Archie and I just have a quick chat.'

'Okay. Can you get me a cup of tea before we go?'

'Of course,' Ruby said, wandering over to the kitchen area. Archie followed. 'Quick? Haven't we got lots to discuss?' His eyes looked glazed glassy-eyed from reading Phyllis' letter.

Ruby shrugged. 'I've not seen her this good since she came here. I've got quiche and salad here for our lunch, but she keeps going on about chippy supper so why don't we go over to Rick Stein's fish and chip shop in Padstow for lunch? The tides going out now, I'll be able to drive the Land Rover across in half-an-hour or so.'

Archie looked panic stricken. 'But what about us?'

Ruby filled the kettle and set it down to boil. She took a deep breath. 'Is there an us?'

Archie rubbed his jawline and settled himself on one of the kitchen barstools.

'Yes.' He nodded. 'There is, I think, if you are prepared to help and support me.'

'Is that not what Phyllis asked in her letter?'

Archie laughed. 'She was so wise. I was angry when she made me write that letter but now, I can read it and smile.' He rested his elbows on the island and clasped his hands together. 'And cry, of course.'

Ruby rushed around the island and embraced him in a hug. She squeezed him tight and he kissed her cheek. 'I've never wanted to do anything else.'

'I know,' he said, still holding her. 'Phyllis was right; I have been the one to blame all these years. I blamed you for not telling me about the baby, but we had a relationship and then I left you to face the consequences alone. It was cowardly of me.'

Ruby broke away to face him. She rested her hands on his shoulders. 'Archie,' she said softly, 'if it helps you, I don't blame you either. I could have easily told you I was pregnant, but I didn't.'

'Out of interest, why didn't you?'

'Because we'd broken up and I was afraid that if I told you, you would have married me out of pity. I didn't want to be anyone's sloppy seconds. As you soon as you told me you were engaged to Phyllis, I knew there was no future for us; you'd chosen her.'

Archie looked down at his hands and twiddled his thumbs.

'I have behaved cowardly, haven't I?'

Ruby nodded. 'Perhaps, but now's your opportunity to put it right. We can tell Elaine together and if she doesn't like it, well, we'll wait for her to come around. At least we'll have each other.'

Archie got up from his stool, his tall frame towering above Ruby's petite one. He put his arms around her neck and slowly bent down to kiss her. His lips, which she had longed to touch hers again, for so many years, reciprocated yearningly.

Eventually they broke away.

'Thank you,' he said.

'For what?'

'For being patient with me, until I came to my senses. Phyllis is right; I am stubborn.'

'Where's my tea?' Lil called out.

Ruby rolled her eyes. 'Coming,' she called as the kettle whistled it was ready. Ruby kissed Archie again and disentangled herself from his arms, feeling like she was walking on air. *This* was finally happening; she was going to have a relationship with Archie Fairclough!

'Anyway, I don't know what you're worried about; Tilly will welcome the news with open arms.'

'You think? You don't think she'll be angry her real grandfather has been living next door all these years?'

'That girl doesn't have a negative bone in her body; she'll be delighted,' Ruby said, popping a couple of teabags into the pot.

'Elaine might take some coaxing. *Elaine darling, sit down a minute, I've got something to tell you before I rush off to work; I'm actually your father.*'

Ruby laughed. 'I'm not sure that's the best approach, I think you'd better have me there to hold your hand.'

'Music to my ears.' Archie laughed.

'Ruby,' Lil called.

'Yes?' Ruby replied, pouring hot water from the pot into the cups.

'Is Archie your baby's dad?'

Ruby looked at Archie who looked as panic stricken as she suddenly felt. 'Oh, shit,' she said, spilling tea all over the kitchen surface.

CHAPTER FORTY-

FIVE

Tilly knocked the door of Ruby's flat and entered with a loud, 'Helloooo!'

Silence.

With gentle footsteps she crossed the kitchen into the dining area. A loud snore alerted her attention to Gran, slumped over on Ruby's sofa, in the corner by the floor-to-ceiling windows.

'Gran,' Tilly called gently, stroking her shoulder. 'You okay?'

Gran jumped and came to. She looked up at Tilly, squinting through her glasses. She looked healthier than Tilly had seen her look in years, her glossy white hair in a new wavy perm, a flowery shirtdress, without bits of food and tea stains all down it and she even smelled of that pleasant, old lady scent of talcum powder and sweet perfume.

She carried on squinting up at Tilly. 'Oh, it's you!' she said, her face full of relief presumably for remembering who her granddaughter was. 'Here, come and sit down a minute our Tilly, I've got something to tell you.'

Tilly looked around the large, open plan apartment to check where Ruby was. It was her she had really come to see. To get some answers about what was really going on between her and Archie but looking at the sheer excitement on Gran's face made Tilly realise she'd left it too long since her last visit.

'Okay,' she said, slumping down onto the sofa next to her. She looked out the window and a light bulb moment pinged in her mind. Gran might have some answers! She was much better at remembering things in the past than what she'd had for breakfast; maybe she would remember when Archie came into their lives.

'I've got a secret.' Gran looked like a little school girl, rubbing her hands together, fidgeting to tell someone what she knew.

'Oh really?' Tilly wasn't sure what game Gran was playing today. Perhaps the schizophrenia was overriding the dementia.

'Gran, can I ask you something?'

Gran tutted. 'Oh, all right, as long as I can tell you my secret afterwards.'

Tilly nodded, playing along. 'Of course. I just wondered when you first met Archie.'

'Ohhh,' Gran clapped her hand over her mouth and looked into the middle distance. Tilly felt on edge. If Ruby came back any moment and found Tilly quizzing Gran about the past, she might not be too happy. 'Well, he moved in next door when our Elaine were a tot. Maybe nearly two?'

'Hmmm,' Tilly said. That confirmed what she'd always known, but no more.

'Can I tell you my secret now, it's about Archie,' Gran said, her body contorting with excitement.

'Go on,' said Tilly, leaning in.

Gran leaned in. 'He's Ruby's, baby's dad,' she whispered.

Bingo.

'Really?' Tilly tried to sound as astonished as she could muster. 'How did you find that out?'

'The other day, when Archie was here.' She frowned. 'Maybe it was yesterday.'

Tilly wasn't sure if Gran was making this up now. Surely if Gran knew the identity of her grandfather, then she had known all along.

'So, Archie is Elaine's real dad?'

Gran drew her breath in. 'No!' She shouted. 'Archie is Ruby's baby's dad, not Elaine's. Elaine's dad is Stan!'

'Now I'm confused.'

'Would you like me to explain?'

Tilly almost jumped out of her skin. She turned around to see Ruby standing there, looking pale, not her normal bright, enthusiastic self at all.

'Erm, if you don't mind,' Tilly replied.

'Come over to the kitchen with me,' she beckoned Tilly to follow. 'I'll just make a cup of coffee Lil, then we need to take you downstairs for Naughty Knitters.'

'What's that?' Tilly asked, following Ruby.

'Oh, just their weekly knitting group. It's become Naughty Knitters because the naughty residents are reluctant to get any knitting done.'

Tilly laughed but it came out as a nervous titter, apprehensive of the conversation she was about to have.

'Take a seat,' Ruby said, beckoning to the stools.

'How did you get onto the conversation about Archie?'

Tilly averted her eyes from Ruby's questioning stare. 'I asked her.'

'Well, that's a relief. I was worried she was proffering up her gossip to anyone who came through the door.'

Tilly risked making eye contact again, relieved Ruby wasn't cross. 'She wanted me to know she had a secret.'

'Oh,' Ruby's shoulders slumped as she spooned ground coffee into the cafetière. 'I think Archie might need to get on and tell Elaine before this information is half way around the village.'

'I think she has her suspicions. That's what brought me here today, together with Winstone's. Oh, and Emma's.'

'What?! Has half the village been discussing me and Archie?'

'In a nice way,' Tilly grimaced.

Ruby burst into a fit of giggles and Tilly felt a sense of relief.

'I'm not sure why I expected anything less from the residents of Hope Cove.'

'I think you may have offered yourselves up for discussion, waltzing around arm-in-arm all the time,' Tilly said, feeling a little more confident.

'I suppose so, but when you've waited fifty years for something that can finally be yours, you become a bit eager to just get on with it.'

'So, are you and Archie an item now?'

'Since yesterday. He's taken some persuading.'

'I bet,' said Tilly, marvelling at how Ruby – at nearly seventy – could get her man when Tilly still felt she was floundering with Winstone. 'I bet he didn't want to give up Phyllis' memory in a hurry.'

'If it wasn't for Phyllis, I don't think it would have happened even now.'

'How?'

'Long story short; Archie and I met at British Aerospace the year before your mother was born. Travel was expensive in those days, so he would stay in digs for up to four weeks at a time and only venture back to Leeds once a month. I didn't know he was engaged to Phyllis when we embarked on our relationship. I was only sixteen; I should have known better than to sleep with him out of wedlock, but you know.' She shrugged. 'Anyway, we did, you know—' she gesticulated to demonstrate the art of lovemaking, '—only a couple of times before he casually mentioned that he had a fiancée in Leeds who he would be marrying in a few months' time and he should never have taken advantage of me. I was heartbroken; I truly loved him, in fact, I'm not sure I've really ever loved another man, definitely not with the same love I have for Archie. But when I found out I was pregnant, I certainly wasn't going to tell him and face further rejection. Or, even worse, him offer to marry me out of duty and us both be trapped in a potentially loveless marriage. Abortion was still illegal then, so I took the only plausible way out, where I escaped with my dignity intact and Lil got to have the one thing it seemed her and Stan may never have; a baby.'

Tilly could feel her eyes welling up. 'Do you think something similar happened to Mum?' She was drawn back to her conversation with Laura; *pursue this only for you.* She'd buried the notion and focused on Laura's notion that she felt a lot of blame and guilt around Elaine and Winstone. It was awful to think that Elaine had made the same decision as Ruby and denied Tilly of a relationship with her own father all these years.

Ruby fixed Tilly with a meaningful stare. 'I don't know. As you know, I tried to get through to her, tried to make sure she didn't make the same mistakes I did, and make the father accountable, but she was adamant it was her business and I was not her mother. None of it was handled very well.'

'If you didn't want to make Archie accountable, why did you tell Archie where Gran and Grandad lived? I'm assuming you must have told them for Archie and Phyllis to move next door. Did Phyllis know who mum really was then?'

All these secrets and lies.

'Phyllis worked it out.' Ruby sighed. A happy sigh with smile and a wistful expression on her face. 'I said to Archie yesterday that under different circumstances, Phyllis and I could have been real friends, I know it.'

Tilly brought an image of cheery Phyllis to her mind, always at home after school, ready to offer Tilly a glass of milk and a biscuit from her tin. She'd been a proper Nana to Tilly; Gran had never been that interested.

'She was lovely. Both her and Archie were like grandparents to me, and all the time Archie really was; no wonder they cared so much about us.'

'Phyllis couldn't have children. In a way it's a shame I hadn't adopted your mum to them but,' she shrugged, 'hindsight is a wonderful thing and I doubt Phyllis would have been so welcoming about Archie's lovechild in 1966 when she still didn't know she would never be able to conceive.' Ruby busied herself with pouring the coffee.

Tilly frowned. 'But if Archie's known all these years, why hasn't he said anything? You could have told Mum years ago he was her dad and maybe all these years of misery and her being so depressed may never have happened.'

Ruby looked up with a remonstrative stare. 'You might not even be here.'

'Oh,' Tilly said, wondering what cosmic interference made all their lives entwine the way they did. It was lust of course. That and a willingness to jump into bed. Thank goodness contraception had prevented her from befalling the same fate and being a single mum with an estranged ex-partner.

'It wasn't my secret to tell; it's Archie's.'

'So, why hasn't he told anyone?'

'Well, that brings us back to the beginning of our conversation really,' Ruby said, handing Tilly a mug of coffee. 'He is too afraid and that's why we have been arguing so much.'

Tilly stopped mid-coffee-sip. 'Why? I think it's absolutely wonderful news! All these years, he's felt like a proper Grampy to me and now he finally is!'

Ruby beamed. 'I knew you'd say that. Your mother is another matter.'

'Do you think that's why Mum won't disclose the identity of my dad? Because she doesn't think it's her secret to tell. Does that mean he actually knows about my existence?'

'Would you be happy to know who he was?'

'I don't really know. I've spent most of my life pretending he didn't exist. I used to tell the other girls at school he worked on oil rigs to explain why he was so absent but by secondary school they knew I was lying. Then I just pretended he'd died before I was born.' It was always easier not to think about his existence, then she didn't need to worry about rejection. Another memory flashed to the forefront of her mind; different to the one she'd had talking to Winstone the other night, but certainly another one she'd buried deep at the back of her mind where it was unreachable to her conscious, most of the time. She really needed to move her next appointment forward with Laura. All this stuff, Mum behaving peculiarly, not Archie being her real grandad; it was making her feel unsettled. And, if she really admitted it, feeling unsettled is when she was most likely to go *off the rails* as Mum would put it and she couldn't afford to do that now, not with *Tilly's Kitchen* and friends, like Emma and Winstone, and family, like Ruby, who she really valued.

Was that why she'd behaved the way she had in the past? Because she didn't value Mum and Gran. It was all very unsettling.

'Oh, my darling,' Ruby said, circumnavigating the kitchen island to give Tilly a hug. 'If you want questions answering, you must keep asking the questions, even if Elaine doesn't like it.'

'Thank you,' Tilly said, nestling her head onto Ruby's chest, 'but I'm a bit afraid of the consequences. I'm not sure Mum would cope if I went onto find my father and have a relationship.'

There she went with the guilt, again.

CHAPTER FORTY-SIX

'This is awesome!' Tilly called over the roar of the engine as Winstone's car raced along the winding, narrow, Cornish lanes, vibrant, violet foxgloves swaying as it zoomed past. 'I'm glad I didn't bother drying my hair now!' She had run back from Ruby's over the beach and showered, when his knock had come at the door, inviting her out for lunch. After a morning of bombshells from Ruby and Gran, she was glad not to be left alone with her thoughts. Plus, it was Monday; her day off. She was allowed to let her hair down, once in a while, wasn't she?

Winstone briefly glanced at her behind his sunglasses, a massive grin spreading across his face, before he returned to concentrating on the road again. 'I'm glad you approve.'

'I didn't realise your Maserati was a convertible.'

'There's lots you don't know about me,' he said, signalling and turning off the lane. The car rumbled over a cattle grid.

'Oh, wow,' Tilly said as the landscape sprawled out in all directions, with rows upon rows of vines in fields, leading down to a farm holding and the Camel estuary beyond. 'Is this a vineyard?'

'Correct, but don't panic, we'll have more than a liquid lunch.'

'I've never been to a vineyard,' Tilly said, looking in all directions as the car slowly descended down the dusty gravel lane into the Camel valley.

'A chalet girl, a cruise line entertainer, now a restauranteur and never been to a vineyard?'

Tilly playfully punched him on the arm, 'Oi!'

'I'm teasing.'

He pulled the car up in the car park alongside a few other expensive looking motors. 'Is it pricey here?' Tilly whispered.

Winstone raised an eyebrow. 'What if it is, I'm paying?'

They were greeted by the Matrèdi and seated on the terrace overlooking more vineyards and the estuary at a table covered in a crisp white tablecloth and expensive, swanky looking cutlery. The waiter ensured Tilly was comfortably seated with her menu before seating Winstone.

Tilly let out a low whistle. 'This place *is* posh.'

'It's Ruby's favourite.'

'Why doesn't that surprise me? How come you know that?'

'As I said, there's a lot you don't know about me,' he winked.

Tilly felt a bit like a fish which Winstone was out to catch. Part of her was flattered, if that was the case, and part of her – the *old* Tilly – would have willingly reciprocated. But new Tilly knew not to go diving in head first, even if old Tilly felt like was starting to lose it a bit and losing herself, getting drunk here with Winstone and possibly finding her way back to his place later, would not solve her problems. Behaving like that was a symptom of her problems; she realised that now. She really couldn't wait for her next appointment with Laura. Some many thoughts were crashing around in her head and amongst all of them were horrible ones beginning to resurface. Mum lying lifeless in her bed, flashed about with that feeling of being drowned, desperate to come up for air but they wouldn't let her.

'Shall we share the lobster?' He said, perusing the menu. 'A bottle of their sparkling wine will go down nicely with it.'

'Pardon?' Tilly refocused, glad to be rescued from her thoughts by Winstone. She registered what he'd just suggested and her eyebrows shot-up. 'You're driving!'

He shrugged. 'We can always get a taxi home.'

Tilly eyed him warily. 'So, have you dined here with Ruby?' She didn't know why she kept bringing the conversation back around to Ruby. Perhaps it was safe ground, away from the thoughts being fired off like canons in her head.

'A few times. Ruby's a genuine friend; she was a great help to me when I first moved here.'

'Really?'

'Excuse, Monsieur, may I take your drinks order?' The waiter interrupted.

Tilly inwardly groaned. As much as her brain felt overloaded and addled at the moment, her curiosity about Winstone was winning out; he was like an enigma to her, he so rarely opened up.

'Thanks, a bottle of your 2016 dry, sparkling white and some still water, would be great thanks,' said Winstone.

'Of course,' said the waiter, formally dressed in a suit and tie. 'And are you ready to order your meal or shall I give you a few more moments?'

Please order so we can get back to our conversation.

'Shall we get something to share?'

Desperate to get back to their conversation, Tilly eagerly nodded.

'Great, the sharing platter to start then please and we'll share the lobster with a side of green salad and fries please.'

The waiter, writing furiously, dotted his biro onto the pad, before waving his hand in a flourish. 'Coming up,' he said, efficiently disappearing as quickly as he had arrived.

'So, what was it like for you, when you first moved here?' Tilly asked, eager to go back to talking about Winstone's mysterious past.

Winstone's mouth opened, but no words for forthcoming. As if he was trying to formulate what he really wanted to say, in his head. 'It's complicated. I came to Cornwall to escape.'

Tilly scowled. 'I know that feeling,' she said. 'I thought coming here would solve all my problems, not create new ones.'

'Oh?' Winstone sounded genuinely concerned.

Tilly shook her head and her now dry, frizzy hair, angrily swept over her shoulders. 'You first. What were you escaping?' Tilly recalled the conversation with Emma when she'd first started cookery classes. Tilly didn't want to let on she knew; she didn't want Winstone thinking she was a gossip.

Winstone pursed his lips together and looked out over the valley where row upon row of vines spread down the Camel estuary in the distance. 'Someone,' he said, not meeting Tilly's gaze. 'A special someone; my girlfriend.'

Tilly nodded and looked down at the empty plate in front of her, a crisp, white napkin resting on top, waiting to be used.

'I'll guess by your silence, you already know she died.'

Tilly kept staring at the napkin, unable to reach his gaze. She was conscious the that the guilt she was feeling now was different to before. She felt guilty for being alive when Winstone's girlfriend wasn't.

She risked a glance up at him. 'Emma told me.'

Solemnly, he nodded, his eyes looking anguished; something she'd never seen reflected in them before.

'I'm sorry,' she said, softly, not sure what else to say. She was the greedy bitch who'd ditched her fiancé to runaway to Hope Cove. Not because she'd lost him and didn't know how she'd ever live without him again.

Winstone sighed and stretched his arms up, behind his neck. 'Don't be. I've carried enough guilt for years; it was Laura who eventually made me see things differently. I felt all my actions led to the consequence of Tory dying but, overtime, I see I couldn't be responsible; we are all responsible for ourselves, our own actions, but we only see that when we're strong enough.'

A stabbing pain surged through Tilly's stomach. She really hoped the waiter would hurry up with some water, she felt like she was going to be sick. That's exactly how Tilly felt about Elaine; that it was her actions which led Elaine to being anxious and depressed. That was where the guilt came from!

Tilly frowned, trying to keep in the moment and not worry about her Mum. 'Why did you feel so responsible?' Would it help her answer why she felt the way she did? Behaved the way she did.

Winstone sighed again, keeping his stare directed at Tilly. 'She took her own life, Tilly.'

Tears welled in Tilly's eyes. She picked up the napkin and placed it to her mouth, to keep in any escaping sick, from the bile she could feel rising in her throat. 'Excuse me,' she mumbled through the napkin, standing up and rushing towards the main house in search of the bathroom. Poor Winstone would think it was empathy for his situation which was making her feel this way. But it wasn't. Sadly, it was selfish pity. And the realisation that it wasn't her fault that she'd behaved the way she had for the past twenty years, but because she'd been made to believe it was.

She really needed to see Laura.

CHAPTER FORTY-

SEVEN

1998

'I'm home!' Tilly called out, shutting the back door behind her. She dumped the Spice Girls new single, she'd just been down into the city centre to buy, on the kitchen side and reached into the larder for some squash. 'It's blistering out there,' she called out, pouring the squash into a glass and screwing the top back on. She frowned and peered through the door into the living room.

Silence.

Strange; she couldn't even hear the hubbub from Gran's TV. She filled the glass with water, necked it down and wiped her mouth with the back of her hand. Grabbing the little plastic bag with her new tape in it, she wandered through to the living room. There was a note on the table in Grandad's spirally writing.

Tilly,
I've taken your Gran to Weston for the day, as the weather's
so nice. Your mum should be home by three-thirty. Phyllis
says to go and see her if you're hungry.
Love Grandad X.

Tilly smiled to herself as she put the note back on the table. Gran and Grandad were meant to be looking after her in the six-weeks-holidays – well, Grandad anyway; Gran could barely manage herself these days; she didn't know what day of the week it was, let alone if Tilly should be at school or not – while Mum still carried on with her shifts at the Co-Op. Tilly smiled to herself at the thought of putting her new tape on at full blast with no Mum or Grandad to complain about the noise; bliss. If Mum came home before Gran and Grandad, there might be time to bring up her Dad again. She'd tried a couple of days ago, in the kitchen, when Mum was preparing tea, but she'd got the usual, stony faced, silent treatment with a generous helping of, *you don't understand, Tilly, what sort of can of worms that would open. It's better to let sleeping dogs lie.* Better for who? Tilly was fed-up with it. The girls at school were getting worse. At primary school it had been teasing about not having a dad. In Year Seven, she'd lied to the new girls in her tutor and said her dad worked on the oil rigs – who knew, maybe he did? If she ever got to find him – but by Year Eight, they'd found out she was lying over the past year and, really, she lived with her mum and grandparents, and, by Year Nine, it got really bad. Ripping her school jumper, pulling her bag, writing *Tilly Henshaw is a bastard* on the toilet walls. There was one girl in particular, Vicki Rust, who liked to pick on Tilly for not having a dad and the fact they lived with Gran and Grandad. Secretly, Tilly felt it was because she was living in similar circumstances – or worse, foster care even – but she was so secretive about her home life and instead had got the other girls in Tilly's tutor on board that Tilly was public enemy number for being so sad. It was all so pathetic, and it made Tilly soooo angry, but what could she do? After them flushing her head down the toilet at the end of last term, she *really* wasn't looking forward to going back to school in

September, but who could she tell? Who could she explain it all to? Archie and Phyllis, perhaps, but they didn't need to be burdened with her problems. There was certainly no point in telling Mum, either; she was just as likely to say it was Tilly's fault and what had she done to provoke the Vicki Rust and her crones in the first place.

Oh, well, there was another three weeks of the summer holidays before she needed to worry about that. In the meantime, she'd file those vile bullies to the back of her mind along with thoughts of when Mum made onion, liver and mashed potato for tea, *bleugh*. She made her way to the other end of the living room, heading for her bedroom at the end of the hall, which used to be Mum's, until Gran and Grandad converted had the loft into a third bedroom. Mum's door was slightly ajar, which was odd. She *always* left it shut, with strict instructions for it not to be opened in her absence. Many a time, Tilly had contemplated having a snoop, seeing if she could find any clues to who her dad might be but the fear of Mum coming down on her like a tonne of bricks always prevented her. Still, seeing it was ajar, it wouldn't hurt to take a quick peek would it?

Tilly gently pushed the door with her index finger and peered into Mum's room. Her stomach clenched as the image on Mum's bed embedded itself into her eyes. Mum was lying there, eyes open wide, vomit coming out of her mouth in pools on her precious, white linen. Tilly dropped her little plastic bag, her hands shaking. 'Mum?' her voice was so wobbly, it sounded like she was going to cry. 'Are you poorly?' She took a tentative step into the room, scared of whether Mum was alive, equally scared of being told off for being in her room. 'Mum,' she said, still walking so tentatively towards her mum, bile rising in the throat at the smell of sick. Mum's eyes were so vacant. Like she wasn't there.

Please don't be dead, please don't be dead.

Hand trembling, Tilly reached out to touch Elaine's neck. It was cold. 'Oh, God, Mum! What's happened?' she cried, her initially anxiety giving way to sheer panic. She pressed her fingers harder into Mum's neck. There was a pulse! What to do, what to do? She looked around the room as if it was going to give her some answers. Her eyes settled on the bedside table. There were at least six bottles of empty pills.

'Oh, heck!' What to do? What to do?

Think Tilly, think!

It wasn't a sickness bug; it was a suicide attempt. Why would Mum want to leave her?

'There's no time to think about that now!' Tilly shouted to no-one but the bedroom walls. 'Mum!' she shouted at Elaine as she shook her shoulders. 'Come back, Mum! I need you!'

Elaine remained limp and lifeless, in her Snoopy nightdress, on the bed.

As quick as a flash, she moved Mum's fragile body into the best recovery position she could attempt – at least she had been paying attention that day at school – and ran into the hall where the telephone was kept on its little table.

Trying to steady her finger as much as possible, she punched out 999.

'Hello, which service do you require?'

'Ambulance, please!' She could hardly speak; her breathing was so erratic. She longed to run next door to Archie and Phyllis and ask them to sort this horrible, terrible mess out, but she knew there wasn't time.

The phone went dead, and Tilly's heart almost leapt out of its chest.

'Hello, can I take your name please?'

'Yes, um, it's Tilly Henshaw, oh!' She broke into a series of sobs. How was this happening?

'Okay, Tilly, it's okay, my names' Gina, how can I help you?'

'It's my mum, she's unconscious, with her eyes open. She's got a pulse, but she's cold and lying on the bed with sick everywhere and I can't get her to wake up. There's lots of empty pill bottles on her bedside table too.'

'Right, what's your address?' Gina asked.

Tilly gave it, feeling like her body was disengaging from her brain. Like she was floating above this surreal situation. Gina told her to open the front door and go and talk to Elaine, keep talking to her, until the paramedics arrived.

Tilly did what she was told, like she always did. Stepping over her new Spice Girls tape, she made her way back to her mum, sitting down on the bed, stroking her hair, holding her hand, squeezing it, telling her it was all going to be okay; the ambulance would be here soon.

Tears silently slid down Tilly's face. It was all her fault. She should never have brought up the subject of her dad. She knew that now; it was all too much for Mum to bear.

CHAPTER FORTY-

EIGHT

'So, you were right,' Tilly said, dabbing the corners of her eyes with one of the copious amounts of tissues she'd used in her session so far, 'I did have trauma around the time I was diagnosed with ADHD.' Tilly sniffed.

Laura had made her wait the three days until her next appointment. Tilly had to compartmentalise the time between her lunch with Winstone on Monday, when all her memories had coming flooding back to her, to this Thursday morning session. With no *Tilly's Kitchen* to run until lunchtime today, there had been a lot of hours — sixty-eight to be precise — until she could let all pent-up frustration, fear and anxieties out at Laura. Funnily enough, the hour was flying by today.

'It was lunch with Winstone which made me realise. What he had experienced with Tory. I found myself almost jealous that he could admit what had happened when I've buried the stuff about Mum, and about those bitches at school, all these years.'

'About Winstone—'

Tilly raised her hand up. 'Look, I know you can't discuss him with me; I know he's a client of yours and after my CBT finished, I can't see you again, because he was your client first—' Tilly could feel her speech speeding up. '—but this isn't really about Winstone; just what he told me has triggered how I'm feeling.'

Laura nodded. Silence filled the room. Tilly was conscious of the clock ticking on and an increasing feeling of panic that she might not get the resolution she so desperately wanted in today's session.

'That's a massive thing to happen to fourteen-year-old Tilly, don't you think? Have to say her mum's life. Have to supress her feelings, how she felt about her mum almost leaving her forever. Not to be able to tell anyone she was being bullied. And, perhaps worst of all, have to supress her curiosity as to who her biological father was. That is a one heck of a challenge for a fourteen-year-old.'

Tear silently flooded down Tilly's cheeks again. *Yes, it was!* She wanted to scream. 'Why did you talk about me in the third person then?' she asked.

Laura crossed her legs, as if biding time to get her answer straight. 'Because you are not that Tilly anymore, are you? That Tilly is still part of you, but she was a child then and I think she needed protecting. And, I wonder if, perhaps, the Tilly sitting opposite me today has been doing that for the past two decades? I wonder if she's been protecting young Tilly by trying to forget the awful things that she saw, that she experienced by the hands of her bullies and the fact she does have a father out there somewhere.'

'Oh!' Tilly let out a little sob. 'You are so right; that's exactly what I've been doing, but not just to protect me but protect Mum and her feelings too.'

'Are your Mum's feelings more important than yours?'

Tilly shook her head and dabbed her eyes. 'I don't know. I feel like they should be, but I guess that's why you asked me to analyse why I always feel so guilty where Mum's concerned, why I always feel a burden.'

Laura nodded and pressed her lips together. More silence. The ticking of the clock was so unbearable, but Tilly didn't know what to say really, the truth just hurt so much.

'Perhaps, when she tried to take her life, that's when you began to feel a burden? That if you annoyed her too much, she might try to do it again?'

'Oh, yes…' Tilly broke into a cacophony of sobs. 'That is, it! That's exactly how it feels! Is that why I've been such a headcase all these years? Because I've not dealt with my shit and I've allowed it to come out in other ways?' She started sobbing uncontrollably again.

Laura waited for her crying to subside. 'I think only you know the answer to that, Tilly.'

Tilly nodded. She knew. She knew why she'd run away on the cruise ships now, spent money she didn't have, always ended up back at home, feeling a failure and a nuisance to Mum; because she was trying to escape from the feeling of being a burden to Mum and attempting to fill the big hole that was the question mark over who her dad really was.

'What does drive someone to take their own life?' Tilly asked, unsure of why she was expecting Laura to have the answer.

'In my experience, there are so many different reasons that it's difficult to tell what brings an individual to that conclusion. But, I do feel that with many of my clients that have experienced even the thought of taking their own life, even if they haven't acted upon it, is because they feel there's no other solution; there's no way they can cope, continuing with the emotions they are feeling. They can't see light at the end of the tunnel; they cannot imagine a future which is bearable, let alone bright or positive.'

'Do you ever think I'll be in a position like Winstone?'

'Tilly, I—'

'I know you said we can't talk about him but, what I mean is, will I ever be normal again? He said he's finally able to look beyond what happened with Tory, to a future. I think he likes me, and I think I like him, but my brain is so fuddled at the moment, so jumbled with thoughts, I don't have the head space for him.'

Laura nodded but said nothing.

'I've just answered my own question, haven't I?' Tilly managed a rue smile.

Laura simply nodded again.

'I need to focus on my immediate problems first, don't I? Then perhaps I can fully commit to Winstone.'

A glimmer of a smile twitched at Laura's lips.

'So, what do I do? Deal with my behaviour or deal with what's causing it?'

Laura pressed her lips together. 'I think you already know the answer to that, Tilly.'

Tilly nodded gravely. 'Mum's not going to like it though.'

Laura held Tilly's gaze as they both took in the enormity of what Tilly needed to do, the thing she had been putting off for twenty years because it was too unbearable for Elaine to deal with. But, Tilly contemplated as the minute hand ticked away to the end of the session, Tilly had feelings too and it really was time to start putting her own feelings above those of her mum, even it would be painful for both them.

She needed to know her father was. She wanted to know. It was the missing piece of her jigsaw.

CHAPTER FORTY-NINE

'Hello Mum!' Elaine said, a little too enthusiastically as she entered the drawing room at Hope Home. A table had been set up, in the large bay window, with a gaggle of elderly women sitting around it, all painting – with what looked like cotton ear buds – whilst the sun shone down over the view of Hope Cove through the window.

Lil turned around. 'Oh, it's you,' she said, returning to her painting.

Elaine felt almost crushed. The woman who had depended on her for the past decade, as her health had deteriorated, was now sitting at a table full of women full of independence.

Julie, the Home Manager, smiled her normal warm and welcoming smile at Elaine. 'Want to join in?'

'Oh, I—'

'Oh, come on Laney,' Lil said, still concentrating on the paint and card in front of her. 'I need to tell you all about our Ruby's baby.'

Elaine rolled her eyes. For a second there she thought Lil's dementia had seriously improved. She was sitting, carrying out a relatively dexterous task and for once, sounded completely compos mentis.

Elaine walked up to Lil's chair. '*I am* Ruby's baby, remember?'

'Oh, we've heard all about Ruby's baby.' Julie chuckled. She lowered her voice. 'I think Lil thinks it's arriving any day.'

'Yes, and you'll never guess who the dad is!' Lil looked like a little school girl, desperate to spill the beans.

'Oh, go on, Lil, tell us who it is today.' Julie laughed.

Elaine watched all the women stop dot painting their flowers to listen to Lil's exciting gossip. Elaine's heart was almost in her mouth, blood thudding through her ears. She might actually find out who her father was.

'Who's who,' Ruby's voice commanded. Elaine turned to watch her float into the room in a pair of cream, wide-leg trousers, with a pink camisole and a dove grey waterfall cardigan. She came to a halt by Elaine with a waft of Channel No5.

Why had this woman, this dazzlingly glamorous and capable woman, abandoned her?

'Lil was about to spill the beans on who your baby's father is today,' said Julie.

Ruby laughed awkwardly. 'Ha, yesterday it was Elvis Presley.'

All the ladies around the table laughed.

'Elaine, darling, I'm glad you're here; I've got something to ask you.'

'Oh?'

'Shall we go and have coffee in my office?'

Elaine looked at Lil who'd returned to her dotty flower painting. 'Okay,' she said, reluctantly conceding that the moment of mental clarity Lil was having, had passed.

Ruby glided in her swishy trousers out of the room and Elaine followed, feeling rather dowdy in the new denim skirt she had bought which, for once, was above the knee.

'Can I get you a coffee?' Ruby asked, flicking on the posh coffee machine in her office.

Elaine was about to say 'no' but something at the back of her mind asked, *why not*? She'd accepted Ruby was her mother; wasn't it about time she finally got to know her?

Plus, she had more pressing matters to discuss…

Sitting down in one of the chairs opposite Ruby's desk, Elaine looked out of the window at the view over the gardens and across the coastline towards Newquay.

'I don't know how you get any work done with a view like that.' She sighed. Wouldn't it be wonderful to work somewhere where you were at one with nature? It was as if you could see every element that the world was from, in one view. It was relaxing. All of her recent, jittery nerves, calmed. She loved working in the bakery and, having given up her job in the Co-Op so long ago, she'd forgotten how much she missed that daily interaction with people. A simple chat about the weather or an old lady's forthcoming operation for her varicose veins, made all the difference in keeping her sane.

Which essentially meant it stopped her obsessing about the whole Anthony-Tilly situation.

'Lil's making real progress, don't you think?' Ruby said, over the noise of the coffee machine.

Elaine smiled. 'She really is.' She marvelled at the fact that a couple of months ago, when she'd arrived here, she would have been incensed that Ruby had managed to achieve what she hadn't with Lil. If it wasn't for the whole avoiding Anthony situation, she had a feeling she could be very happy in Hope Cove. She'd missed the review appointment he'd made for her and now had his receptionist chasing her pretty much every other day to rebook. Every time the bakery door chimed, she held her breath that it wasn't him, come looking for her. He wanted a relationship with Tilly; that situation wasn't going to go away forever, however much she attempted to avoid it.

Her eyes fell upon a photo of Nana Jean and Grandad Bob, taking pride of place under an ornate Art Deco lamp on Ruby's desk.

She picked it up. 'You keep this, even though they treated you so badly?'

Ruby brought the steaming cups and saucers over, sitting down in her office chair, opposite Elaine.

'It's funny but that same photo caught Tilly's eye the first time she came to see me. They're still my parents,' she said, setting the cups down. 'Times were different back then. I shamed my father; he was born in 1920 and brought up in a different world to the one where I got pregnant in the sixties. If he hadn't had a heart attack when he did, he certainly would have done with the way we all live our lives today.'

Elaine shook her head. 'It's madness, isn't it? There's no shame in bringing up a baby on your own.'

Ruby raised an eyebrow. 'Not now, no.'

Elaine nodded, knowing what she was getting at. 'I know; it wasn't much better in the early eighties when I had Tilly. I hate to concede it, but you were right; I should have told the father. I should have taken your help when you offered it too.' What she would give to ask for her real mother's help now, too. But she was too proud to really admit that to herself, let alone Ruby.

Ruby smiled. Her sparkly blue eyes glistened like jewels. 'Hindsight is a wonderful thing, don't you think?'

This was her opportunity to ask what she had really come to ask, while Ruby's guard was down. Something which had been nagging at the back of her mind, occasionally overtaking the obsessing over whether Anthony would press for her to tell Tilly. 'Are you and Archie an item now?'

Ruby laughed, setting her coffee cup down and pushing her blonde curls away from her face. 'Yes, I guess we are, if that's what you young folk call it these days.'

'I have to say, I'm very surprised. I thought he would still consider himself married to Phyllis, even in death.'

If Ruby was shocked at Elaine's directness, she didn't show it.

'How long have you and Archie known each other, exactly?' Elaine continued.

'Oh, a long time.' She leaned forward and rested her arms on her desk. 'He was my go-between.'

Elaine frowned. 'Go between?'

'Stan was too proud to take money for your upbringing, but I was determined to contribute, so Archie smuggled envelopes of money I sent, every payday, to Lil.'

Elaine suddenly felt sick. This wasn't the answer she'd been expecting at all. Ruby had kept in touch all these years because she cared. Not because of the guilt of abandoning her.

Ruby studied Elaine's face. 'You do know that if the circumstances had been different, I would have kept you?'

Elaine nodded, feeling for the first time in her life that she finally understood the situation.

'When you had Tilly, I upped the contributions, but I had a sneaky suspicion Lil wasn't passing my contributions on. Archie discovered her love of the gee-gees—'

'Gee-gees?'

'Yes, betting on racehorses. She was obsessed with it. I think Stan was turning a blind eye to it all. I suspect it was another form of her schizophrenia, but the money I was sending was disposable cash to her; it wasn't affecting their household budget, so Archie took matters into his own hands. He started buying the things you needed for Tilly—'

'Ugh! The Silvercross pram?'

Ruby nodded. 'It was the only way to see you got what you needed.'

'But why? Why would Archie and Phyllis get involved?' She scrutinised Ruby's face, hoping she would give something away.

Ruby shrugged. 'Because they cared about you too.'

'And my father? He didn't care enough to be involved?'

Ruby shrugged again. 'I've told you before, I wasn't in a position to tell the father.'

'And you're not prepared to tell me now?'

'Have you told Tilly who her father is?'

'Goddamit, Ruby, you are so frustrating! Every time you throw that back at me!'

Whatever Ruby was feeling on the inside, she was showing no emotion on the outside.

'We both have our reasons. We must respect each other for that.'

Elaine nodded, blinking back tears at drawing a blank again. The problem was that until she was ready to admit Anthony's identity to Tilly, she couldn't very well push the matter of her own father's identity.

'I've been thinking about you a lot, you know,' Ruby said as if drawing a metaphorical full-stop on their disagreement.

'Oh?'

'You gave up a promising career in nursing to have Tilly and never went back to it.'

'How do you know all these things?'

'I told you,' Ruby winked, 'Archie was my go-between.'

'I regret it, but you can't change the past.'

'But, you can change the future. I know you've got your job at the bakery, but I'd be happy for you to come and work here. You could enrol at college, in Wadebridge, for September. I know you've had your own experiences with mental health, so you'd certainly have empathy with some of the residents here.'

Elaine beamed, like a child being told by her mother she was actually good at something. Then she realised that was exactly what was happening.

'Do you really think so?'

Ruby nodded. 'I do, plus one day all of this will be yours so it would be beneficial for you to learn the ropes.'

Elaine looked around the office, out of the view she found so relaxing and then back at Ruby. 'All mine?'

'Well, who else am I going to leave it all to?'

'I could run this place?' Elaine whispered, marvelling that she wasn't hyperventilating at the thought of all that responsibility.

'Yes, and for what it's worth, I think you could do an excellent job. Will you think about it?'

'I certainly will, thank you,' she said, taking a sip of her coffee. She may still not know the real identity of her father and she may have a massive hurdle to overcome where Tilly and Anthony were concerned but, for now, she was coming away from her morning with Ruby with something much more valuable than any of that; a future.

CHAPTER FIFTY

With a lull in customers, Tilly took a moment to stare out to sea and watch the shimmering sunlight catch on the calm waves out into the Atlantic. She sighed. What she would give to sail away today. Only, she had come to Hope Cove to escape her problems and all they'd done was catch her up so sailing away wasn't exactly going to help her, was it? She'd done that on the cruise ships and look where that had left her; broke. Perhaps not just financially but mentally too. Her mind cast back to the day she had left Bristol for Hope Cove, when she and Elaine had argued, and Elaine had accused her of going *off the rails*. She realised now, it was Elaine that had derailed her in the first place by attempting to take her own life, to leave her. Was that what she'd been running away from all her life? That memory? Or the fear that at any time, Elaine might attempt to leave her again? Perhaps that's why she always ran away. Before Elaine had the opportunity to try and leave Tilly again. Either way, there was no running away this time; she was just going to have to face this, whatever the consequences. She was stuck in ever decreasing circles until she broke the cycle and could move forward. She was going to have to ask Elaine about her real dad.

'Quiet today is it, Tilly?'

'Hmmm?' Shaking herself from her thoughts, Tilly looked down to see her mother standing on the harbour. 'Um, not really, I've been run off my feet up until now.' It was coming up to two o'clock when the number of customers usually dropped off, but it was the Friday of Whitsun Bank Holiday weekend and the beginning of half-term which meant there had been more customers than usual.

'Oh, right, well, you'll never guess what?!'

Tilly looked blankly at the woman, formerly known as her mother, who appeared to have undergone a total transformation, wearing new clothes and make-up. Was now perhaps a good time to ask? Elaine couldn't kick-off so easily in a public place, could she? 'No, I can't guess, sorry.' There she went with the apologising again. Why did her mum have this effect on her?

'Ruby says I'll inherit Hope Home one day! And she says she'll pay for me to go back to college in September and retrain again as a nurse. Of course, it means I'll have to give up the bakery, but isn't it fantastic news!'

'Amazing!' Tilly managed to remember to close her mouth, so no flies flew in. Where was the real Elaine? What had happened to her?

'I can't believe it; this really could be the start of something for me.' Elaine smiled coyly to herself.

'It really is. Listen, Mum—' Tilly was keen to strike while the iron was hot or, in this case, while Elaine was in a rare good mood. '—there's something I'd really like to ask you.'

Elaine smiled. A genuinely, broad, excited smile which Tilly hadn't seen Elaine wear for a long time. 'Yes?'

It seemed insensitive to ask now but her mind returned to yesterday's session with Laura. She couldn't move on without knowing. It was time to put her needs before her mum's. 'It's about my real dad.'

The smile instantly dropped.

The sound of running feet distracted both women as they turned to see a teenage boy skid to a halt by her menu of ice cream flavours. Behind him came Doctor Dare and a girl who looked vaguely familiar to Tilly, a tall and skinny girl with mountains of long, curly hair.

Goddamit!

'Hello, Tilly,' the Doctor said, coming closer to Tilly's stand. 'Miss Henshaw.' He nodded at Elaine.

'Hello,' Elaine almost barked.

Tilly tried to smile at her most recent customers, but she was confused as to why Doctor Dare was calling her by her first name, and Mum so formally. 'What can I get you?' she asked, smiling at the boy and girl with the Doctor.

'Can I get a tub of salted caramel, double chocolate chip and clotted cream ice cream, please, with chocolate sauce and cookie sprinkles?' asked the boy.

'Sure.' Tilly grabbed a tub and scoop.

'I'm sorry, I should have introduced you.' The doctor seemed to be talking more to Elaine than to Tilly. 'This is my daughter, Libby—' Tilly noticed Libby didn't even look up from her phone '—and this is my son, Tom—'

'Hi!' Tom raised a hand and waved at Tilly. She reciprocated with a smile.

'—They're down for half-term, aren't you guys?' The doctor beamed, clearly proud of his children. Tilly assumed they must live with their mother elsewhere. Something, in the pit of her stomach, growled that even living with separated parents was a choice which had been denied to her.

'What about you, Libby, can we tempt you?' Doctor Dare asked his daughter.

Libby patted her stomach. 'No thanks, Dad.'

'Libby's going to be revising most of the week for her A-Level exams. She's hoping to leave education behind to grace the catwalks of Milan,' Anthony said, sounding anything but the proud father.

'Wow, really?' Tilly asked.

'Yes, I've been recruited by *Thunder*; one of the model agencies in London.'

Tilly let out a low whistle. 'That *is* impressive,' she said, squirting chocolate sauce all over Tom's ice cream. If Tilly had ever wanted to be a model it would have been out of the question with her height. She would have been more likely to have got on walk-on role in The Hobbit.

'Yes, but what happens when her looks fade and the work dries up? Who's going to pay the mortgage then?'

'Here you go!' Tilly said brightly to Tom, passing over the ice cream tub. She sensed the modelling thing was a bone of contention and she had no interest in getting involved in Doctor Dare's parenting. She was currently dealing with a truculent parent of her own who was standing there, crossed armed, looking out to sea, her body language oozing *please don't talk to me*.

'What about you Doctor, can I tempt you?'

'I'm good thanks; how much do I owe you?' He asked, reaching for his wallet.

'On the house.' Tilly didn't know why she wanted to offer the doctor free ice cream but he was here, playing the attentive single-dad and she admired him for that.

'Oh, Tilly, that's very kind of you.' He smiled.

'Thanks!' said Tom, rushing off over to the rock pools emerging as the tide drew out. Libby followed him.

'Elaine.' Anthony turned in, towards Elaine and spoke in hushed tones. 'Tina's been trying to contact you—'

Tilly busied herself washing out her ice cream scoop, so it didn't sound like she was eavesdropping.

Which she totally was.

'I don't want to do this here.' Elaine spoke in a shouty-whisper, if such a thing was possible.

'Then come and see me at the surgery, please?'

Out of the corner of her eye, she saw Elaine silently nod, keeping her gaze fixed firmly on the concrete slope of the harbour.

'Okay, well thanks Tilly!' The doctor called and waved as he set off towards the rock pools. 'Better check what Tom's up to; only child I know who could probably drown himself in shallow water.'

'Ha.' Tilly let out a nervous titter. 'Bye!' she waved, watching father catch up with son and daughter, still racking her brains as to why Libby had seemed so familiar. Perhaps she had visited her dad in Hope Cove before but Tilly hadn't realised the connection?

She waited for him to be a safe enough distance away before rounding on Elaine. 'What was all that about?'

Elaine shrugged, still looking down at the ground. 'All what?'

'All that with the doctor. Why does he need to see you?'

'What is it with you and your curiosity, Tilly!' Elaine sounded venomous as she hurriedly stepped towards Tilly's stand, looking up at Tilly with her eyes full of anguish, completely different to how she had arrived on the harbour fifteen minutes ago.

'I don't know,' Tilly said, quietly, feeling like guilt-ridden, fourteen-year-old Tilly again.

'Not everything is about you,' Elaine snapped, 'and you can drop the questioning about your father too. I don't know who mine is either. Sometimes life isn't fair, Tilly, and we just have to live with that.' And with that, Elaine pushed her handbag up her shoulder, turned on her heel at fled at almost a run up towards the high street.

Tears welled in Tilly's eyes again. 'Well, I for one don't want to live like that,' Tilly whispered watching, through blurry vision, Anthony Dare and his children frolic in the rock pools.

CHAPTER FIFTY-ONE

For the first time in a long-time, Archie was feeling quite chipper about life. With the tide out, he and Hector had had a leisurely stroll back over from Gull Island in the afternoon sun and he had even taken his jumper off to enjoy the warmth of sunrays on his old bones. He didn't feel lonely anymore. He and Ruby got on so well that, like a moth to the flame, he found himself wanting to be over on the island more and more. He had even found himself spending more time with Lil than he'd ever done, and the care Ruby was giving her was bringing her back to life. Not completely without the dementia but something resembling the smiley, chatty woman she once was.

He still thought about Phyllis, but he had eventually made peace with the situation. Phyllis had told him to enjoy life without her and, remarkably, with Ruby now properly in his life, he could look back on his life with Phyllis fondly and not with that gut-wrenching burden of guilt. Not that the pain of guilt had gone away all together, he thought, reaching the top of the cliff steps and looking over at Hope Cottage.

Not everything was resolved.

He knew he needed to tell Elaine, of course he did; it was the first question Ruby asked every time she bloody saw him, but he just hadn't found the right moment.

'All these secrets and lies, Hector,' he said, clipping the dog's lead before crossing the road. 'Where will it ever end?'

He'd stopped having that heavy heart every time he turned the key to the cottage these days. Mainly because he knew he could escape back to Ruby's flat whenever he wanted. But partly because he was hopeful of catching Elaine on her own. Part of him was ready to tell her now. The major part of him was scared, but now he had Ruby's support, he felt ready to do it. Ready to face the consequences that might come from Elaine knowing the truth. Even the shame he carried all these years didn't seem so shameful now. He wanted a relationship with his daughter *and* his granddaughter.

He paused from hanging his anorak on the hooks and looked down at Hector.

'Is that you sniffing, old chap?'

Hector stared at him expectantly.

'Hmm, not you.' He followed the sound through the living room door to find Elaine curled up in a foetal position on the sofa. 'Elaine!' Archie said, rushing into the room and sitting down next to her. He wanted to reach out and rub her shoulder, but it was as if his arm had frozen. 'What's the matter?'

'I...' she said between sobs, 'I don't want to talk about it.'

'Right,' he said, wondering what approach to take. 'I'll go and make us a cup of tea.'

By the time he had faffed about in the kitchen, with his hands shaking like leaves, considering whether this was the moment and deciding most probably not, Elaine had calmed down somewhat and was sitting up wiping her eyes with a tissue.

'Here you go,' he said, setting the tray down on the coffee table. He had been too apprehensive to carry two mugs. At least the tray caught any spillage.

'Thanks,' she said, curling her legs under her. 'All my life you've always been here to mop up the tears, haven't you, Archie?'

Archie swallowed hard as flashbacks of giving Elaine a cuddle every time there had been a fall-out and Lil and Stan's came to the forefront of his mind.

'I guess so, probably more Phyllis than me, but you'll have to make do with me today,' he said, sitting down. 'Are you going to tell me what's up?'

She looked away, out of the bay window and across to the island.

They sat in companionable silence, both watching the gulls swoop over the beach, Elaine deep in her thoughts, Archie, waiting for her to speak.

'I don't think you'll even believe me,' she finally said, 'I can hardly believe it myself,' she whispered.

'Well, why don't you try me? Do you remember the time you came to tell Phyllis and I you'd failed your mock o-level Maths and didn't know how to tell Lil and Stan?'

She turned around and smiled through her tears. 'I do, you were both so understanding,' she said, taking his hand and squeezing it.

'So, perhaps I can be just as understanding now.'

Elaine took a deep breath. 'Tilly's asked me about her real father again.'

Archie's heartrate began to rise. He took a deep breath. 'Oh?'

Elaine nodded. 'I told her I wasn't going to tell her, and she needed to live with it, but now I feel bad.'

'Oh, love, don't feel bad, I know how hard it is for you.'

Elaine shook her head and tears began to well in her eyes again. 'You don't understand, you're just trying to be nice. The thing is, I feel jealous, if I tell her.'

'Jealous?'

'Yes, because, she'll know but I still won't know who my real father is.'

She looked up at Archie, her face full of anguish and he knew this was his moment.

'I understand,' he said, quietly.

'No, you don't.' She shook her head. 'You can't; it's so complicated. Of all the places to find him.'

'Find who?'

'Tilly's father.'

'I don't understand what you're saying, lass? Tilly's father's here, in Hope Cove?'

'Yes, I've been lying to her all these years and now my lies have finally caught up with me.'

'You and me both, love. The thing is, Elaine—'

'Anthony's Tilly's father.'

'—I'm your real father.'

They spoke in unison.

'What?' Elaine immediately withdrew her hand. She started shaking her head. 'Don't lie to me, Archie.'

Archie's heart was beating nineteen-to-the-dozen, his arms and legs had frozen. Was he suffering a stroke?

'I'm not,' he managed to stammer. 'I should have told you years ago, but there never seemed an opportunity. You were Lil and Stan's daughter.'

'Is that why you moved next door?'

He nodded. He couldn't be having a stroke, could he? 'Elaine, I don't feel so well.'

'Oh, don't give me that Archie,' she said, standing up and pacing the room. 'So, you've known Ruby all these years?'

He took another deep breath. 'Yes, but she never told me about you!' He could hear his voice rising, like he needed to get his point across. 'She didn't tell me about you until after she'd let Lil adopt you. It was too late then!'

'So, you left her alone and pregnant?

'It wasn't like that!' He wanted to stand up, but his legs were like jelly.

'What was it like then?'

Something snapped. If Elaine could be accusatory, so could he. 'What was it like for you? You never told Anthony, did you? So, how's he going to feel when he finds out? Or Tilly for that matter!'

'Arrrgh!' Elaine put her hands over her ears. 'Stoppit!'

'Elaine, I should have told you before now, I know. God knows it's eaten me up all these years! But you weren't our daughter to tell, so we had to do the next best thing and be Uncle Archie and Auntie Phyllis next door.'

'Phyllis knew?' Elaine said, sitting down in an armchair, her voice finally calming.

Archie nodded. 'She figured it out. Smart girl was our Phyllis.'

'And she went along with it?'

'She couldn't have children; it was the next best thing. Elaine,' Archie whispered, 'she loved you so much.'

Tears slipped down Elaine's face. 'I know. She was wonderful to me.' She looked up at Archie. 'And you too.'

He smiled through his watery eyes. 'Thank you.'

'Anthony's guessed Tilly is his,' Elaine said, looking down at the tissue she was tearing to pieces in her hands.

'And is he happy?'

'Delighted. He's so glad to have met me again, but I feel so guilty! He eants me to tell Tilly.' She sighed. 'But I don't know how to,' she said, dissolving into tears again.

Archie edged his way along the sofa, so he was sitting opposite her. He took her hands.

'You think you're doing the right thing at the time but all you're doing is building up a pressure pot that is going to explode at some point. Best get it done with. I think Tilly might surprise you.'

Elaine looked up, searching his eyes for answers again. 'You think she'll be happy?'

'Tilly just wants everyone to be happy. It's her missing piece of the jigsaw, finding out who her dad is; it might just put everything together for her.'

'Why didn't Ruby tell you she was pregnant?'

'I did a bad thing,' Archie looked down at his feet. 'I was engaged to Phyllis but working away a lot in Bristol.' He shrugged. 'We clicked; I fell for her. Ruby can be very enchanting when she wants to be.'

Elaine laughed. 'Not to mention interfering and manipulative.'

'All with her heart in the right place. We had a fling. My engagement to Phyllis had been arranged by our fathers, a coming-together to two industrious families in Leeds. I'd only had a few dates with her. Perhaps I panicked. I don't know really, but I got scared and ended it with Ruby and told her I had to marry Phyllis.' He took Elaine's hands. 'You must know that if I'd known about you, I would have called it off with Phyllis.'

Elaine nodded. 'Life might have been very different if I'd been brought up by you and Ruby.'

'Aye, it might, but then you may never have had Tilly.'

'True. Or had Phyllis in my life. She never, ever showed any malice towards me.'

Archie laughed. 'She wasn't jealous of you! She loved you, lass; you were the daughter she never had.'

'Thank you, Archie,' Elaine said, her voice wobbling. She stood up. 'I think I'll go for a walk now and digest all of this.' Her hands dropped.

Archie wanted to hug her, but he didn't want to feel rejection if she stepped back.

'Okay. Would you like me to come?'

'No, it's fine, thank you.' She made her way out into the hall and popped her shoes on.

'Don't you need your handbag?' He asked, searching around for it.

'What? Oh, no, it's fine, I won't need it.' She smiled, a weary smile which didn't quite reach her eyes.

Archie nodded. 'Are you sure you're okay love?'

She went to open the door and paused, looking back. 'I will be.'

With that she was gone. Archie took some deep breaths and wandered back into the living room to find his tea. He looked out of the bay window to watch Elaine's slumped-shoulder figure wander off in the direction of the lighthouse and struggled to find the reason that why, instead of feeling relief at telling Elaine, he had this nagging, foreboding feeling settling in his stomach.

Chapter Fifty-Two

The basement was heaving, which was surprising seeing the clouds had descended this afternoon and the patter of rain had started, less than an hour ago, across the harbour and incoming tide. Tilly had noticed that when the weather was good, the Friday night disco was pumping and when the weather was pants the disco was usually sparse. Tonight, was different though. Along with the regular locals – girls from the village giggling at the local lads – there were some newcomers. Many newcomers. Tilly looked around her as she squeezed her way through the masses to Winstone's stage area. He looked down at her and grinned.

'Hi,' she said, taking his hand as he pulled her up onto the stage.

'Hello, you,' he said, 'how are you? I haven't seen you all week.'

It was true, she had avoided him since their lunch on Monday. It must have come across as incredibly rude when he'd taken her for an expensive lunch, but she just hadn't had the headspace to talk to Winstone. She needed to sort this shit out with her mum; it was totally doing her head in, especially Elaine's avoidance of anything to do with Tilly's dad.

'I'm sorry, I've had a lot to think about—'

'Hey, no biggie,' Winstone interrupted, 'as long as what I told you on Monday didn't scare you.'

Tilly vehemently shook her head. 'No, it didn't.' Now wasn't the time to tell Winstone about her mum's attempt, once, to take her own life. 'It just brought up a lot of stuff for me and I needed to talk to Laura.'

Winstone's smile dropped and his face took on a gesture of total concern. 'I'm sorry,' he shouted over the noisy music and banter from the crowd, 'that was the last thing I intended to do.'

Tilly nodded. 'I know.' She smiled but she couldn't quite muster up a proper, full one. 'Anyway, I'd better get back to collecting the empties.' Her voice sounded falsely enthusiastic, even to herself.

'Okay, catch you later,' Winstone said, watching Tilly as she jumped down off the stage and disappeared into the crowd. He mixed the music into the next song, noticing there were lots of new faces. If these Friday nights carried on growing the way they were, he was going to have to consider a bigger venue.

'Hi, are you Winstone?' A giggling girl, probably in her late twenties, tapped Winstone's arm.

'I am.' Winstone smiled, removing his headphones.

'Oh, we lived for our Friday nights with you! We've come all the way down from Billericay for the weekend just so we could see you.' The second girl said.

'Oh, right.' Winstone frowned. 'So, how did you find out about our little Friday night discos then?'

'Instagram! Some food place called *Tilly's Kitchen* was promoting you, they used #WinstoneChambers and I said to Shar, here, oh my God, babe, we have got to go and see him, for old times!'

Winstone ran his hand over her stubble, feeling irritation and frustration surfacing. Why had Tilly done that? The last thing he needed was the life he had tried to escape catching up on the new life he'd made for himself.

'Can we get a selfie?' Shar asked, proffering her phone.

'Sure,' said Winstone, thinking there was nothing he would like to do less. His face would be plastered all over social-fucking-media in the next ten seconds.

He managed a pleasant goodbye to his 'fans', lined up the next two songs and jumped down into the crowd, in search of Tilly, trying to quelle his rage at what she had done before he heard her out.

'Tilly!' An arm grabbed Tilly's and pulled her away into the harbour.

So, engrossed in her thoughts, as she almost sleepwalked her way around the edge of the disco collecting empties, she didn't see who it was man-handling her.

'It's your mum.' Tilly looked up to see a very ashen looking Doctor Dare scanning her face for answers.

'What about her?' she asked, feeling mildly irritated. She still hadn't forgiven Elaine for telling her she'd have to *live with it* on the harbour earlier. Anthony's children were standing behind him. Libby was looking bored and impatient, winding a stray ringlet around her finger, while Tom looked excitedly on at the crowd, his body looking as if he wanted to dive in and dance with all the other gyrating disco-goers.

'Archie phoned me. He gave her some news—'

'Oh, finally! Now she knows who her father is perhaps she won't mind telling me who mine is!'

She watched Anthony Dare flinch, before frowning. 'Archie is Elaine's father?'

'Yes,' Tilly said impatiently, 'it's so obvious, I'm not sure how it's taken her so long to figure out.'

'You knew?'

'I worked it out; from his behaviour with Ruby.'

'Oh.' The urgent anxiety in Doctor Dare seemed to have abated. He cleared his throat. 'Look, Tilly, I'm really worried about your mum.'

'Okay.' Tilly reached into her back pocket, for her phone, remembering Doctor Dare showing his concern for her mum on the harbour earlier. 'I'll phone her.' She tried to quell the rising feeling of panic that was coming over her. She'd pressed to know about her real dad again and suddenly Elaine had disappeared. She wouldn't try it again, would she? 'Did you try Hope Home?'

'Archie was phoning Ruby as I left. I'm really concerned about her, Tilly.'

'TILLY!' Winstone's voice raged over the crowd inside the disco.

Tilly paused from connecting the call, caught off guard by how angry Winstone sounded.

'Come on, Tilly, you need to phone your mum.' Doctor Dare said, dragging Tilly away from Winstone's accusing stare.

She was beginning to feel sick. She took deep breaths to try and calm herself but Winstone's face was haunting her. He looked hurt, wounded even and she had no idea what had happened to put him into such rage.

'Come on, ring her,' Doctor Dare instructed as the fine drizzle fell, out on the harbour, coating her in a chilly, wet mist.

'Okay,' she said, trembling as she reached for her phone from her back pocket.

'Voicemail,' she said, as the call connected. 'Hi, Mum, it's me, Tilly. Look, everyone's a bit worried about you; can you call me back please?'

She didn't have time to analyse her words because the tornado which was Winstone was storming out onto the harbour.

'What were you thinking?' he shouted.

Her phone started ringing.

'Is it Elaine?' Doctor Dare asked, rushing to look.

'I'm sorry—'

'Tilly, do you have any idea why I moved here?' Winstone continued.

'I do, but—'

'I wanted to get away from that life, not drag it all down here with me!'

'Tilly, who is it?' Anthony asked impatiently.

'Archie,' Tilly said rejecting the call. She couldn't think straight. A nagging concern was beginning to descend about where her mum was, coupled with an overriding feeling of nausea that she had inadvertently upset Winstone. 'What have I done?' she asked, quietly.

'Put the pub and me all over social media! Why, Tilly? Why? After everything I've told you!'

Tears sprang to her eyes. 'I, um,' she stumbled over her words, 'I thought it would help bring a few more locals into the pub. I didn't know about, um… I didn't know anything when I was promoting the discos. You only told me on Monday.'

Her phone sprang to life again.

'Tilly, you need to answer that!' Doctor Dare said, grabbing her arm to make her look at the phone.

Tilly batted back tears as Winstone angrily paced and the crowd sang and whooped along to the medley of songs Winstone had left on play inside.

'Archie?'

'Tilly is that you? Oh, thank God I got through. Your mum went out of a walk at four o'clock and no-one's seen her since. It's all my fault.'

A sudden sense of clarity washed over her. 'No,' she said, firmly. 'This is not your fault.'

'Oh, but it is, I told her who I really am.'

'I know who you really are, Grandad,' she smiled, trying to ignore both Winstone and the doctor's impatience in her peripheral vision.

'Thank you,' Archie said, obviously sensing the warmth in her voice. 'I've tried Ruby but she's not at the home. The tide's in now, what if Elaine's stuck somewhere?'

'Sulking somewhere more like. Look, you get off the phone in case she calls. I'll get the doctor to go in one direction and I'll go in the other. I'll phone you in half-an-hour to tell you where I am.'

'Okay,' Archie said, sounding fretful.

'Archie, *this is not your fault.* In fact, it's wonderful news is far as I'm concerned.'

'Thank you, Tilly,' he said, his voice sounding wobbly.

'Where do we start looking?' the Doctor asked, as soon as she disconnected the call.

'Tilly, we need to talk,' Winstone said, appearing calmer from his pacing up and down the seafront.

'You go the coastal path to the lighthouse; she likes to sit there and look out to sea. If she's not there, carry on past the surfers shack, by the cottage, towards the headland which looks over to Newquay. I'll try the path to Port Trillick.'

'The reception isn't very good over that way.'

'Don't worry, if I find her, I call as soon as I get back into reception.'

'Okay,' Anthony nodded, before setting off into the drizzly dusk, with Libby and Tom, slumped shouldered, following behind.

Tilly's heart sank as she turned to see Winstone standing, hands on hips. 'Why did you do it Tilly?' His voice was softer now.

'Because I thought it would bring some business into the village! How was I to know that people would flock from all over the land, to our sleepy little village, to see you DJ?'

'Because I disappeared off the face of the earth! Fans wanted more and now they know where to find me and I will be forever faced with the question of *why did I let Tory die?*'

Tilly gasped. Tears pricked her eyes. 'That was never my intention.' She whispered.

'And yet it's the consequence of your actions.'

Tilly began shaking her head but no more words to come to defend herself. What did it matter anyway? Winstone had clearly made up his mind.

'Whatever,' Winstone said, kicking a stone. 'I can't deal with this. I'll go back in there and finish the set and then I'm through. No more discos.' He stalked back through the cellar doors.

Tilly watched him go, her heart breaking just like the crowd was parting to let him through. Salty tears trickled down her face, mixing with the dewy rain collecting on her cheeks how guilty she felt at letting Winstone down.

CHAPTER FIFTY-

THREE

Tilly must have just stood in the drizzle for a good ten minutes, watching Winstone throw himself into the music, listening to the increasingly, angry crashing waves on the shore when her phone sprung to life.

'Tilly, darling, it's Ruby.'

'Oh, hello,' Tilly said, trying not to sound as if she'd been crying.

Which she had.

Constantly for ten minutes.

'Look, I can't get across to the mainland as the tide's in and the water's too choppy for the ferryman. I'm worried sick about Archie, he sounds out of his mind with worry.'

'He's not the only one.'

'Of, sorry, how insensitive of me! Of course, you are too.'

Tilly was about to say it wasn't her, that it was Doctor Dare who seemed overly worried, when a sudden sense of guilt crashed over her, like the waves on the beach, that she wasn't as worried about her mum as everyone else.

'Tilly are you still there?'

'Um, yes, sorry.'

'Are you all right my love?'

Tilly watched Winstone, head down, focused on the music and the music alone. He hadn't looked up once to see if Tilly was still standing there.

She mentally shook herself. 'Yes, fine.'

'Okay.' Ruby didn't sound convinced. 'Well, what's the plan? I feel useless over here. I just want to comfort Archie.'

The noise of the music and the singing dancers made it difficult for Tilly to hear so she moved away from the cellar doors, trying hard to focus on the urgent matter of finding Elaine and not at the heartache of walking away from an angry Winstone.

'You're not useless at all,' Tilly said, pacing up and down and focusing her mind in the fading light. 'Mum might have walked across to the island while the tide was out and got stuck. Get a torch and do a scout of the island. Are there any paths apart from the drive up the home?'

'Yes, right, I'm on it, darling! What are you going to do?'

'Anthony's headed up towards the lighthouse and I'm going to take the coastal path to Port Trillick. Actually, you could do one other thing, Ruby.'

'Yes?'

'Phone the police. I know she's only been gone a few hours but wasn't in a good place this afternoon; we argued on the harbour.'

There was silence at the end of the phone. 'What about?' Ruby finally asked.

'That's not important now. What you should know—' gosh, could she do this? She'd never told anyone before '—is that once, a long time ago, she tried to take her life.' Tilly heard Ruby's gasp at the end of the phone.

'When?'

'When I was fourteen.'

'Why didn't I know about this?'

Tilly was about to explain about Elaine's shame and how the five people who did know – Lil, Stan, Tilly, Archie and Phyllis – had all been sworn to secrecy when she realised none of that mattered now. 'Just get off the phone, ring the police and start searching. I told Archie I'd phone him in just under an hour, I'll update you then too.'

'Tilly,' Ruby said, her voice full of concern.

'Yes?'

'Go careful, it's brewing up a storm quickly out there.'

'I will. Bye,' Tilly said, disconnecting the call and looking down at her Havanias. Perhaps she should pop home and change into better clothes and footwear, more appropriate for walking a coastal path, but the more Tilly pushed her argument with Winstone to the back of her mind, the more fear of Elaine might be up to was moving to the forefront.

Elaine looked over the cliff edge. Colossal waves were crashing onto the rocks below, making a pool of white foam at the edge of the ocean. It looked like jacuzzi, frothy, inviting, especially if you were running out of options.

She had been angry when Archie had told her this afternoon. Fuming in fact. She still was, but the angriness she felt had made way by the paralysis of fear.

She knew who her father was now.

So, there was no reason for Tilly not to know who hers was.

She closed her eyes again and imagined taking off like a bird in flight, allowing the foaminess of the ocean to envelop her and take her away from all her worries.

Would it hurt?

Probably.

Not for long though. She'd be free. Free of it all. Free of her worry for Mum, Lil, whoever she was these days. Free from thinking how different life could have been if Ruby had told Archie. Free from the lies she'd told Tilly *and* free from facing Anthony again.

Anthony. He was the one glimmer of hope in this desperately sad situation but if he found how what she was thinking right now, what would he think of her then? It wasn't the first time she'd had these thoughts, but it was the same reason; not being able to tell Tilly the truth.

'Mum!'

Elaine wondered if she was hallucinating, as it sounded very much like Tilly's voice being carried on the wind.

'Mum, are you here?'

Elaine turned, careful of her footing, to see a tiny white light shining through the rain.

'Tilly?'

'Mum! Oh, thank goodness, we've all been worried about you!'

Elaine watched elation turn to sheer horror as Tilly saw how close Elaine was to the cliff edge and stopped in her tracks.

'What are you doing?' She called over the sound of the crashing waves below.

'I could ask you the same! Look at you with hardly any clothes on, you'll catch your death!'

If Tilly wasn't scared all ready, Elaine's choice of words sent a chill down her spine.

'Not before you fall to yours,' she said, feeling the need to tackle the issue head on.

Elaine laughed. 'I'm just clearing my head.'

'In the wind and rain, as daylight fades?'

Elaine turned to look back out to sea.

'I had a lot to think about.'

'Well, if you're just thinking, you won't mind stepping back and coming to do it, a bit closer to me,' Tilly said, now feeling sicker than she thought was possible.

'I'd rather stay over here for now, thanks,' Elaine said, without looking back.

'Mum, you're scaring me.'

Elaine said nothing.

Tilly could hardly breathe for her beating heart, hammering like a piston. She took some deep breaths and tried to think. Her phone had no reception, she couldn't phone for back up.

Think Tilly, think.

It was crucial she didn't say the wrong thing. She didn't dare move towards mum in case she leapt off the edge.

What would Laura do? What made someone want to take their own life? Laura's words from yesterday ran through her mind, *feel there's no other solution; there's no way they can cope, continuing with the emotions they are feeling. They can't see light at the end of the tunnel; they cannot imagine a future which is bearable, let alone bright or positive.*

She knew what she needed to do; she needed to get on board with how Mum was feeling, and once Mum knew Tilly understood, then she could show her it doesn't have to be this way, they could have a future, together.

'Tell me, then,' Tilly called, aware her voice was being carried on the wind away from Elaine, not towards her. 'Tell me what's so awful, you're standing on a cliff edge.'

Elaine's face crumpled and she shook her head. 'I can't. I can't tell you.'

Could she bring it up? Dare she bring it up? Laura was always banging on about her being more autonomous; Tilly was just going to have to say what felt right to her. 'Is it the same thing that made you take all those pills that time?'

'No,' Elaine barked. 'It's nothing to do with that; why are you bringing that up?'

Because it's why I've behaved so erratically and been a nuisance to you, ever since.

'Um, no reason.' She was thinking on her feet, no clue of where to go next, only focused on keeping Elaine talking so she couldn't throw herself off that cliff edge.

'It's a good thing, you know. You might not think it now, but there are worse dads to have than Archie.'

'What?' Elaine turned around looking confused.

'I'm just saying, er—' what was she saying? *Please don't kill yourself!* '—it's all going to be okay.' Tilly could have kicked herself for sounding so cliched.

'How, Tilly? How is it *all* going to be okay?'

Tilly could hear Elaine sounded angry, but she also sounded like a truculent teenager; something Tilly recalled Laura accusing her of at the beginning of her sessions. Tilly had been offended, but Laura had been right. Was that what was happening here? Was Elaine stuck in teen-mode acting all defensive and thinking irrationally?

'Archie is the loveliest man I think I've ever met,' Tilly continued, suddenly aware that she was soaked through to the bone. 'He is positive, kind, clever, all the things I aspire to be, and I for one and am glad he is my grandad! If you want to be angry with anyone, take it up with Ruby; she lied to him in the first place.'

Something flickered across Elaine's face. Tilly wasn't sure what it was and in the dusk it could have just been a trick of the light, but it looked very much like guilt to Tilly. 'It's not about Archie.' Elaine said, sulkily.

'Then what's making you stand on a cliff edge, Mum?'

'You, Tilly! You are!' She sounded angry. Really angry.

Tilly was stunned. 'I don't understand?' she said, as calmly as she could muster.

'Because now I know,' Elaine said, more softly, 'I haven't got the excuse not to tell you who your father is, have I?'

Tilly thought back to their conversation earlier today, on the harbour. 'You told me on the harbour this afternoon, I'd have to *live with it.*'

Elaine let out a little sob. 'But I know now, so, now, I have to tell you.' She began to cry.

Tilly tried to quell the rising anger within her. The two weren't inextricably linked. Had she been punished all these years by her mother? Because Elaine didn't know the identity of her real father, then Tilly wasn't allowed to know hers? It didn't make sense. At least Elaine had had Grandad Stan, her adoptive father. Who did Tilly have growing up, as a father figure?

No-one.

'I haven't asked, have I? You don't have to tell me if you don't want to.' *Although I do bloody want to know!* Tilly wanted to shout. But quizzing Elaine could wait until she was safely away from a cliff edge.

'But you have asked Tilly. So many times. Why do you think I tried to take my own life all those years ago? Why do you think it's so unbearable for me now?'

It came from deep within. 'I DON'T KNOW!' Tilly screamed. 'None of it makes sense! Why have I never had a right to know who my father is?!'

'Because I didn't want to share you!' Elaine shouted back.

'What?' Tilly whispered.

'I didn't want to share you with him,' Elaine whispered. 'I was so confused when Ruby told me who she really was, and I didn't want anyone taking you away like I'd be taken away from her and given to Lil and Stan! I wanted to keep you safe—'

Tears welled in Tilly's eyes at the thought of a young Elaine trying to protect her.

'—but now I know I've got to tell you and share you with him and it's all so scary.'

Tilly shivered. The rain was icy and the wind cold, even on a June evening approaching midsummer.

'Look Mum, it doesn't matter, tell me when you're ready—'

Elaine shook her head, her face full of anguish. She was as soaked through and shivering in her cardigan and denim skirt as Tilly was. 'It's too late Tilly, you need to know, before you find out.'

'Find out? How am I going to find out? I doubt either of us would even know where to start looking for him.'

Elaine stared out across the angry ocean. 'He's here, in the village.'

Tilly had never had a lightbulb moment. She'd heard people say that in the face of death your life flashes before you, but she had never believed it. Yet, here she was with images flashing through her mind. Of Libby, Doctor Dare's daughter, of all people. Her hair. The way she twizzled it around her finger and her posture. She was taller than Tilly, much taller, but she made the same pose, almost leaning back over her hips so they jutted out, her arms tucked in around her body.'

'Oh, my God,' she whispered.

'Tilly, are you okay?' Elaine asked, taking a step back in-land.

'It's Doctor Dare, isn't it?' She knew now, she knew for sure. She'd felt a connection to him from that first appointment in his surgery. Then he'd started coming for lunch in the pub more frequently. It all made sense.

Elaine, who'd tentatively been making steps towards Tilly, stopped in her tracks, closed her eyes and nodded while tears silently streamed down her face.

The rain was stinging Tilly's skin now, but she didn't care. The pain felt good. Numbing the feeling that Winstone was disappointed in her and that her Mum had been lying to her, her whole damn life.

'Does he know? How long has he known? Why didn't you tell me?' So many questions.

'I didn't know how to,' Elaine squeaked.

'It's quite easy you know. Oh, Tilly, you know that new doctor you went to, well, you probably shouldn't go again because he is, in fact, your dad!'

'It's not like that!' Elaine screeched.

'Pah!' Anger was rising inside Tilly's chest. 'Is this the real reason you followed me down here? Because of him? Have you been in contact all these years and didn't tell me? Were you afraid I'd find out?' None of it made sense.

'No, Tilly, it's nothing like that, I didn't even know he was living here! I hadn't seen him since 1983! I—'

'Save it, Mum. I've had a crap day, I've stopped you throwing yourself off a cliff, so now I'm going home,' she said, turning around. She was fuming. She'd have to think about all of this in a hot bath and consider whether she just packed her bags and went back to Bristol. She could probably continue her therapy there. There was plenty of student life; she could set up *Tilly's Kitchen* at Harbourside, probably, make a decent profit nearly every night of the week.

Most importantly she could escape her catastrophically fucked-up family.

Her flipflop slipped on the wet, sandy gravel, as she descended back down the coastal path, sending her skidding precariously close to the edge. 'Woah!' She tried to correct her balance, but it was all happening so fast.

'Tilly!' Elaine screamed.

'Arrrghh!' cried Tilly, as she tumbled over the cliff edge, bottom first. '*Fuuccck!*'

Chapter Fifty-

Four

Winstone knocked back the last swig of his whisky when the hammering started on the door. He'd told the staff they could all go; he just wanted to clear up on his own. Clear his thoughts, really. Instead, all he'd done was sit amongst the empties at the bar and drown his sorrows at how badly he'd behaved. He'd overreacted for sure. Tilly had thought she was doing something kind, which she had been, and he'd come down on her like a tonne of bricks.

He'd panicked.

There was no other explanation. He'd moved here to forget his old life; he didn't want the past turning up for a good time at his expense.

The hammering carried on.

'We're closed!' Winstone shouted, pouring more whisky into the tumbler.

'Winstone, it's Elaine!'

Winstone stopped pouring. That was all he needed. An angry mother coming to protect her child. He dragged the stool backwards and walked across to the front door. He unlocked it to find a very wet and tearstained Elaine on the doorstep.

'Look,' he said holding up his hands. 'I'm sorry, okay? I overreacted; I shouldn't have behaved the way I did. I'll come and see her in the morning and—'

'There's been an accident,' Elaine blurted out. 'I didn't know where else to go. I left my mobile at home and—'

'Woah!' The hairs on Winstone's neck were all standing on end. 'What kind of accident?'

'It's Tilly. I need an ambulance, or the Coastguard perhaps. I knocked on the Lifeboat door but no-one's there and—'

'Elaine!' Winstone put his hands on Elaine's shoulders to shut her up. 'What kind of accident?'

'Tilly's fallen off the cliff, she's stuck on a ledge, oh,' she sobbed, 'it's all my fault!' she managed to gabble out before dissolving into tears and sitting down at the nearest bench.

Winstone took hold of her shoulders again. 'Ssssh,' he said, trying to soothe her, feeling anything but inside. He needed to get information out of her. 'Where, Elaine? Where did it happen?'

'On the headland between here and Port Trillick.' She started crying again. 'It's all my fault!'

'Elaine,' Winstone shook her shoulders this time trying to stop her hysteria. 'Was she conscious?'

Elaine shook her head. 'She was lying still.' Tears slid silently down her face.

'Bollocks.' Winstone reached for the phone from his back pocket and dialled 999. He asked for an ambulance knowing they would notify the coastguard and explained the situation to the lady on the other end. There was no-way of taking a car up to that point and he'd been drinking anyway.

This called for drastic measures.

'Elaine,' he said, grabbing her and dragging her up. 'You need to go to the cottage and tell Archie what's happened. Tell him I'm going to find Tilly now. Tell him he needs to round-up as many people with torches and meet where Tilly is. Do you understand?'

Elaine was sobbing hysterically.

'Elaine!' Winstone said, impatiently.

'Yes, I will,' she said between sobs.

'Then go,' he said, thrusting her out of the door and locking it again. He quickly moved through the pub and made his way down to the cellar. He kept rope for cordoning off extra outside seating area in the harbour during the summer months and a small generator he used for outside lights and playing music on summer evenings. He gathered it all together and went to grab some of the disco lights and an extension lead. The weight of it all would slow him down, but the Coastguard would need to see where he was.

It felt like an eternity to get the relatively short distance out of the cove and over the headland to where he thought Tilly was. In his rush to get to Tilly he had forgotten a torch so had to rely on the one on his phone, which wasn't very effective in the pitch dark. Arriving at the headland he started walking along the cliff edge, looking down into the swirling abyss of the sea and feeling grateful that at least Tilly hadn't fallen into the angry sounding waves.

Please let her be alive.

Guilt washed over him that he had argued with her.

Please don't let her die.

'Tilly!' He shouted, noticing a cliff and making out her white denim shorts in the dark. 'TILLY!'

Nothing. She lay completely still. He had to get down there. First things first, he needed to power up those lights so the Coastguard could where they were. He flung everything to the floor and flicked the generator on. It started humming over the sound of the wind and the waves as he frantically connected the extension leads to the lights. Time was of the essence; he could at least give Tilly basic CPR.

Anything to keep her alive.

Lights on and dancing into the night, he started to look for something he could tie the rope to securely to get down to the ledge. The nearest tree was too far away, it would take up too much of the length of the rope. It wasn't easy to search in the dark. The nearest bramble bushes were too far along, he would never swing at that angle towards the ledge.

Tilly needs your help.

'Fuck it,' he said, hooking the wound-up rope onto his shoulder and walking towards the edge. He'd just have to scramble down himself. There were a few branches on the way, and he was six-foot-two; the drop could only be three times his height.

Easy-peasy.

He took one more look and then knelt to the floor as if he was going to dip down into a swimming pool. He looked to where the nearest branch was and lowered his foot down until he reached it, hanging onto the edge of the cliff for support. His t-shirt tore on another branch sticking out but, tongue between his teeth, he used the crags in the cliff to climb down, until all his weight was balancing on the branch as he moved his left foot down onto another branch further down. Before he knew it, he was lowering himself onto the ledge, avoiding stepping on Tilly.

He knelt down next to her, praying the ledge had enough support under it to take the weight of both of them.

She didn't move.

He reached in to find her pulse. Relief coursed over him to find she was still alive.

'Tilly,' he said, gently, moving her hair from her face to reveal blood trickling down her forehead. 'Shit.' He hadn't thought to bring tissues or something as useful as a first aid kit.

'Hmmm,' Tilly groaned. Coming to, she partially opened her eyes. 'Winstone,' she whispered.

'What am I going to do with you?' He smiled to stop himself from crying. She was alive.

'I was arguing with Mum and I fell.' She tried to move. 'Oooh!' She groaned.

'Where does it hurt?'

'In my side,' she whispered. 'Under here.' She used her right hand to point under her left side.

'Don't move,' he said, stroking her shoulder. 'Here,' he said, taking his t-shirt, 'let's put this over you to keep you warm.'

'Thanks,' she said, shivering.

'Look, Tilly, I—'

'Hello!' A voice shouted from above. 'Winstone, are you there?'

Winstone looked up to see Archie peering over the cliff top with a torch.

'Yes, we're here!'

'Is she all right?'

'She's conscious but her side hurts. Can you pass me anything to keep her warm?'

Archie took off his coat and threw it down.

Winstone caught it and tucked it over Tilly.

'Any news on the Coastguard? She needs to get to hospital!'

'They're on their way. Half the village is coming up with torches.'

In the distance, Winstone could hear the hum of a helicopter.

'Okay, thanks, I'll keep talking to her,' he said, focusing his attention back on Tilly. 'Did you hear that? They're coming to get us off this ledge.'

'I'm sorry, Winstone,' Tilly said, her eyes shutting again.

Tears leaked from the corner of his eyes. He was finding it hard to breathe.

'Don't you go dying on me, Tilly Henshaw,' he said, stroking her hair.

'I won't,' she mumbled.

'What were you doing up here?"

'Mum was losing it. She was trying to kill herself, again.'

Tilly's speech was slightly slurred, and it was hard to make out what she was saying. 'Again?'

'She tried to once before, when I was younger. She just didn't want me to know who my dad is.' Her eyes closed as she dipped into unconsciousness again.

Guilt washed over Winstone, as angrily as the waves below. In all his years, consumed with all his grief and guilt over Tory, it had never occurred to him that someone might have suffered a similar experience.

Poor, poor Tilly.

'Tilly! *Don't die.*' He gently shook her shoulder. He checked her pulse again. It was still going but slowing. 'I think I love you,' he whispered.

'Keep talking to her, Winstone,' Archie called down.

'JUST GET THAT FUCKING HELICOPTER TO HURRY UP!!' Winstone shouted out to the ocean.

CHAPTER FIFTY-FIVE

The other night dear, as I lay sleeping
I dreamed I held you in my arms
But when I awoke, dear, I was mistaken
So I hung my head and I cried
You are my sunshine, my only sunshine
You make me happy when skies are grey
You'll never know dear, how much I love you
Please don't take my sunshine away

Standing in the doorway, listening to Archie sing, Elaine was reminded of when he used to sing that song to her. Four days Tilly had been in an induced coma since her operation. She had ruptured her spleen. Anthony said it was standard procedure, nothing to worry about and most importantly, you could live without a spleen.

Elaine still couldn't wait for her to actually wake up.

'I remember the first time you ever sang that to me.'

Archie jumped and turned around. 'Oh, hello,' he said, pulling out the chair next to him. 'Come and sit down.'

'Do you remember?

'I have never forgiven Lil for locking you in that bathroom. But,' he took a deep breath, 'she didn't know her own mind at the time, so I guess her actions were understandable.'

'She didn't know I'd try and escape. Now I feel I've done exactly the same to Tilly.'

Archie frowned. 'How?'

'It's my fault, my own madness, why we were even up on that cliff edge. Mum's actions made me break my collar bone and now my selfish actions left Tilly to almost die.'

Archie took Elaine's hand and squeezed it. 'She's going to be fine. As soon as she wakes up, she'll be itching to get out of here.'

They were in the Royal Cornwall Hospital at Truro. Anthony had driven her for the fourth day in a row. It was nearly an hour's drive from Hope Cove, so Anthony dropped Elaine off before surgery commenced and came to collect her in the evenings. Archie had set up a camp bed next to Tilly's in the little room she'd been given off the main ward.

Elaine felt her eyes welling up. 'Oh, Archie, what have I done?'

Archie took her hand. 'Hey, now, let's not have any of that. Look at your mum.'

'Which one?'

Archie chuckled. 'Lil, of course. It doesn't matter what's in the past, what really matters is what you do now.'

Elaine frowned. 'I don't know what you mean?'

'Lil turned it around. She started taking medication after your fall in the bathroom; she tried her hardest to be the best mum she could be.'

Elaine shook her head. 'I already take medication though. Doesn't look as if it's made a blind bit of difference. I still panicked and tried to kill myself, Archie. I'm just like her, aren't I?'

'Is Ruby like that?'

'No.'

'Then look to her for guidance.'

Elaine nodded. It was hard to ask Ruby for help. It all stemmed back to when Ruby had turned up offering her help, when she was pregnant with Tilly, and Elaine had rejected her. She felt like she wasn't allowed to ask for help again. But, then, Ruby had recently offered her the olive branch of returning to college. 'I guess pride comes before a fall.'

Archie frowned. 'What do you mean, lass?'

'Well, I've refused Ruby's help in the past, so I guess I'm finding it hard to reach out and ask for it now.'

Archie rubbed his hand over his rather overgrown stubble. 'Has Ruby ever told you about her depression?'

Elaine's head shot up. 'No?'

'When you wouldn't let her help, when you were expecting Tilly, she felt rejected. She almost fell apart by all accounts.'

'Oh.' Elaine didn't really know what to say to that. She hated to concede that if even happy-go-luck, knock 'em dead Ruby could get depression that normalised it. It was just another emotion.

'Counselling,' came Tilly's croaky voice.

Elaine and Archie both swung their heads around.

Tilly was lying with her eyes open, smiling at them.

'Pardon?' Elaine asked.

'You need to go to counselling,' Tilly whispered again. 'Can I get some water please, Grampy?'

Elaine watched Archie frown before a wide smile spread across his face.

'Grampy?'

'That's what you are now, aren't you?'

Elaine watched Archie nod while tears silently escaped from the corners of his eyes.

'Aye, I guess I am.'

Elaine thought of the song he had been singing to Tilly when she came in and all those nights where it wasn't safe to stay at home, and he would read her Enid Blyton and kiss her goodnight.

'She's right you know, Dad,' Elaine whispered. 'And you always have been.'

'Thank you,' Archie stifled a sob whilst pouring Tilly's water. 'I can't tell you how much this means to me.'

CHAPTER FIFTY-SIX

Tilly packed the last of her toiletries and squashed them into her bag, which was no mean feat when she was doing it one-handed, having fractured her left wrist which was now held in a splint. She looked at the clock which had moved about two minutes since she last checked. It had just gone midday. She'd been elated this morning when the consultant had said she could be discharged today. It was nearly a week since the accident had happened. Last Friday, around this time she was on the harbour serving up burgers and tortillas, working towards a career in her own right, a sense of purpose. Now, she was incapacitated, wouldn't be able to open *Tilly's Kitchen* for another few weeks, had a new dad who Elaine had told her was going to go at 'her pace', so would wait until she was ready to sit down and talk with him, and a boss (or possible ex-boss) who she thought had become a friend but hadn't texted, phoned or visited her once since their argument at the disco.

It was all hugely depressing.

Still at least it gave her plenty to discuss with Laura at tomorrow's session. She believed her mum now too, she really did. It was all pure coincidence. She had no more a clue that Anthony lived here than Tilly knew posting about the discos on social media would bring back so much trauma for Winstone over Tory.

Tilly looked at the clock again and her heart sank. She thought someone would be here by now. Her phone had somehow been lost. Probably on the cliff ledge, so she had asked the hospital to phone Hope Home where she knew someone would answer. Hopefully Ruby would come and collect her, but almost a week away from Hope Cove meant Tilly wasn't exactly sure of the tide times and whether Ruby could cross over in the Land Rover.

A gentle knock at the door was followed by a 'Hi.'

Tilly's heart leapt into her mouth as she recognised who the voice belonged to.

'Um, hello,' she stammered.

She knew Winstone had been the one to save her from the cliff ledge and help the Coastguard winch her to safety, but she couldn't remember anything after falling down the cliff. Her last thought as she slipped down the craggy rocks was, *I'm going to die!* Before she felt a searing pain in her side and had passed out.

She'd assumed his absence meant he was still angry with her.

He smiled. A warm, reassuring smile, but Tilly felt anything but. She tried to breathe steadily to calm her nerves.

'How are you?' She found herself asking.

He lowered himself onto the edge of the bed. 'I think it's me who should be asking you that.' He smiled again.

'Thank you for saving my life,' she stammered, fiddling with her splint, not daring to look at him.

He laughed. She didn't know what it meant but he was here, so that must mean something.

She dared to look up at him and he was still laughing. 'What's so funny?'

'Can you remember what I said to you, on the cliff ledge?'

She shook her head. 'I can't remember anything.'

He nodded. 'Okay. Ready to get out of here?'

'Yes please,' she said, unsure if he was still pissed off about all that Instagram hash tagging or not.

'Cool, I've got something I really want to show you.'

They left the hospital at high speed, Winstone constantly asking all the way home whether his fast driving on all the windy, country lanes, was causing her pain. Tilly didn't care; her hair was flying along in the wind of his open-top sports and if felt so good to be alive. As the car roared down the lanes, off the main road and into the village, Tilly saw the sea come into view and she breathed a sigh of relief that it didn't fill her with fear.

'You okay?' Winstone asked, again, glancing at her briefly whilst the road was straight.

Tilly looked over to Gull Island and smiled. 'I think I'm going to be,' she said. There was a lot to sort out but Winstone appeared to be her friend again, she finally knew who her dad was and now Elaine knew that Archie was her father, perhaps they could all move on with their lives, together, like she had always hoped for.

Tilly frowned as they descended the High Street into the village. 'I thought you never brought your car down to the harbour?'

'I'm making an exception for my poorly friend.'

Tilly smiled; they were friends again.

Winstone slowed to navigate tourists wandering up and down the high street. They sailed past the harbour and up towards the lighthouse.

'Are we going to the cottage?'

'You'll see.' He was grinning from ear to ear.

He indicated and swung the car onto the open driveway of the disused building on the opposite side of the cove to the Lobster Pot.

'Why are you parking here?' she asked, looking up at the disused building, still as dilapidated as the first time she had noticed it, that very first day she had arrived in Hope Cove.

'What's with all the questions?'

The tide was half-out and weak sunlight was burning through the clouds. It was shaping up to be a hot summers day in Hope Cove. She watched Winstone get out of the car and come to open the door for her.

'Thanks,' she said, finding it difficult to get out with the use of just one arm. He carefully guided her out and took her good hand to go and stand by the wall which looked out over the cove. She didn't refuse it, enjoying Winstone's touch. She realised she couldn't remember the last time someone had physically touched her, who wasn't taking her blood pressure.

From here, she could just make out the headland to Port Trillick. She wasn't sure she ever wanted to walk up that way again and be reminded of that awful night.

'I think I might need to go back to the cottage and change. I feel a bit hot in these clothes.'

Elaine, in her infinite, motherly wisdom had packed Tilly mainly hoodies, long sleeve tops and jeans because she didn't want to get cold, in a stifling hot hospital, and catch an infection.

'Let's go and have a look inside first, shall we?' he said, pulling her away from the view.

'Okay,' she said, still holding his hand, enjoying their connection. It actually sounded quite noisy inside. Wrapped up in her concerns about returning to the coast, where she had almost lost her life only a few days ago, she hadn't noticed that there were vans outside the disused building too and inside was a hive of activity. 'Wow!' Tilly took in the smell of freshly sawed wood, amongst the loud drilling.

Winstone let go of her hand and she was overcome with a sense of loss. 'This—' he said, standing in the middle of the room, '—is going to be the dance floor. The bar will be here—' he walked to the end of the room and splayed his arms out, '—behind will be the kitchen, and come with me—' he said, stepping out through some rather posh looking bi-fold, aluminium doors which had been installed across the entire front of the building.

Tilly followed him out onto the balcony which had been jet blasted and was looking limestone fresh.

'This will be where we'll serve elevenses, and lunch, and light snacks in the evening, before the music cranks up and it's just a bar.'

Tilly looked up at the misty cloud.

'I'm having a veranda installed, so it'll be undercover.'

She grinned. 'You've got all bases covered then?'

Winstone grinned back. 'And can you see those workmen over in the cellar at the Lobster?'

Tilly narrowed her eyes. 'Yes.'

'They're starting on works to turn it into a separate restaurant to the pub. A restaurant you're going to run.'

'Me?' Tilly swivelled around. 'What about *Tilly's Kitchen*?'

'That's going on the road.' He grinned.

'With who?'

'Ruby's got it all in hand and you'll be involved with the recruiting process. It's off on its travels to Padstow, St Ives, Charlestown, all the tourist places, reflecting dishes you create in the new restaurant.'

Tilly's mouth was open wide. She couldn't find the muscles to close it. 'But what about this place?'

'You made me realise that we should follow our dreams, aspire and achieve. For the past seven years I've been hiding here, trying to forget the life I had before.'

Now was her opportunity to bring their argument up. 'Look, Winstone, about the Instagram thing, I—'

Winstone held his hand up. 'You don't need to apologise!'

'But I *need* to explain,' she pressed on. 'I didn't know about Tory when I promoted the disco nights, you have to believe me, I am—'

Winstone rushed forward and took her good hand. 'I know,' he said, looking deeply into her eyes, as if trying to explain that he did really understand now. 'I overreacted, it's me that should be sorry. That's why I decided to get on and purchase the lease for this place. I wanted to prove to you how sorry I am.'

Woah. She didn't see that coming; Winstone feeling as guilty as she did.

She nodded and bit her lip, not sure of what to say next. It was such a kind gesture. No-one, apart from Ruby perhaps, had ever been so generous to her in all of her life.

'Do you remember what I said to you on the cliff ledge.'

Tilly's mind flashed back to falling off that bloody cliff, almost losing her life. She never wanted to think about it again as long as she lived. But then she remembered the buried memory of Elaine trying to kill herself the first time. Look what good that had done her; none. Perhaps it was better to embrace what frightened the most, deal with it and *then* move on.

'No,' she said, quietly, hoping they could change the subject.

'I said I think I love you,' Winstone said, softly.

The builders clanged and banged around them, but Winstone's words rang in her ears. A few weeks ago, she wouldn't have wanted him telling her this, but somehow it felt different now.

'But I got it wrong.'

Tilly's heart sank.

'I *know* I love you, now.'

Tilly looked up at him and saw his face full of hope, full of anticipation of how she might react.

She broke into a grin. 'You know,' she said, squeezing his hand tighter, 'I think I might be in love with you too.' She knew. She known it from the night he'd been angry with her, all over a misunderstanding, but it had mattered to her, how upset he'd been. She nodded determinedly. 'Actually, no, I know too; I love you.'

He smiled. Gently, oh, so, slowly, he reached in to kiss her. She didn't hold back, even if it was hard to balance and kiss with one arm out of action. It was going to be okay. Life was never going to be perfect, she realised that now, and there were still, most likely, more tears to come with Mum, Anthony, no doubt restaurant renovations. But Winstone loved her and finally she had found someone she really wanted to love back. She'd come to Hope Cove to escape, but it had never occurred to her that it might finally feel like coming home.

The End

Arthur: Shadow of a God
By Richard Denham

Arthur: Shadow of a God gives a fascinating overview of Britain's lost hero and casts a light over an often-overlooked and somewhat inconvenient truth; Arthur was almost certainly not a man at all, but a god. He is linked inextricably to the world of Celtic folklore and Druidic traditions. Whereas tyrants like Nero and Caligula were men who fancied themselves gods; is it not possible that Arthur was a god we have turned into a man? Perhaps then there is a truth here. Arthur, 'The King under the Mountain'; sleeping until his return will never return, after all, because he doesn't need to. Arthur the god never left in the first place and remains as popular today as he ever was. His legend echoes in stories, films and games that are every bit as imaginative and fanciful as that which the minds of talented bards such as Taliesin and Aneirin came up with when the mists of the 'dark ages' still swirled over Britain – and perhaps that is a good thing after all, most at home in the imaginations of children and adults alike – being the Arthur his believers want him to be.

A Storm of Magic
By Ashley Laino

Being brought back from the dead is an impressive trick, even for magician Darien Burron. Now he must try and use his sleight of hand to swindle modern-day witch, Mirah, to sign her power away, or end up a tormented demon in the afterlife.

Meanwhile, sixteen-year-old Mirah is starting to lose control of her powers. After an incident at her aunt's Witchery store, Mirah is sent to a secret coven to learn to control her abilities. While away, Mirah meets up with a soft-spoken clairvoyant, a brazen storm witch, and the creator of dark magic itself. The young woman must learn to trust in herself before she loses herself entirely to the darkness that hunts her.

Weirder War Two
By Richard Denham & Michael Jecks

Did a Warner Bros. cartoon prophesize the use of the atom bomb? Did the Allies really plan to use stink bombs on the enemy? Why did the Nazis make their own version of Titanic and why were polar bear photographs appearing throughout Europe?

The Second World War was the bloodiest of all wars. Mass armies of men trudged, flew or rode from battlefields as far away as North Africa to central Europe, from India to Burma, from the Philippines to the borders of Japan. It saw the first aircraft carrier sea battle, and the indiscriminate use of terror against civilian populations in ways not seen since the Thirty Years War. Nuclear and incendiary bombs erased entire cities. V weapons brought new horror from the skies: the V1 with their hideous grumbling engines, the V2 with sudden, unexpected death. People were systematically starved: in Britain food had to be rationed because of the stranglehold of U-Boats, while in Holland the German blockage of food and fuel saw 30,000 die of starvation in the winter of 1944/5. It was a catastrophe for millions.

At a time of such enormous crisis, scientists sought ever more inventive weapons, or devices to help halt the war.

Civilians were involved as never before, with women taking up new trades, proving themselves as capable as their male predecessors whether in the factories or the fields.

The stories in this book are of courage, of ingenuity, of hilarity in some cases, or of great sadness, but they are all thought-provoking - and rather weird. So whether you are interested in the last Polish cavalry charge, the Blackout Ripper, Dada, or Ghandi's attempt to stop the bloodshed, welcome to the Weirder War Two!

Click Bait
By Gillian Philip

A funny joke's a funny joke. Eddie Doolan doesn't think twice about adapting it to fit a tragic local news story and posting it on social media.

It's less of a joke when his drunken post goes viral. It stops being funny altogether when Eddie ends up jobless, friendless and ostracised by the whole town of Langburn. This isn't how he wanted to achieve fame.

Under siege from the press, and facing charges not just for the joke but for a history of abusive behaviour on the internet, Eddie grows increasingly paranoid and desperate. The only people still speaking to him are Crow, a neglected kid who relies on Eddie for food and company, and Sid, the local gamekeeper's granddaughter. It's Sid who offers Eddie a refuge and an understanding ear.

But she also offers him an illegal shotgun - and as Eddie's life spirals downwards, and his efforts at redemption are thwarted at every turn, the gun starts to look like the answer to all his problems.

Burning Bridges
By Chris Bedell

They've always said that three's a crowd...

24-year-old Sasha didn't anticipate her identical twin Riley killing herself upon their reconciliation after years of estrangement. But Sasha senses an opportunity and assumes Riley's identity so she can escape her old life.

Playing Riley isn't without complications, though. Riley's had a strained relationship with her wife and stepson so Sasha must do whatever she can to make her newfound family love and accept her. If Sasha's arrangement ends, then she'll have nothing protecting her from her past. However, when one of Sasha's former clients tracks her down, Sasha must choose between her new life and the only person who cared about her.

But things are about to become even more complicated, as a third sister, Katrina, enters the scene...

www.ingramcontent.com/pod-product-compliance
Lightning Source LLC
Chambersburg PA
CBHW032041050726
47590CB00001B/80